TYRANT

FORCE
OF KINGS

TYRANT

FORCE
OF KINGS

CHRISTIAN CAMERON

First published in Great Britain in 2014 by Orion Books,
an imprint of The Orion Publishing Group Ltd
Orion House, 5 Upper Saint Martin's Lane
London WC2H 9EA

An Hachette UK Company

1 3 5 7 9 10 8 6 4 2

A CIP catalogue record for this book
is available from the British Library.

ISBN (Hardback) 978 1 4091 0460 5
ISBN (Export Trade Paperback) 978 1 4091 0461 2
ISBN (Ebook) 978 1 4091 1086 6

Typeset by Deltatype Ltd, Birkenhead, Merseyside

Printed in Great Britain by CPI Group (UK) Ltd,
Croydon, CR0 4YY

The Orion Publishing Group's policy is to use papers that
are natural, renewable and recyclable products and made
from wood grown in sustainable forests. The logging and
manufacturing processes are expected to conform to the
environmental regulations of the country of origin.

www.orionbooks.co.uk

For Shelley Power and Bill Massey,
without whom, I would not be a writer

GLOSSARY

Airyanãm (Avestan) Noble, heroic.

Aspis (Classical Greek) A large round shield, deeply dished, commonly carried by Greek (but not Macedonian) *hoplites*.

Baqca (Siberian) Shaman, mage, dream-shaper.

Chiton (Classical Greek) A garment like a tunic, made from a single piece of fabric folded in half and pinned down the side, then pinned again at the neck and shoulders and belted above the hips. A men's *chiton* might be worn long or short. Worn very short, or made of a small piece of cloth, it was sometimes called a 'chitoniskos'. Our guess is that most *chitons* were made from a piece of cloth roughly 60 × 90 inches, and then belted or roped to fit, long or short. Pins, pleating, and belting could be simple or elaborate. Most of these garments would, in Greece, have been made of wool. In the East, linen might have been preferred.

Chlamys (Classical Greek) A garment like a cloak, made from a single piece of fabric woven tightly and perhaps even boiled. The *chlamys* was usually pinned at the neck and worn as a cloak, but could also be thrown over the shoulder and pinned under the right or left arm and worn as a garment. Free men are sometimes shown naked with a *chlamys*, but rarely shown in a *chiton* without a *chlamys* – the *chlamys*, not the *chiton*, was the essential garment, or so it appears. Men and women both wear the *chlamys*, although differently. Again, a 60 × 90 piece of cloth seems to drape correctly and have the right lines and length.

Daimon (Classical Greek) Spirit.

Ephebe (Classical Greek) A new *hoplite*; a young man just training to join the forces of his city.

Epilektoi (Classical Greek) The chosen men of the city or of the *phalanx*; elite soldiers.

Eudaimia (Classical Greek) Well-being. Literally, 'well-spirited'. See *daimon*, above.

Gamelia (Classical Greek) A Greek holiday.

Gorytos (Classical Greek and possibly Scythian) The open-topped quiver carried by the Scythians, often highly decorated.

Himation (Classical Greek) A heavy garment consisting of a single piece of cloth at least 120 inches long by 60 inches wide, draped over the body and one shoulder, worn by both men and women.

Hipparch (Classical Greek) The commander of the cavalry.

Hippeis (Classical Greek) Militarily, the cavalry of a Greek army. Generally, the cavalry class, synonymous with 'knights'. Usually the richest men in a city.

Hoplite (Classical Greek) A Greek soldier, the heavy infantry who carry an *aspis* (the big round shield) and fight in the *phalanx*. They represent the middle class of free men in most cities, and while sometimes they seem like medieval knights in their outlook, they are also like town militia, and made up of craftsmen and small farmers. In the early Classical period, a man with as little as twelve acres under cultivation could be expected to own the *aspis* and serve as a *hoplite*.

Hoplomachos (Classical Greek) A man who taught fighting in armour.

Hyperetes (Classical Greek) The *Hipparch*'s trumpeter, servant, or supporter. Perhaps a sort of NCO.

Kithara (Classical Greek) A musical instrument like a lyre.

Kline (Classical Greek) A couch or bed on which Hellenic men and women took meals and perhaps slept, as well.

Kopis (Classical Greek) A bent bladed knife or sword, rather like a modern Ghurka kukri. They appear commonly in Greek art, and even some small eating knives were apparently made to this pattern.

Machaira (Classical Greek) The heavy Greek cavalry sword, longer and stronger than the short infantry sword. Meant to give a longer reach on horseback, and not useful in the *phalanx*. The word could also be used for any knife.

Parasang (Classical Greek from Persian) About thirty *stades*. See below.

Phalanx (Classical Greek) The infantry formation used by Greek *hoplites* in warfare, eight to ten deep and as wide as circumstance allowed. Greek commanders experimented with deeper and shallower formations, but the *phalanx* was solid and very difficult to break, presenting the enemy with a veritable wall of spear points and shields, whether the Macedonian style with pikes or the Greek style with spears. Also, *phalanx* can refer to the body of fighting men. A Macedonian *phalanx* was deeper, with longer spears called *sarissas* that we assume to be like the pikes used in more recent times. Members of a *phalanx*, especially a Macedonian *phalanx*, are sometimes called *Phalangites*.

Phylarch (Classical Greek) The commander of one file of *hoplites*. Could be as many as sixteen men.

Porne (Classical Greek) A prostitute.

Pous (Classical Greek) About one foot.

Prodromoi (Classical Greek) Scouts; those who run before or run first.

Psiloi (Classical Greek) Light infantry skirmishers, usually men with bows and slings, or perhaps javelins, or even thrown rocks. In Greek city-state warfare, the *psiloi* were supplied by the poorest free men, those who could not afford the financial burden of *hoplite* armour and daily training in the gymnasium.

Sastar (Avestan) Tyrannical. A tyrant.

Spola (Classical Greek) Body armour of leather. Herakles in heroic depiction has a spola in the form of a lion's skin, but soldiers might wear anything from a light leather tunic to stiffened abdominal protection and call it a spola.

Stade (Classical Greek) About 1/8 of a mile. The distance run in a 'stadium'. 178 meters. Sometimes written as *Stadia* or *Stades* by me. Thirty *Stadia* make a *Parasang*.

Taxeis (Classical Greek) The sections of a Macedonian *phalanx*. Can refer to any group, but often used as a 'company' or a 'battalion'. My *taxeis* has between 500 and 2,000 men, depending on losses and detachments. Roughly synonymous with *phalanx* above, although a *phalanx* may be composed of a dozen *taxeis* in a great battle.

Thorax/Thorakes (Classical Greek) Body armour – literally, that which covered the abdomen. Could be bronze, quilted wool or linen or a mixture of textile and metal armour; could also refer to a leather armour like a spola. The so-called 'muscle cuirass' forged by the armourer to look like the male abdomen was one form, and probably the most expensive.

Xiphos (Classical Greek) A straight-bladed infantry sword, usually carried by *hoplites* or *psiloi*. Classical Greek art, especially red-figure ware, shows many *hoplites* wearing them, but only a handful have been recovered and there's much debate about the shape and use. They seem very like a Roman gladius.

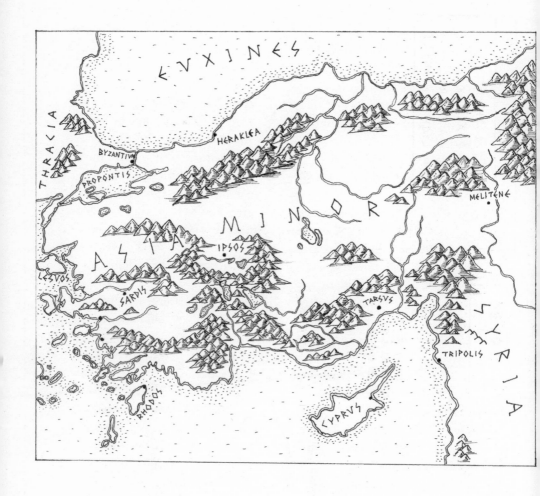

BATTLE OF IPSOS 301 BC

MACEDONIANS

ANTIGONIDS

ELEPHANTS
PHALANX
CAVALRY
LIGHT INFANTRY

SELEUCUS

LYSIMACUS

SATYRUS

FARM

MELITTA

DIODORUS

ANTIOCHUS

DEMETRIUS

ANTIGONUS ONE-EYE

PROLOGUE

It should have been the day of his greatest triumph.

Stratokles was dressed in his very best – a chiton with flames of Tyrian red licking up the shining white wool from the hems, themselves so thick with embroidery that the gold pins that held it together were difficult to push through the cloth. Over his shoulder hung a chlamys of pure red-purple, embroidered in gold, and on his brow sat a diadem of gold and red-purple amethysts, worth the value of a heavy penteres all by itself, without reckoning the other accoutrements he wore – gold sandals with gold buckles, gold mountings on the dagger under his armpit, gold rings on his fingers.

The extravagance of his costume was matched – or exceeded – by every other person in the temple of Hera. Despite being Herakles' foe, Hera was well represented at Heraklea, and her temple shone with white marble columns and magnificently painted statues. The vault of the portico had inlaid panels of lapis with bands of hammered gold around every panel, so that the recessed coffers seemed to radiate light. Cunning engines – engines that Stratokles had devised himself – allowed alternating coffers to be opened or shut, allowing rays of the sun to fall straight to the temple's polished, inlaid floor.

And standing on that floor were the guests; the wedding party of the bridegroom. They stood in shadow, carefully arranged by Stratokles with due concern for precedence. They represented a dramatic shift in policy and five tense months of desperate diplomacy; Stratokles had had to sail a stolen warship through Demetrios's siege lines at Rhodes, and later he'd had to ride across Greece with his mistress, Amastris, Queen of Heraklea, in his arms.

But he'd pulled it off, and the reward stood at the head of the procession. Lysimachos, Satrap of Thrace. Soon to be King of Thrace. One of the leading players in the war for Alexander's empire – a near neighbour, and a dangerous professional soldier with all the resources of the Thracian silver mines and the Thracian war-tribes at his back. And at his back, Cassander, King of Macedon, still, despite the best efforts of Antigonus and his son Demetrios, the lord of most of Greece. And just behind him, Amyntas, brother of Ptolemy of Aegypt. And behind *him*, resplendent in purple and gold, stood Seleucus's brother Philip of Babylon. Together, the four men represented the alliance that faced Antigonus, lord of Asia, and his son, Demetrios the besieger. Stratokles had arranged to bring them all here, to Heraklea, to celebrate the marriage of his carefully fostered pupil, Amastris, who stood almost alone in a shaft of golden sunlight that he had carefully arranged to fall like the benison of heaven on her golden head. She looked like Aphrodite come to earth, dressed in a long chiton of shining gold embroidery over linen so fine that the sun shone straight through it. And Amastris had the body to bear the scrutiny of the most critical of men.

And the mind to use that body as she needed, to accomplish what she desired for the good of her city, and her own power.

Stratokles watched her with approval – approval and a distant tinge of desire. He'd loved her from their first meeting, but the years had mellowed his love into a kind of golden servitude. She rewarded him with trust and a thorough practice of the principles he instilled. And money. Stratokles was now a very rich man.

It should have been the day of his greatest triumph.

But the woman standing at Cassander's elbow was not his wife, Penelope. Nor the woman most Macedonians accepted as his mistress: Euridyke of Athens. The woman on his arm was a courtesan named Phiale, and when her downcast eyes flicked up to touch Stratokles' eyes, it was like the lightest possible cut from a razor-sharp xiphos at the start of a fight.

Stratokles had used Phiale – years before – in a failed plot to assassinate Ptolemy of Aegypt. The irony – and this wedding was full of historic irony – was that Stratokles had undertaken the assassination of Ptolemy at Cassander's behest, to win favours for Stratokles' beloved home city, Athens.

But the world had turned, and Cassander and Ptolemy needed each other against the power of Antigonus.

Stratokles struggled to remember how he had used Phiale and whether she had cause to hold it against him as he crossed the floor to her. He had warned her to leave Alexandria – that Leon the Numidian would certainly catch on to her eventually.

Why, then, did she look at him with such hate? Odd. But Stratokles had long since learned to attack a dangerous opponent and never leave one behind him, so he crossed the floor to her in a few strides, noting the averted glances of the courtiers around her.

'Phiale?' he said.

Cassander had stepped away from her to speak to Philip of Babylon and an older man by his side.

'Stratokles the Informer,' she breathed huskily. 'What a pleasure to see you.'

Her eyes, carefully controlled, stroked him. There was no message of hate now. A far different message.

Stratokles stroked his beard. 'We were friends, once,' he said.

She laughed and put an arm on his. 'Oh, my dear, we are still friends. What do you hear of Satyrus of Tanais?'

He noticed that her glance sharpened back into a sword when she said the name.

'He remains something like a force of nature. Beloved of the gods.' He managed a smile – there was something wrong, something he couldn't pin down, something to do with someone he had just seen and the absence of men seeking his good will. He was isolated in the middle of his own party. And Phiale knew something.

Stratokles didn't turn his head – but he managed to glance to his left, where the guards were. Plenty of them, good men – most men he'd picked himself. He rubbed his chin, flipped his cloak over his shoulder, and turned back to Phiale as if everything was fine.

'Although,' he said somewhat at random, 'Satyrus is harmless enough,' and saw her flush.

'Really?' she asked. 'Last time you and I were *friends*, you wanted him dead.'

'That is the way of politics, isn't it? And may I say how very beautiful you are?' Stratokles smiled at her.

She returned the smile, but it didn't touch the tiny lines at the edges of her eyes. 'You didn't used to be so easy about Satyrus,' she said.

Stratokles smiled, his eyes still scanning the room over her head. *What in Tartarus had happened?* Running on automatic, his mind put words into his mouth.

'He didn't used to supply grain to Athens,' he said. 'This season his ships escort our ships to Athens. Hence, we are friends.'

Phiale smiled again. 'You are selling his bride to Lysimachos and you think he'll escort your ships to Athens?'

Stratokles smiled back. 'I made sure he was at sea before I let the news of the wedding out,' he said. 'Besides – he knows. He and Amastris have been estranged for a year. I made sure of it. She doesn't need, or want, a military master. She wants a peer.'

Phiale controlled her face. Stratokles watched her do it, and read, in the careful play of the muscles in her jaw, his own doom.

She knew something. The word *peer* triggered her reaction.

'So Satyrus is on his way to Athens?' she asked.

'Rhodes first, and then Athens,' Stratokles said. 'Will you excuse me, fair lady?'

Stratokles bowed and walked across the temple portico to where his second, the Latin, Lucius, waited. Lucius was as well dressed as he, and a handsomer man. Stratokles had a magnificent physique and a strong jaw, but his face was marred by a vicious old wound that left him looking like he had a comedian's nose rather than a human one. Lucius was handsome by any standard – but his hair was bright red and that was not accounted a mark of beauty among Greeks.

'Something feels wrong,' Stratokles said.

Lucius nodded. 'No one is licking your arse, lord,' he said.

That settled it. Crude as he could be, Lucius had hit the rivet square. On a day like this – a day that capped a generation of clever diplomacy and careful betrayal, Stratokles should have been surrounded by sycophants and flatterers and great men seeking favour.

Instead, he'd been left alone, and his involvement with the details of the costumes and the lighting and the ceremony had fooled him.

'I'm for the axe,' he said. 'I can feel it.'

'You see Phiale?' Lucius asked.

'Like seeing a ghost.' Stratokles risked a glance over his shoulder. He was a realist, but his heart was pounding and he still couldn't believe it. Why – *why*? Why would his beloved mistress sacrifice him? But Phiale's controlled reactions told him an answer. His mistress was to be used, not courted. Lysimachos wanted him gone.

His glance happened to intercept that of one of the bodyguards. The man flinched – visibly. He was a man Stratokles had chosen

4

himself – a Macedonian left behind by one of Satyrus of Tanais's military adventures, a man who owed Stratokles his very life. And the man wouldn't meet his eye.

'Arse-cunt,' Stratokles said softly. If the guards were in on it, then Amastris herself had sold him.

The wedding was heartbeats from commencement. He could see the two priestesses of Hera at the head of the procession of religious figures and Heraklean gentry, most of them awestruck to be in the presence of the leading figures of their day.

'We need to go,' Stratokles said.

Lucius nodded.

Phiale pressured her lover's arm gently. 'My lord?'

Cassander turned to her, and waved at a handsome, dark-faced man by his side. 'My lady, the Courtesan Phiale of Athens. This is Mithridates, lord of Bithynia. A new ally against Antigonus.'

'I have long *desired* to be your ally, my lord.' Mithridates looked Persian, with a long, straight nose and perfect skin. Phiale found him attractive – she wanted to touch that skin. 'But this wedding puts your forces on my side of the Bosporus, and makes our cooperation possible. If I can evict my uncle from the throne.'

'It was very clever indeed of Stratokles to have seen that you could be enticed to join us.' Cassander smiled brilliantly. 'He outdoes himself. Sometimes I think that we are all merely his puppets. Have you seen him?' Cassander asked.

Phiale turned her head slightly. 'There he is, lord. Talking to the red-haired man.'

'Herakles, how can a man live, being so ugly? You have met him, Mithridates?' Cassander's eyes were moving rapidly around the room. 'What did he have to say to *you*, my dear?'

Mithridates bowed. 'I have met him. My lord, I must make my introductions to Philip of Babylon. Phiale, you are the most beautiful woman in the room.' His eyes lay on hers for a moment, and she sighed at the unexpected compliment. Mithridates stepped away into the throng, and Cassander pulled her wrist until they were beside a pillar – the closest to privacy a king could manage at the edge of a great wedding.

'What did he say to you?' Cassander hissed.

'You know him, my lord?' Phiale asked.

'I know him, my dear. I have – hmm – made use of him in my day.' Cassander smiled, a handsome, charming man at the height of his powers. 'You are no friend of his, I take it?'

Phiale smiled brilliantly at Seleucus's brother, causing the younger man to spill some wine. 'I hate him. He used me – ill.'

'Then you'll be pleased to know that he's living his last hour,' Cassander said. He gave her a thin smile. 'He is a dangerous man who has outlived his usefulness. He arranged this wedding, and Lysimachos wants him gone. Lysimachos wants this city and its trade and its back door into Asia to lie like a woman, ready to his will – not to have ideas of its own. Stratokles must go. He is too good.' Cassander sighed. 'So good that I will miss him. Even when he fails, he owns up. Few of my tools are so apt to the hand as he.'

Phiale gave Cassander a brief look. 'And Satyrus of Tanais?' she asked.

Cassander laughed. The Priestess of Hera was at the head of her procession, visible just across the temple portico, and the ceremony was ready. His laugh carried easily over the temple, and heads turned. 'Lysimachos will settle him,' Cassander said.

'If I told you that I could rid you of him – with no repercussions?' she asked.

Cassander kissed her. 'Then I would love you more, if possible, than I do now.'

She smiled. 'After the wedding, I will require a fast ship for Athens.'

'After the wedding I had other plans for us, my dear.' He ran a finger under her chin.

'Does Socrates not say that the pleasures of revenge are more beautiful than the pleasures of love?' Phiale asked.

'Not that I'm aware of,' Cassander said.

'He should have,' Phiale answered.

'Well?' Lucius asked. 'Do you have a brilliant plan?'

Stratokles didn't have the energy to laugh. He was angry, and under the anger was the start of a bleak depression. *How could Amastris have betrayed him?* He wanted to confront her – but that was madness. If he was wrong, she would be very angry, and if he was right, she would kill him.

6

'No brilliant plan. Just start walking. Come on.' He began to walk with a purposeful stride towards the inner temple. He was careful to keep his head down, as if he was listening attentively to Lucius.

'They won't just let us walk away,' Lucius said.

'They may,' Stratokles opined. 'Listen – the procession of priests is at the portico. Custom holds men rigid – better than chains. No one will interrupt the ceremony. Keep walking.'

A few steps from the inner temple – almost safe – he saw the flicker of a cloak and his peripheral vision caught a nose, an eyebrow shape.

'Zeus Meilichios,' Stratokles said. 'It's the doctor.'

Leon paused for a moment, savouring the weight of the white stones in his hand. He examined the board carefully, and then chose to make his capture rather than move. He took another white stone off the board and rattled them in his hand.

Ptolemy laughed his gruff, farmer's laugh. 'You know,' he said, rolling his knucklebones, 'I *have* courtiers who know enough to lose to me.'

Leon watched the king roll a four. 'You should play with them, then,' he said.

Ptolemy moved two stones and removed one of Leon's black stones. He hesitated a long time over his fourth move, and finally, with enormous hesitation, he advanced a single stone. 'It's different,' he said.

Leon rolled his knucklebone without a moment's hesitation. It came up a six. As the king of Aegypt groaned, he moved his forces swiftly, isolating Ptolemy's latest, hesitant attack, capturing two white stones, and leaving the result of the game in no doubt.

Ptolemy shook his head. 'More wine?'

Leon shook his, too. 'No. I have all my accounts to review tomorrow, and ships in the yard to inspect.' He rose. 'I could tell you how to play better,' he said.

'Bah, you could no doubt tell me how to run my kingdom better,' Ptolemy said. 'I recommend you don't.' He took a drink of wine while slaves rushed about – some getting Leon's sandals, others his mantle.

Leon paused for a moment. 'Did you ever think, when you were fighting in the Kush with Alexander, that someday you'd have all this?'

Ptolemy grinned. 'Remember when Kineas took me prisoner? I didn't know you then – were you there?'

Leon nodded. 'I was at the fire when Philokles brought you in.'

'There was a fine man,' Ptolemy said.

'The best,' Leon agreed.

'I think of it often. When I was taken – after the skirmish – I was sure I was for it. The locals always tortured prisoners to death – we'd find them staked out on the roads. I thought that I was a dead man – dead for nothing, in a lost campaign, in a particularly nasty way. Then Philokles picked me up, and he was a Greek, and I knew I was going to live.' The king took a long drink of wine. 'But if I'd been taken by your Sakje – well, it would have been pretty ugly, eh?'

Leon shrugged. 'Hard to tell. But yes – especially young people. They like to see what they can do.'

Ptolemy swirled the wine in his golden cup. 'I think of it often. Because – when things look bad, I think, *Thank the gods, I could be old bones at Marakanda now.*'

'Very Pythagorean of you,' Leon said.

Ptolemy shrugged. 'I do more thinking about … about things. Old age, I guess. How's your nephew?'

Leon's 'nephew' was Satyrus of Tanais. They weren't related in any real way, but Leon had been part of Satyrus's father's household, and Leon had taken Satyrus into his own household, and all the world called them uncle and nephew.

'Thriving, since the siege. He's up in the Euxine, seeing to his own people.' Leon smiled. 'I'll change my mind to the tune of half a cup of wine.'

Instantly, a slave placed a cup in his hand.

He tasted it – good Chian wine, but nothing fancy.

'He's not,' Ptolemy said. 'Galon told me this morning. He's headed back to Rhodes – probably there now.'

Leon, whose intelligence service was one of the finest in the world, was surprised. 'He's got the grain fleet? So early? Whatever for?'

Ptolemy nodded. 'That's just what I'm asking you. It's not that I distrust the boy, he's served me as if he was a subject – more loyal than half my captains. But the last time his grain fleet sailed, he landed three thousand soldiers and seized control of the Propontus for a year. Zeus – he must have made a fortune on tolls.'

Leon smiled. 'He did. I have reason to know.'

'So,' Ptolemy said. 'What's the game this time?'

Leon stared at his wine. 'He hasn't told me,' he said, and there was anger in his voice. 'How many ships, have you heard?' he asked mildly.

'Forty grain ships from Tanais and Pantecapaeaum, another ten from Olbia, and fifteen more from Heraklea. The word is that he'll take half of his grain to Rhodes and sell the other half in Athens.' Ptolemy sat back, having delivered his thunderbolt.

'Athens?' Leon asked. 'We don't do business there now. Demetrios holds Athens.'

'Precisely,' Ptolemy said. 'He's not ... contemplating a change?'

Leon sipped his wine. Ptolemy was the best dissimulator he knew – the king had played two games merely to put him at ease for this moment.

'Poseidon,' Leon swore, 'I would never believe it of him.'

Ptolemy nodded. 'Good – good. That's what I needed to hear. Galon had a theory – I'll tell you as one suspicious bastard to another – that when Amastris jilted him, Satyrus had to go running to the other side. She's marrying Lysimachos – you know that.'

'I imagine everyone in the Mediterranean knows that now,' Leon said. 'But he – that is, my nephew – has known that she has other interests – well, for a year. Perhaps more. Before the siege, anyway.' He paused. 'You know that by the terms of the truce after the siege, my nephew cannot engage in open war against Demetrios for one full year.'

'Of course,' said Ptolemy. 'My brother helped negotiate it. But at the end of the year, I need him – at my side, in spirit if not in the flesh.' The king clapped him on the shoulder. 'With Satyrus's fleet, the fleet of Rhodos, and my fleet, we can keep Antigonus and Demetrios at arm's length.' He nodded. 'If Satyrus were to go over to Demetrios ...'

Leon rose to his feet. 'I'll get you a firm answer, lord. But don't accept gossip. Satyrus has never given you cause. You allow your captains to openly court Cassander and Antigonus – you allow companies of mercenaries to cross the lines when their contracts expire. By Artemis, you let your own brother flirt with Demetrios.'

'My brother doesn't have twenty brand-new triremes and a squadron of penteres building right here in my own port,' the king said. 'I'd be a lot more careful of him if he had the money and the power that young Satyrus controls now. And the name. Since the siege, your nephew has a name.'

Leon nodded.

'I'm not voicing these suspicions anywhere but this room. Herakles, Leon! I don't want to distrust the boy. But these are bad times. I have to raise taxes this year. Seleucus and Lysimachos want me to invade Syria. The bastards want *me* to take the brunt of Antigonus's forces while they whittle down his provinces. Cassander just wants us all to die. Sometimes I wonder if I'm on the wrong side. Am I the only king who doesn't want anything more? I want to rule Aegypt. No one could rule the whole world – not me, not Antigonus, and not Alexander.' The king combed his beard with his fingers and a slave poured him another cup of wine.

Leon finished his wine and rose. 'The fellahin can't take much more taxation,' he said. 'Invading Syria would be a mistake. Although something might be done with the Jews. They love you – and hate Antigonus.'

Ptolemy nodded. 'I don't *want* Syria. I don't want to raise taxes. Do you know how much the expenses of war have climbed since Alexander died?' He looked at Leon for a long moment and then laughed. 'Of course you do.'

Leon turned his cup over. 'I'll see what's going on with Satyrus. I'm sure it is innocent.'

Ptolemy nodded. 'I pray it is. But who takes thirty warships to do something innocent? I dread one of those lightning strokes that changes the game. Satyrus wouldn't see himself as a third side, would he?'

Leon sighed. 'I hope not,' he said.

'The doctor,' Lucius said, drawing his blade. Two rows of columns hid them from the wedding, but the first sound of combat would break the spell, turn every head.

Sophokles of Athens, a man who studied medicine at the Lyceum, a man who accepted money to kill – quite possibly the most dangerous man in the Hellenic world. He came to a stop and leaned against a pillar, his long, festive cloak covering him – and any weapons he bore – from head to foot.

'Stratokles,' he said.

'Sophokles,' the informer nodded. 'The blessings of Lady Hera on you and your doings this day.'

The doctor nodded. 'And yours, my dear. Cassander has given you up – traded you like a prime slave to Lysimachos. Who has given me a good purse of gold to remove you from the game.'

Lucius had already seen the men coming up the steps.

Stratokles shrugged. 'I won't pretend that the whole matter doesn't make me angry,' he said. 'On balance, I've served well.'

Sophokles nodded. He looked at Lucius. 'Steady on, there, sir. If you threaten them, we could have trouble. Put that blade away.' To Stratokles, he said, 'Cassander's decision to dispense with you threatens all of us. On the other hand, I owe you for Alexandria. You abandoned me.'

Stratokles shrugged. 'You were in place, close to the king, and undetected. I had no way of knowing that Phiale would sell you to Satyrus and Leon. Besides, sir – this is ancient history. If you will kill me, then get it done.'

'I don't think that Phiale actually sold me,' the doctor said. 'But I wanted to hear your denial. I tried for Melitta – the girl. Satyrus of Tanais's sister. I failed, but it was close. The very gods protect that pair.'

Stratokles managed a smile, despite the circumstances. 'The blood and gold I've wasted on them – Herakles holds them in the palm of his hand.' He shook his head. 'Satyrus is quite likeable.'

'There remains an enormous price on his head,' the doctor said.

'Surely not? Eumeles is dead and rotted. At Satyrus's hand, I believe.' Stratokles was trying to calculate – did the doctor mean to kill him? This was a curiously long conversation, and even he would hesitate to kill him inside the sacred precincts.

'Eumeles is not the customer. He was, but the contract now is far larger. I wondered if you would join me in taking it up.' The doctor bowed his head, one peer to another. 'You have resources that I lack. People will deal with you who will not deal with me.'

'That's a sad comment on one of us, doctor,' Stratokles said. 'I don't suppose you'd like to give me time to consider?'

The doctor glanced at the wedding. 'No,' he said.

Stratokles nodded, more to himself than to the doctor. 'Does your contract include young Lucius here?' he asked.

Sophokles nodded. 'I'm afraid so.'

Lucius looked around. 'I'm right here, and I'm pretty sure I can do the lot of these rabble.'

The doctor looked at Stratokles. 'I'd really rather not have a demonstration either way.'

Stratokles had made some terrible errors in the last weeks – he must have missed a thousand clues of the coming betrayal – but just at that moment he didn't care. A life of dissimulation had brought him to this – death on the steps of a temple, at the hand of a former ally, at the behest of his own master.

He shrugged, and mostly he was tired. 'You know,' he said, 'I'd like to save Lucius. He's been very loyal, and he is no part of our little ways – he's a Latin. Let him go.'

The doctor looked him over. 'I'm proposing that we let you both go, and you join us,' he said.

Stratokles shook his head. It was impulsive, but by all the furies, he was done with that kind of life. 'No,' he said. 'I don't want to kill young Satyrus for money.'

The doctor nodded. 'I could see you heading there,' he said, 'but I wouldn't have believed it. You've lost your edge.'

'So much so that I will stand here and let you kill me,' Stratokles said, with a smile that he hoped was noble. 'I'll even walk down and cross over the boundary into those trees, without a struggle – if you let Lucius go. No impiety for you. No religious impurity over your heads.'

The doctor looked him over. 'You are a surprising man,' he said. He glanced at Lucius. 'Go,' he said. 'He has bought your life. Don't indulge in some petty fake nobility. Run.'

Lucius's only farewell to his master of ten years was a raised eyebrow. Then he turned and walked away.

Stratokles didn't know what he felt. Relief, at having accomplished something good? Or complete failure – he was to die. Die. Right now. It made his knees tremble, and he forced himself to think of all the other times he'd cheated death. Really, for a man of his profession, he'd done rather well. He squared his shoulders. 'Let's take a walk, doctor,' he said.

They strolled together, down the steps and across the open ground where all two hundred of the visiting dignitaries could watch them.

The sight caused many different reactions that Stratokles couldn't see – Phiale smiled in a way that made her ugly, and Amastris turned her face away, the joy of her day of triumph clouded, and a number of men Stratokles had made felt the churn of the stomach that tells a man he has done very, very wrong. But no one stirred a foot to save him.

He crossed the boundary wall, and vanished.

Miriam pulled the cloak tighter around her shoulders and raised an eyebrow at her brother. 'Where in God's name are we?' she asked.

They were looking out through a ruined rower's port in the side of a damaged penteres that was moving slowly. They'd been put in a locked cabin, almost like a cage, too small for them to stand or sit, in the stern of the lowest rowing deck – really just a set of heavy boards nailed across the tiny space, sometimes called the aft-tabernacle. The helmsman's feet were just over their heads.

Abraham put his eye to the small opening again. 'Asia, I'm sure of it. I don't know the headland, but we're close to Cos, or I'm a gentile – don't ask me how I know, dear sister. I know.'

Miriam was afraid – terrified, really – but she had long practice in not showing terror. 'Are we to be sold as slaves?' she asked.

Abraham put an arm around her. 'I don't think so, Miriam. We're citizens of Rhodes – and hostages. Killing us would be … well, it would be insane.'

At the end of the siege of Rhodos, Demetrios had insisted on a hundred hostages, and he had chosen them from among Satyrus's closest friends. He had demanded the payment of a tribute and, most importantly, the hostages were to guarantee that neither Rhodes nor the Euxine cities took an active role against him in the field or at sea.

The two of them had been 'held' in a very pleasant captivity at Athens – in the house of a Jewish metic, Belshazzar, until just two weeks before, when they had been hurried aboard a heavy warship. Even then, they'd been used with dignity, even deference – until the night before last, when they'd been imprisoned in this box by marines in full armour.

There were other ships out there – merchantmen all, as far as he could see. Some were very large, and others quite small – a convoy. His angle of vision was limited, but a suspicion began to form in his mind – he pushed so hard against the view-hole that he ground his ocular bone against the wood.

Just at the edge of his vision, a heavy warship was approaching fast from behind them – he was pretty sure the warship was coming from the north. A triemiola – a Rhodian, then, or—

The heavy bronze lock on their small cage grated, and a marine appeared in full armour. He put his spear to Miriam's throat.

Stratokles climbed up the precinct wall, took a last look at the world, and jumped down into the olive grove on the far side like a small boy on an olive raid, intent on eating his fill. He'd be dead in heartbeats, now. Even the air tasted wonderful. The olive grove was the most beautiful he'd ever seen.

I expected more of a farewell from Lucius, I guess.

He looked back to where Sophokles was jumping down from the precinct walls. Then he walked deeper into the grove. The doctor's retinue of killers followed him, oddly ill-assorted types in finery that they weren't used to wearing.

The doctor caught up with him and they walked side by side in silence until they were midway into the grove, well hidden from the temple.

'Care to close your eyes?' the doctor asked.

Stratokles shook his head. 'Not particularly,' he said.

'I really would like you to reconsider. What is this Satyrus to you?' The doctor cocked his head a little, like a curious cat.

Stratokles managed a smile. 'Nothing. I'm not fond of him, and he's not fond of me. But I'm done, Sophokles. I don't want to play. I don't want to hide, I don't want to run about. I liked serving Amastris. This city is the better for my hand at the tiller, and men eat grain in Athens because I tended these fields.' He shrugged. 'After that, killing for money – well, it has very little appeal.'

Sophokles nodded. 'You are not my first victim to refuse an offer. Nor my first brave victim.' He drew his sword, a particularly fine Chalkidian blade, a xiphos with a heavy central ridge.

'Throat or guts?' he asked.

One of the doctor's thugs grunted. 'Just fucking do it!' he said.

'No need to be in a hurry, Laertes,' the doctor said. His voice carried a sibilant warning, and the man – Laertes – flinched. It was the first sign Stratokles had seen that the doctor was still the monster he'd always been.

'Just go watch the temple,' the doctor said quietly.

'Yes, sir,' Laertes answered.

'I appreciate the professional courtesy, but I'm going to shit myself soon. Just get it done.' Stratokles stood straight, pulled his light chlamys off his shoulders and swirled it over his head.

The doctor had stepped back two steps.

'Not going to fight back,' Stratokles said with satisfaction. He'd made the man flinch. He dropped the chlamys.

The doctor nodded. 'Somehow I feel that killing you will only weaken me. He's going to kill me eventually, too.'

Stratokles nodded. 'So he is. Isn't that my line – when I plead for my life? I tell you that you're next? You do it anyway? Let me make a different suggestion. Take the money for killing me and run. Babylon – no one there has ever heard of you. Live out your life.'

Now the doctor smiled. 'Would you? What would you do if I let you walk away?'

Stratokles shrugged. 'You are a cruel bastard, Sophokles. You haven't the least intention of letting me walk away.'

'I'm giving you another minute of life, ingrate. Humour me.' The doctor gestured with his sword.

'Remember Banugul?' Stratokles said.

'I've heard of her.' Sophokles shrugged, looked around at some fancied noise.

'I have her. Or rather, I know where she is, and her son. Her son by Alexander.' He laughed.

'This sounds like a way of buying your life, doesn't it?' Sophokles nodded. 'I know this tune. You offer me something of great value. And I confess: a son of Alexander, even a bastard, is of great value.'

'Well, he's not for you. The management that would be required to propel that young man into the arena – to bring him to the moment where he could unseat Cassander – I don't know if it could be done.' Stratokles shrugged. 'I'm not even sure that I want to do it. He and his mother live far away – off the stage, out of the game. For all I know, the boy's dead, or deformed.'

'He must be, what, twenty-three? Twenty-four?' Sophokles looked over his shoulder. 'Are you by any chance double-dealing me, Stratokles?'

Stratokles frowned. 'I'm standing here ready to die, you're the one talking – and you think I'm betraying you?'

'Laertes?' the doctor asked.

'Dead as a fucking sacrificial lamb,' Lucius said, emerging from the trees. His sword was red in his left hand, and he had a javelin in his right hand, cocked and ready on the throwing cord. His gaze flicked over Stratokles. 'Thanks for saving my life. But I don't run. I ran once – that was enough for my whole life.'

'You killed my whole group?' the doctor asked. 'I'm very impressed.'

Lucius spat. 'Don't be. They weren't worth sheep-shit.'

The doctor nodded. 'They were more for colour than for muscle, anyway.'

Stratokles felt the tension draining from his shoulders.

'Walk away, Sophokles,' he said. The doctor was getting ready to spring; his feet were angled oddly, his limbs formed in a crouch. 'If you come for me, we all fight. People die – most likely you and me both.'

The doctor didn't slacken his physical stance. 'I'm listening.'

'We all back away. A step at a time.' Sophokles risked a look at Lucius.

'He has a distance weapon and I do not,' the doctor said. 'Distance only aids you, and taking you as a hostage is my only viable response.'

Stratokles took a deep breath. 'You didn't want to kill me anyway, Sophokles. I guarantee your life. You have my oath on it before the furies. Walk away, and consider this a fair return for my error of judgment in Alexandria.'

No one could call Sophokles of Athens indecisive. 'I accept,' he said, and stood up straight. He turned his back and walked away. He took a dozen steps, then sheathed his sword after a small flourish at Lucius, who spat again. He bowed to Stratokles. Then he turned and sprinted away.

Stratokles watched him until he was out of sight.

'Well,' said Stratokles. He turned away and struggled with the urge to vomit. It was all he could do to speak.

Lucius waited for him and held out a canteen of wine. 'I thought I was too late,' he said.

'He didn't want to do it. He's a strange man.' Stratokles shook his head.

'You offered your life to save me,' Lucius said. 'I *never* would have expected that.'

'I'm getting old,' Stratokles said.

'Where to?' Lucius said. 'I have a pair of horses – and we should get moving.'

Stratokles spat the sour wine. 'Hyrkania. We can be there in ten days.'

Lucius raised an eyebrow.

Stratokles shrugged. 'I'm going to throw another piece on the game board. If I accomplish nothing but to give fucking Cassander some bad nights – that will be enough for me.'

The blade rested, cool as a stone in her father's cellar, against Miriam's throat.

'Not a word, now,' the marine said. His voice was steady, almost apologetic. 'Trierarch says, if you say anything, I'm to off the pair of you. Sorry, despoina. Orders.'

Abraham lay perfectly still, and Miriam lay next to him. Over the silence, they could hear gulls, the rush of feet on the catwalk of the main oar deck, and the helmsman over their heads. The steering oars creaked, and then creaked again. The navarch spoke – the decking muffled his words.

'... right there,' the helmsman said.

'Like they own the whole world,' the navarch said. 'Wave like we're friends.'

Miriam tried to keep from shaking – tried to keep her mind from racing off into the abyss.

'Ten days out of Athens!' roared the helmsman over their heads. He was shouting to another ship – that much penetrated her terror and her anger.

'Where bound?' carried to her from the other ship, clear as a new day. The sound of the voice went through her like hot soup on a cold day. She felt her brother's hand close on hers like a vice, saw the marine's eyes glitter.

'Ephesus!' the helmsman replied.

'Safe voyage, then!' called Satyrus of Tanais from his own command deck.

And helpless in their cage, Abraham and Miriam held each other and lay in silence as they were rowed further and further away.

PART I

1

'By Herakles! This little worthless instrument will not defeat me!' Satyrus growled.

'Put your fingers on the strings again, and stop trying to be perfect,' Anaxagoras insisted.

'I promised Miriam that I would learn to play this before I saw her,' Satyrus said. He was sitting on a folding stool just forward of the helmsman's station, and Anaxagoras was sitting with his back to the light aft-mast that they had mounted to catch the light airs of late summer. They were an hour off their breakfast beach, cruising south of Lesbos en route to Rhodos.

'Your promise won't be worth the spit you put in it if you don't allow yourself to be human,' Anaxagoras said. He played the first measures flawlessly. 'It comes with practice. Like fighting with the sword, or pankration.'

Satyrus's eyes went back to the Antigonid penteres, now just a nick on the horizon.

'I thought that they behaved oddly. Too damned cheerful. There ought to have been catcalls and curses.'

Anaxagoras nodded. 'Perhaps. But you have thirty merchant ships and half as many warships in your tail, brother, and I dare say they were daunted by the sight.'

Satyrus laughed. 'I'll keep the truce – they have half my friends as hostages.'

Anaxagoras raised an eyebrow. 'I'm sure that the Antigonid navarch knew that in his intellect, my friend, but I suspect that your line of battle made his arse pucker nonetheless. Give the poor man his due. He was polite, and so were you, and now we're done.'

Satyrus shifted his seat on the deck. The weather was already hot, humid as only the surface of the sea can be humid, and the salt in the air burned in every minute laceration on his shoulders and back from practising in armour. He was thoroughly dissatisfied.

'I want to be away for Athens,' he said.

Anaxagoras laughed. 'I want to be back in Tanais, or perhaps Pantecapaeaum.'

Now Satyrus had to laugh. 'She won't be in either. She's off to the high plains – she was away from her people three-quarters of a year and she needs to be seen.' He was speaking of his sister, who was, by birth and inclination, Queen of the Assagetae, the western clans of the Sakje, the Scythian tribes of the Western Door of the Sea of Grass.

Anaxagoras nodded. 'I should be riding with her.'

Satyrus smiled. 'No,' he said. 'You should be right here with me. Selling grain like merchants, playing our lyres, having adventures. Tonight we can beach on the south of Chios. I know an islet that can take the whole fleet. Besides, you can barely ride.'

Anaxagoras bowed his head to acknowledge the truth of that. 'If only I'd known as a child that my future happiness depended on my ability to ride,' he said.

'You can be such a sophist,' Satyrus said.

'I was only speaking the truth,' Anaxagoras returned.

'No, you are implying that riding is a worthless accomplishment,' Satyrus said.

'No more than you imply to me every day that playing the lyre is the action of a dilettante and not a proper gentleman,' Anaxagoras said. 'You will not tame the lyre by force, brother.'

Silence reigned for as long as it took the oarsmen to pull ten times.

'When you take that superior tone, you sound just exactly like Philokles, minus the Lacedaemonian accent.' Satyrus clambered to his feet.

'I shall take that as a compliment, since I know you loved him. Perhaps he, too, used logic to debate you, instead of raw emotions from the gut?' Anaxagoras raised an eyebrow.

'Sometimes he simply hit me,' Satyrus agreed. 'Which had its own logic. I do not enjoy being as bad at anything as I am at playing the lyre.'

'I can't imagine you were born to your skills at pankration?' Anaxagoras asked wickedly.

'Xenophon says all men are born natural swordsmen. Old Socrates used to say that men are born to natural wisdom.' Satyrus grinned. 'But no. Your point is fair and well taken. I came to my skill in pankration down a long, hard road. And as you saw in Pantecapaeaum, I'm still hard-pressed to tumble Theron, even when he's past forty and I'm in my prime.'

Anaxagoras nodded. 'That was something to see. I could have watched all day – every man present felt the same. Like watching lions fight.'

Satyrus stuck out a discoloured shin. 'My bruises haven't healed yet.' He looked up at the masthead, and back at his helmsman, Thrassos, a red-haired barbarian and now a citizen of Rhodos. 'Wind is backing, Thrassos,' Satyrus said.

'Aye,' the Keltoi said. He wasn't a big man, but his tattoos, the scars around his eyes and his red hair made him a fearsome sight, and despite holding citizenship in three cities, no one would ever have mistaken him for a Greek.

'Planning to do anything about it?' Satyrus asked.

'Ain't steady yet,' Thrassos said.

As if to prove his weather-sense, a gust from the west tossed the bow and almost cost the rowers their stroke.

Satyrus shook his head. 'I feel as if the god tried to tell me something this morning and I ignored it,' he said. 'But for my life, I've no idea what. Did I commit impiety? Oh, forgive me, Anaxagoras. I'm in a foul mood.'

His friend used the mast to push to his feet. 'No apology required between friends, philos. You'll feel better when we're clear of Rhodes and headed towards Athens and Miriam.'

Rhodes was not the same as he had left it, just four months earlier. The Rhodians were pouring treasure into the restoration of their city, and the whole north end of the port, pounded nearly flat by siege engines, had begun to grow roofs and walls like a particularly colourful crop of forest mushrooms; new whitewashed houses with red and brown tiled roofs, and here and there a daring man had a yellow roof or a blue one, made from the new coloured ceramic tiles that were all the rage from Sicily to Asia.

The temple of Poseidon was almost fully restored, all his columns standing tall, and the new roof almost half complete – a better roof

23

than it had had before the siege, with the tiles and beams of solid marble, like the Parthenon on the Acropolis in Athens. The harbour was clear of hulks, and forty warships lay, warped alongside a pair of stone piers, ready for sea in a few moments, while another twenty were in ship-sheds up the beach – all new construction that included a rebuilt harbour wall with a dozen strong towers.

Satyrus took in the harbour in a single glance, and smiled despite the remnants of yesterday's foul mood. Rhodes had survived the mightiest siege since the Achaeans went to Troy. And he'd done his part to see them victorious.

When his ship dropped its anchor stone off the beach, the pilot tried to insist that as a hero of the town, Satyrus could lie alongside the stone piers, but Satyrus didn't need the space, and he waited while his oar master and his helmsman made the ship fast and then watched as his grain ships – those designated for Rhodes – came into the inner harbour and made for the great pier, one after another.

Menedemos, the serving archon, came down from his offices in the harbour tower to greet him when he waded ashore.

'A great man like you could keep his feet dry,' he said.

'Not if it would slow the unloading by a heartbeat,' Satyrus laughed. 'I'm away on the wind for Athens with the balance of my grain.'

Menedemos raised an eyebrow.

Satyrus shrugged. 'All right, I admit I'll be lucky to be out of here in two days, and even then I'll leave rowers in your brothels.'

Menedemos laughed and clasped his hand. 'It is good to have you back. You'll have no trouble getting lodgings – in fact, I'd be delighted to host you.'

'I promised Abraham I'd see how his house was coming along,' Satyrus said.

'I assumed as much, but the offer is there. Any problems on the way?' Menedemos asked.

'None. I'm assuming that, as a signatory to the truce, I'm safe – besides, having guaranteed half my grain to Athens, it is rather in Demetrios's best interest for me to be well treated. We came across one of his penteres off Chios, sailing on the wind, bound for Ephesus. The navarch was perfectly polite.'

'Pirates?' asked Menedemos.

'Menedemos, we must have killed half the pirates on the ocean, this last year.' Satyrus laughed. 'There's not a pirate in the Bosporus, nor the Pontus. Word in the Pontus is that the survivors went west, to Sicily and Corsica.' He looked around. 'But Demetrios's fleet is in the Pontus – charging tolls and hemming Lysimachos out of Asia.'

'That's news. How bad are the tolls?' Menedemos asked.

Satyrus made a face. 'Since half my grain was for Athens, I was excused. Which was probably best for everyone concerned. But watch out for your own, Menedemos. Demetrios can squeeze you without breaking the truce.'

'He can squeeze,' Menedemos said, 'but he needs to sell his products from Asia, too. He needs us. Hades, if Antigonus would see sense, he'd see that he needs Alexandria, too. We could all make money – no need for this endless squabble.'

Satyrus smiled. 'I think that Demetrios has other interests besides a healthy trade balance,' he said.

The last time he'd been at Abraham's house, the tile floor of the andron had been naked to the stars. Now the walls were back up, and the whole house smelled of fresh clay and fresh plaster – an earthy smell with a hint of lime and acid under it.

Jacob, Abraham's steward, let him inside the courtyard. 'My lord!' he said, and took Satyrus's hand.

'Jacob,' Satyrus said. He embraced the older man. 'I sent a letter.'

'We had it, lord. The plaster is still wet, but everything is to order. I have hardly any slaves, lord – Abraham freed most of them during the siege. But I have enough staff to move furniture and make food.' Jacob bowed to Menedemos. 'May I fetch you gentlemen a cup of wine?'

Satyrus nodded. 'And something for Anaxagoras and Apollodorus, as well, Jacob. They'll be along shortly. Do you have a shortage of slaves, then?'

Menedemos nodded. 'The city – that's me – we're buying almost every load that comes into town. We need them just to rebuild the walls – and level the besiegers' camp.'

Satyrus grimaced. 'I'd hoped to get myself a new hypaspist. Or at least a body slave.'

Jacob shook his head while an older woman served wine. 'Perhaps at Delos, lord. Not here.'

Later, Satyrus walked out of the house alone – a rare moment for a king – and along the newly restored back streets towards the back of the temple of Poseidon, where the agora was.

It was late in the day. Down at the piers, his ships were disgorging grain as fast as slaves and oarsmen could empty the holds, and his marines and sailors were already filling the wine ships and taverns on the waterfront. Anaxagoras was sound asleep in the heavy heat of late summer.

Satyrus had a hard time moving on the streets, because everyone in the town knew him, and men would stop to embrace his arm, or bow. Women raised their eyes to him, and men smiled and pointed him out to their children.

He wondered if he were better known in Rhodes than in Pantecapaeaum. Theron had told him that this was going to be his last adventure – that it was time for him to stay home and act like a king.

Satyrus had every intention of acting like a king – when he had Miriam by his side. He was cruising the Mediterranean to honour his commitments to Demetrios – grain for Athens – and to get his hostages back. When his duty was done, and when Miriam was free, Satyrus was ready to go back to his kingdom and never, ever leave. He smiled at the thought.

Even this trip ... Tanais had never looked finer, and his new ships being built at the new slips had been a sight he wanted to stay and enjoy. He'd come to enjoy giving justice, and walking in the agora, and having men listen to his opinions.

He smiled at another veteran of the siege, and bowed a little to a trio of women – widows – by the wall of the temple, where he and Miriam had curled side by side in the first light of morning, preparing for another day of siege. He felt close to her here – illogical, as she was in Athens, but he felt as if she might step out of the back streets, or emerge with her women behind her from the market.

Then he walked across the agora, where his own statue stood near those of Demetrios and Antigonus and Lysimachos. The Rhodians were great ones for dedicating statues, and even at the height of the siege they hadn't destroyed the statues of the men laying the siege. And now he had his own. He stood looking at it.

There was no echo in it, and he felt an obscure disappointment. What had he expected? A conversation with himself?

Past the statues. Small boys were trailing him, more than a dozen of them, some begging and more just shouting his name.

At the far western end of the market there was a small grove of olives, just six or eight trees, and the entrance to an underground temple of vast antiquity, where the city's reserve grain supply had been stored during the siege. Now there was a new altar atop the underground temple, a large, ornate marble with a deeply indented top and scrolled sides. In front of the altar were placed a dozen stele, markers for the dead of the siege.

Jubal, his oar master and sometime siege engineer, sat on his haunches by one of them. He had some teeth missing, and his face had the deep brown of old, salt-stained leather. His dusty cheeks were marked by the tracks of tears.

Satyrus ignored the boys and squatted by Jubal.

'Neiron,' Jubal said.

'Helios,' Satyrus added.

One by one, they traced the names of their own dead on the newly cut stele. Even the boys were silent.

When they were done, they paid the priestess to sacrifice a young ox, and gave most of the meat away. Before the smoke from the fat and bones began to rise to the gods, Anaxagoras came, and Apollodorus. They, too, looked at the stones. They, too, wept.

Other men came forward – some drawn by the free meat, and others by the observance, and hours passed before they were free to walk, arm in arm, back to Abraham's house.

Menedemos was with them by then, and the five of them held a small symposium under the stars in the restored garden.

Apollodorus grew drunk quickly, and he cried and cried – a fountain of tears. Anaxagoras watched him cry like a man watched a dangerous stranger.

'I have never seen him cry,' he said.

Satyrus took another drink. 'I doubt he cries while the enemy are still on his deck,' he said.

'Men don't cry for lost friends, they cry for themselves,' Anaxagoras said.

Satyrus shook his head. 'Easy to say, philos. But when I think of Helios, I don't think just of what I lost – good hot wine every morning. Clothes ready when I wanted them. A spear at my shoulder I could trust. By the gods – if that were all, I'd be a pitiful specimen. Apollodorus, too. What does Achilles say? Better a slave to a bad master than a king in Hades? Helios is gone to the land of shades. I'll be there soon enough, myself.'

'Maudlin, too.' Anaxagoras held out his cup for more wine and flopped on his stomach.

'What do you do when you aren't criticising me?' Satyrus asked.

'I criticise myself. The unexamined life is not worth living.' Anaxagoras laughed. 'Where is young Charmides?'

'Out in a brothel putting all that youth and beauty to good use, I suspect. Or perhaps wooing under some lucky maiden's balcony.' Satyrus spilled wine. 'Here's to him.'

'Ares, you sound like some forty-year-old with a paunch and no hair,' Anaxagoras said. 'You are, what, five years older than Charmides?'

Across the couches, Jubal had managed to stand. He embraced Jacob, or perhaps just fell against him, and went off to bed. Satyrus rose, and so did Anaxagoras, and they left Apollodorus, face down on his kline, weeping as if he would never cease.

2

'This is all taking too long,' Satyrus muttered. He hoped that he was keeping his thoughts to himself – his ships were lading and unlading as fast as the well-bribed slaves could work, and he'd already received payment, and still it seemed to him that every jar of grain was taking an age to move.

Anaxagoras, standing next to him on the great stone pier, his ruddy skin almost white in the full glare of the sun, made an expression with his mouth – wry, deprecating, knowing, amused, all in a single pull of the lips.

Satyrus caught the expression and knew that he was transparent.

'You know perfectly well that she's capable of entertaining herself,' Anaxagoras said. Unforgivably accurate, damningly exact and on the topic of his thoughts. 'She's not some foolish dancing girl who will pine for you a day or two and then spread herself for the next pretty young king who wanders by.'

'You're not as funny as you think you are,' Satyrus said. He tried to keep his tone light.

Both of them had been in love with Miriam – at the same time. To some remarkable degree, their friendship was based on that rivalry, and how they had risen above it. But Satyrus still avoided discussing Miriam with his friend, sometimes from a sense of propriety, and sometimes because he feared ridicule. Anaxagoras had – apparently – transferred his attentions to Satyrus's own sister, Melitta.

'I am,' Anaxagoras said. 'You're just not in the mood to laugh. I can turn the knife on myself – your sister is out on the plains right now, with at least one former lover and ten men who want her to wife – every one of whom can ride a horse like the wind and shoot a bow.'

'If my sister had wanted a Sakje, she'd have had one,' Satyrus said.

'That was rather my point,' Anaxagoras said. 'I know that I have

29

nothing to fear.' He looked at Satyrus. His tone, his expression, admitted that the exact opposite was the case, and he laughed ruefully.

'At least you'll see Miriam in Athens,' Anaxagoras said.

'If we ever get there,' Satyrus allowed.

It was cooler on the palaestra, the sand beautiful between his toes, the sea breeze curling through the colonnade to cool his sweat-slicked skin.

He and Anaxagoras had wrestled, boxed, fought two throws of pankration, and were now facing each other with short swords made of wood and their chlamyses wrapped around their shield arms. Satyrus had the feeling one gets from heavy exercise, a few bruises, a body in the peak of condition.

Anaxagoras had had a year-long siege to make a swordsman of himself, and he was excellent – taught by the same tutor who had helped Satyrus to restore his muscles after a wasting disease. So they circled each other warily, and Anaxagoras, once an aggressive but clumsy swordsman, now bided his time, aware that, as the inferior fighter – although not by much – he needed to launch counter-strikes rather than trying to move in on Satyrus's longer arms and greater experience.

Satyrus knew this as well, and he was tired – pleasantly tired, but with enough fatigue in his muscles to restrain him. He circled; side-stepped, and subsided again. For several long moments, both men were perfectly still.

'This is the last touch. I want a massage,' Satyrus said. It could be hard to be the king, all the time. Even Anaxagoras, who had the artist's ability to be any man's equal, deferred to him in matters of training. Anaxagoras would spar until he dropped of exhaustion – it was always left to Satyrus to call quits.

Anaxagoras nodded slightly.

He stepped to the left again, as Satyrus expected him to, and Satyrus launched a slow attack – so slow as to be almost languorous. His wrapped cloak flew off his arm like a live thing, fluttering out to snap, the cloak weight dragging the heavy cloth out flat for a fraction of a heartbeat.

Anaxagoras pivoted on both feet, rotating his hips to avoid the weight with his face, and his own cloaked arm snapped out to bat the incoming sword, but found no weapon, and dropped lower, seeking it.

Satyrus's blow was *so* slow that Anaxagoras's parry, blinded by the swirl of cloak, missed it entirely, and the wooden blade smacked him in the side of the neck – a trifle too hard. He dropped to one knee, his hand to his neck.

Satyrus was at his side, sword dropped. 'Apollo! A thousand apologies, Anaxagoras!'

The musician shook his head. 'It's nothing. Or rather, it is a fitting accompaniment to my sense of humiliation. How, exactly, did you land that blow?'

Assured of his friend's health, Satyrus was suffused with pride. 'It is a timing blow. It would never work without the cloak – it simply baffles the opponent's notions of the speed of the fight.'

'Devastating!' Anaxagoras said.

'Not if your opponent strikes fast – expects the blow, cuts at the sword arm,' Apollodorus commented from the colonnade.

'Look who's recovered from his wine!' Anaxagoras said, clearly piqued that the other man had seen him hit so easily.

Satyrus smiled inwardly at the ease with which men – men who were friends and comrades – could nonetheless cause each other offence. Satyrus was almost never offended by Apollodorus and his abrasive commentary on all fields of martial endeavour – the man was a professional, and his comments were meant only as professional criticism, no more. But the small, sharp-featured man had never mastered the art of giving criticism.

'Let's fight a bout and see,' Apollodorus said, coming onto the sand. He pulled his chlamys off and wrapped it around his arm, disclosing a body laced with scars the way barbarians wore tattoos. Satyrus had never counted them, but he expected that his captain of marines had at least a hundred scars, most of them on his forearms and lower legs, a few on his back, and one that indented his neck, where his heavy shoulder muscle met his collarbone, and ran, red, shiny and deep, across his chest to his hip.

Apollodorus was a small man, but neatly built, heavily muscled, and fast. Satyrus tossed him his practice sword, and he and Anaxagoras began to circle.

Anaxagoras remained cautious and defensive, which Satyrus read as a sign of anger. In combat, Anaxagoras was dangerously aggressive, almost as if he knew the hour of his fate and had little care until that time. Apollodorus was usually the cautious fighter – a man only survives as much combat as Apollodorus had seen by virtue of some caution. But today he was the one committed to attack.

'We are at the end of our workout,' Satyrus said. 'Wine-bibbers have to take the consequences of their excess.'

'You're next,' Apollodorus said. As he spoke, his chlamys-arm snapped out in a feint, and his sword followed, a fraction of a heart-beat behind.

As fast as thought, Anaxagoras parried, the two swords clicking together hard.

But Apollodorus didn't maintain the pressure. Instead, he dropped his weapon, stepped in, and grappled, his now free sword-hand seizing Anaxagoras's wrist expertly, his cloak over the musician's head.

Anaxagoras raised his left hand, indicating he'd lost, and Apollodorus unwrapped him from the folds of his cloak. 'I needed last night,' he said. The words held no apology, but the tone did.

'I have been thoroughly put in my place,' Anaxagoras said. 'I'll go back to the lyre and leave the sword to you two.'

'Nonsense,' Apollodorus said. 'If you could beat me, I'd be a pretty poor specimen. I've fought for twenty years – and practised ten years before that.' He nodded to Satyrus. 'Your turn.'

Satyrus caught the sword that Anaxagoras tossed him – and found that Apollodorus was on him immediately, sword and cloak weaving like a pair of dancers. He reacted without thought, ducking, backing – got his cloak on the other man's sword and tried for a seizure and missed, tried snapping a kick to the other man's shin and connected – a glancing blow, but it put him in the pattern and Apollodorus fell back, and Satyrus snapped his chlamys, his sword hidden behind it, and stepped back himself to breathe – and Apollodorus's sword hit his wrist hard enough to cause him to drop his own sword.

Anaxagoras clapped his hands together. There were other men standing under the colonnade and they applauded as well. 'Splendid!' called a younger man – Satyrus couldn't remember his name, but the man had been an Ephebe during the siege. He was still thin. Satyrus wondered if any of them would return to their full weight after a year on starvation rations.

He rubbed his wrist and smiled at Apollodorus. 'You are still the master,' he said.

Apollodorus rubbed his shin. 'If you had kicked for real, I might never have launched that blow,' he said.

Satyrus found his hands were shaking – muscle fatigue and the daimon of combat together. 'I'm done,' he said, showing his shaking hands.

Other men went out onto the sands, wrestling or boxing, and Satyrus realised that they had all been waiting for him – giving him the sand, as men said of someone they respected. He smiled around, trying to catch every eye – thanking them for their good opinion of him.

It was good to be a hero.

He went in to get a massage and a bath.

Later, after a review of his accounts with Abraham's steward, he met Anaxagoras in the courtyard, his lyre tucked under his arm as a much younger man would.

'Revenge is sweet,' Anaxagoras said with an evil smile.

Indeed, Anaxagoras was the very best of teachers – endlessly patient, his voice carefully modulated, slow to praise and slow to anger – so that when he did praise, a student knew he had done well indeed, and when his cheeks did mottle red, a student knew he'd been very foolish indeed.

Nor was this in any way a reversal of their bouts on the palaestra. Anaxagoras was a competent wrestler, an excellent boxer, a quick study at pankration, and now a brilliant swordsman. Satyrus was, at best, an indifferent musician. He loved to play – enjoyed any music, was constantly and pleasantly surprised that he could play anything at all – but seldom practised hard, so that simple fingerings were still the limit of his powers, and it was rare that duties – and pleasures – allowed him the time or the inclination to take a complete lesson.

'Play the scale again. This time, every other note,' Anaxagoras said.

Satyrus did as he was told.

'Now again, with regard to the tempo. Every note exactly the same *length*,' Anaxagoras said.

The control of his face suggested he was hiding a smile. Satyrus tended to play all the notes in a tune, but without the strict adherence to time essential to make the music correctly.

'And again,' Anaxagoras said. 'Your habit of resting your thumb on the sound board is part of the reason you cannot make your transition correctly.'

Satyrus turned his head sharply, a retort on his lips. And relented, reason telling him that anger at a teacher who was trying to help him was unworthy – foolish and boyish. Besides, his teacher's carefully controlled face suggested that this was, in fact, a form of revenge.

The third day in port. Miriam seemed a thousand Parasanges away, and a newly arrived Cyprian ore-freighter had somehow got ahead of his last three grain ships at the pier, and even when the confusion was sorted out, he'd lost another day. In his irritation, he slipped and got the tip of Anaxagoras's sword in his throat – hard enough to make him feel the front of his gorge with the back, and it ached all day.

'When we're on campaign somewhere, in our tenth or eleventh straight day of rain, and I feel like crap, and there's no wine, I'll wish I'd enjoyed these days more,' Satyrus said to Anaxagoras. He was sitting with his lyre in his lap. His throat hurt and he had no interest in playing. Or rather, he had every interest in playing well, and no interest in doing the work to get there, today.

'You are a king, not a mercenary,' Anaxagoras said. 'Surely sooner or later you will stop fighting.'

Satyrus shrugged. 'Unlikely. When Lysimachos and Ptolemy and Seleucus and Cassander and Demetrios and all the busy, scheming bastards are dead, perhaps. But there'll be more of them, I expect. Perhaps worse. The rumour is that Lysimachos is getting ready to march into my territory – claiming that he only seeks to march his army around the Euxine to Asia.'

'Now that he is to marry Amastris?' Anaxagoras said.

Satyrus looked out at the sea, blue as his former lover's eyes in the bright sunlight. 'They're married now,' he said, 'unless something happened to prevent it.'

'Shall we drink to them?' Anaxagoras asked. 'Is this why you are so far away from us?'

Satyrus spilled a libation. 'To Hera, goddess of the marriage bed. May Amastris be blessed. May they both be happy.'

'You mean that?' Anaxagoras asked.

Satyrus smiled. It was a crooked smile, but not a mean one. 'I think I do. I'm doing my best to mean it.'

Anaxagoras chuckled. 'Listen, philos. When I was young—'

'Look at the grey beard!' Satyrus said.

Anaxagoras glanced at Charmides, who was admiring a serving girl as she, quite self-consciously, carried water on her head across the street. 'Charmides makes all of us feel old,' he said, and they both laughed. The younger man glanced at them and smiled.

Satyrus smiled back at him. 'Will Charmides ever be old?' he asked.

Anaxagoras shook his head, dismissing the topic. 'At any rate, when I was young I wanted to marry a beautiful girl – a free girl. A local farmer's daughter. She was modest and clever and her legs – oh, even now, I think of her—'

'Aphrodite, philos, this was, what, six years ago? Stop telling it as if you were decades from her!' Satyrus laughed.

'And my father forbade it, of course. Rich men's sons do not wed farmer's daughters, no matter how good their legs are.' He laughed, but his eyes were far away.

Satyrus felt a prickle of unease.

'And the worst of it was that I knew – *I knew from the first* that my pater was right, and that I would never marry her. But I was stubborn, and romantic, and I pursued her. Long enough to convince her father I meant business.' He shrugged. 'And then I realised that she was merely clever, not actually intelligent. That she cared deeply for money and fine things.'

'It is easy to sneer at such thoughts, when you are rich,' Satyrus said.

'Too true. This is not a pretty story, nor one that shows me to best advantage.' Anaxagoras poured himself more wine. 'Eventually, I sopped seeing her. It was easy to do – after all, she was a free woman and modest, so that seeing her at all had required enormous effort. You understand?'

'Of course,' Satyrus said.

'And then – within a year – she married. She married well – better, in fact, than me. An aristocrat's son – a powerful man with powerful connections and an old, old family. And to this day I cannot decide what my role in all of this was – did I love her? Do I bless her success? Should I have wed her myself?' Anaxagoras drank off his wine. 'See? No great lesson there. Just real life.'

Satyrus nodded. The silence floated between them, easy enough. Easy silence had been the first sign they were friends, and now it endured, a token of esteem.

'I worry that I cannot marry Miriam,' Satyrus said.

The connection was obvious enough. Miriam was a Jew, not a Hellene. The daughter of one of the Middle Sea's richest merchants, no one could suggest that marrying her was marrying *down*. But she was a barbarian, a foreigner, an alien.

'I know,' Anaxagoras said. 'I wondered the same. I even wondered if, by courting her, I was – oh, I don't know. A foolish thought.'

Satyrus smiled. 'Redeeming yourself, brother?'

'Proving that I wasn't such a snob, more like. Although Miriam does rather rise above snobbery.' Their eyes met, and Satyrus grinned.

'My mother was more of a barbarian than Miriam will ever manage to be,' he said.

'Your father was not a king, of course. Were they married? Your parents?' Anaxagoras asked.

'Before Greeks and Sakje,' Satyrus said. 'I almost feel as if I was there, I've heard the tale so often. Pater was campaigning against Alexander, out on the Sea of Grass.' He poured wine to the shade of his father. 'Do you know that most of our sailors and marines worship my father as a god?'

Anaxagoras nodded. 'I know that Apollodorus wears his amulet, and so does Charmides.' He smiled. 'Does it trouble you?'

Satyrus shrugged. 'When I was a boy, I thought that he spoke to me. And when I was sick last year, he and Philokles seemed to visit me constantly. And yet Philokles never suggested to me that my father was anything but a good man. A difficult standard by which to measure myself, a worthy one, but no more.' He shrugged again. 'As I grow older, I find ... how can I say this? I find the idea of my father's deification a little offensive. Obscene.'

Anaxagoras nodded. 'I'm trying to imagine how I would feel if my own father were deified.' He laughed. 'And I can't. A good man of business – a pious man and a good father for a ne'er-do-well son. But godhood is not in him, and when he passes, his shade will not reach to the heavens for apotheosis.' Anaxagoras rubbed his beard. 'I'm not sure he'd want it even if offered.'

Satyrus took a deep breath. Then he changed his mind. 'Tomorrow?' he asked.

Apollodorus nodded. 'Why don't we stop being so serious, walk down to the pier, and see?'

The land breeze of the early morning found them already clear of the harbour mouth, the great mainsail rigged to catch the world's wind, a gentle Boreas blowing them west, almost dead astern on their track for Athens after they weathered the northern promontory of Rhodos. The ships that had been laden with grain for Rhodes were full now of copper from Cyprus, cedar planks from Lebanon, skilled slaves who would become freemen in a year or two at Tanais or Pantecapaeaum, marble, spices and even a consignment of fine Aegyptian furniture for a rich merchant in Olbia. They also had the hard silver specie that had paid for the abundance of grain. Two days later, he sent them away north off Lesbos, under guard of half his ships, with Diokles, his most trusted trierarch, in command.

Aekes, a small, fiery man, brought his *Ephesian Artemis* off the beach in style and rowed away west – the scout ship. Satyrus followed him with two penteres, two triemiolas, and six triremes; almost a quarter of his full fleet, and some of the best ships – and some of his rawest, too.

He missed Diokles already, having seen little enough of the man in Rhodos, but keeping all of his best captains at his side all the time was poor strategy and unfair to them. He kept Aekes, though, because he could be trusted with anything – he had worked his way up to trierarch from the starting position of a Spartan helot, and he owed Satyrus his status, his citizenship, and his fortune.

Steering his own penteres – not his beloved *Arete*, lost to fire in the siege of Rhodos, but *Medea*, a smaller, lighter fiver built in Olbia – Satyrus pondered on Athens as a destination and what this visit meant to him. More than just seeing Miriam – although seeing Miriam was the greatest part of it, he admitted to himself. He must decide, before his prow touched the great pier at Piraeus, whether he meant to marry her. But there were other opportunities in Athens, other perils – he was a citizen there, and one whose activities made him both famous and infamous; a hero and a monster. Demetrios the besieger was the city's current lord. Satyrus wanted to land in Athens ready for anything that might transpire. He wanted to be done with his state of war against Demetrios because, among other things, he expected shortly to be at war with Lysimachos.

Looking at Anaxagoras, taking a nap in the sun, Satyrus thought back to their last conversation in Rhodes and frowned to himself. *Hard to lie to a friend. Harder to hide from yourself.* Satyrus's sense of bitterness – betrayal, even – over Amastris's change of heart was deeper than he wanted to admit to another man. He told himself that the feeling was *not* just the jealousy of the jilted lover. He reminded himself that he would have lain with Miriam a hundred times – a thousand – during the siege, had she only been willing. He allowed that Amastris was a ruler, as he was, and had duties to her city, as he did.

Despite all of that, he couldn't think of her without a rush of anger. Her decision to marry the Satrap of Thrace – a major player in the war against Antigonus – made war with Lysimachos almost certain; a war that would pit him against Ptolemy, if not in immediate fact, then in form, and would have repercussions across his personal, professional and mercantile life. It was this that had caused him to be so very careful of the trierarchs he chose to take to Athens. He wanted only his most trustworthy men, men who would look after his interests even when offered major bribes, even when threatened. He had no idea what the city might try to do. But he needed to keep the door opened by the truce with Demetrios ajar, at least, even if it meant trading with the enemy. Amastris's wedding had put him there, and he had no choice but to react this way.

Or that's what he told himself.

So he had Aekes scouting ahead, and Anaxilaus and his brother Gelon – both aristocrats from Sicily, wealthy men and no friends to Athens. They had *Oinoe* and *Plataea*. And Daedelus of Halicarnassus brought up the rear of the column in another heavy penteres – *Glory of Demeter*, a famous ship.

He could not take only his most trustworthy captains, however. None of the rest of his captains were remarkable men, and all of them were new to him – he had Eumenes of Olbia's son Ajax, a fine young man with a fine new ship called *Apollo of Olbia*, and two ships from Pantecapaeaum commanded by relatives of his former adversary, Heron, the last Tyrant of Pantecapaeaum – Lykeles son of Draco, and

Eumeles son of Tirseus, both too young to have reputations. They had light triremes – *Tanais* and *Pantecapaeaum*.

And finally, he had a pair of Rhodian-built triemiolas, decked triremes with a half deck for carrying full sail and more sailors – or marines. Their captains were prosperous men who had been made by Leon: Sandokes of Lesbos, a foppish man famed for his daring navigation, trierarch of the powerful *Marathon* and the Etruscan; and Sarpax, whom Leon had employed for twenty years. Satyrus could see Sarpax from the helm, because the tall Etruscan was standing in the bow of his *Desert Rose* just a few horse lengths astern of *Medea*.

He put the inexperienced men in the middle of his line, the way a good strategos would place them in the phalanx. They had expert helmsmen to help them – his money and reputation now attracted some of the best on the ocean.

It was all very satisfying. He looked back down the line of his fighting ships, all heeling well to starboard with the press of wind, sails well set, the ropes that crossed them appearing to be restraints on mighty Boreas himself. And behind his warships, sixteen heavy merchants – six Athenian grain ships, towering over the rest, and ten of his own. A fortune in grain, carefully guarded, representing the wealth of his kingdom and a new avenue of diplomacy. Grain for Athens.

Where Stratokles had begged him to take it. Stratokles, who had single-handedly engineered Amastris's betrayal – her wedding to Lysimachos.

On the bench built under the rising strakes of the stern by the helmsman's station, Anaxagoras opened his eyes. 'Who could doubt the gods on a day like this one?' he asked.

Satyrus smiled and looked away.

'Aha,' Anaxagoras said, swinging his feet onto the planks of the deck. 'You could. Thinking of Miriam?'

Satyrus shook his head. 'Lysimachos. Cassander. Stratokles.' The last name he spat.

'He has done you no disservice,' Anaxagoras said.

'Hmm,' Satyrus said.

'None, philos. You need to keep everyone a little further away – arm's length, I think Coenus said.' Anaxagoras nodded north, towards distant Tanais, where Coenus was regent. 'The appearance of alliance with Athens will give everyone pause.'

Satyrus shrugged. 'I know.'

'And you don't like it,' Anaxagoras said. 'Do you ever think that men make war because they don't want to go through the tedious process of keeping peace?'

Satyrus laughed. 'You have me exactly. I was just thinking how much simpler open war was than peace. We overawe Athens with our fine warships while we sell her grain from our fine merchant fleet – while selling to Rhodes and offering our ships to Ptolemy. At least when Demetrios was firing his huge rocks at us, we knew which way the enemy lay.'

Anaxagoras shook his head. 'No we didn't. Think of Nestor's betrayal. Think of all the idiots who would have sold Rhodes for some cash and a guarantee of survival. Think of the welter of cross-purposes – slaves, mercenaries, soldiers, your men, Rhodians, old versus young – all the factions, all the sides. That was war.' Anaxagoras smiled when his eye caught that of Charmides, who was exercising amidships. 'What you wish for, *lord*, is the freedom that man has to pretend that the world is simple, when you and I both know that in war and in peace the world is very, very complicated.'

Satyrus nodded. 'Who made you so wise?' he asked.

'Dionysus,' Anaxagoras said. 'And old Aristotle played his part, I expect.'

'We could go wrestle at the Lyceum,' Satyrus said. 'There's glory for you.'

'Now you're talking, brother. Wrestling at the Lyceum, and the finest courtesans in the world. Oh – I didn't mean to say that aloud.' He roared with laughter at Satyrus's reaction. 'Got you, got you.'

Satyrus laughed too. Astern, Sarpax waved. He was laughing, too.

They made landfall at Delos in late afternoon. Satyrus was a pious man, and the opportunity to revisit the temple complex was appealing, even with Athens looming – or rather, the more appealing because Athens was looming – just a few days away. And he told himself that he needed a body slave.

He beached his ships on the windward side of the island, and paid a fisherman to take him around the point to the temples. Sandokes and Aekes and their helmsmen came, as did Apollodorus and Charmides. Anaxagoras had eaten bad shellfish on the beach and was busy returning it to Poseidon, or so he croaked between bouts of being sick.

This time, Satyrus sent Apollodorus ashore first to make sure that the priests knew that his visit was religious and not official, and then waded ashore himself, paying the fisherman a gold daric to stay on the beach waiting. The man bit it, looked at it carefully, and then gave him a pleased smile.

'I'd a' sold you my boat for it,' he said cheerfully.

'Don't tell the priests or they'll find a way to take it from you,' Satyrus said, only half joking.

The fisherman laughed and rowed away down the beach to where poorer men waited in lines for a turn in the temple.

No waiting for kings, of course, even those not on official visits.

Satyrus sat in the anteroom to the oracle, trying to put his mind in a state receptive to the god. He had wrestled with Anaxagoras before crossing, and the bout was very much in his mind – Anaxagoras had thrown him with an outstretched arm and what had seemed the gentlest nudge to his hip, and Satyrus found in the move a whole new expression of balance in combat. It filled his mind, kept him from the meditative state.

With apologies to the two men waiting with him – an Athenian from one of the priestly families and a Corinthian – he stepped out onto the porch of the temple and took up a fighting stance and began to rotate his foot at odd angles.

The hierophant was watching him when he stopped. 'I have seen a woman offer her dancing to the god, but never a man offer his foot-work at the pankration. Nonetheless, yours is fine.' He grinned – not the grave, dignified high priest at all, just for a moment, but a Greek man with an appreciation for a fine sport and a fine body.

Satyrus was abashed – a very rare feeling for him. 'My apologies, I meant no disrespect. I *have* been practising the lyre . . .' He trailed off, feeling like a teenage boy caught nuzzling a slave girl.

The hierophant cackled. 'Your lyre work will probably never match your fighting skills, my lord. Will you come with me?'

'It is not my turn,' Satyrus said.

'I gave you my turn,' the Athenian priest said, inclining his head. 'I am here for my city on a very minor matter of religious law.' He smiled. 'Had I known that I would see a famous pankrationist, I'd have come sooner.'

The Athenian priest was plainly dressed, and yet clearly a man of enormous worth. He also had a fine physique – barrel-chested and tall.

Satyrus smiled at the compliment and inclined his head in return. 'Sir, I am on my way to Athens, where, I, too, am a citizen. Perhaps we might have a bout at the Lyceum?'

'Polycrates, son of Lysander,' the Athenian said, and they clasped hands. 'We are keeping the hierophant waiting.'

The hierophant nodded. 'It seems to me that this meeting was the reason the god brought you here. This may have been the only moment that the god required.' He nodded at their confusion. 'It is often thus. Brasidas met the King of the Thracians here. He was coming to ask, "By what means may I defeat the Athenians in Thrace?" I understand that he never even had to ask the question.'

He led Satyrus by the hand to the sacred lake, and prayed aloud to Apollo – a very old prayer in the old Ionian style, with his arms spread wide. Satyrus assumed the same pose and waited.

'Ask your question,' the high priest said.

'*Do not go to Athens!*' called a hoarse, low voice in the distance. And there was laughter. Satyrus turned his head and saw a group of retainers – possibly Polycrates' men – playing by the side of the temple.

The omen was clear to Satyrus. He looked at the priest, who looked back at him, arms outstretched. 'Were you contemplating a trip to Athens?' he asked mildly enough.

'I have a fleet of grain ships, fully laden, en route to Athens. The woman ... that is, my best friend is a hostage there. My grain ships are the guarantee of my good behaviour. I *must* go to Athens.'

The priest nodded curtly. 'I wish that I had a drachma for every time a supplicant has received a direct order from the god and then informed me, and my lord Apollo, that he cannot possibly obey,' he said. 'I would be a rich man.'

Satyrus had meant to ask something grand – to ask how he might best serve his people, or something equally vague. Delos was, he thought, best at vague questions. But now he went with the divine inspiration. 'Lord Apollo, Lord of the Silver Bow, God of the Lyre, what must I do to survive Athens?'

The hoarse voice down in the temple yard floated across the temple lake: '*Guest ... friendship is still sacred... even in Athens.*' as clear as if the priest had spoken it himself. In the distance, men laughed. Many conversations merged into the voice of the god.

Satyrus considered running outside to find the men – to ask what they were discussing, what joke was being told, what ribald story gave rise to these pronouncements, so like the voice of the god. But only to see the mechanism of the god's breath. For Satyrus was as sure as anything he'd ever known that he'd heard the voice of the god floating over the sacred lake.

'You are very close to the gods,' the hierophant said.

Satyrus raised an eyebrow. 'I have been told so,' he said.

'I know men who would kill for an answer as clear as that,' he said. 'Come.'

Together they walked back to the anteroom on the temple porch. The Athenian was moving his feet in just the way that Satyrus had been. He grinned, also like a much younger man caught in some secret sin.

'I see it,' he said. 'A very small movement of the hips can be as powerful as a much larger movement.'

Satyrus shrugged. 'Perhaps not as powerful,' he said. 'But good enough in a confined space, or a real fight.'

Polycrates nodded. 'May I hold you to our bout at the Lyceum?'

Satyrus narrowed his eyes. 'Allow me to go one better, sir. Let us swear a guest friendship here, and I'll give you a ride back to Athens. We can fight on every beach from here to there.'

Polycrates' eyes sparkled. 'Nothing would give me greater pleasure,' he said. 'The more especially as it would allow me to dispense with a particularly annoying pup of a trierarch who has made my life a misery. Now I can send him on his way to Corinth. You are no friend to Demetrios, as I remember?'

Satyrus bowed. 'We are not at war, he and I,' he answered carefully.

Polycrates nodded. 'Well – best you know – I am his friend. Perhaps his greatest supporter in Athens. Will you still carry me home?'

Satyrus extended his hand.

Polycrates took it. 'Let us go before the god.'

Arm in arm, with the hierophant behind them, obviously pleased, they walked into the divine presence, where the flame burned. They made their gestures to the god, and then, with the hierophant leading them, they swore guest friendship. Satyrus undertook it as King of the

Bosporus, with full solemnity, and Polycrates answered him in kind, as high priest of Herakles in Athens.

When they were done, Satyrus nodded to his new friend. 'So you are the priest of Herakles,' he said.

'And you are his descendant, are you not?' asked Polycrates. 'As are we – Heraklidae all.'

The grain fleet might have made Athens in two long, hard days, but Satyrus allowed three – he was suddenly in less of a hurry, and more determined to know Polycrates, and to gather what news he could from fishermen. The most likely threat came from Demetrios – it seemed obvious, when he thought of it, lying on the sand at Syros watching the wheel of the stars over his head, that Demetrios meant to take him and hold him. No surer way of preventing his re-entering the war when the truce sworn at the end of the siege of Rhodes expired.

Besides, Polycrates was a wonderful close-in fighter, and Satyrus found that the man had things to teach him. He had a technique for fighting from the ground – a technique that Satyrus had seen Theron use, but had never been taught. Polycrates could lever himself up on his shoulders and neck and grasp with his legs like a pair of blacksmith's tongs, seizing his opponent and pulling him to a ground grapple which Polycrates, built like a large rock, would inevitably win.

Charmides was annoyed by the technique. 'What is to keep me from walking away as soon as you go to ground?' he asked the older Athenian.

Satyrus shook his head. 'We do not always fight by choice, Charmides. What if circumstance or Tyche places you on the ground? What if you are attacked *after* being knocked down? We do not always fight from a position of advantage.'

'In fact,' Apollodorus said with a quick smile, 'we *never* seem to fight from a position of advantage. No one attacks you because you are ready to be attacked, young man.'

Charmides was abashed, and blushed. 'Of course not. I should have held my tongue.'

In fact, there was quite a crowd to spar with the big Athenian man. He was courteous, careful, and very good.

So good that he won the first night against Satyrus, three throws to two. Satyrus lay watching the stars. It was a long time since anyone had beaten him. He could console himself that he had not used all of his skill – but neither had the other man, he was sure. No one would, in a friendly grapple on the beach. And it was a long time since he had lost, and he was trying to bear it with good grace.

After lying awake an hour, he rolled off his cloak and his two furs and walked up the beach to where his kit lay under his aspis, and took out his canteen. It was full of wine. He sat with his back against the stern, and said some poetry to himself, and then he fetched his travelling lyre and went around the headland and played it for half an hour.

He fell into the playing – some of the best he had ever done. When he had finished with his practices and his hymn to Apollo, he was sleepy, so he went back to his cloak and fell immediately asleep.

'Am I growing more arrogant?' Satyrus asked.

He was between the steering oars of his *Medea*, an hour off the beach at Syros, driving along over the choppy sea with the wind dead astern, all the rowers enjoying being passengers while the deck crew worked like ants to keep the mainsail and the boatsail trimmed and drawing in a tricky wind.

Anaxagoras grinned. 'I'm sorry – how would I know? I mean, if one throws pitch on a black statue—'

Satyrus swatted him with an open hand. 'I'm serious,' he said.

Anaxagoras frowned. 'Are you? All the tragedies seem to have this moment held in them, brother. And have you ever known a woman to ask you if she was gaining weight, and to want a genuine answer?'

Satyrus looked away in consternation. 'So the answer is – yes.'

Anaxagoras shrugged. 'Yes. That is, the siege hardened something in you. You used to be somewhat hesitant about giving some opinions – now you take for granted that your opinion is necessary in all situations.' He held up a hand to forestall Satyrus's explanations. 'Now, to be sure, philos, you *are* a king, and you *are* a commander. But since you asked, may I say by way of allegory that I am a famous musician, and that I find that this does not particularly increase my ability to pronounce on how this ship sails?'

Satyrus tried to laugh – he got a smile to his face, at least. 'Whereas I feel that my expertise as king justifies voicing my opinion on all subjects?' he asked.

Anaxagoras shook his head. 'See? You don't really fancy my opinion.' He rolled his eyes. 'I expect I'll be executed.'

Satyrus looked at the horizon. 'Fuck off,' he said. 'I asked. I was hoping for a less adamant answer.'

Anaxagoras shook his head. 'You knew the answer before you asked.'

Satyrus sighed. 'I'm not taking the losses at pankration at all well.'

Anaxagoras grinned. 'There, I can put your mind at rest. I think that you are bearing them splendidly, in that you haven't cursed or shouted out loud. When did you last lose?'

'Lose outright?' Satyrus thought. 'Three or four years, anyway.'

Anaxagoras nodded. 'Well, it's good for you. Builds character.'

'My tutor, Philokles, used to say that.' Satyrus nodded. He was stung, and trying very hard not to show it.

'All tutors say that,' Anaxagoras said. He put a hand on Satyrus's shoulder. 'May I say – at the risk of hurting you further – that it's brave of you to ask? And that you can remedy this simply by being silent on occasion?'

Satyrus looked away, and a variety of responses occurred to him. But again, he managed a smile. 'I'll see what I can do,' he said.

Polycrates came back from the bow, where he'd gone to catch the breeze. 'What a perfect morning!' he said. He nodded to Anaxagoras. 'My lord, you keep very good company – good men, with good manners and real excellence. That Charmides ...'

Satyrus raised both eyebrows.

Anaxagoras smiled. 'Everyone loves Charmides,' he said.

'Where is he from?' asked Polycrates. 'Is he of a good family?'

Apollodorus appeared on deck in armour. 'Very good,' he said curtly. 'Swords, Satyrus?'

It was days since Satyrus had practised in armour. Charmides came forward and assisted him in putting on his thorax of bronze, and he and Apollodorus began to move up and down the central gangway.

Satyrus fought with restraint, fighting the temptation to work too hard to vindicate the loss of the night before. And in a few hits, he was too deep in the moment to worry about such stuff. Apollodorus had always stretched him to his limit, and today was no different – if anything, the smaller man was better than usual, leaping high in the air, stepping up off an oarsman's bench to land a cunning blow along the back of Satyrus's neck.

But Satyrus, after a slow start, rose to his level. He fought so well that when the two of them came to a stop, they were on the amidships fighting platform, neither man having pushed the other to the bow or stern. Each landed a simple blow, and almost as one they removed their helmets, panting hard, and laughed.

'Well fought,' Apollodorus said. 'You've winded me.'

Satyrus had to use his will to keep from bending double to take bigger breaths. He didn't risk talking, but merely laughed and slapped his marine captain on the back.

Polycrates clapped his hands together. 'May I?' he asked. 'I don't have armour ...'

Satyrus felt much better. He grinned. 'You may have mine if you don't mind the sweat.'

Polycrates sent his body slave for a chitoniskos. 'I should say something nice about the sweat of a king,' he said, taking the thorax, 'but you have about soaked the thing through.'

'You go that long against Apollodorus,' Satyrus said. In fact, he meant no rivalry by it – Apollodorus was the best fighter and the fittest man.

'Ah,' Polycrates said. 'Then I should wait until tomorrow, when he's fresh.'

Apollodorus bridled – perhaps at being discussed in the third person. 'I'm fresh enough right now, Athenian,' he said. 'Let's see what you have.'

Polycrates wasn't sure he liked that response – it showed in his face – and Satyrus had a moment to see what a powerful man looked like when he was displeased. He looked pompous and silly – and Satyrus knew that he had looked the same the night before when he had lost at pankration. He nodded to no one in particular. He was a day from Athens, with all the danger of the prophecy combined with his anxiety on seeing Miriam – it seems a good time to honour the gods and work on excellence.

Polycrates' slave brought him a linen chitoniskos, a fine one with a red stripe. The Athenian stripped and put it on, and then Satyrus helped him into his scale thorax, which fitted him well enough, if a

47

little small in the chest. Satyrus tied the cords a full two fingers looser than he would on himself – when he tied it, the rings touched.

Polycrates picked up Satyrus's practice aspis, and moved it around. 'Heavy,' he said, sounding human.

'I practise with a heavier shield ...' Satyrus began.

'Of course you do – you fight for real.' Polycrates flexed his knees, picked up the wooden sword, and saluted Apollodorus. 'At your service. And I meant no slight, sir, when I said I'd wait for you to be fresh. I feel very much at a disadvantage here – you are professional soldiers, athletes, men who live like heroes from Homer, and I am a rich politician from Athens. If I spoke badly, please accept my apologies.'

Apollodorus hooked his cheek-plates down. 'Not necessary,' he said simply, and turned to walk down the command catwalk to the amidships command platform.

Satyrus caught a glance from the Athenian which suggested that he felt he'd been rebuffed.

'It was a handsome apology,' Anaxagoras said.

'He can be a prick, though,' Satyrus said.

Anaxagoras pursed his lips. 'If you were alone on his ship, surrounded by killers ...'

Satyrus rocked his head from side to side. 'Good point. Hadn't seen it that way.'

After a few moments of staring, the two contestants came together – two cautious blows, one each, both easily turned on the shield rim, and they were apart.

They batted at each other for as long as it took for the ship to sail the length of a tiny islet, and then Polycrates closed.

Or rather, he attempted to close, pushing forward with his back leg and levering his hips to shield-slam his opponent.

Apollodorus met him, but his shield was angled to the impact, and his sword arm shot out, past the Athenian's head, and then the bigger man was on the deck, the point of Apollodorus's wooden sword at his throat.

Polycrates slapped the deck in surrender and got smoothly to his feet – a fine display of muscle for an older man. He rubbed his hip where it had hit the wood planking.

But he was on his guard in heartbeats, and they came together again, and the next time Apollodorus tried a simple throw, the Athenian blocked it and stepped back. Each of them landed some hits – a few more to Apollodorus – and then Polycrates hit Apollodorus in the forearm, hard enough to draw blood.

In the time it takes a man to say a single word, he had his helmet off and was apologising.

'Too damn hard – I'm sorry, comrade. You're beating me easily and I'm trying too hard.' He shook his head.

Apollodorus smiled. 'I'd be a poor man if I couldn't take the cut of a wooden sword, Polycrates. But I think I'm done for the day.'

They embraced, though, and Polycrates was more human, and better received, after the fighting on the deck.

That night they fought again on the beach – pankration again – and this time Polycrates won three straight bouts. Other men were waiting for a turn with him, and Satyrus didn't feel he could ask for a fourth. It wasn't just a matter of size, although the man's reach was impressive – so was Theron's, and Satyrus could hold Theron to a draw.

'You are very good,' Polycrates said, reaching to embrace him.

Something about the compliment angered Satyrus, but he accepted the embrace and went off to his lyre. He sang Sappho's songs to the waves and the sunset, and thought of Miriam, and wondered what surprise was waiting for him in Athens.

In the morning, he called all his fighting captains together, and walked them around the headland to where the merchant ships were gathered off the beach. 'Apollo told me that Athens will be a danger to me,' he said. 'I've given this a certain amount of thought, and if I have understood the god's words, then Demetrios will seek to take me in Athens,' he said.

If he expected consternation, he was disappointed. His captains knew the gossip, had heard more about his visit to Delos than might have made him comfortable.

'We'll be right there behind you,' Apollodorus said.

Satyrus shook his head, seeing in his mind the punishment Demetrios might mete out on the hostages if Satyrus landed armed marines in Athens. 'No. I don't want to seem a threat at all. So the fighting fleet will not enter the harbour. In fact, I want to see all the warships drop off when we have Piraeus in sight. I'll signal with my shield – all of you sail for Aegina. If all is well, I'll meet you there in three days. If all is not well, Apollodorus has the command and must do as he sees fit. No rescues – even if Demetrios takes me, it will only be as a prelude to further negotiation.' He looked around. 'Let me say that again, friends: if Demetrios takes me, it is *not* an act of war. No seizing Athenian shipping, no striking at his fleet up at Corinth. You hear me, friends?'

They growled – all except Aekes, who simply nodded.

Satyrus looked around. 'If for some reason, Demetrios has me killed – well, you are all released from your oaths, but I'd take it as a favour if you would do all the damage to his shipping that you possibly can.' He grinned.

No one grinned back. 'Is it that bad?' asked Apollodorus.

Satyrus shook his head. 'No,' he said. 'If not for the prophecy, I'd have no fears for myself at all. It would be the height of folly for Demetrios to attack me. But Apollo does not speak lightly to mortals.'

Aekes shook his head. 'Makes no sense at all,' he said. 'If he grabs you, you forfeit very little – and Rhodes is free to break the treaty.'

'Not while he has all their hostages,' Satyrus answered. 'But still – I agree, Aekes. I've thought about it every night – I can't get my head around it.'

'Why not stay here?' Anaxilaus asked. 'Camp on this beach – we take the grain fleet into Athens, sell the grain, meet you here. You can wrestle with Charmides.'

They all laughed.

Satyrus shook his head. 'I have private business in Athens,' he said.

'Business with long legs?' Aekes asked, but his voice was very low. 'Listen, lord,' he said louder. 'I'm not a pious man, but if the god spoke to you direct, why not just obey? Stay here? Tell us who you want to meet and we'll bring him to you.'

'Abraham is a hostage,' Satyrus said. 'You can't bring him out of Athens, and I need to see him.'

His captains looked at him with something like suspicion.

'I'm going to Athens,' he insisted.

'Without your fleet?' Sandokes asked. 'Haven't you got this backward, lord? If you must go, why not lead with a show of force?'

'Can you go three days armed and ready to fight?' Satyrus asked. 'In the midst of the Athenian fleet? No. Trust me on this, friends. And obey – I pay your wages. Go to Aegina and wait.'

Sandokes was dissatisfied and he wasn't interested in hiding it. 'Lord, we do obey. We're good captains and good fighters, and most of us have been with you a few years. Long enough to earn the right to tell you when you are just plain wrong.' He took a breath. 'Lord, you're wrong. Take us into Athens – ten ships full of fighting men, and no man will dare raise a finger to you. Or better yet, stay here, or *you* go to Aegina and *we'll* sail into Athens.'

Satyrus shrugged, angered. 'You all feel this way?' he asked.

Sarpax shook his head. 'No,' he said. 'Aekes and Sandokes have a point, but I'll obey you. I don't know exactly what your relationship with Demetrios is, and you do.' He looked at the other captains. 'We don't know.'

Sandokes shook his head. 'I'll obey, lord – surely I'm allowed to disagree?'

Satyrus bit his lip. After a flash of anger passed, he chose his words carefully. 'I appreciate that you are all trying to help. I hope that you'll trust that I've thought this through as carefully as I can, and I have a more complete appreciation of the forces at work than any of you can have.'

Sandokes didn't back down. 'I hope that you appreciate that we have only your best interests at heart, lord. And that we don't want to look elsewhere for employment while your corpse cools.' He shrugged. 'Our oarsmen are hardening up, we have good helmsmen and good clean ships. I wager we can take any twenty ships in these waters. No one – no one with any sense – will mess with you while we're in the harbour.'

Satyrus managed a smile. 'If you are right, I'll happily allow you to tell me that you told me so,' he said.

Sandokes turned away. Aekes caught his shoulder.

'There's no changing my mind on this,' Satyrus said.

Sandokes shrugged.

'We'll sail for Aegina when you tell us,' Aekes said.

Satyrus had never felt such a premonition of disaster in all his life. He was ignoring the advice of a god, and all of his best fighting captains, and sailing into Athens, unprotected. But his sense – the same sense that helped him block a thrust in a fight – told him that the last thing he wanted was to provoke Demetrios.

He explained as much to Anaxagoras as the oarsmen ran the ships into the water. Anaxagoras just shook his head.

'I feel like a fool,' Satyrus said. 'But I won't change my mind.'

Anaxagoras sighed.

'When we're off Piraeus, I'll go off in *Miranda* or one of the other grain ships. I want you to stay with the fleet,' Satyrus said. 'Just in case.'

Anaxagoras picked up the leather bag with his armour and the heavy wool bag with his sea clothes and his lyre. 'Very well,' he said crisply.

'You think I'm a fool,' Satyrus said.

'I think you are risking your life and your kingdom to see Miriam, and you know perfectly well you don't have to. She loves you. She'll wait. So yes, I think you are being a fool.'

Satyrus narrowed his eyes.

'You asked,' Anaxagoras said sweetly, and walked away.

3

Attika appeared first out of the sea haze; a haze so fine and so thin that a landsman would not even have noticed how restricted was his visibility. Satyrus saw the mountains, but the coast was still lost.

'I have a favour to ask,' Polycrates murmured, suddenly at his side.

Satyrus was standing at the rail. His helmsman, Thrassos, had the steering oars, the length of a sword thrust away.

He turned to the Athenian priest. 'We are guest friends,' Satyrus said. 'Whatever I can do for you, I will.'

Polycrates flushed. 'I am in your debt, then. I need you to land my slave at the Temple of Poseidon. At Sounion. It is a religious matter – the matter that took me to Delos. And he is . . . very good at running messages.'

Satyrus had barely noticed the young man, a gangly youth with a face full of spots and pimples. He was, now that Satyrus looked at him, well-muscled for such slim bones. His hair was black. He was older than he seemed at first glance.

'He looks like a Greek,' Satyrus said. He nodded to the man. He liked the look of him, despite the pimples.

'Theban mother and father.' Polycrates took his turn to look out over the rail. 'Friends of mine, really. What Alexander did there – brutal. Horrible. Jason is not really a slave, but I protect him. And he serves me.' Polycrates looked around. 'He serves me in political ways. If you take my meaning.'

Satyrus thought that it was remarkable how little information the man had just conveyed, given that he had lowered his voice to a pitch that was virtually inaudible.

He smiled at the young man – Charmides' age or a little younger, he stood straight, but with that indefinable air of slavery about him. His demeanour caused Satyrus to look at Polycrates in a new way.

You can judge a man by his dogs. Or his slaves. Satyrus hoped that none of his own slaves ever looked like this young man. *I am looking for reasons to dislike Polycrates*, he thought. *Because he can beat me at my best game.*

'It will be our pleasure to land him at Sounion.' Satyrus turned to Thrassos. 'Tell me when you can see the Temple of Poseidon clear,' he said.

Thrassos raised an eyebrow. Satyrus wanted to ask the gods why all helmsmen were self-important argumentative arrogant pricks – but he knew the answer. 'Mind your wake,' he said, with no justice.

I am surly this morning, he thought.

Satyrus had his *Medea* lead the way into the cove below the temple. He flashed his shield at the other ships, raised and showed a red flag at the stern, and hoped that they understood; his war captains knew most of the signals, but not as well as the men who'd served in the seas off Aegypt the year before, like Aekes – and the merchant captains didn't know them well at all.

Medea raced in towards the beach under oars, and Polycrates was in the bow with young Jason, whispering to him urgently.

'He's a fucking spy,' Thrassos said, pointing with his chin at Polycrates.

Charmides nodded agreement. 'He is not a good man, for all his skill at pankration.'

'Spoken by the very paragon of Greek manhood,' Satyrus said.

Charmides blushed and looked away.

'Fucking spy,' Thrassos said again.

'Apollo himself told me to make him my guest friend,' Satyrus said.

'Never been a big follower of the Lord of Light, myself,' Thrassos put in. 'Not exactly a god for *men*.'

Anaxagoras was just completing his exercises. He executed a snap kick – a shin attack – with his left foot, punched with his right, and turned his head slightly.

'Who's not a god for men, Thrassos? And who healed you when you had a certain, hmm, complaint?' he asked.

Thrassos turned bright red – a flame of colour from the middle of his chest to his fire-red hair, making his dark tattoos stand out like brands. 'Meant no disrespect,' he said. 'Just not my favourite.'

Anaxagoras raised an eyebrow. 'You, my barbarian friend, worship a storm god who isn't even included in most civilised pantheons and you believe that the amulet around your neck will protect you from drowning better than learning to swim would protect you. Eh? Have some respect for our gods.'

'Someone's in a mood today,' Thrassos muttered.

'You weren't exactly respectful of his beliefs,' Satyrus said. In the bow, Jason had received his instructions.

'We won't run up the beach,' Satyrus said. 'We'll heave to as soon as you can see the sand under the water.'

'Aye, aye. Sand line it is.' Thrassos sent a boy forward to call the depth under the ram-bow.

Polycrates came aft. 'May I thank you again for this, my lord? Your whole fleet delayed – this is guest friendship, indeed. But my boy can swim. He's ready.'

Satyrus saw that the young man was naked in the bow, all his clothes in a leather bag. He gave a salute, like an athlete beginning a contest – a gesture that raised him in Satyrus's estimation – and leapt into the water, straight off the rail of the marine box, vanishing under the water for a long time, a truly surprising amount of time, enough time that Satyrus began to scan the sea, wondering where the dark head had come up, and then began to fear for the boy.

'He's a wonderful swimmer,' Polycrates said. 'And a good fighter. A good man in every respect. I really couldn't live without him.' He sighed.

The young man surfaced way in, further than Satyrus would have thought to look, halfway to the beach.

'Ready about,' Satyrus said.

Thrassos grinned. They had already started their turn.

'Fine, know-it-all. Lay me alongside *Miranda*.' To Polycrates, he said, 'Your Jason reminds me that I meant to buy a body slave on Delos.'

'I'll be happy to loan you one from my house,' Polycrates said. 'If you fancy him, you can buy him. What kind of body do you fancy?'

Satyrus laughed. 'Not that kind of body slave, friend. I mean a servant – a man to watch my clothes and braid my hair and clean my weapons and stand at my shoulder in a fight.'

Polycrates shook his head. 'A slave? In a fight?'

'Oh, I'd free him if he suited me.' Satyrus found that some acerbity had crept into his tone.

That seemed to silence Polycrates, which was unfortunate, as they had some hours of sailing left. The rowers were hard at work today, and Satyrus walked down the waist of the *Medea*, talking to his upper deck men, making sure that they knew he'd be away – and that he was going to be back.

He felt the change as the ship came out of a tight turn, and he was up the forward ladder from the thranites deck in no time. He picked up his sea bag from under the helmsman's bench, embraced Thrassos, and waved to Anaxagoras and Charmides.

'Don't get yourself killed,' Anaxagoras said. 'And take your lyre. Nothing like a spot of time in a cell to practise.'

'Fuck off,' Satyrus said, but he took the lyre and he embraced this man – this outspoken bastard who had become his friend. Then he embraced Charmides and Apollodorus.

'I think you should have me with you,' Apollodorus said. 'Me, at the very least.'

'You are all laying far too much emphasis on this,' Satyrus said. 'And Apollodorus, you are my designated commander. I need you with the fleet.'

He embraced the smaller man, picked up his bags, and made the leap from the rail of the *Medea* up onto the waist of the much higher-sided *Miranda*. Polycrates followed him, and then Philaeus, his oar master, threw Polycrates' bags aboard, his muscles powering the bags high into the air before they came down with a smack on the smooth planks of the merchant ship.

And then his friends were just a ship length away for another two hours as they ran up the coast of Attika, Anaxagoras clearly visible as he played his lyre in the bow, and then his kithara, and then sang for the rowers. During the entire time he made music, the oars worked flawlessly – the timing was precise, and Anaxagoras's emphasis on rhythm and meter in playing had a visible effect on the working of the oars. And he heard Charmides singing – taking lessons from Anaxagoras. And Thrassos laugh, and Apollodorus's voice, punishing a marine for what he called 'wilfulness', a crime that could be manipulated by Apollodorus to suit any occasion.

'I don't usually find it suits – freeing slaves,' Polycrates said, eventually. 'But I can tell that you are of the opposite view, and I am not seeking a quarrel.'

Satyrus found the working of the merchant ship interesting enough. They had twenty oars in the water, but they also manipulated the big, square mainsail on the standing mast with a good deal more delicacy – the mast came out of a bigger hull, and had many more brail ropes to it, allowing it to be brailed up to many different points, and allowing the massive yard which held it to be rotated through half a circle. No individual item of tackle was very different from its equivalent on a warship, but the total was easier to manipulate and allowed a slightly broader set of angles of sailing. Satyrus was attempting to measure just how a warship might be rigged the same way when Polycrates interrupted his thoughts.

'Hmm?' he asked.

'You think that I should free Jason,' Polycrates said.

Satyrus made a face. 'Not my business,' he said.

'It was plain enough. And your helmsman took the time to inform me that you free almost all the slaves you buy.' The Athenian had his shoulders square like a man preparing for a fight.

'I do, at that. When we were children, my sister and I swore to have as few slaves as ever we might. I'm aware that no society can live without them but it seems like a piece of arete to improve their lot if I may.' Satyrus could see Aegina now, clear on the port bow. He turned his head – indeed, *Medea* was already signalling, and the line of warships was reacting. It was prettily done – the column of ships all turned together, and suddenly they were a fighting line, their oars flashing in the sun.

'Apollodorus is giving us a demonstration,' Satyrus said.

'Your men fear you'll be taken in Athens.' It wasn't a question.

Satyrus shrugged. 'Yes,' he answered.

Polycrates shook his head. 'I can't imagine it,' he said. 'Demetrios thinks as highly of you as he does of any man in the circle of the world.'

Satyrus smiled. 'I can't tell you how much you put me at my ease,' he said. In his heart he wondered, suddenly, if this was all a put-up job – the priest, Delos, the whole prepared to lure him ...

Foolishness. No one but the gods knew he was going to Delos. And as he was headed for Athens either way – as in his heart he knew

57

that it was Miriam, and only Miriam, that brought him in person to Athens – no plot could have been laid. He needed no lure. And no one could know the power of his attraction to Miriam, unless . . .

'Why don't you stay with me, guest friend?' Polycrates asked. 'You need have no fears in *my* house – I have guards and men and all that, and besides, everyone knows me.'

'I'd be delighted,' Satyrus said. 'But I am a citizen – I have my own house.'

Polycrates nodded, a distant look in his eye. 'I had forgotten. But I must add – you are welcome. Perhaps until you can settle in, engage staff?'

Satyrus laughed. 'I only plan to be here for three days – and now that I consider it, it would be foolish to sleep in a musty farmhouse outside the walls when I could be snug in a well-appointed house of a friend. So yes – I'll accept your offer.'

'You have business beyond merely landing your grain? I'm sure that King Demetrios would be delighted if you would visit him but I suspect that he is off at Corinth. He has the Acrocorinth under siege.'

Satyrus hadn't known that. The most impregnable place in Greece. *You didn't take Rhodos, so you're having a go here. Rather the way I had to win with the sword what I lost at pankration.*

'I don't think I have time this trip,' he said. 'Besides – my allies would probably not take the message correctly if I were to pay Demetrios a social call.'

Polycrates nodded. 'I had wondered.'

'Wondered?' Satyrus asked.

'Hmm.' Polycrates gave a small smile. 'All this about having business in Athens. I had wondered what you were about.' The Athenian raised his hand. 'Please – I'm not asking for your secrets. But people will talk.'

Satyrus shook his head. 'Personal business. My friend Abraham Ben Zion – a citizen of Rhodes – is here as a hostage. I need to see him.'

Polycrates' smile remained in place. 'Of course,' he said, in a tone of voice that suggested that he didn't believe a word.

Satyrus had no intention of telling anyone about Miriam. The complications of their relationship would only grow with sharing. And for a political animal like Polycrates – guest oath notwithstanding – such knowledge would give him immense power . . . and a hold over Satyrus.

Yet again it occurred to him that what he was doing was foolish. If he did manage to see her, it would not be private. It would not be easy. And it would be all too apparent to an observer that he had come to see her.

The safest thing would be not to see her, of course.

Satyrus smiled. He was not going to do the safe thing. Since Rhodos, he had become familiar with his own mortality. Life was, in fact, likely to be short.

I want her now, he thought. *There may not be a tomorrow.*

'Piraeus,' Polycrates said. 'Athens.'

And there was the port, and the Parthenons gleaming in the sun, far away atop the acropolis, one of the noblest sights in the world.

Miranda was the last ship to come in – Kleosthenes, her captain, was the senior merchant officer from Olbia, and he wanted to see all the cargoes safe before she landed, which raised him in Satyrus's estimation. The warships were gone – lost in the haze off Aegina – and Satyrus knew that, by now, Apollodorus and all the trierarchs were paying the oarsmen, and soon they'd be drinking, rutting, or, just possibly, visiting family ashore. He knew that Aegina provided a good few oarsmen.

Piraeus had more piers than any other city in the world except perhaps Alexandria, and the grain fleet was expected – announced by every fishing craft who had seen them in the early morning. Two piers were cleared end to end, and all was ready – two hundred city slaves waiting in squads to help the longshoremen unload the vases of grain, wagons, donkeys – and almost at Satyrus's feet as the *Miranda* pulled alongside stood Leo's factor in Athens, Harmonius, a freed man from Alexandria. Satyrus had known him from boyhood. He was neither tall nor physically imposing, but he had a head for figures unmatched in Leon's counting house and he had designed many of the ciphers that Leon and his men used throughout their trade. He had dark brown skin like polished leather – good expensive leather – and curly dark hair, and despite an early life of slavery – or perhaps because he'd been freed – he wore a perpetual smile that made him easy to talk to and easy to learn from; Satyrus had had his geometry from Harmonius in Tanais and Athens, before Philokles came back from campaigning with Diodorus to be his tutor.

Satyrus waved, and Harmonius waved back, pointed Satyrus out to another man.

'Wait where you are, my lord!' he called.

Satyrus wanted to laugh. Harmonius had flayed his backside with a stick for inattention – being called 'my lord' had a certain wrongness to it.

The man with him was wearing armour. He came up the gangplank, and he and Harmonius bowed respectfully to Satyrus. 'Lord, let me present an officer from the citadel: Lysander, son of Nicomedes of Athens. He is in charge of collecting the ship tax on foreign ships. I have explained that we owe no tax, and that this was guaranteed by Demetrios himself – and I have a letter to that effect.'

Satyrus shrugged. 'What seems to be the problem, Lysander? This is my grain, and I am a citizen of Athens. And you can see for yourself that half these ships are Athenian hulls with Athenian crews.'

The young man took his helmet off and wiped his brow. Satyrus got a good look at him, and he was not as young as he had expected. He had a broad scar running across the bridge of his nose – almost like the wound Stratokles had. It was an odd, random thought.

'I'm sorry, my lord, but orders are orders. The law has changed – or my captain has made an error. But we are ordered to collect the ship tax from you.' He shrugged by way of apology.

Satyrus felt his brow furrowing and he fought the expression, struggling to remain calm and cheerful. 'Lad, with all the good will in the world, please tell your captain that if he persists, Harmonius here will see him in court. I'm not a difficult man, but neither am I a petty merchant, that the citadel can summon me.' Satyrus looked at Polycrates, who nodded.

'Perhaps I can help,' Polycrates said, stepping forward for the first time. 'You know me, sir?'

The soldier shook his head. 'Can't say that I do, sir.'

Polycrates raised an eyebrow. 'You do go to assembly, don't you? Very well. I'm Polycrates – priest of Herakles. I will stand surety for these cargoes until such time as Lord Demetrios can be contacted.'

The soldier didn't budge. 'That would be – at least sixty talents of silver,' he said.

Polycrates shrugged, now openly dismissive. 'See my steward, then.

He'll show it to you. And that's as close as you'll get to it until I've seen some people.'

The soldier shook his head. 'I'm sorry, but I am not going to allow this. You must stop unloading.'

Polycrates shook his head. 'Your pardon, son, but you are an idiot. These are important men – this grain is important to the city. Go tell your captain – that's my *friend* Isokles, yes? Go tell Isokles he has the wrong end of the stick, and if he comes up to my house tonight for a cup of *good* wine, he can thrash it through with us. Got that, lad?'

'People don't call me "lad",' the man said.

'I do.' Polycrates stood his ground. 'Who the fuck are you, and where do you get this attitude?'

Satyrus stepped between them. 'Clearly there's some misunderstanding. Go back and check with your captain. I'll wait.'

The soldier turned on his heel and walked away, the hobnails on his sandals crackling against the gangplank.

'City soldiers – ephebes and washed up mercenaries. I apologise on behalf of the city,' Polycrates said.

Satyrus turned to Harmonius and embraced him. 'Old teacher – your hair's all white!'

Harmonius laughed. Then he looked at the soldier, now well up the pier, with his squad. 'Even when Athens was technically at war with Alexandria, I never had this kind of trouble with cargoes.' He shook his head. 'I keep up on changes in the law but I'm only a metic and he wouldn't listen to me.'

Satyrus smiled. 'Not to worry. As Polycrates says – some mercenary feeling a little power. Let's get our things ashore. Then I'll practise my lyre while I wait for him.'

'You can't be serious,' Polycrates said. 'We shan't wait a moment. I know his captain – by Herakles our common ancestor, I know every man in this town. No need for the King of the Bosporus to cool his heels like a merchant! We'll ride up to my house, and if Isokles needs you, he can come calling. You are a king!'

Satyrus gave a wry smile in return. 'Here in Athens, I'm just another citizen,' he said. Then he nodded. 'But thanks. You are right. Let us go.'

They rented a small cart drawn by a donkey, and two horses – average beasts by the standards of a cavalryman, but fine animals to an

Athenian. Their owner was right on the pier, anxious to serve and delighted to be paid full price.

'You must allow me!' Polycrates said. 'But you are too polite. I'm sorry you didn't bring Charmides or Anaxagoras – fine men.'

Satyrus looked up the pier through eyes narrowed in the bright sun. 'I had to take some precautions.'

'You should have opened your mind to me,' Polycrates said. 'I'd have set you at ease.'

Satyrus mounted, his body switching from aquatic to equine in that one motion, and despite the horse's tendency to shy to the right, he found that she was responsive – a decent mount for a beast rented on the dock.

He paid the farmer to deliver his bags to Polycrates' house, and the two of them rode easily up the wharf, picking their way among the longshoremen.

The soldiers on the wall gave them a hard look, and Polycrates dismounted to talk to the phylarch at the gate. When they were through, he shrugged.

'They know who you are, and they didn't know anything about Isokles demanding ship tax,' he said. 'It is the damnedest thing, Satyrus. If Isokles is so hot to talk to you, why weren't we stopped at the gate?'

Satyrus shook his head. 'No idea,' he said. The two of them trotted along, passing carts – a dozen carts, already loaded with vases of Euxine grain.

'Is there someone here who would try to steal my grain?' Satyrus asked.

Polycrates shook his head. 'Anyone who attacked you would have to be insane,' he said. 'Demetrios would exact *such* a revenge.'

They rode on – the summer was just gilding the grass, and there were flowers everywhere, so that the earth seemed particularly alive to a man who had been at sea for weeks. Satyrus was just smiling at a clump of jasmine when Polycrates gave a cry and fell from his horse.

It took far too long for Satyrus to register that his guest friend had just taken a slung stone to the head, and was clutching his brow, blood flowing around his fingers, mouth opening and closing like a fish. A dozen men surrounded him. And two of them grabbed his bridle – they all had swords and some had spears.

One man kicked Polycrates viciously. 'That'll teach you to backtalk me, arse-cunt,' said the man with the scar on his face. He kicked Polycrates again.

Satyrus held up his hands. 'Whatever you want, you are killing an important man.' He looked around. 'Stop at once!'

Such was the power of his voice that all the soldiers stepped back – even the scarred man. But then he sneered. 'Fuck you,' he spat, and rammed his spear into Polycrates' heart.

Satyrus froze – the world seemed to stop, just for a moment. Then he slipped off his horse, as much because he wanted to think he might save the man, his sworn guest friend.

He was beyond saving.

Satyrus whirled. 'You have killed a friend of Demetrios. How stupid are you?'

But the spell was broken. Scarface stepped forward. 'Stop where you are,' he said.

Arms grabbed Satyrus from behind. There was nothing he could do – not productively, not against a dozen men. He wasn't even wearing a sword – not allowed in the confines of Athens. His sword was with his bags in the donkey cart, somewhere on the road behind them.

The officer was wearing a sword. He drew it, leaned down, and cut Polycrates' throat. 'Arse-cunt,' he said. He giggled. 'Now you, so-called king, you can just come along with—'

Satyrus lunged. He got a hand on someone's elbow and he put his feet under him – struggled, and someone hit him, and he was stumbling, but free of one confining arm ... free of the other, and training took over.

He got a man's arm and broke it, the bone going with a dull crack like a green limb breaking on an olive tree. The man screamed, and Satyrus kicked him into two more men who stumbled back. Satyrus ducked – instinct alone – as a club tagged his shoulder instead of his head. Pain, but no permanent damage. He rolled to his right, ignoring another blow to his thigh, and kicked out as he changed stance – flexed the man's knee right back so that his leg curved the wrong way, spun on his grounded foot – no time for close engagements or grappling – punched out: left, right, landed half of each blow by sheer speed.

Now he'd been free of them long enough to form a plan – which

63

was to get back on a horse and ride. Men who didn't live with horses didn't know how quickly a Sakje-trained man could mount. He got a hand behind an adversary's head, swung his hips and threw the man head first into the ground.

The officer, who Satyrus had christened 'Arse-Cunt', screamed at his men. 'All together!' he shouted.

His shout gave them pause, and while they paused, Satyrus put his palm into another man's chin, breaking his jaw, and the crowd was getting thinner.

I can do this, he thought.

He put the crown of his forehead into another man's nose, felt the satisfying crunch, took a hard blow across the shoulders, and stepped through his downed opponent, stepping hard on his crotch. He'd put quite a few of them down.

He got his back to his horse but the untrained animal shied away where a Sakje horse would have pressed in against his back – or even put a hoof into an attacker.

He stumbled, turned to mount, and a staff caught him in the side. He had no choice but to abandon his attempt to mount, and he rolled under the horse. No blow he'd taken yet was enough to stop him – he was a trained pankration fighter, after all – but the aggregate of the beating he was taking had begun to hang on him like a bull on his shoulders. He got to his feet but he was slow, and there was Arse-Cunt, who cut at him with the sword – quite competently. That limited his options. Satyrus stepped left, and by sheer bad luck his horse went the same way, snorting and backing, and he went down under its hooves – was up, but slowly, having been kicked, but now he had the horse between him and the sword.

Arse-Cunt killed the horse with one solid cut, his blade neatly severing the artery at the base of the horse's neck – Satyrus saw the rising cut and the man's hip-roll and knew that he was a trained fighter. The horse blood was everywhere.

The other horse bolted, and Satyrus's options narrowed sharply.

He was panting, and the nearest opponent took it as a sign that he was done, and came in, club raised. Satyrus stepped into the blow, caught the man's elbow, and rammed his thumb into the man's left eye, killing him instantly.

There were only five of them still on their feet, but the horses were gone, and the five remaining were no doubt the best of the lot, and they moved to surround him. Satyrus made himself grin, because grinning opponents are scary, and he decided to go for Arse-Cunt, because if he could get the sword, he was reasonably sure he could kill the rest of them. He took a breath—

A club swished so close to his ear that he felt the breeze and the tug at his hair as he leapt forward – right foot, left foot, balance, set – hip feint, and he had his hand on Arse-Cunt's wrist – turned him on his hips and stripped the sword out of his hands, but Arse-Cunt punched him in the gut instead of standing slack-jawed in surprise, and another unlucky blow from one of the other men caught the sword and spun it away.

And then the fight was lost. He had time to think of Herakles – to hope that he had honoured the god in his last fight – and to wonder, even as he went down, how Demetrios could ever have ordered this. But the third blow to his head took him down into the dark. It was odd: he didn't go right away, but lingered, as if outside his body, while Arse-Cunt killed his own wounded.

I would like to have killed that man, he thought, and then he was gone.

4

Stratokles had meant to ride all the way to Hyrkania, but events conspired to ease his passage, and he arrived at the settlement at Namastae on a fishing boat that carried him, Lucius, and their horses – six of them – crammed so tight that Stratokles slept with his head on his horse's rump.

But the wind was fair and the sea calm, and he was riding up the hill to the citadel just eleven days after fleeing Heraklea. His purse was almost empty. It would have been as flat as salt-bread if he and Lucius hadn't had the good luck to be attacked by bandits who were richer and better mounted than they. Their horses and their darics had solved most of their travel problems.

'You haven't said much about what we're doing here,' Lucius said, as they rode up the hill to the stone citadel on the height.

'Kineas of Olbia stormed this,' Stratokles said. 'Perhaps he was a god, at that. How in the name of all the gods did he storm this?'

Lucius looked up the steep slope, and shrugged. 'Crap defenders, superb attackers – the usual story. Like most, I expect he won the fight back when he was training his legion, not here while they were fighting.'

Stratokles smiled. 'You are not just a pretty face,' he said.

Lucius shook his head. 'If we could drop all this back-stabbing and fight a war, you and I might prosper,' he said.

Stratokles nodded. 'My thoughts exactly. The question is, which side? And the answer – *let's start our own.*'

Banugul was no longer young. Unlike many beautiful women, she didn't trouble to hide her age. She did not redden her lips or apply too much kohl or other cosmetics to smooth out the tiny wrinkles or hide the years.

In fact, despite – or even because of – the crow's feet at the corners of her eyes and lips, the skin at the top of her chin, the infinitely slight sign of a jowl under her jaw, she was still Banugul, from the top of her fine light head to the base of her slim, arched feet; feet that wore slight golden sandals because the wearer was not afraid to emphasise rather than hide. Under her Greek matron's chiton, her body was hard and muscled, her breasts swelled in proportion to her hips and shoulders, and when she moved, all the temple dancers in Heraklea could not have competed with her.

'Stratokles,' she said, rising from her carved chair to take his hand.

'My lady,' he said formally.

'And who is your beautiful friend?' she asked.

Stratokles bowed. 'This is Lucius, a Latin from far-off Italia. He has served me for some years – indeed, he was with me when we rescued your son.'

Banugul smiled, and her smile decorated the room. Even from the side, Stratokles caught its force, but Lucius, who was the intended recipient, all but staggered.

She stepped down off her dais and caught his hands. 'I understand that Stratokles – and you, sir – no doubt took my son for your own ends. And yet as a mother I know that your actions saved his life. Demetrios would have executed him – or Cassander would have, or Ptolemy.' She turned the smile on Stratokles, like the beam of a lamp turned on a moth, and Stratokles found himself grinning like a fool.

'I've come to talk about your son,' Stratokles said.

'The answer is "no".' She smiled a very different smile. 'You want him for some scheme. I am done with schemes, Stratokles. Once, in this very room, Kineas of Olbia told me to be satisfied with what I had. And now have again. And you know? I have built a life here, my dear. I have killed most of my enemies and I rule a goodly piece of the coast, and the satrap and I are old friends, and Antigonus and Seleucus both court me.'

Stratokles twitched his lips.

Lucius was pinned by her gaze the way a butterfly might be pinned to a piece of parchment, as a specimen for a rich man's collection. Or perhaps a rich woman's.

Stratokles had noted on arrival in the mosaicked throne room that there was an eyehole behind the throne – an eyehole he'd noted on earlier visits. In former times, it had appeared to be a flaw in the black hair of a naked nymph who was enjoying, or being enjoyed by, a particularly ardent and well-endowed satyr, but the mosaics had changed with the tastes of their owner, and the eyehole was now in the dark fur of a luxuriating panther. Stratokles smiled to himself, looking for something witty to say about the change in decoration.

The slaves wore clothes, too.

But there was an eye at the eyehole, and that eye could only belong to one person.

Satyrus looked back to where Banugul was busy conquering Lucius without a word being said. He ate her with his eyes, and she merely accepted his homage without promise or denial – and spurred him to greater surrenders.

'He is old enough to make his own decisions, is he not, your son?' Stratokles said.

'A pox on you, you Athenian intriguer!' she said, without asperity. 'Why can't you be entranced by my charms like other men?'

'Despoina, I am as entranced as other men. I just look for more practical ways of finding my way into your bed.' He smiled – she smiled. Lucius looked stunned.

Aside, Stratokles said, 'Nothing those eyes promise is ever fulfilled, Lucius.'

'For you, perhaps, but not for all men,' Banugul said.

Stratokles shrugged.

The silence went on too long.

'He's twenty-three, is he not? Old enough to make a name for himself?' Stratokles asked.

'No,' Banugul said. Her eyes flicked nervously to the wall, and Stratokles knew that his suspicions – all of them – were confirmed.

'Herakles must be the last scion of Alexander left on the board,' he mused. 'I wonder if he has any of his father's talents? The prowess? The strategic thinking?'

'The binge drinking?' Banugul said. 'Can you stop this? You and I both know that he is listening. You are playing on him.'

In fact, after a pause, the young man in question emerged from the door hidden in the tapestries.

He was short, by Greek standards, but well formed, with a head slightly too big for his shoulders but with a fine shock of dark blond hair and a good face – strong chin, good nose. His carriage was not as erect as Stratokles would have liked to see – too much riding and not enough gymnasium work.

He inclined his head to Stratokles. 'I remember both of you,' he said. 'You took me from Demetrios.'

Stratokles nodded. 'So we did, lad. And now we're back. I want to ask your mother to take you from here and put you on the board. Take you out into the world – command some troops – fight. The major players are heading towards the big fight – perhaps the last. Antigonus is old. Demetrios took a heavy defeat at Rhodos, whether he knows it or not. If you wish to make a life out in the world, now is the time. In a year or two, the board may be cleared, and then … well, the winner will only want you dead, lad. Because any fool can see that you are the image of your father.'

Herakles grinned.

'Do not, I pray you, my son, *do not* fall victim to this man's accurate and deadly flattery.' She tried to make the comment light-hearted, but the words had an edge.

'As you have yourself, Mother? And yet,' Herakles shook his head, 'I already have this man's measure. I *like* him. He rescued me.'

'For his own ends,' Banugul said.

'Of course!' Herakles shook his head. 'If I go with you, sir, will I be your lord?'

Stratokles hadn't thought that the difficult child of ten years ago would turn into something this accomplished – for all that his shoulders slumped. He twitched his lips and rubbed the knot where a chunk had been cut out of his nose.

'We'll be partners,' Stratokles said. 'I'll be your tutor and mentor – and sometimes, your prime minister. In time – at least three years, and perhaps a great deal more – I will serve you and call you lord.'

Herakles nodded pensively. 'I do not like taking orders or instructions,' he said haughtily.

'You never did,' Stratokles said, with a smile.

'I'm too old to strike with your hand, now,' the young man said.

Lucius snorted.

Herakles turned on him. 'And you. I remember you. You spanked me!'

'And I could again,' Lucius said. 'But only if you deserve it.' His eyes were already back on Banugul.

'I forbid it. Stratokles, you are not taking my son out of this castle. And that is my word – as queen and as a mother.' She stared at him – dark blue eyes like lapis that could melt a man's ethics.

Stratokles feigned to meet her eyes with indifference, as it was the only weapon a man could wield in such an unequal contest. 'Then Lucius and I have had a long trip for nothing,' he said.

Late that night, he lay on a couch with young Herakles, drinking wine, while Lucius shared another couch with Banugul. Stratokles had never seen Lucius so completely undone by a woman, and it amused him. It also made him feel a little sorry. Lucius's imperturbability was his greatest asset; his sense of dignity – *gravitas*, he called it in his own tongue – was one of his most endearing qualities.

But it was entertaining, and would last for years as a source of teasing. Best of all, Lucius was already squirming at his own bemusement.

After dinner, Stratokles resolutely resisted the urge to talk about politics or to seduce young Herakles with anything as banal as promises of greatness. So instead, he talked about Satyrus of Tanais.

'Kineas's son!' Banugul said with real pleasure. 'His sister was here last year with a raiding party, headed back west. She got her man,' she added, with just a tinge of wickedness.

'She often does,' Stratokles agreed.

'She's very beautiful, of course,' Banugul said.

'Not half as beautiful as you,' Lucius said, and looked stricken.

Banugul rolled onto one hip and struck him lightly. 'If that is the best you can do, keep it to yourself, Latin. Melitta of Tanais has the perfect skin of a maiden, eyes as fine as mine, her mother's excellent breasts, good muscles, and a scar on her face that shows that she is no plaything.' She smiled, stretched, rolled on her stomach and kicked her heels over her head, showing off her own excellent muscles. 'You men think we're all like cats – but it is not true. Worthy women admire worthy women.'

'You sound as if you fancy her yourself, Mother,' Herakles said.

'I can't hide that I would have liked to see the two of you together,' Banugul admitted. 'As her husband, you would have place and protection. And none of the curs who compete for Alexander's empire have the balls to go onto the Sea of Grass.' Wine brought out her crudity.

Stratokles liked her better that way.

70

'She treated me like a child,' Herakles said.

'She is a queen and a warrior,' Stratokles said. 'She's no friend of mine, but I'll say this for her – if she treated you like a child, it is because that's what you seemed to her.'

Herakles sprang off the kline, his back straight in outrage.

Stratokles shrugged. 'You've never commanded an army – she has. Never fought hand to hand, have you? She's a notorious fighter – she's probably killed more men than her brother. Her archery is famous from one end of the steppe to another. She rules the Assagetae of the Western Door with a strong hand, but a fair one, and they love her. I couldn't displace her with money or hired killers. You let your mother rule this small wolf-state while she is the Lady of the Sea of Grass. In her world, a man is rated by his accomplishments. What have you accomplished? Hence,' Stratokles finished, relentless as the attack of a phalanx, 'hence, you are like a child to her.'

Herakles held up an arm like a man trying to block a blow. His face worked, but nothing came out, and then he whirled, crashing into a slave and spilling wine everywhere, and fled from the room.

Banugul applauded. She sat up, clapping. Terrified slaves hurried to clean the floor, and still she applauded.

'Well done, Stratokles. And don't think that I don't see right through you.'

Stratokles shook his head. 'As I am making no attempt to dissimulate, you don't have to "see" through me. I want him to come to his senses, get out of his mother's boudoir and come out into the world.'

Banugul laughed. 'I think you have come on too strong, my friend. He will never forgive you.'

Lucius shook his head. 'He used to worship Stratokles. I'd watch the two of them at the camp fire when we were coming here – when was that? The year of Gaza? Yes?' He looked into her eyes and lost the thread of his discourse.

Stratokles almost snorted wine through his nose. 'Lucius, come back,' he said.

Later still, Stratokles lay on a wide bed with good linen sheets, and Banugul lay in the circle of his sword arm, her head pillowed on the heavy muscles of his bicep. 'I missed you,' she said. 'Why do you never come? Did that harlot at Heraklea love you better?'

71

Stratokles smiled at the ceiling – at the gods.

'Amastris of Heraklea never made love to me in any way,' he said. 'I served her. She betrayed me, arranged for my death, and failed.' He shrugged, a comfortable movement that caused him to appreciate her body all the more. 'I used her as well, my dear. And I cannot serve Athens as your bed-mate. Athens cares nothing for Hyrkania.'

She lay for a little while. 'Must I tell you again that I missed you?' she said.

He kissed her – not passionately, as he had a few moments before, but lightly, with friendship. 'As I missed you – not every day, but deeply, at times.'

'And other times you forgot I existed? And you the ugliest man in creation?' she spat, but there was no real malevolence in her words – going through the motions than aiming to cut.

He laughed. 'How often have you thought of me?'

'At least once a year. And whenever I see a particularly ugly old goat.' She laughed into his chest.

And then they were kissing, slowly at first, exploring forgotten territory, and then faster and deeper as they discovered more things they had forgotten, or only laid aside – the taste of the inside of his mouth and the sharpness of his teeth, the warm heaviness of her breasts and the texture of her nipples …

Stratokles ceased to plot, or even to plan, and the couch became, for a while, the circle of the world, her hair the edge of the universe.

'If you take him away,' she said, much later, after they'd surprised themselves by making love twice, like youths, 'if you take him away, I'll have nothing.' She didn't sob, or seduce. Her words had a chilling truth to them.

'He needs to be in the world.' Stratokles sighed.

'No!' she said, and rolled on top of him. 'Aphrodite, I'll be sore in the morning, and my cheeks are rubbed raw from your beard. But no – he does not need to be in the world. You need him in the world. You need him as a pawn in your revenge.'

Stratokles watched her in the lamplight – the kindest light to all women, young and old – and she was magnificent, and again he silently thanked the gods for this, for this woman, for a rest from his endless life of struggle. 'Yes,' he said. 'It's true. I want to spring him on Cassander and watch him sweat.'

She lay back down. 'That's better.' She stretched languorously. 'If we could manage a third time, I would feel quite young, I think.'

He rubbed a knowledgeable thumb around her nipple and licked the side of her ear. 'You'll be the one doing all the work,' he said. 'The last time I made love three times in a night, I was here. And ten years younger.'

She laughed – and her laugh alone took him halfway to arousal. 'I do believe that was the nicest compliment you've ever paid me.'

'What, better than "she's not half as beautiful as you"?' Stratokles laughed into her neck, and they wrestled for a moment, he seeking to pin her with his legs and she seeking to roll atop him – and then he lay still as she began to stroke him with her hands, bit his shoulder.

'Well, well,' he said quietly into the storm cloud of her hair.

'Why didn't you tell me she was your woman!' Lucius said bitterly. They were exercising in the yard. Stratokles showed the marks of his night, nor had he any interest in hiding them. In fact, he felt twenty years younger.

Stratokles blocked the wooden sword with his cloaked arm, stepped to the left, and rocked back, ready to kick. Lucius changed his guard. They sparred together so often that most of what they did was to show each other their guards – they'd long since run out of surprises, like an old married couple with their fights.

'She is not my woman. She is very much her own woman,' Stratokles said. 'And if she had wanted it, she would have been in your bed last night, nor would I have been allowed to protest in the slightest.'

'She is a harlot?' Lucius asked.

'She is the queen of this little country. She is the daughter of a great Persian nobleman – she was Alexander's mistress, and perhaps Antigonus's as well. She has survived when all about her, her family and friends have died. Her son is the last get of Alexander on the circle of the world, and he is only alive because she and I are both brilliant plotters – and because Antigonus thinks the boy is no threat.' Stratokles shrugged. 'Besides, I thought you knew that we ... were friends.'

'Damn me, you are a close one, Athenian.' Lucius shrugged. 'She is remarkable. Like a great lady in my country – very like them. You are not jealous?'

'Who could be jealous of sharing the sun?' Stratokles said. 'The heat warms us both, and cares as much for our desires.'

'Well put!' Banugul said. She clapped. 'You are both so *elegant* naked.'

Lucius made a face, and whirled, but when he caught her eye he was hers, and no amount of discomfort could hide his feelings. Still, his flush went from the middle of his stomach to his hair.

Stratokles feinted and tapped his man on the head. 'Pay attention, Lucius,' he said.

'Fuck you,' Lucius said, quietly. But then he stepped back and saluted. 'I'm getting old,' he said. 'And you've found some sort of youth potion.'

'Perhaps,' Stratokles agreed, with a grin. And hit him again.

A week later, Stratokles rode west, with ten men-at-arms furnished by the queen, all Macedonians, as well as Lucius and Herakles. The young man rode out with armour on his back, a fine sword at his side, a beautiful gilt helmet with a pair of eagle wings at his saddle bow, and four servants to attend him. Behind him, his mother waved once from the gate, saw his raised hand in answer, and then went calmly inside to see to the business of her little kingdom. She was too proud to cry in public.

Stratokles didn't try to kiss her in public, but they'd already exchanged words. She was angry, and he understood, but took her son anyway.

But cry she did, night after night. Nor was she weeping for the loss of her lover. He did this – he rode away to conquer the world, and came back when he was beaten, and rode away again. What she loved best in him was that she could heal him.

But her feelings for her son were fifty times as strong, or a hundred times. And after her fifth night of sleepless tears, she dragged herself to her shrine to Aphrodite, and threw herself on the floor – a full prokinesis –and swore to the goddess.

'Blessed Lady of the Cyprian Shore, foam born, goddess of lovers – may my son live, and thrive, out there in the world! And if Stratokles the Athenian leads him out to his death, may he, in turn, die, and all those who caused his death – my curse on them, and him! And if he lives, may he go from glory to glory – but first, Lady, let him live!' She wept, and crawled to the foot of the goddess's statue. 'Let him live! Let him have his glory and live!'

She lay there, until she felt that she had received an answer.

Artaxata, in Media Atropatene, eight days south and west of Hyrkania, travelling more than ten parasanges a day. Artaxata, where Stratokles' route finally cut the old Royal Road, and they could make better time.

'When do we rest?' Herakles whined. 'By the gods, Stratokles, give me a rest!'

'Rest when you are king of the western world,' Stratokles said. 'We've been slowed by mountains, fog and bad luck, and now I want to move. With a little luck, we can be on the coast and raising mercenaries before any word of us gets out.'

Lucius shook his head. 'Even for you, this is a desperate throw. This boy is not ready to play Alexander for you.'

Stratokles shook his head. 'I can feel it. Come!' he said, and they galloped off up the Royal Road.

Antigonus and Seleucus sparred constantly for the possession of the northern satrapies, so the posting houses were not all in order – but many of them were, and for as long as they were, Stratokles squandered money on horses and speed. His beautiful clothes from the wedding – his diadem and jewelled belt – vanished like spring mist under a summer sun.

Every evening, no matter how tired their prince claimed to be, Lucius and Stratokles took turns teaching him – swordsmanship and pankration, mostly. He was unwilling, even defiant, at first. Later, simply truculent, until Lucius punched him hard enough to knock him down.

'Good looks and good birth will not overcome a single enemy,' Lucius said to the angry young man, 'and if you burst into tears in front of your Macedonians, you can count on their deserting you. There's no amount of gold darics that will make a Macedonian stand for a cry-baby. In that, at least, they are like Romans.'

If he wept, he did it in secret.

And after ten days on the road, his back was straighter, and he had ceased to whine.

*

On the eleventh day, he was almost killed. He was bursting to try his newly learned combat arts, and when a wrangler spat on him – haughty airs win no friends on the Royal Road – he whirled, drew his sword, and cut at the man. Lucius had to admit later that he had drawn and cut with skill.

But Herakles had the bad luck to choose a Persian nobleman fallen on hard times – an older man who had been fighting for thirty years – who sprang back, his whip shooting out and disarming the eager prince, and then *his* sword was free.

Herakles froze.

Luckily, Lucius had seen the whole thing coming. He was behind the Persian – armlock, disarm, trip – and he had his sword against the other man's neck.

Stratokles stood aloof, shaking his head. He'd come within a few heartbeats of losing his new master. And the boy tried to hide it, but he wept in mortification at being disarmed. They were a quiet party as they rode away.

East of Sardis, Stratokles heard a rumour that Antigonus was marching, and that Demetrios was at the point of taking Corinth.

He shook his head that night, over the camp fire. 'If Ptolemy and Seleucus don't act soon, Cassander's going to be caught between the hammer and anvil.'

Lucius laughed. 'You sound unhappy. You want Cassander dead.'

Stratokles frowned. 'I'd like him punished, but only at my own hand. I've miscalculated – I thought that after the failure of the siege of Rhodos, Demetrios would fold like a house of cards, but he's rebuilt himself.'

'Lysimachos?' asked Lucius.

'The best of the lot, even if he's the one who sold me down the river – or demanded my head. I should have seen that coming. He's wily and he's a good diplomat, but he hasn't the generalship to stop Antigonus – nor does he have the troops. He'll be besieged in Heraklea before the year is out. Trapped, unless something can end the truce Demetrios has with Rhodes and bring the Rhodians back into the war.'

'So what are *we* doing?' asked Herakles. He had recovered – the best thing you could say about him is that he didn't stay beaten long.

Stratokles shook his head and rubbed his nose. 'I don't know yet. Ask me at Sardis.'

Sardis – and all memory of the comforts of Banugul's bed were lost in the dust of twenty-five days on the road.

'Swordsmith in the agora says Satyrus of Tanais was murdered in Athens by Demetrios,' Lucius reported after a scouting trip inside the gates. They'd been on the road long enough now that Stratokles was taking every precaution – including watching his young prince's bodyguards for defection.

'Satyrus has been reported dead more times than a porne plays flutes at a symposium,' Stratokles quipped, pushing a sausage down on a stick. 'But if Demetrios attacked him – kidnapped him? Whichever – he's made a bad mistake.' He hunkered down and started to cook the sausage, and Lucius handed him a wineskin full of drinkable wine. 'I hate it when the big players make stupid mistakes,' Stratokles complained. 'I can't plan for other men to behave like children.'

'I don't understand,' Herakles said. He didn't whine when he said it, though.

'Nor should you, lad. Satyrus of Tanais helped break the siege of Rhodos. He's part of the truce that came out of the end of the siege – he swore to the gods not to attack Demetrios. And he has a powerful fleet. If Demetrios killed him, he's voided the truce, and Melitta will go for his jugular.' Stratokles shook his head. 'If she acts quickly, she'll retake the Bosporus, or simply allow Lysimachos and Cassander to move freely. Why on earth would Demetrios do such a fool thing?' He rubbed the bridge of his nose.

Herakles pursed his lips. 'Perhaps,' he said slowly, clearly afraid to be ridiculed, 'perhaps it wasn't Demetrios who did it?'

He flushed with pleasure – his fair skin showed the flush even by firelight – when Lucius and Stratokles both looked at him with new attention.

'Ahh!' said Stratokles. He sat back on his haunches, and took a bite of sausage. Then a drink of wine. He passed the wineskin to Herakles, who took it with pleasure. 'Not bad, young man.'

Lucius smiled. 'The wine, or the notion?'

Stratokles nodded. 'Either. Both. If Cassander arranged it – ah, master-stroke. Revenge for an old failure, all suspicion on Demetrios, and Melitta coming over to his side even though my Amastris just jilted her brother.' He rubbed his nose, belched, and held out a hand for the wineskin. 'I wonder if a word of it is true, though.'

Five days to the coast. They came down to Miletus, no longer a major port since her roadstead began to silt up, but the citadel was still strong, and the commander, an Antigonid captain of forty years' experience, was an old friend – or at least, an occasional ally. Miletus was the third largest entrepôt for the hiring of mercenaries. Antigonus allowed it because it was better than having them go somewhere else.

Stratokles was preparing to introduce his charge when the older man, yet another Philip (Philip, son of Alexander), raised an eyebrow. 'You planning to stay long?'

'I was planning to see what I could hire here,' Stratokles said vaguely.

'Not much right now. You heard that Satyrus of Tanais was taken by Demetrios?' Philip asked.

'I heard he was dead,' Stratokles said.

'Aye, taken or dead, or soon to be dead.' Philip shrugged. 'Odd – I thought young Demetrios and Satyrus were friends – they looked it last year, believe me. But his navarch has the young king's fleet right across the water – Lesbos. Mytilene. He's hiring all the men. Above my pay grade, but if Golden Boy did this, he'll rue it. That Apollodorus is no fool. With a few thousand of the best and twenty ships, he can make a lot of trouble.'

'Why don't you stop him?' Stratokles asked. 'You are one of One-Eye's men, aren't you?'

The older Macedonian gave him a level stare. 'Antigonus won't last the winter. You know it as well as I. And his son – well, he's brave. But he's not much for the likes of me. There's a rumour that Lysimachos is across the Euxine with some men – not many – but that he's marching this way.' He let the rest dangle.

It was almost comic. Two months before, Stratokles would have bought this man's loyalty on the spot – for Lysimachos. *You fool*, he thought. But he hadn't suspected how rotten the inside of Antigonus's system really was.

'Well,' he said. 'If the mercenaries are all in Mytilene, I guess that's where I'm bound.'

*

Mytilene was the same small city he remembered – a pleasant town with beautiful women, handsome men, and good wine. Superb olives. 'I could retire here,' Stratokles said.

'You'll retire with two feet of steel in your thorax,' Lucius said.

'Hah! Too true,' Stratokles said. 'But until then, I can daydream.'

Herakles looked at Mytilene as if he'd arrived in paradise. Miletus had been too big for a man who'd grown to adulthood in a town with four thousand inhabitants including slaves. But Mytilene was ideal.

Besides, Stratokles was allowing him to ride abroad, well dressed. If they were going to make this work, it was going to start here.

They brought horses across – always a good investment, taking horses to Lesbos, especially big, well-bred warhorses from Persia. So they rode up from the port, looking like a prince and his retinue.

Herakles was in his element, and he positively sparkled – like his mother – when it became clear to all of them that the mercenaries could see a resemblance. Heads turned, all the way from the beach.

Stratokles arranged lodgings with a guest friend – the Athenian proxenos, in fact. But before he could try the wine or the olives, much less the women, he received a summons, from a source he chose not to ignore.

'So,' Apollodorus said. 'Are you a raven come to pick the bones, or an ally?'

Stratokles rolled the wine around in his cup. 'We've been adversaries more times than allies,' he said.

Apollodorus nodded. 'True enough.'

Stratokles took a deep breath. 'I came to hire men for another purpose,' he said. 'But ...'

'But you could be tempted to help me?' Apollodorus said.

'If you'll help me,' Stratokles answered. 'And I have to warn you that Leon and I have never been friends.'

The Numidian came in from behind a tapestry. 'Well shot, snake. I told him as much. But I'm the one who sent to bring you here.'

'Sent?' Stratokles asked. 'Where?'

'Why, Heraklea, of course. Although I wondered at first if you had done this yourself.' Leon shook his head. His hair was almost all white. It made Stratokles feel old.

Stratokles shook his head. 'Amastris—'

Leon smiled. 'Cut you loose.'

'Tried to have me killed, actually.' He shrugged.

Leon smiled again. 'I understand the feeling,' he said.

'She failed. I went east for a while.' He raised an eyebrow.

Leon took a deep breath. 'You mean you are *not* here at my invitation?' he asked.

Stratokles shook his head. 'I gather that's the wrong answer,' he said. 'Too bad, because I think I'm willing to help.' He looked around. 'Surely the Lady Melitta is here, as well?'

'She's got the rest of the fleet,' Leon said. Apollodorus was shaking his head. Leon drank some wine, leaned forward, and said, 'I think he can help. So do you. Why not tell him?'

'Because everything we say to him will go straight to Demetrios,' Apollodorus said. 'Now that he's sitting here, I remember how much I hate the bastard.'

Stratokles laid both of his hands on the table. 'Apollodorus, if Leon and I can do business, I don't think you have any right to pretend your rivalry is older and deeper. I don't think we've even crossed blades. In fact, I think we've been comrades – at Tanais.'

'I almost gutted you at Rhodos,' Apollodorus said.

'Bah – we're all professionals. Leon, tell me what you want from me. I swear to you – by any gods you wish – that I have no employer just now and that I won't sell what you tell me for one month from today.' He stood up.

Leon took him at his word. 'Bring the image of Herakles,' he said. 'Swear on Lord Herakles and the heroic dead of Marathon, where Athens proved her greatness, may their shades come to haunt you if you break your oath, that you will keep anything we tell you here to yourself for one full lunar month from today.'

Stratokles met Leon's eye. 'I swear on Lord Herakles and the heroic dead of Marathon, where Athens proved her greatness, may their shades come to haunt me if I break my oath, that I will keep anything you tell me here to myself and my lieutenant Lucius, who will be bound by the same oath, for one full lunar month from today.'

Apollodorus leapt from his chair. 'You heard him change the oath!' he said.

Leon nodded. 'He meant us to hear that he's a truthful man. If he helps us, he has to explain to his henchmen.' He nodded.

Stratokles thought it was unfair how handsome Leon remained. It lent him a dignity that Stratokles was never likely to have.

'So?' he said. 'I've sworn.'

Leon passed him a cup of wine. 'Here. It's a long story.'

Later, the two men shocked each other by clasping hands.

That night, Stratokles wrote a long letter to Hyrkania, and sent two of Herakles' Macedonians and six recently hired mercenaries to carry it over land. And then he sat down to a symposium with Lucius and all of Satyrus's captains and, odd as it felt, he enjoyed himself.

PART II

5

'Plistias of Cos,' Diokles said, peering into the sun under both hands. 'See the funny little break above the beak of his penteres? That's for ripping oars. He had it cast for his flagship.'

'Anyone could cast one,' Melitta muttered, also shading her eyes with her hands.

Diokles just shrugged. It was an eloquent shrug – it suggested that while anyone could, only one man would.

It was a hazy summer day in the Dardanelles, and Diokles' flagship led a line of twenty-four warships. Down the channel, mostly hidden by the Point of Winds, lay the northern fleet of Demetrios and Antigonus, sixty warships.

Diokles turned to his helmsman, an older Italiote, Leonidas of Tarentum. 'Steady. I want to come within easy hail of him.'

'Easy hail it is,' Leonidas answered.

Melitta turned back to her navarch. 'Should we be getting into armour?' she asked.

Diokles pursed his lips. 'Despoina, I don't know. That's for you to answer. It's all about what signal you want you want to send. Peace? War?'

Melitta admired his calm. 'We will fight if he does not move,' she said.

Diokles nodded. 'I know.'

She nodded, twisted her mouth – very like her brother, really.

She vanished under the tent-like awning she'd installed amidships – like having a Sakje yurt on a ship – and re-emerged wearing a coat of pale caribou with blue elk-hair work and golden plaques and bells. She pulled it on and belted it, hung her akinakes from her hip, and went to the stern.

Diokles smiled, but he didn't do it where the Lady of the Assagetae could see him.

Plistias stood his ground, his ship well out in the current with two triremes on station behind him, well warned that there was another squadron in the channel.

Diokles had not matched his force – he came forward alone, confident that the high state of training and the superior construction of his ship would see him clear if Plistias behaved badly.

He chewed the ends of his moustache. *Confident* wasn't the right word. His crew and his ship would give him a chance—

'How did it come to this?' Melitta asked. 'I hate not knowing.'

Diokles shrugged. 'If Demetrios really has taken your brother or killed him, he is counting on the "not knowing" to slow us.'

Coenus and Theron emerged from the tent amidships, wearing simple chitons like farmers.

Coenus looked under his hand at Plistias's flagship. Shook his head. 'I wish the odds were better,' he said.

Theron snorted. 'I was brought up to understand that in narrow waters, the smaller fleet has no disadvantage,' he said. 'Look at Salamis.'

Diokles and Coenus both shrugged simultaneously.

Coenus smiled. 'I'd rather test that theory from the position of a massive advantage of force,' he said. 'And as I think Diokles will agree, in early spring we had a massive advantage in rowers – ours work year-round, and theirs do not. But now? We have an advantage in spirit, perhaps. But his fleet is worked up, now. Look at his oars work. It's not beautiful, but it is well enough done.'

Diokles grinned. 'I thought that you were a cavalryman.'

Coenus raised an eyebrow. 'What part of Greece is more than a day's walk from the sea? Certainly not Megara.'

'Nor Corinth,' Theron said.

A stade away, and Plistias's oarsmen only pulled to hold their station.

'He's waiting for something,' Coenus muttered.

Diokles didn't like the waiting, the *not knowing*. Especially as there were warships launching past the headland and masts coming down, readying for a fight – or that's what it appeared to him.

Melitta turned to him. 'If he attacks us, I will shoot him dead. Let my arrow be the signal for the ballistas to let fly.'

'You may already be dead,' Diokles said with brutal honesty.

Melitta shrugged. 'Then my mother's line will have ended, and what happens will be of little moment to gods or men.'

'I may still be alive,' joked Theron, amused by her view of the world. 'Diokles, here, might care to live.'

She rolled her shoulders in irritation. It was easy to forget how young she really was, until she showed irritation, or beamed with happiness. Not much of the latter, lately.

A quarter stade, and they could hear the oar beat on the other ship as clear as if their oar master was on Diokles' ship.

'What ship?' asked one of Plistias's men in a brightly burnished bronze thorax.

'*Atlantae*,' Diokles called, his voice like a trumpet. 'Of Tanais and Pantecapaeaum.'

Half a hundred pous, now – point-blank shot for the ballistae. The archers on the *Atlantae* were armed and had arrows to their bows, but they stood amidships, well clear of the rails. But the ballistae were loaded, and Jubal's new invention, the crank-repeaters, were fully tensioned.

Plistias of Cos's ship, *Golden Demeter*, was also fully ready. His two forward ballistae were cranking even as the two ships sailed on, closer and closer, not quite nose to nose.

'Oars in,' Diokles said in a calm, clear voice, and the oar master, Milos, repeated the order quietly.

Melitta found the quiet more dangerous than the noise. Quiet, to her steppe-trained ears, meant ambush. She stood, fully exposed in white caribou, on the stern platform, and she could hear the sound of almost two hundred oars being dragged into oar ports and crossed between benches – a manoeuvre endlessly practised, but never quiet.

By bringing in their oars, they signalled that they were not going to fight. The time it would take to get their oars in the water would be critical, in a fight.

Twenty pous or less separated the ships – almost close enough to jump. Melitta smiled.

'Closer,' she said quietly to the helmsman.

He tapped the steering oars with the flats of his hands, and the bow twitched to port.

Before she could change her mind, or her councillors could dissuade her, Melitta stepped up onto the rail, a long leg flashing in the summer sun, and leapt for Plistias's ship.

87

She landed easily, a little shorter than she had intended, balanced, and stepped down off the rail onto the helmsman's deck of the *Golden Demeter*. Half a dozen marines looked at her as if she'd grown wings and flown.

While they gaped, she glided forward. 'Plistias of Cos?' she asked.

He nodded, his mouth still a little open.

'Melitta, Lady of the Assagetae. My brother is King of the Bosporons.'

'Despoina,' he said politely. The man's marines were just reacting.

'Your master, Demetrios, has taken my brother against the provisions of the Truce of Rhodes —'

'What?' Plistias shook his head. 'Despoina, I have—'

She put a hand in his face. 'Please, be silent.'

Another man on the deck inclined his head. 'Despoina, we have heard nothing to suggest ... that is, King Demetrios has the highest opinion—'

The sharp movement of her hand would have beheaded the man, had she held a sword. She took a deep breath. 'You will take your fleet out of the straits and retire to the Aegean, or we fight. No room for negotiation. If your king has not taken my brother, I will allow you back into the straits when I know this. If your king has him, he can have access to the straits by restoring my brother to me.'

Plistias shrugged. 'Despoina, you have too few ships to make good your threats.'

Melitta shrugged right back. 'I'll give you until tomorrow to retire. You have been warned.' She smiled her *killer of the steppe* smile, the smile that had earned her the name *Smells Like Death*. 'If I had had my way, we would simply have attacked you this morning. But my brother's people believe in talk. So I have spoken.'

She stepped between two of the marines as if they weren't there, vaulted onto the rail, and was across to her own ship in another breath.

'Oars out,' Diokles said.

'We do not respond to threats!' Plistias called.

'Back water,' Diokles said to the oar master as soon as the oars were out. Across the water, he could see men with bows at full stretch. It didn't require an order to start the war – just a mistake.

Four strokes, five strokes, and the distance started to open. Already, only the bow-mounted heavy weapons would bear.

'That was ... not what we agreed to,' Coenus said carefully.

'I changed my mind,' Melitta said cheerfully. 'Now that man, at least, knows who I am.'

'He will think you are a barbarian,' Theron said gently.

Melitta shrugged a shoulder out of the caribou coat. 'But, my dear teacher, I *am* a barbarian.'

Dawn. Smoke rising on the far horizon, probably Imbros. Well beyond the straits – five parasanges or more. Melitta watched it with satisfaction.

'Apollodorus?' Coenus and Nikephorus stood beside her.

She nodded. 'Unless someone has captured our signal book or one of our messengers.'

'Plistias will have seen it too,' Nikephorus said.

Melitta laughed. 'I hope that Lysimachos and Cassander and Antigonus see it, as well. What we are doing is sending a threat, and we need that threat to be seen and understood in every camp.'

She put on a light thorax of iron scales on heavy deer hide; no yoke, in the Sakje way, and a light helmet that allowed her free vision. Today she wore her gorytos openly.

Nikephorus was armed in bronze from head to toe. So were Coenus and Theron. Diokles wore a bronze thorax and a leather Boeotian cap.

They shared a kylix of wine, poured libations to Poseidon and Herakles and all the gods, and went to their ships.

The sun was well above the horizon when they rowed carefully up to Kynossema and lowered their main masts, prepared to fight.

On the other side of the point, around the difficult corner where fleets had waited since the siege of Troy, Plistias's ships manoeuvred into their fighting formations – two lines of heavy ships and a third of lighter ships, well over to the European shore, backs to their beach. It was a surprisingly cautious formation. For one thing, it allowed Melitta's fleet to turn the corner in the channel at Kynossema without opposition.

The Bosporons had twenty-eight ships and they formed two lines, with fifteen in the first line and only thirteen in the second, and then the lines passed the point one at a time, wheeling in unison on the barbed rocks on the European shore like so many hoplites drilling in the agora.

'That was well done,' Diokles commented.

'Because we're past?' Melitta asked.

'Because Plistias just got to see how good we are. See the centre ships in his line still jockeying for position? He has some very green crews.' Diokles nodded.

'See how he waits with his back to the camp?' Coenus said. 'He doesn't want to fight.'

The Bosporon fleet moved slowly down the Hellespont, keeping a crisp formation, until it faced the Antigonid fleet.

A little late, but not unduly so, the first division of Apollodorus's squadrons appeared from the south, headed up the Hellespont.

Diokles grinned.

Apollodorus had twenty-one warships, almost half of them penteres of the new designs – *Glory of Demeter* and *Nile Lilly* and *Oinoe* and all the rest of the ships that had gone to Athens a few weeks before.

'He's raising his boat masts,' Diokles said. 'You going to let him run downstream, or kill him now?'

Melitta looked at Coenus.

Coenus raised an eyebrow. 'I'm not the king,' he said.

Melitta looked at Theron. Theron winked.

'Let him go,' she said.

'Good girl,' Coenus breathed, a little too loudly.

That night, the combined squadrons camped on the same beach where Plistias of Cos had camped the night before. It was a strategic spot. Melitta liked it for its history: in one walk along the muddy beach, she'd found a Sakje arrowhead – a style more than a hundred years old – and an Athenian obol older yet.

Leon and Apollodorus had Stratokles the Informer with them. She had to think about that. The man had been her adversary too often to let him inside her guard – but she could see his utility in this instance, and the Euxine was afire with reports of Amastris's betrayal of him at her wedding to Lysimachos.

Unless the bastard had done it on purpose, spread the reports to gain their confidence.

She shook her head, the way she'd shake it if she had taken a blow in combat. Thinking like this never ended well, in her experience. She turned back towards her camp, eyes still on the beach.

Head clear, she walked up to the circle of men awaiting her.

'So,' she said. 'Is our message sent?'

Stratokles nodded. 'And well sent, despoina. You can close the Hellespont. Demetrios will have to take notice.'

Leon nodded. 'I worry about Ptolemy,' he admitted. 'To the suspicious mind, we are equivocating. Or even changing sides.'

Apollodorus shook his head. 'If we had ejected Lysimachos, Ptolemy might think as much. But Leon, we have ejected Plistias.'

Leon shook his head. 'We have changed the playing board, and that will threaten everyone.'

Stratokles nodded. 'I think you *must* threaten everyone. I don't think that we have enough information to guess who took him. It might *seem* that Demetrios has him, but that would suit Lysimachos or Cassander, too.'

Melitta glared at him. 'You make my head hurt, Athenian. And who is this boy? I remember him – Hyrkania.'

'This is my ward, Herakles.' Stratokles stood back to allow the younger man his place in the ring of commanders.

Old Draco, now captain of marines on the *Atlantae*, did a double-take. 'Herakles of who?'

Melitta nodded at Stratokles. 'Son of Alexander, I think.'

Stratokles nodded.

Draco whistled. 'A pleasure to meet you, my lord. I served your father.'

Herakles flushed, straightened his shoulders. 'Despoina – I have known more than twenty-five winters, and I am no boy.'

Melitta nodded. 'We're of an age, are we not, Herakles?' She looked at Leon. 'Are this wily Athenian and this Macedonian-Hyrkanian using us, Leon?'

Leon took a deep breath. 'By the gods, I hope not. I allowed Stratokles to convince me that the young man's presence with us would serve as much point in threatening both Antigonus and Cassander as our seizure of the Hellespont. Word will spread.'

Melitta looked at Apollodorus. 'And this met with your approval?'

Apollodorus looked around. 'Satyrus gave me the command, and I used it to get his ships to here. With your permission, despoina, I'll lay down my command now and go back to being a marine.' He looked at Stratokles. 'I ... am more hesitant than Leon.'

Melitta nodded. 'My thanks, Apollodorus. And my brother's.'

'He did a good job,' Leon said.

'He wants to tuck into Demetrios's forces and kill,' Stratokles said. 'And he doesn't love me. I return the feeling.'

Melitta looked around. 'So. And so. Here we are. We have a fleet, an army, and a potential King of Macedon. What is our next step?'

Leon crossed his arms. 'Now we wait.'

Stratokles shook his head. 'Not I. With your permission, Anaxagoras and I ... we will go to Athens. All I ask is that you allow anyone who comes to your camp to see my young scapegrace, and that you don't let him wander off or die.'

Herakles looked, if not frightened, then at least deeply hesitant. 'You will leave me, Stratokles?'

Stratokles was growing to like the young man, despite his temper and his uneasy sense of his own importance. And he had always found it difficult to dislike those who liked him. 'I'll be back,' he said.

When the junior officers – the ship trierarchs and the centarchs from the taxeis – had returned to their duties, Melitta summoned Stratokles to her with a gesture. He thought of Banugul's comments about her. She was more imposing than he remembered, and her eyes were darker, and a little wilder. Her muscles were impressive, too.

'I don't like you,' she said.

Stratokles crossed his arms. He smiled. He always smiled when he was fighting. 'I admire you,' he answered.

That stopped her.

'I don't trust you,' she said. 'You killed my mother.'

He shook his head. 'No, despoina. We've been over this ground before. I did not kill your mother. In fact, she gave me this cut to my nose.'

'You helped to have her killed,' Melitta hissed.

Stratokles glanced around for Lucius. 'Yes,' he said. He liked this new tactic – just tell the truth. It was easy to remember and saved a great deal of energy. 'I acted under orders from the man who was my master at the time, and on behalf of my city.' He shrugged.

She narrowed her eyes. 'I can kill you,' she said.

He had the most ridiculous impulse to smile again. 'Despoina,' he said, 'you don't relish me as an ally. But really, if I may? You risk nothing by sending me to Athens. If I am secretly in league with

92

Demetrios, what do I gain? I leave you the most valuable hostage in the world today. And if I return with your brother, then I will expect something by way of apology.'

She watched him, the way a cat watches a mouse. It was fascinating, considering that he was a man, and eight inches taller, how very imposing she was. She allowed the slightest smile to touch her eyes, just the corners of her mouth. 'No,' she said. 'You bring me my brother, and I'll call us even.'

Stratokles cursed his fickle heart, because he was attracted to this unsheathed knife of a woman even while he could feel her hate like the warmth of a flame against his face. Now he let himself smile. 'I will settle for even,' he said.

She shook her head. 'No, you won't. You will play some game, some very clever game. And then I will kill you.'

Stratokles shook his head. 'No games,' he said.

Now it was her turn to smile. 'Stratokles, do I know you better than you know yourself?' She nodded. 'In truth – if you bring me back my brother, I might forgive a game or two.'

He liked this play. Melitta of Tanais was far more interesting in her way than Amastris. It occurred to him – in an oblique, revenge-bound way – that serving Melitta would be a revenge of its own. They had been friends, once, Melitta and Amastris – until Amastris's jealousy of Melitta's freedom parted them. Or something like that.

'Let's see what I bring back,' he said mischievously.

He felt *alive*.

6

Satyrus awoke with all the pains of a man who has lost a fight. His head pounded, he could feel the blood matted in his hair, and when he put his right hand tenderly against the right side of his scalp, it *moved*, and the flesh squelched like a bathing sponge.

His right elbow hurt, and when he tried to roll over, his ribs ... at least one was broken. A spike of agony rolled him back, and the combination of his injuries went off like a series of internal fires.

'He's awake,' said Arse-Cunt.

You ought to be dead, Satyrus thought. So damned close.

Satyrus smelled her before he saw her, and he knew immediately who had him, and why, and he was afraid.

'My poor Satyrus,' Phiale said. She came to the side of the box upon which he'd been laid out. She rested a light hand on his forehead. 'Poor Satyrus.'

'You,' he managed.

'Me,' she replied. 'How very satisfying. Money is a wonderful thing, Satyrus. I paid this man a sum, and he produced you. Very little effort.' Satyrus assumed that she was smiling. His vision was too blurry to be sure.

She had a knife, though. He felt it when she laid it against his cheek. 'You sent me out of Alexandria as if I was a disposable thing,' she said, her voice thick. 'I cannot decide which I would prefer: to cut your nose and your penis clear of your body and then send you back to your whore of a sister, or simply to execute you.'

Satyrus grunted. He wanted to say something – to tell her that she was insane, for instance. She was insane – Satyrus was confident of that much, not that it seemed very relevant from where he was, her knife cool against his cheek.

'Well,' she said, 'to be honest, I'd like you in a little better shape than this, Satyrus. I'm afraid you are such a wreck that cutting you seems a waste of time.' Her knife licked at his cheek. It was sharp; he felt the blood flow before he felt the sting of the cut.

'See, Tenedos, he's all but ruined. I just cut a slice out of his face and he hasn't even cried out.' Phiale got to her feet and he could hear her dusting her hands together as if his blood was dirty – perhaps it was, to her. 'Sticky,' she said, and giggled. 'Call me when he's better,' she said. 'You know where to find me.'

Arse-Cunt grunted. 'As you say, despoina.'

'Yes,' she answered. 'As I say.'

The next day, his cheek was infected where she'd opened it almost to the bone, and he was weaker – loss of blood, he expected. His whole face was hot, and he couldn't move his shoulders much, either, and he didn't even know why.

'She's mad as a tanner,' Arse-Cunt said. 'And she's going to hurt you. It's funny – I worked so hard not to kill you, back outside Piraeus. You killed quite a number of my men – worthless fucks, most of them, but Aeneas was a good man. If I'd killed you right away, I'd have done us *both* a favour.' He laughed merrily. 'I'd like to off you for Aeneas, but I'd be doing you a favour. See the irony?'

Arse-Cunt settled for kicking him in the ribs.

When Satyrus next approached consciousness, he was aware that he had dreamed of his father, and Herakles, and Olympus. The dream empowered him.

He determined to escape. He didn't have a plan, or any idea where he was, but only the determination to escape, immediately. He swung to a sitting position, and his lungs pressed against his broken rib, and he fell to the floor ... a wave of pain washed over him ...

Do not surrender now!

He was on the floor, a floor of fire, his head had been cut from his body and floated above him, a separate thing from his headless corpse – he crawled, his hands burned by the fires rising from the floor every time he moved his arms. His elbow touched something – he kept going, the pain in his knee and the pain in his right shoulder nothing to the pain of his head, cut clear of his shoulders and burning in the golden haze over the stump of his neck.

Keep going.

His hands were in something cool. He didn't know what it was, but he dragged his body into it. He pulled himself by his arms when his legs refused to answer. Now his hands were hot and his knees were passing though the cool thing.

He allowed himself to sink down on his stomach.

No! Now! Go now!

He raised himself onto his elbows – infinite agony – and dragged himself, one arm-reach at a time, until there was *nothing* under his hands. He wriggled, pushed with one trapped foot ... and fell.

The feeling of falling was disassociated from movement, and for one long heartbeat, he was not in pain, as no part of his damaged body was pressing against the ground. And then he hit the ground.

Wake up! Almost there! Go!

He came to in the fetal position. He didn't feel any worse – or better. He lifted his head, rolled on his stomach – efforts of will – raised himself, and crawled towards what seemed to him to be an opening, although his eyes were nearly swollen shut.

Arm over arm. And then a push with a knee, with a foot. Another. Another.

Nothing under his hands. Again. This time, he was more lucid and thus more afraid, and he reached down ... and felt stone. Not a long drop. A step – a single step. He levered himself on his arms, winced as his ribs passed over the sill, collapsed panting in what had to be sunlight.

'Apollo!' said a woman's voice. 'There's a fucking corpse in the street – it's moving!'

'Pluto, he looks like donkey shit,' said a boy's voice. 'Been stripped, too.'

'And beat. Hey – you alive?' said the woman. A hand touched his shoulder. Rolled him over so he gave a small scream.

Satyrus rallied his will, licked his lips. One chance.

'Gold!' he hissed. 'Get me clear of here.'

And then he was gone. Again. And no voice came to tell him how he had done.

He came to in pain: hot pain, like spikes of ice and fire into his head and back, and dull aches over everything; cold, dull aches that were always there between the spikes. He was being bounced – up, down, up, down. His eyes wouldn't open. People talked, all around him. It was as if half the human race was shouting, all around him, but two voices came clear.

'Wide-arse weighs like a double sack of grain!' said a voice under him.

'Worth more, sweetie.'

A bed. He was on a bed, in the narrowest room he'd ever seen. He was on a low, narrow bed with clean sheets, and the walls weren't much wider than his shoulders. The cushion at his head was covered in pus.

That pus was coming from his face. It felt wet, and sticky, and hot. But at least he could feel, and the swelling had to be down, because he could see from his left eye. He flexed his shoulders, felt the edges of the pain of broken ribs under a tight bandage. A good, workmanlike job.

If he had a fever, it was a light one – he could think. See. Move, a little.

There was a curtain at the end of the narrow room, and it was lifted, and a stoop-shouldered man came in with a satchel over his shoulder and a mop of curly white hair. 'Still alive,' he said, with a smile. 'I had you marked as a tough one.'

Satyrus tried to return the grin, but his attempt was lost in a wash of pain and some sort of bursting on his face, and hot fluid ran down his chin, and he coughed.

'Pus,' the man said, and opened his satchel. 'Someone really didn't like you, son. I'll do what I can, but your face is never going to be what we call right. Lie still, now. I've seen worse – when a sarissa goes right through a man's cheek, puncture wounds on both sides, all the teeth ruined.'

'Did,' Satyrus managed. His voice was rough, the word incomprehensible. 'Did he live?'

Curly Hair laughed. 'No. Starved to death. I kept him alive a long time, though. He didn't really want to live. His boy left him for another man.'

'You – are – doctor?' Satyrus managed.

'Hmm. Yes. Although I don't know if Hippocrates would have me if he saw my practice. You have a name, lad? The whores who brought you in want to be paid. You said gold.' The man winked. 'Beat as bad as you were beat, I'd have claimed to have gold, too. My advice? Don't be too eager to pay.'

Satyrus coughed. 'Why?' he asked weakly.

'Because you're bleeding internally, son. Pissing blood right and left. Pay if you live, that's my advice. You have family in Athens?' he asked.

'No,' Satyrus said.

'Don't be telling me you're a slave. You had two rings on until some cocksucker – and I use the term precisely – took them.' He began to unwind Satyrus's bandage. 'This is going to hurt. Anything you want to say, first?'

'Kineas,' Satyrus said, on the spur of the moment. He was clear headed enough to know that his own name probably wasn't the wisest idea. 'Alexandria.'

'Ah,' said the doctor. 'So you do have a few darics, eh? I can tell the girls and boys?'

Satyrus nodded.

'In that case,' said the doctor, 'I'll give you some poppy for the pain.'

The god lay by his stream, as he ever did, a magnificent figure – bigger than Theron, bigger than any man Satyrus had ever seen, his skin smooth and unmarked, heavily muscled. He wore a lion skin like a kilt.

Satyrus was healed. He walked to the edge of the stream and sat easily, all of his muscles responding perfectly.

'You will have to make decisions,' the god said. 'You will have a friend – a weak friend.'

Satyrus wanted to bathe his head in the cool stream, not listen to the god. He rolled on his stomach. The ground underneath him was moss – damp and cool and slightly springy. The stream was narrow but swift, and he could see the gravel bottom. He put his hands in the stream, and it was cold as ice. He dipped his head—

'Are you awake, sir? Sir? Awake, sir?' said an insistent voice.

Satyrus rose out of a deep well of sleep and poppy towards the voice.

'Please wake up, sir. Please wake up, sir. Sir, please wake up.' It was an unpleasant voice – a surprisingly unpleasant woman's voice, squeaky, grating, the sound of a sword on rock.

Satyrus tried to respond. A meaningless mumble emerged, and his eyes opened.

'There's a good gentleman, sir. How nice. Lovely morning – very cool. And can you tell me sir, what is your name? Where can we find your ... people?' she asked.

There was a man standing behind her. 'Bankers. Ask if he has bankers.'

Harpy Voice sounded impatient. 'Don't be *stupid*. He can barely talk. We'll be lucky if he's a ship owner.'

Satyrus wasn't thinking very clearly. He was *afraid*, not a common feeling for him. Afraid that this coarse-voiced woman would sell him to Phiale. Afraid that Phiale would find him – he was in a brothel, he assumed. With his left eye open, he could see that Harpy Voice was a plain-faced girl of sixteen or seventeen with short legs and magnificent, prominent breasts and hips worn under a chitoniskos so short as to be indecent. But of course it was indecent. She was a whore. A porne. Her eyes, though, were fierce, independent – interested.

The boy behind her was younger – wide shoulders, narrow waist. Fit, but his face was misshapen, as if he'd been hit hard as a small child, or had his jaw broken and badly set. He looked stupider than an ox. An ox with a broken jaw.

'Maybe a ship's name, then?' Ox Face asked. 'Maybe he's off a ship and they can pay us?'

'Shut up,' Harpy Voice said. She leaned over Satyrus – she had to, as there wasn't room to stand next to the bed. 'A name, sweetie. Just a name, so we can get you help. No offence, sir, but we're not doing this for our arete.'

Her use of the upper-class word made him smile.

'Ooh, sweetie, you know that word, do you?' she said, and she sat by his feet, coiling neatly on her haunches. 'The better for us, Alex.'

'Why?' he asked, in his ox voice.

''Cause idiots and poor men have nothing to do with arete, that's why. Not for the likes of us.' She smiled at Satyrus – a totally false smile, and not a very effective one. 'Give me a name, lover.'

Satyrus couldn't think of a name that would help him without compromising him. Leon had factors in Athens – but surely Phiale would have them watched. Even in one of their houses, he'd be vulnerable to Phiale, or to her master.

Satyrus had to assume that Phiale was working for Demetrios.

The girl leaned down the bed, moving her feet along the bed's edge, crawling over him like a spider – with the ease of long practice, he assumed. Her breasts hung before his eyes, and even through the poppy he was aware of her.

'Oh-ho,' she said. 'So you are alive. Listen to me, sweetie. I need a name and some promise of reward, or I'm clearing this bed. I'm paying four obols a day for this bed, I'm paying for the doctor in blow-jobs, and to be honest, I have plenty of work just now. So ... a name.' She smiled. It was a better smile. 'Come *on*. I don't care what husband beat the crap out of you. You'll live – you won't be pretty, but you'll live. Doctor says you ain't pissing so much blood. So give over, lover. A *name*.'

He was dead, but he was a name, from one of the great families of Athens, and if Demetrios was behind this, the man's family would help him anyway. He didn't pause to check the mushiness of his logic. He could drive an elephant through the flaws, but he needed out of this brothel before Phiale, who'd come out of one of these and knew them like he knew the plains below Tanais, looked for him.

'Polycrates of Lysander,' he croaked.

'Ooh, dearie,' she said, and clapped her hands. 'Ooh, sweetie. For that name, I'd keep you for a week.' She leaned down and kissed his forehead – he had a flash of his mother, and she bounded off the bed.

'Come on, Alex,' she said. 'We're going to be rich.'

She was gone, and her ox-faced partner with her.

Once she was gone, Satyrus had a long time to examine what he'd done and doubt it. After all, the man was dead. It was possible that the news wasn't out yet. Satyrus lay in his narrow bed and couldn't decide how many days had passed. Two? At least two. Perhaps as many as ... he really didn't know.

It was possible that Polycrates' body hadn't been found. In which case, his family would still be loyal to Demetrios – Satyrus grunted. He could follow this line of thinking to one disaster after another.

The skin under the heavy linen wrap around his torso itched as if he had a dozen mosquito bites wrapped under there, but his arms were better. He tried to scratch, and found that he could move his shoulders and neck – real improvement.

He watched the shadows roll down the curtain. Somewhere over his head was a small, unglazed window – there was no breeze, but somehow the air in the room was alive.

When he lay still, he could listen to the sounds of the house. As the shadows lengthened on the curtain, customers began to arrive. Many of them tramped right past his curtain – feet both loud and soft, aggressive and secretive, hurried and measured. Some were talkative – enquiring after their partner's health, as if a chance-met friend in the agora – others were silent, or pre-emptive, or demanding.

His first evening of lucidity. He wondered how many times his sheets had been changed. His mouth was dry, and he needed to urinate so badly that it made his back hurt, and he suspected from the smell that he'd relieved himself into the bed up until now.

Down the hall, a man was beating his whore. The boy's sin was failing to give the man an erection – a hideous scene, played out through thin walls. Satyrus had little experience of brothels. Listening made him feel ill – right though his pain and his bladder.

Right next to him, a woman was moaning with pleasure, her voice getting higher and faster. Satyrus had never heard a woman make such noises while making love, and he had to assume that they were simulated.

Simulated from what knowledge of pleasure, he wondered. Clearly the brothel had rules of its own. Certainly the porne had to thank his customer, or her customer, when he was finished.

The pain on his bladder was now too much to bear. And no one was going to come, he could tell. The whores were all working, and the doctor …

He got his elbows under him and wriggled down the bed, his hips almost free from pain and his ribs protesting, but bearably. He managed to get his feet on the floor at the end of the bed, then he had to lie and watch the fly specks on the ceiling – the room spun for a moment when he raised his head. But he saw an old, deep amphora with the top smashed in, in the corner – a makeshift chamber pot.

He got his feet on the floor again and wriggled his hips towards the end of the bed again. Raised his head. Bad.

He was going to do this.

He raised his head and got his hands against the walls. His wrists hurt – his right shoulder felt as if it had been dislocated.

Herakles, stand by me, he thought – a war cry to go and urinate. It made him laugh – a low gurgle.

'Hey! You're not running off on me, are you?' Harpy Voice poked her head through his curtain.

'Must ... piss,' Satyrus managed.

'Oh! Sweetie, I'm sorry. You usually just wet the bed. And the poor slaves clean up after you. Here, that's it, honey, let me get my shoulder in there.'

She got him up and off the bed – she was strong. But when he stood over the makeshift chamber pot, he untangled his left arm from her shoulder. 'Thanks,' he said.

'You are a gent,' she said. 'I've seen a few pricks in my day, sweetie. Just piss.'

'Go,' he said. He felt his face flushing, and his bladder was on fire, but he couldn't get a drop out while she stood there.

She giggled – a genuine reaction, he thought. 'I'll just wait in the hall,' she said.

It came out of him in a rush – orange and red. Blood in it, but no more than when he'd taken a blow in the kidneys through his armour. Not enough for despair, anyway. Enough to take seriously.

The process went on and on – embarrassingly – and he had to use the corner walls to hold himself up.

'You having a symposium, lover?' Harpy Voice called, and she laughed. Next door, the same crescendo of passion was being acted out for the second time that evening.

'Tell me how big I am,' demanded a male voice.

'Ooh. You fill me up!' answered the porne in the next cubicle.

'Now lick my ear,' said the male voice.

Satyrus shook his head.

'Are you through yet?' Harpy Voice asked.

'My time isn't fucking up yet!' called a male customer.

'Not talking to you, sweetie,' Harpy Voice said.

Satyrus wiped himself on a rag provided for the purpose and was appalled to see how red, bruised, and swollen his penis was. He'd been beaten before, he'd been hit in his genitals before, but never like this. No wonder it all hurt so much.

He turned to stumble back to the bed, misjudged the distance, and fell.

'Damn you, sir,' Harpy Voice said. 'All you had to do was call, you know. Can't let a working girl see your yard, can't be seen to piss? Men are fools.' She got him to his feet with her legs, a lift that a wrestler might have envied, and he flopped onto his back on the bed.

In the distance a bell rang. 'Eurydike!' called a charming, cultured voice.

'Ah. Sorry, sweetie. Customer for me,' she said. She patted his foot. 'Tell me you are going to make me rich, sweetie. Please.'

Satyrus grunted. He hurt. But he managed to twitch the right side of his face. 'Rich,' he said.

'Hmm. I might be falling in love with you,' she said cheerfully, in her grating voice. 'See ya!'

And she was gone.

It was hours before he slept. He heard several porne beaten – some by customers who just wanted to hit someone. But other customers were tender, solicitous, and thus sounded just as foolish as the lusty ones and the violent ones.

At one point, every bed on the hall must have been working at the same time. Satyrus could *smell* the sex. He could hear it all around him. It was ... curious.

Eventually the sounds began to die away. It was quite late – in fact, in farmer's hours, it was more *very early*. Satyrus had slept – he had trouble ungumming his eyes, and now he was desperately thirsty.

He tried to swallow, tried to raise saliva. Decided he would have to get up. He was sure he could do it.

He had started to wriggle down the bed when the curtain opened. Ox-head glanced at him.

'You doing all right?' the boy, a young man, really, old enough to be a junior *ephebe*, asked.

Satyrus raised a hand. 'Water,' he said.

'Oh, sure!' the young man responded. 'I was supposed to bring it to you when I came on shift, but I was sent to a party.' He vanished.

Somehow, waiting for him to return was harder than all the waiting until then.

He came back through the curtain with a whole water jar, plain black ware, full to the brim. He dipped a sponge in and handed it to Satyrus, who slurped it dry.

Satyrus repeated this three times, and he felt immensely better.

'Help me sit up,' he said.

Young Alex got an arm around him and lifted. He was gentle, and strong and Satyrus leaned back against the wall, took the water jug and drank. 'Of course,' he said, to no one in particular, 'now I'll have to piss again.'

Alex laughed. 'Happens to me whenever I have to stay over at a party,' he said. 'When they're done with me, I get sent to the kitchen. I won't go to the slave quarters – I'm not a slave. But they always lock me in – as if I'd steal from my customers? And when I have to piss?' He laughed.

'Not a slave?' Satyrus asked.

'Oh, no, sir. I'm a citizen. Both my parents were citizens.' Despite his face, the boy sounded quite intelligent.

Satyrus drank more water. 'What do you do at parties?' he asked.

Alex rolled his head back and forth. 'I dance, usually. Sometimes I play drums for one of the girls. Some parties pay for us to fuck – me and Aella, usually, which is fun. We do it well.' He nodded. 'At a good party, after we dance, someone will take me aside, and then it's just business. Right?' he smiled. 'At a bad party, the men get drunk, and then they all want to fuck me at once. Sometimes it hurts, and sometimes the idiotes don't pay.' He shrugged. 'My hair's coming in, so my days of parties are about over, and that's as well. I've made a bundle.'

Satyrus nodded. He'd been at parties with flute girls and boys. Now he was talking to the other side of the coin.

Aella poked her head through the curtain. 'How's our gentleman?' she asked.

'Better,' Satyrus said.

'Good for you, sweetie. I have some bread and honey for you, and some dates. What the doctor said to try.' She came in, and she was naked. Satyrus smiled.

'I will certainly try to make you both rich,' he said. He had to get their loyalty, right away – before they sold him to someone else. Demetrios.

Aella grinned. 'Do you know how many men have promised to make me rich, honey?' she said. 'But the only purse they want to deposit in never seems to hold any cash. Eh?' she laughed.

Alex rolled his eyes.

'I need to go to bed,' Aella said. 'Alex will go and find your friend Polycrates tomorrow, won't you, Alex?'

'Day off, after a party,' Alex said. He shrugged. 'A bad party.'

'Oh, honey,' Aella said – the first *actual* empathy she'd shown, Satyrus thought.

Alex shrugged. 'I was well oiled – Sappho took care of me. But none of them wanted her and all of them wanted me, and some of them were bastards.' He shrugged. 'Let's get to bed.'

They left the narrow room. Satyrus, who would have ignored them, scarcely even seen them as human under other circumstances, missed them instantly. He was bored and lonely, and afraid. He lay and thought about these things. Eventually, instead of passing out, he fell asleep, craving opium.

He awoke to a quiet brothel. From the angle of the sun, he knew it was morning – late morning, and the beds were quiet. He lay and listened, and all he heard was some distant laughter and the cry of a baby. Two babies.

He thought about young Alexander. About how bad a bad party might be – bad enough when you were a guest. He'd seen how a group of Macedonian officers could behave; to each other, to any man they might use. Worse if you were a porne. Probably much worse.

The swelling in his cheek was down. The pus was crusted over.

Alex or Aella had put more water in his jug, and he drank some. He made it to the amphora unaided. It hadn't been emptied.

He was just back on the bed when the doctor came in.

'Up and about, are we? Excellent.' He opened his bag and took out a small alabaster jar.

'No more poppy, thanks,' Satyrus said.

'Really? Don't tell me you're a miser.' The doctor put the jar away, rolled in a piece of soft leather.

'I've had quite a lot of it,' Satyrus said. 'Too much, for one life.'

'Soldier?' asked the doctor.

'Something like that,' Satyrus said.

The doctor nodded. 'Well. You'd know best. But when I take that bandage off, it's going to hurt like Hades.'

He was right. It did.

He didn't pass out, but the pain was remarkable. He cried out – not once but twice. Then he was wrapped up again.

'Somebody really doesn't like you,' the doctor said.

Satyrus nodded.

The doctor grinned. 'Well. Hope you make the whores rich, lad. You can keep this bandage wrapped, I assume, and if you don't want poppy ... well, your cheek wound is clean and dry, and you'll hurt for weeks – but I'm done with you. I've crotches to look at.'

Satyrus offered his hand, but the man vanished through the curtain.

Satyrus began to think that he could tell the difference between different sex acts by the sounds. He was appalled – sometimes amused – by the frankness of the vulgarity and the customers. Men asked for the crudest things – some in sing-song, little boy voices, some in harsh demands. Aella came in to check on him, and stayed to chat while washing and rubbing olive oil into her vagina, an act she performed without the least coyness or shame.

'No girl can make enough juice to last a whole night – not during the feast of Aphrodite,' she said. 'That's my bell!' And she was off out the curtain.

Feast of Aphrodite! Satyrus thought. *I've been here two weeks.*

Afternoons were slow. The boys and girls talked, or bathed, sulked, read, debated – they were Athenians, and Satyrus had to laugh at how very Athenian they were: debating political matters, arguing the relative merits of Cassander and Lysimachos, Ptolemy and Antigonus. Aella was a confirmed supporter of Demetrios, who she had seen in person.

'He's like one of the gods,' he heard her say as she walked down the hall. 'His father has captured Mithridates – not the good one. The bad one. The one who's against us.' She laughed like the supporter of a winning sports team. No one disagreed.

Satyrus lay and wondered about how easily men could be labelled 'good' and 'bad' because of their beliefs, or which side in a civil war they backed. It was ... fathomless. He philosophised on it until he heard the proprietress inspecting the girls.

The proprietress was an older woman, with wide-set, large eyes and hair dyed jet black. In some lights she could be quite hideous, with a large nose and bad teeth – but when evening came, she was lovely, attractive the way an older matron is attractive, with a sense of dignity that Satyrus would never have associated with this world of porne and sex. Her name – frequently called out – was Lysistrada.

He knew her by voice and by glimpses through his curtain, but that afternoon she entered his cubicle.

'Medea!' she called – the voice of command, or of a mother.

A young woman came in. Her Sakje blood was obvious – her cheekbones were high, and besides, she had tribal scars on her right shoulder and down her arms. She had a strong face, not a pretty one. 'Yes, despoina?' she asked. She was meek, and her eyes were downcast.

'Empty this pot. It stinks. The smell of urine is not an aphrodisiac, young lady.'

'Yes, despoina.' The Sakje girl flicked her eyes at Satyrus.

'Good afternoon,' Satyrus said, in Assagetae.

She started, eyes wide. Then she fled, carrying the broken amphora full of waste. In moments, she could he heard sobbing in the hall.

'That was a fine trick to play me, sir, and my house footing your bills.' Lysistrada glared at him. 'I came to see to your well-being, and – what did you say to her?'

'I gave her good afternoon, in the language of her folk.' Satyrus suddenly felt exposed. Traders from Alexandria don't know Sakje languages.

'She's the worst slave imaginable,' she sniffed. 'She's injured two gentlemen. I should sell her as a nurse but some of those households are ... well, worse than brothels.' Lysistrada smiled. 'And it took me for ever to break her to our ways. I'll make my investment back – and you, sir. I will make my investment back on you, as well. I under-stand from my young people that you have a connection with our Polycrates.'

Satyrus nodded.

She crossed her arms. 'Only, dear, there's another rumour on the street that someone is offering a very large sum of money in cash for the location of a man from Olbia or Pantecapaeaum. A man with a cut on his cheek like an alpha, and tall.' She smiled.

Satyrus knew he was taken. She'd sent the Sakje girl in on purpose. His brain ran on – he was fit enough to grab her. Perhaps ... use her as a hostage?

No. Phiale would care nothing for that. He had to run. Immediately.

He was naked on the stained sheets of a cot in a brothel – no clothes, no money ...

'What is it worth to you – in cash, not promises – for me to continue to hide you? Sir?' she asked.

Satyrus struggled for a calm he really didn't have. He took a breath, as if squaring off on the palaestra. 'Polycrates will pay for me,' he said, more to buy time than anything. The most likely result was that she would sell him to Phiale *and* to Polycrates. Except that Polycrates was dead, and unless he managed to meet with, and talk to, a family member, they'd have no reason to help him.

Two weeks! His grain ships would be gone. Leon's factor would have the grain money – plenty to ransom a king or two.

A bold front was the essence of the thing. He managed a smile. 'There is a woman seeking to have me killed,' he said, succinctly. 'If she succeeds, and your house is blamed ...' Satyrus left the threat unspoken. 'Whereas, if I make it to my friends, I would expect that you might receive a great deal of money, and perhaps something more.'

'Empty threats and promises I might receive from any agora ruffler,' she said – but she was interested.

Satyrus had seen Leon and Diodorus do this – had watched Philokles do it a thousand times, using a person's cupidity and greed against their better judgement. But Philokles, sometime spy and spymaster, had spoken against it for a king. 'Manipulation is the poorest form of management,' he was wont to say.

Satyrus had no options. 'My promises are not empty. You be the judge – do I look to you like a man of worth?'

'Give me a name,' she said.

'I have. Polycrates. Bring me a member of his family.' Satyrus paused – this woman was intelligent, and he didn't want to give away his weaknesses. 'Or the man himself, and I will see you paid – an enormous amount. A shocking amount.'

'My dear sir, your rival is offering a shocking amount. And you may even have multiple rivals.' She laughed – a harridan's laugh. 'Maybe they will bid for you, like men bid for a beautiful slave.'

He'd misjudged her. Somehow she was personifying in him all the men she disliked – all the men who had bought and sold her. Or perhaps that's how she reacted to all men. 'I can pay more,' Satyrus said, with a confidence he didn't feel. 'And my death – you would feel it.'

'I know every politician in this crooked city,' she said. 'I have most of them by the balls.'

Satyrus shrugged. 'It would be a pity to see you sold back to slavery,' he said.

She started, went white and then red. 'Fuck you, you rich ponce.' She was gone through the curtain before he could retract.

The moment her cork sandal soles had gone down the steps, Aella appeared. 'Bitch,' she said. 'She's trying to cut me and Alex out of our money, ain't she, sir?'

Satyrus nodded. 'Help me up.'

Aella looked out in the hall. 'She's gone out.'

'She's gone for my enemies. Please – this is life and death.'

Aella paused. 'Swear!' she said. 'Swear by Styx that you'll make me rich, and Alex too.'

Satyrus raised his hand. 'I swear on Styx, and on my father's grave, and on all the gods, may the furies plague me, that I will raise you and your friend Alex, and make you rich.'

She pursed her lips. 'It's a beating for me, or worse, if she catches me.'

Satyrus smiled. 'It's death, for me.' He took a breath – having failed miserably as a manipulator, he tried a different tack with Aella. 'How long will you be able to live like this, honey? Before ... before your skin coarsens and your breasts sag? What *other* chance do you have?'

Outside, in the street, there was a stir.

'Aella!' came Alex's voice.

She ran out through the curtain.

Satyrus got himself to his feet. If Phiale was close by, her people would be here any moment.

He used the wall, moving as fast as he could, until he reached the curtain.

'He looks rich enough, I suppose,' he heard Aella say.

'He's Polycrates' slave – his boy.' Alex's harsh whisper carried up the stairs. Satyrus was in the hall – a hall he knew only from sounds. Whitewashed, swept clean with tiles underfoot, it was narrow and ran the length of the second floor – probably had twenty small rooms.

The rooms on the other side of the hall opened on the street – some of them had an exedra, or second storey balcony.

'Fuck!' Aella said. 'She's coming back. With thugs.'

109

Alex made a noise of despair. Another voice spoke, urgently.

'Try!' Aella said. 'Go – go before she sees us!'

Now Satyrus was paralysed, standing at the head of the stairs. He didn't even know if there was another access to this level. Exedras often had their own stairs, but in a brothel that seemed unlikely.

Aella came pounding up the steps, her bare feet ringing on the stone flags. 'By Aphrodite,' she said. 'You're up! You look like shit. Here, come with me.' She grabbed his hand, tugged him along he hall, and he stumbled, and almost fell.

'Top of the stairs,' Lysistrada said, outside. 'Big man.'

'Oh, I know him,' said Arse-Cunt.

Aella pulled him along the hall, past the only three cubicles that were occupied. Near the end of the hall was a door, where all the other rooms only had curtains.

'Hers,' Aella said. She took a breath. 'I'm fucked if she catches me at this,' she said.

There were rapid steps on the stairs.

She opened the door, and the two of them went through. Aella slammed the door back, but Satyrus caught it and closed it softly. There was a bar. He dropped it carefully.

It was a fine room – a woman's room, with an unused loom and two fine tapestries, a Persian rug, a scroll basket full of scrolls.

'She lets us read here, when we're in favour,' Aella whispered.

'Gone!' roared Arse-Cunt. 'Can't be far. Search the rooms!'

'Always wanted to search a brothel,' said another voice. 'Hey, open up!'

The unmistakable sound of a sword pommel on a wall.

Lysistrada was shrill. 'You may *not* search where my customers are!'

'Don't be shy,' Arse-Cunt said. 'I've fucked every girl here!' He laughed. 'They won't care if my boys watch 'em a little.'

'Back off, bastard. This is my house. Theo!' she called. Her bouncer.

'Fuck you, bitch,' Arse-Cunt said. 'Search all the rooms. Kill anyone who tries to stop you.'

The sound of a heavy slap, and Lysistrada shrieked again, and then feet were pounding.

'Is there another way out?' Satyrus asked. His heart was hammering inside his chest.

'Yes. Off the exedra. She has her own steps.' Aella was having trouble breathing. 'Go!'

'You first,' Satyrus ordered. He was just about able to hold himself up, but he wanted a weapon.

He held himself up with his arms and moved from surface to surface, but there was nothing. Out in the hall there was the sound of fighting, and an angry customer was shouting at someone – chaos.

Satyrus followed Aella out onto the exedra, which ran across the side of the house, overlooking an alley no wider than his shoulders.

'Whose room is this?' A whiny voice – not Arse-Cunt. One of his men.

'That's my room,' Lysistrada said. 'You stay out of it!'

A mistake to have barred the door. Too late to regret. Satyrus got down the steps well enough. Aella was there, and Alex, and another man who looked familiar.

'He's in there!' shrieked Lysistrada. 'My door is locked. You bastard!' Her voice sounded close. She must be on the other side of the door.

'Follow me, lord,' said the familiar-looking man. 'Not far. Come.'

The four of them moved as fast as Satyrus could manage. They went from alley to alley, with Aella scouting ahead and the two young men holding Satyrus up – after twenty steps, he needed a shoulder under each arm just to keep him upright.

'Jason!' Satyrus managed.

'That's right, lord.' Jason was panting with the exertion of carrying half of a big man.

Two alleys, and a cross street with pedestrian traffic and a donkey cart, and four men standing by an enormous breadbasket at the mouth of an alley. Jason led them into a donkey shed, and in moments – and not without pain – Satyrus was inside the breadbasket and the top was bound on.

'You two go back to work,' Jason said. 'You know where I live. Come tomorrow.'

It was Jason – Polycrates' body slave. He was well dressed, clean and neat and had silver pins in his chiton – the slave of a very rich man, or a well-off middle-class man himself.

Aella sounded fierce. 'He promised us gold.'

Jason nodded to her. 'And he will. But girl, if we don't get him out of here soon, he'll be dead.'

'I'm no girl,' she protested.

'When do we get paid?' Alex asked.

'When I have him safe at my house,' Jason said.

'You're a slave, ain't you?' Aella asked Jason.

'I am,' Jason answered. For the first time, he sounded less than confident.

'Thought so. We're not slaves, see? So if you fuck us, we'll fuck you right back.' She sniffed. 'We'll be by tomorrow. Better have some money for us.'

Then silence – sounds in the street – and then many men, all together, and the basket was lifted.

'Heaviest fucking bread I ever carried,' said a porter.

'It's a body, idiot. That pretty boy ain't no baker's apprentice – silver pins in his chiton? This is politics. Just take the money, carry the basket, and wait and find out who was murdered. Tomorrow. When we's safe.'

Now they moved fast. Satyrus could feel the speed, and he could see a little bit through the basket – changes in light and shade, mostly, but sometimes, when the sun was at the right angle, he could see figures.

They went a long way. Satyrus had time to get thirsty, to feel the need to urinate, to get cool as the evening air came on his naked skin. Fighting on the deck of a warship was much better than this helplessness.

An hour passed, at least. Or so it seemed.

'Zeus Panhellenios, where are we going?'

'What are we getting for this, boss?'

'Four drachma a man. Don't be such a crew of faggots.' Voice change. 'Sir? Young sir? Are we close?'

'Right here,' Jason said. 'My farm wagon will be along any time now. Thanks. Here's your money. Here you go.' Clink of coins. 'And here you go.' More coins.

Grumbles and mutters. Farewells.

'Where is my master?' Jason asked, from outside the basket.

'Dead,' Satyrus managed.

The top came off the basket. 'I had to make sure that they were gone. I'm making this up as I go. Who killed him?'

Satyrus got his head out of the basket and drank in some better air.

'I don't know. A courtesan, Phiale – she was the agent, I think.' He shook his head.

Jason helped Satyrus to a sitting position. 'Who was behind her? There's men searching everywhere for you, lord. I paid men to find my master – my informers run across them everywhere. I guessed … well, I guessed that they killed Master and you got away. It was a possibility that fitted the facts. They're looking for a "man from Olbia".'

Satyrus nodded. 'I was taken. I … escaped.'

Jason looked at him. 'I heard from Master you are a famous fighter. Listen – please. I have found you, and I will get you to Master's house. Yes? Then I beg you to do something for me.'

Satyrus nodded. 'Anything I can, boy.'

'Take me with you,' Jason said. 'Master kept me safe. From some things. I want free of them.'

Satyrus wondered how desperate the world of slaves and freedmen was. Constant bargaining. And how tempted Alex or Aella would be when they learned what he was worth to Demetrios.

'I'll free you,' Satyrus said. He meant it, but he also knew that it was an offer that would trump most offers of money.

Jason smiled. Satyrus hadn't seen him smile. It made him look much younger.

'I want more than that,' Jason said. 'I want to be a citizen. Not here – too much baggage here.'

Satyrus, naked, and almost unable to walk, had to smile. 'I can make you a citizen of Olbia or Tanais of Pantecapaeaum just by saying that you are,' he said.

Jason nodded. 'I know you can, lord. My master is dead. I can serve you.'

Satyrus took a deep breath. 'You have not told me anything of your troubles – or your master's plots,' he said. 'Get me clear of this, and I'll see you have your freedom. I cannot promise more than that.'

Jason nodded. 'Lean on me. Let's go.'

They went through a farm gate, along a stone wall, through an olive grove, up a hill and down through another grove, and this time they had to endure the barking of dogs and the angry stares of a herd of sheep.

They came down a low ridge to a great house, and by then Satyrus was hobbling, but he felt better, not worse, as if stretching his muscles healed them.

'Can you ride, lord?' Jason asked.

Satyrus nodded. His breath was short.

Into the yard of the great house, where there were four men – big men, all wearing swords. Satyrus wanted to shy away, but Jason merely gave them a nod. 'Usual rates,' he said.

The biggest man chuckled. 'We *love* working for you, Jas.'

Jason turned to Satyrus. 'I had to arrange this on the fly. This is Achilles, and his friends Ajax, Memnon, and Odysseus. Gentlemen, this man needs your protection. Take him somewhere, and tell me where when you can. I have some loose ends to tidy up. He can pay – and he can be a good friend. Lord, just do as they say.'

Satyrus shrugged. 'I would like clothes and a sword,' he said. Achilles was tall and might have been handsome, if he didn't have a rip a finger broad across his face that left his mouth in a permanent leer. Even with the big scar, he had carriage – dignity. Ajax was taller and heavier, with a paunch, and legs as big as a small man's chest – and a disarming grin. Memnon was African, thin and hard, and Odysseus had a mouthful of gold teeth and a wispy beard, and looked altogether more like a lout than the other three, who might easily have passed for gentlemen.

Achilles looked him over. 'You may have mine, lord, if you insist, but right now, you don't look like you're worth spit in a fight.'

Satyrus had to agree with that.

Jason broke in. 'I can get him a couple of chitons and a chlamys,' he said. 'I doubt there's a sword in the house.'

He vanished inside.

Memnon gave him a long look. 'Who's hunting you? And why do we have to call you "lord"?'

Satyrus sat heavily on a farm bench. 'You don't have to call me lord. Jason seems to do it too easily.'

Jason came back with a basket, a leather satchel, and a bundle. 'No sandals – but good boots. Put your legs out, lord.' Satyrus stretched his legs out, and Jason laced the boots on, and they fitted well enough – tall Boeotian boots, well tooled.

Jason then helped him into a chitoniskos – the wool was well-washed, and soft, but raising his arms over his head made him grunt.

'Those is some amazing bruises, boss,' Odysseus said. 'I used to fight barehand in taverns – never got me no bruise like yon.' He was pointing to the mark of a heavy oak staff on Satyrus's left bicep – still purple after more than two weeks, a deep bruise indeed.

'You win or lose?' Ajax asked.

'Lost,' Satyrus said.

All four of them nodded.

'Let me see your hands,' Odysseus said.

Satyrus stuck out his hands.

'I need you to get moving,' Jason said. 'Those porters will be easy to trace.'

Achilles held up his hand. 'A moment, Jas. We don't call this brute Odysseus for nothing.'

The gold-toothed man felt Satyrus's palms. 'Hard enough. Swordsman? Hoplite fighter?'

'Yes,' Satyrus said.

'Can you talk low and act – like us?' Odysseus asked.

'Hopeless,' Ajax said. 'Look at him. Fucking gymnasiums every day. Manners.'

Satyrus grinned, spat to one side the way he remembered Neiron doing, and bobbed his head. 'Fuck off,' he said.

Odysseus smiled. 'Not bad. Don't talk much, and try *not* to keep your back straight all the time. Ride by me. We're sell-swords looking for work with Demetrios, and you've known all of us since ...'

'Rhodos,' Satyrus said.

'We weren't at Rhodos, sorry. We don't get out of Attika much.' Achilles smiled, and his scar moved. 'Never mind. Just spit and look angry and injured. Let's get moving.'

Memnon brought six horses out of the barns and Jason helped Satyrus mount.

He felt better on a horse. 'You didn't ask me if I could ride,' he said to Odysseus.

The man's teeth winked in the last of the midsummer sun. 'Didn't need to,' he said. 'We know who you are.' He pulled at his reins as Jason came up to them.

'Leave word for me in the usual way,' he said. 'I don't expect to be a public man after today.'

Achilles nodded. 'So it's true? Polycrates is dead? Who got him?'

Jason shook his head. 'Still trying to find out. Likely need you lot to sort that out, too.'

Satyrus was amused to note that his rescue – if indeed he was being rescued – was not centre stage. Polycrates' death was centre stage.

'You are Polycrates' men?' Satyrus asked.

'Hmm,' Achilles answered. 'Hmm. Some would say we was, and some would say we wasn't, like.'

Odysseus nodded. 'We're our own men. Polycrates pays – paid, I guess – well, and he'd stand up when we asked 'im to.'

'Not like fucking Demetrios of Phaleron,' Memnon muttered.

They began to ride – first downhill, through a wheat field, and then along a donkey path through a vineyard, through a gate in a high stone wall, and out to a road.

Satyrus didn't know Athens really well, but he could see the Parthenon as clear as the moon – the last of the sun was shining on the roof, eight or ten stades to the south. They rode west, into a red sky, and they rode as fast as he could handle. No part of him was badly hurt any more – but he was tired and his hips hurt.

He didn't complain.

The moon rose and the sky went from dark blue to black, and the stars came out, and still they rode. They crossed two small rivers, and swung more south than west, and when Satyrus had almost fallen asleep in the saddle, Achilles called a halt, and they all dismounted and onion sausage was handed out by Odysseus.

Satyrus had his bearings. 'Headed for the Eleusian Way,' he said.

'Got it in one,' Odysseus replied.

They all relieved themselves, drank water, and got mounted, riding more quickly. Achilles and Ajax, the two biggest men, changed horses.

They began to climb steeply, and hills, heavy with rock, loomed on either side, even in moonlight. Twice they passed villages – not a light to be seen – and then, well after moon rise, when Satyrus didn't feel that his discomfort could be greater, they entered a third village. This one had a big inn, and the yard gate opened when Achilles spoke a phrase from the mysteries.

Slaves took their horses – cursing, surly slaves called from their pallets.

'Yer late,' said a shrewish voice.

Achilles made a bow, like a priest before his god. 'Despoina, Tyche affects all men, even heroes.'

Satyrus couldn't see her, whoever she was. Since Odysseus was holding his arm lightly, and had cast the hem of his chlamys over his head, he assumed they didn't want the woman to see him.

'The room over the stable – just as you requested. Let's see the shine of some silver.' He heard the clink of coins, saw the shape bite one. 'World is full of thieves,' she said. 'That's full payment, boys. Thankee. Sleep well. There's bread and opson and a nice piece of venison waiting for you.'

Up steep, narrow steps with no handholds, and there was a low trestle table. Satyrus sat down, and a small clay cup of wine was pressed into his hands. Downstairs, Achilles was still talking to the woman – the the woman who owned the taverna, he assumed. The wine was wonderful – full of flavour, dark as blood in the lamplight.

Ajax ate quietly, quickly, efficiently, while Memnon watched from the barred window and Odysseus curried the horses and fed them – quite an efficient team. As soon as Ajax had eaten, he took Memnon's spot and the black man ate the same way – pushing food into his mouth, chewing quickly, every motion efficient. The only sign of enjoyment of the excellent venison came when Memnon finished his and had his first gulp of wine.

'Lessa's a good hostess,' he said. He gave Satyrus a nod, and walked down the steep steps.

Achilles came back up. He went to a chest in the corner, a big enough box for a body, and opened it. From it he fetched a Sakje bow, a Greek quiver, and a Spartan sword.

'All I have,' he said, handing the long knife to Satyrus. 'But you know how to use it, right?'

Satyrus put the cord of the scabbard over his shoulder. At worst, now, he could see to it that he wasn't taken alive. He nodded. 'Thanks,' he said.

'Don't thank me till you pay,' Achilles said. 'We need to get some things straight. There's a mort of people lookin' for you. Right?'

Satyrus nodded.

'Now, Odysseus says you're the King of the Bosporons. That right?' he asked.

Satyrus nodded.

Achilles nodded a few times back, and winked at Ajax.

'I can retire on a farm in Attika right now – all four of us can – for selling you on.' Achilles sat back, arms crossed.

'So everyone tells me,' Satyrus said. 'Until I get back to my people, I have nothing to offer you.'

'And when you get back to your people?' Achilles asked. 'Then what? Make us an offer.'

Satyrus shook his head. 'You gave me the knife,' he said. 'And you already have a deal with Jason. Why should I make a new deal?'

Achilles nodded. 'I'm a fair man. I won't sell you straight – but me and mine, we might just ride away. Jason said this was escort work. But we know who you are, and the old witch who keeps this place says the roads are full of men looking for you.'

'Whose men?' Satyrus said.

'Demetrios's men,' Achilles said.

'Soldiers?' Satyrus asked.

'Exactly.' Achilles said. 'So?'

'A silver talent each?' Satyrus said.

'Zeus Panhellenios!' Ajax said. 'We'd get you out of Tartarus for that.'

'Shush, you.' Achilles laughed. 'No head for negotiating. But fine. For that fee, we'll see you clear of Attika and put you up in one of our hidey holes for a week, until the excitement dies down. It always does.'

Satyrus nodded.

Six days on the road, as his muscle tone returned, and they climbed out of Attika, over the shoulder of Mount Kimeron, past Eleutherai, to Plataea.

Boeotia was beautiful at high summer, the dance floor of Ares stretching away, a patchwork of fields in gold and green, like a tilled version of the Sea of Grass. Plataea sat high on the shoulders of Kimeron, looking out over the valley, down to the Asopus – the walls were new, and shone in the sun. The Spartans and the Thebans together had destroyed the town twice, and Alexander of Macedon had ordered it rebuilt at considerable expense – fair recompense for the men and women who had fought among the hardest to preserve Greek liberty, or so Alexander said.

'Land here was cheap as dirt when we were new to the business,' Odysseus said as they rode along Asopus and started up a low ridge. 'We had a little windfall early on – bought us this farm.' He grinned.

The farm was on a hilltop, with a low stone tower and an old forge building, a fine vineyard and some scraggly apple trees. Several slave families lived in a hamlet behind the main house.

'Here, we're like lords,' Achilles admitted. 'Hey, Tegara! We're home.'

Women came out of the tower – some attractive, and some looking as hard as bronze, and two of them older than the rest. Two boys emerged from the shed and took all six horses.

'This one is a guest,' Achilles said to the gathered women. 'See to it he has a pleasant stay. He's a paying customer.'

From this, Satyrus gathered that not all visitors were welcome, or voluntary.

The next morning, Odysseus was gone.

'Other business,' Achilles said with a casual wave. 'But he'll put us in touch with Jason, if the boy's still alive.'

Satyrus slept in a bed and took some exercise the next day, shooting arrows with Achilles and Memnon outside the walls of the courtyard. It fatigued him more than it should have, and he took a nap under the old olive trees. Tegara, the older of the women, brought them olives and cheese. She sat down by him, gathering her chiton under her hips as she sat, a very ladylike gesture.

'Who are you, really?' she asked. She had a beautiful, husky voice, far richer than her farm-matron appearance.

'No one important, despoina,' he said.

She smiled at him, her eyes bold. 'I beg leave to doubt that. You look exotic, to me.' Without another word, she shifted behind him and started to massage his back and shoulders – not an erotic job, but a workmanlike job, the kind of thing a man might expect at a gymnasium.

Achilles rumbled a laugh. 'You've made an odd convert, there, lord. Tegara never likes anyone!'

Satyrus slept better that night, and the next morning he met Achilles in the courtyard with Tegara pouring water over his head. She winked at Satyrus, who winked back. There was something about the woman that transcended age or sex – she was easy to like, untrammelled, somehow, by convention.

'Swords?' Satyrus asked Achilles while he bathed himself.

Achilles grinned. 'I have a few.'

'Practice?' Satyrus asked. A bucket of cold water hit him from the side – Tegara tittered. He spluttered.

'Happy to – but I'd like to see you work through some exercises first.' He nodded.

Satyrus understood – no man wants to play at wooden swords with a stranger, who may not pull his blows or behave with decency. He nodded. After he bathed, and took oil from Achilles' aryballos and anointed himself, he picked up a stick and began his own exercises – the six cuts and the two thrusts, the legwork from pankration, the arm blocks and the sword blocks – up and down in front of the well, until Achilles slapped his thigh.

'So you're a hoplomachos, eh? That's what I get for asking, I guess.' He shook his head. 'Promise you won't humiliate an old mercenary, eh?'

Satyrus caught an odd look on Tegara's face. Her impish grin was late to her face when she caught his eye, leaving her looking oddly false.

'I had good teachers,' he said, as much to her as to Achilles.

'You *are* an aristocrat,' she said, without much kindness. Her implied comment was *I thought you were a man.*

She stalked off, head high.

'And she's taken agin' ye as fast as she was for ye,' Memnon said, coming down from the exedra. He shrugged. 'Don' be angry wi' she. She's the real owner here. She's not had an easy life, like enow.'

Achilles nodded at Satyrus. 'Our guest wants to play at the sword.'

Memnon looked surprised. 'Well, well,' he said.

The three of them walked out of the courtyard with half a dozen wooden swords under their arms, and two small Macedonian-style shields. Once they got to a handsome dell of turf below the olive orchard, Memnon dropped the gear he was carrying and sat down.

Satyrus chose a wooden sword he liked – shorter and a bit heavier than most of the rest, and wrapped his chlamys carefully around his arm.

Achilles nodded. 'Let's swear,' he said. 'No man will bear ill will into this ring of grass, nor take ill out when he leaves, despite competition, error or injury. I swear this by Ares and by Athena, God and Goddess of War.'

The words were old-fashioned – Ionic Greek, like the *Iliad*. The oath itself made Satyrus happy, as if he was living in elder days. He repeated it, trying to match Achilles' diction and pronunciation.

Achilles didn't salute. Instead, he simply crouched. 'Ready,' he said.

Up close, he was big – too big for many of Satyrus's tactics of domination. Satyrus was used to being bigger than most men in a fight, and Achilles topped him by a hand. Ajax, absent in the house, was bigger by a head.

'Ready,' Satyrus said.

He had expected a trick – an immediate leap, a lunge, some palaestra trick – but Achilles seemed to relax. He began to circle the dell, his footwork careful but not the trained dance steps of the gymnasium-trained man.

Satyrus didn't react at first, deliberately facing Achilles' initial orientation, allowing the other man to circle him ...

Achilles launched a blow from his left – a high cut.

Satyrus stepped back out of range, and Achilles was already back on his guard. He took another circle step, and Satyrus changed his front in a single turning step, a fluid reorientation from front to back that placed Achilles in easy sword-reach, and Satyrus feinted at his cloak-arm, rolled his wrist, and cut low, but as he had expected, Achilles was a well-trained man, and he ignored the cut at his protected side and parried the real cut at the opening line.

They both smiled. It had been a short exchange with no real contact but Achilles now knew how precisely Satyrus could pull his blows, and Satyrus could feel how good Achilles' balance was in close, and they both sidestepped diagonally left, opening the range.

There was more circling. The sun came through the trees only at one point, and Satyrus considered trying to orient his opponent into it, but it seemed pointless.

Achilles made some internal decision and chose to attack. He pivoted quickly and started a sword-foot forward attack, and Satyrus stepped *into* it, a tough call against a bigger man, isolated the attacker's elbow with his cloak arm and kicked Achilles lightly just above the knee while keeping his sword ready to the real cut that came, as he expected, under his cloak – he pivoted on his own left foot, put his knee into the oncoming cut, and tapped Achilles on the head with his sword.

Achilles stepped back.

Satyrus fell into his guard, and saluted. 'Hit to the knee,' he said.

'Ah, well,' Achilles said. 'Myself, I'm dead.' He grinned. 'To tell the truth, I expect you'd ha' broken my knee with that kick, eh?'

Satyrus shrugged.

Achilles nodded. 'I heard you fought the pankration, but it's another thing to see it.'

Satyrus nodded. 'Kicking in combat is dangerous – your leg is out where you can't defend it. When men are in armour, with swords and spears – not much use, really, unless you are right inside.'

Achilles nodded.

They set again, and both men called 'ready'.

Satyrus felt that it was only fair that he launch the next attack, and he launched a simple one, a rising snap cut that appeared to target the lower shield leg, rolled over into a high cut, and became a thrust to the (hopefully) open chest. It was one of his favourite moves, a routine he had practised for ten years.

Achilles baffled his feint and his whole intention by taking a long step back, out of range, as Satyrus tried to engage, and then the big man moved quickly forward and right, forcing Satyrus to turn and parry with his arm. Achilles played for his sword, trying for a grapple, and Satyrus responded with a strong, stiff arm, backed and cut; the other man caught his cut neatly on his arm and stabbed low, Satyrus blocked the low stab lower and tried to rotate his hips to isolate the sword for a disarm, and got a light smack in the side of his mouth, as Achilles' fist just tapped him.

Satyrus stepped back, and nodded. 'Good blow.'

Achilles looked happy. 'Thanks,' he said, amicably. 'Ready?'

Satyrus nodded, and this time, Achilles was on him before he could draw breath, a flurry of blows, high, middle, and low.

Satyrus backed, and backed again, and then, his wits gathered, he struck out – cloak arm and then right foot kick. The moment he broke the other man's rhythm, he lunged, a powerful step forward with his sword foot, a lightning transition from back foot to forefoot, from long-range cuts to being almost face to face, and his sword point was four inches above the other man's groin.

Achilles jumped back, and he wasn't grinning. 'Hit,' he said.

'Got your measure,' Memnon said.

Achilles came at him with another flurry of blows, this time faster – and stronger.

Satyrus was ready this time, met him body to body, and parried the second cut sword to sword – not a typical block, but a high counter-cut that slapped hard at the opposing sword and then cut down at the opponent's wrist. But Achilles' cut was a feint – the result was both men stepping back and rubbing their wrists.

'Too hard,' Satyrus said. 'I'm sorry.'

'Me, too. Takes two to fuck up that badly.' Achilles had to sit down. Both of them had hit with roughly the speed of both arms hurling together.

Satyrus was clearly the less injured of the two, and he stood, rolling his wrist back and forth.

Memnon got to his feet. 'Got enough in you to try a bout wi' me, sir?' he asked.

Satyrus nodded, and Memnon picked up a longer sword.

Achilles grunted, got to his feet and walked to the other side of the dell, cradling his wrist.

'Broken?' Satyrus asked. 'I'm sorry—'

'Bah,' Achilles said. 'My pride's hurt worse than my wrist.'

Memnon said ready, and Satyrus answered, and they were off. They circled each other a long time – far longer than Satyrus and Achilles had circled. After some time, Memnon began making very cautious feints – always the same feint, leading with his left foot and cutting over his head at Satyrus's sword side. By the time he'd done it for the tenth time, Satyrus had grown impatient – parrying on that side forced him to move his feet and arms in a way that annoyed his rips, at least, and it was a dull move – a move done entirely to measure him and to make him move.

Satyrus counter-cut at the wrist on the eleventh attack, timing to catch the instant after the launching of the feint.

Memnon pulled his feint, stepped sideways, and Satyrus turned to face him again, feeling a new twinge from his ribs.

Memnon gave a small smile, and launched a whole new attack – a left-right combination that started with his rolled chlamys arm thrusting hard, a straight punch to Satyrus's chlamys, and then the black man stepped in – hard – and raised his sword. Suddenly the attack was the same attack he'd feinted so many times – and when Satyrus

123

went to parry, his ribs screamed in sudden pain – and Memnon scored on him, touching him on the head cleanly right over his feeble counter-cut.

Satyrus stepped back, clutching his ribs. 'Good hit,' he spat.

Achilles shook his head. 'Memnon is no gentleman,' he said. 'But he saw you favouring your ribs, and he went for you there. And you let him.'

Memnon took his sword while Satyrus sat heavily. 'There's no "fair" in a sword fight,' he said. 'But I din't mean to hurt ye so bad.'

Satyrus took a deep breath – the pain was already better. 'What you did was well done,' he said.

Memnon grinned. ''Twas!' he said. 'Y'er a fine swordsman. Had to beat you fancy.' He spat. 'Cup o' wine, lord?'

Satyrus drank wine with them, trying to suss them out. Achilles had tried to fight him in a palaestra fight – careful, scholarly. Memnon had ignored such conventions. He wondered what that said about them, since both were sell-swords, hired killers, mercenaries. Which was the more honest? Which was the real swordsman?

Satyrus wasn't sure. But he knew his ribs hurt, and he knew that both men were good company, and that he'd rather have them at his back than across a shield wall.

'How much to hire the four of you?' Satyrus asked. 'For, hmm, a year?'

Memnon laughed. Achilles glanced at him from under his heavy brow and raised an eyebrow. 'Serious?' he asked. 'What's the job?'

'Bodyguards. For me.' Satyrus shrugged. 'I assume you're trust-worthy. For cash, paid down.' He smiled.

Achilles smiled back. 'A year? We work by the day – most of the time.'

Memnon dipped a piece of hard bread in olive oil. 'When we're broke, we rent out of Demetrios or Cassander for soldier's wages,' he said. 'How much are we talking, here?'

Satyrus raised an eyebrow. 'I don't know. I'm not Croesus. What's your daily rate?'

'Jason gives us ten drachma a day, and expenses if we need equip-ment or horses,' he said. 'Double what a hoplite is paid, if he brings his own gear.'

Satyrus nodded. 'And a bonus?'

Achilles shook his head. 'Often, but not always. Sometimes the job comes with its own bonus. Kill a rich man ...' he said, and left the rest of the thought to tail away.

'How long have the four of you been together?' Satyrus asked.

Memnon looked away.

Achilles shook his head. 'Not all that long, eh? Memnon only joined up, what, before the feast of Demeter, eh? It were just me an' Odysseus – time out of mind. Years, anyway. Longer than we've any right to be alive. Ajax ... well, we met him fighting against him, a few years back. Memnon here's the latest recruit.'

'He'll raise an army in a hundred years or so,' Memnon added. He laughed cautiously, the way he fought.

'Well?' Satyrus said. 'If I pay your daily rate for a year, half in advance, for all four of you?'

Achilles raised an eyebrow again, an expression that made him look like a philosopher and not a warrior at all. 'Have to ask the others.' He nodded. 'How dangerous?'

Satyrus shrugged. 'I've been in six ship fights in four years,' he said.

'So ... fucking dangerous,' Achilles said. 'Well, fair enough – at least you tell the truth.' The man glanced at him. 'Spear fightin' is more real than sword. Just sayin'.'

Satyrus's whole face hurt when he smiled, but he managed one. 'I know,' he said. 'But people get hurt—just playing with spear poles.'

Achilles nodded. 'Try me tomorrow,' he said.

Satyrus could see the man's pride as a soldier had been hurt. After his experience with Polycrates, he was more sensitive to another man's feelings. 'I'll try spears,' he said. 'Tomorrow.' He yawned, cursed the pain in his cheek, and then tried again.

'How long's your contract with Jason?' he asked. They picked up the swords and shields and started back to the house.

Achilles shrugged. 'Haven't seen any money yet,' he admitted. 'I assumed it was until Jason came to collect you. I don't really want to linger too long here – folks saw you arrive. But I need to hear word from Odysseus before we move again.'

Satyrus chewed on that as he climbed the stairs of the old tower. He had time – too much time – to think, and he worried about the people in the village, and watched them walk about from the top of the tower – watched the steady flow of traffic up the flank of Kithaeron, and back down the valley of the Asopus – men and women with donkeys or just walking alone or in groups. Plataea wasn't on the main trade route from Attika to Boeotia – that was the road from Thebes to Athens, over Parnassus – but this was the second most-travelled road, and Satyrus saw a potential spy in every traveller.

He also had time to worry about Abraham and Miriam. If Demetrios had tried to take him, he must not intend to release the other hostages. Satyrus spent a day with a borrowed wax tablet and a stylus, trying to work out what he knew of the attack on him and what it might mean.

If Demetrios had attacked him, on purpose, he should have used Polycrates as his tool, and done it at Polycrates' house. Where Satyrus had been headed. The more Satyrus turned this logic over in his head, the less it seemed possible that any set of murderers could possibly have been hired so ineptly that they murdered a major ally of Demetrios – casually – as part of the seizure of a political opponent. The more so as a botched attempt – and it had been close – would have resulted in immediate military consequences. And perhaps it already had; Satyrus hadn't considered it before, but the more he thought about it, the more likely it seemed that Apollodorus and his sister would have taken action by now.

On the other hand, if Demetrios's lieutenants had botched their instructions – and such things happened all too frequently – then the other Rhodian hostages were either dead or under renewed threats, as the only hope Demetrios would have to keep Rhodes in check.

Satyrus drank cup after cup of the excellent well-water in the sweltering heat, watched the roads about the old house, and tried to work through all the different possibilities.

One that he couldn't discount was that the attack had been sponsored by Cassander. He played with the idea, idly making dots with his stylus in the soft wax of his tablet. It was warm, and he was sleepy, and it was too easy to daydream instead about the length of Miriam's body stretched against his ...

Satyrus wondered if there was another man in the world as powerful as he who spent more time pining for women rather than simply mounting them. The slaves Achilles kept were clearly for the very purpose, and some had offered themselves in one way or another. The only one he fancied was Tegara, a free woman, who had something about her he admired, but she had not made herself available – far from it. Satyrus recognised that there was something to that – the unattainable was always to be preferred, he supposed.

He went up on the roof as the sun began to decline. He took a lyre he'd found in the main hall and tuned it, the old gut strings holding despite years of neglect, and he tried his scales and found them waiting for him. He played a simple tune – the opening lines of the *Iliad*, the way the rhapsodes played them. Thought about Anaxagoras.

Really, it was time he stopped being a prisoner of the attack, and took action himself. The obvious course was simple – woo Achilles, buy his services, and get to the Chersonese, where Melitta would be.

Down the valley, he saw a woman talking to a horseman. Horses weren't common in Plataea. Something about her straight back and the carriage of her head alerted him. But the horseman walked his horse along with her for some distance, quite openly, and he lost interest.

The other option was to go to Demetrios.

It was, after all, what had brought him to mainland Greece – the opportunity to see Miriam and to discuss the release of the hostages. And now there was no better way for him to judge the man's intentions – except for the price of being wrong.

It pleased his sense of action, though, and he began to weigh methods of providing for his own safety.

Now the horseman was mounted – well over towards Cithaeron. But he didn't ride over the pass to Athens, rather, he rode west, and Satyrus dismissed him. A boyfriend, a local aristocrat – not that she seemed to like the breed. For surely the woman down at the bridge had been Tegara.

She didn't meet his eye that night, at dinner, which she didn't eat with the men, but merely supervised.

'I think that it is time to move,' Satyrus said. 'Have you considered my offer?'

Satyrus was surprised when Ajax responded. He was the largest, and his face typically wore a look of deep and bovine stupidity.

Not when he spoke, however. 'We like it,' he said, and shrugged his giant shoulders. 'But we await the views of Odysseus. We have sworn oaths – the view of one is the view of all.'

Satyrus nodded. 'I understand,' he said.

Achilles nodded. 'I, too, think it is time to move. There were horse-men up towards Eleutherai today, and down at the bridge, as well.'

Satyrus nodded. 'I saw them. Or rather, I saw one of them.' He looked at Tegara, and had his suspicions confirmed. She looked away, and she was not a great dissimulator.

'Tegara was speaking to one of the horsemen,' Satyrus said quietly.

She stood taller. 'Well?' she said to Achilles. 'What if I was? He was pretty enough, and asked me nicely the road to Corinth.'

Achilles looked at Satyrus.

Satyrus nodded. 'He did ride off towards Corinth,' he said.

Achilles gave her a long look. 'Woman, you have a good life here,' he said. 'And we need you to run the house, so don't ...' He shook his head.

She turned red, then white. 'A good life, is it?' she asked.

Satyrus rose. 'I think we should be gone in the morning,' he said.

Memnon nodded. 'I agree. Demetrios is at Corinth, right?' He looked at Tegara, and she glared at him.

Ajax swore. 'Y'er crazed, woman! This is our business. You ha' no right.' He looked at Achilles, who had her by the arm. 'The man is right – we ought an' be gone. But then Odysseus won't know where to fin' us.' He glared right back at Tegara. 'An' we can't exactly tell her.'

'Kill her?' Achilles said wearily.

They were such pleasant men, in a bluff, soldier-like way, that Satyrus almost missed the moment where their professional needs overbalanced any pretence of morality. Tegara was crying – not dramatically, but simply standing still, sobbing quietly, and Achilles had his sword at her throat.

'Wait!' Satyrus said. 'Why not ask her what she did? And why? And then ... Gods, gentlemen, why kill her?'

Achilles looked puzzled. 'She crossed us,' he said. 'It's on her face.'

'She's just a woman,' Memnon added. 'She's got no one to come back on us.'

Satyrus stood up. 'If you're working for me,' he said, 'then I forbid you to kill her. As long as she tells us who she told and why.'

She drew herself up. 'You lot act like lords,' she said. 'I am a woman of Plataea, and you are robbers, thieves, and war-whores. You think I like watching what you do?' She shrugged. Slumped. 'I think they're Demetrios's men. Cavalrymen.' She looked at Satyrus. 'They was looking for him before you lot got back – except that they called him the "King of the Bosporus".'

Satyrus nodded. 'I am the king,' he said.

Achilles hit her so hard she crumpled to the floor. 'I guess that I am working for you, lord,' he said. 'So I won't kill her – though I think you're being a soft fool.'

'You're hardly the first to think so,' Satyrus said. 'Ethics matter. How matters, not just where and why.' He stepped over, looked at the woman, and sighed. 'If we ride now, can we get clear?'

'Head for Delphi,' Memnon said. 'I'll go up the mountain and hide – no bunch of gentlemen-cavalry will find me. I'll find Odysseus.'

Then they were all business – Satyrus wolfed down the rest of his meal, having long experience with riding hard. He ran to the top floor of the tower, filled a leather bag with clothes and pins, a comb – left the lyre.

The courtyard was dark, even with torches lit, but Memnon took him by the hand.

'Ajax says we're not to light anything else, or watchers'll know what's afoot,' he said. 'Here's your horse.'

Achilles was already mounted. 'I'm going down across Asopus, and cross country to Thebes,' he said. 'Then north to Delphi. I expect to make it there in two days unless we have to hide.'

Memnon gave a rough salute, his dark skin glinting in the fitful torchlight like polished iron. 'I'll find you.'

Then they were away, down the hill, picking their way carefully along the road in moonless darkness. The stars were like distant lamps on the clear night, and the sound of insects was only drowned by the gurgle of the river as they rode to the bridge.

Achilles leaned over and handed Satyrus a spear. 'I don't see anyone on the bridge,' he said, 'but fuck, there could be twenty men behind that house and I wouldn't see them.'

He rode forward first, and Satyrus followed him, feeling freer with a good cavalry spear in his fist. The feeling lasted until their horses' unshod hooves were ringing on the stone bridge, and then Achilles stopped his horse and cursed, filling the narrow bridge, and Satyrus glanced back to find that there were at least a dozen horsemen closing in behind him.

He couldn't see past Achilles, but even over the sound of water he could hear the sounds of a troop of horse – sounds familiar from childhood.

'Boss . . .' Achilles turned in his saddle. He had a sword in his hand, but it wasn't pointed at Satyrus. 'I think we've fucked away your talents of silver, I'm sorry to say.' He shrugged. 'We're surrounded. Demetrios's men, I'd say.'

Satyrus looked back again. 'Damn.'

Achilles shrugged. 'To be honest, it's probably our fault, but I'd rather not die for it. Will you surrender?'

Satyrus patted the blade at his side. He balanced the spear in his hand. The horsemen behind him were sitting – not calm, either. 'Probably not,' he said.

Achilles nodded. 'Try talking to the officer. Look, lord, he probably has a *hundred men* and they've been all around us since afternoon.'

'Satyrus of Tanais?' called an officer. He was tall and blond. Satyrus could remember him from Demetrios's staff. His armour was worth the value of the farm on the hill, or more.

Satyrus nodded. 'Here I am. I have a truce with your master. Why are you here?'

The officer's grin showed obvious relief. 'Lord, I'm so damned glad to find you I could burst. Lord, we're here to *protect* you. Thanks to all the gods you're alive.'

Satyrus looked around. 'This is not what I expected,' he said to Achilles. He looked at the sell-sword. 'You didn't sell me yourself?' he asked quietly.

Achilles frowned. 'No,' he said. 'Bad for my reputation, something like that.'

'Would you four ride with me? If I went with them?' Satyrus pointed at the Aegema. 'My offer is still good.'

'Escort?' Achilles asked.

'If he agrees to it, and leaves us all armed, I learn something,' Satyrus said. 'To be honest, if you and he can't agree to that – I might as well fall on my sword. I'm not going to be taken again. And for whatever reason, I trust you.'

Achilles nodded.

Satyrus called down the bridge, 'I'll come with you if I can take my escort – armed and mounted – with me. I keep my weapons, and he keeps his.'

The officer – Philip? Amyntas? All the Macedonians had the same set of names – nodded eagerly. 'Yes, yes. Anything you like, lord, only come to Corinth with me.'

Achilles shrugged. 'Memnon's sharp enough. He'll figure out we was took, and come, or not.'

'We're coming in, then,' Satyrus called. He loosened his sword in the sheath, and rode down the bridge behind Achilles.

No one grabbed his bridle or made other aggressive motions, which was a good sign. Satyrus rode right up to the officer. 'I'm Satyrus of Tanais,' he said. 'This is my bodyguard, Achilles. He'll be wanting to knock at the ferryman's door, here. You won't stop him, will you?'

'Amyntas son of Philip,' the man said, pulling his helmet off and hanging it from a web of equipment behind his saddle with the ease of long practice. 'You've just earned me a promotion, lord, and no mistake. Rumour is men are trying to kill you – Demetrios addressed us himself, offered a reward to find you.'

Achilles dismounted at the old ferry house, where the ferry had been before Alexander ordered the bridge built. The old man who lived there was wide awake and terrified – every peasant in the village, if not all of Plataea, had to know that the countryside was full of cavalrymen that night. But he accepted Achilles' message, promised that his eldest would take the news up to the Middle Hill Farm in the morning, and that he'd send another son up the mountain. Satyrus gave him a silver owl, and the man managed a smile.

And then they were away, into the dark.

They surprised Satyrus by riding due west – not the straightest way to Corinth, by any means, and very quickly they picked up the Oeroe, at first merely a dry gully on their right, but soon enough a gurgle of water. They stopped once to water their horses, and again at Kreusis – a sleepy village in starlight, with four triremes lying off the beach.

'They want you bad,' Achilles said.

Satyrus could only nod, his mouth dry.

They left their horses with the cavalrymen, and the centarch, Amyntas, came in person. 'No point in pleasing the king if you don't get the reward in person,' he said cheerfully. 'Please come aboard with me.'

'You're not acting as if you're going to kill me in the morning,' Satyrus said.

Amyntas shook his head. 'Oh, I wouldn't think so,' he said, in a voice that was not completely reassuring. But he led them up onto the trireme, and then he lay down by the oarsman's bench and went straight to sleep.

As the sun rose over the Gulf of Corinth, it revealed the ancient city and the ongoing siege in stages, so that Satyrus saw the Acrocorinth and the defenders' citadel first, kissed by the lips of Dawn as she ascended from her lascivious couch to brighten the day, or so some of the oarsmen were asserting in the crudest terms.

The sun caught the temple at the peak of the citadel first, and then the walls, which looked, at the distance of ten stades, as if they were utterly impregnable, towering at an unimaginable height over the plain below, and the rising sun only illuminated the besiegers' works and camp last. But Demetrios's camp was vast, covering the plain below Corinth, and he had not one but two siege lines surrounding the whole of the city. From the height of the stern platform, Satyrus could see that Demetrios had two squadrons – one in the Gulf of Corinth, and another blocking the Aegean beaches to the south, so that, with two military camps, twenty stades of earthen walls, and two fleets, he had the defenders completely blockaded; a difficult feat against mighty two-beached Corinth.

Achilles was as awake as he, and stood at his shoulder. 'The king has them whenever he wants them,' he said. 'A strong place ain't no guarantee, 'gainst the besieger.'

Satyrus had to disagree. 'We had less to defend at Rhodes,' he said. 'And we held him.'

Achilles nodded. 'And well done, I'm sure. But you had citizens with their lives and fortunes on the line. Prepalaus – that's Cassander's strategos in Corinth – he's got mercenaries, and too many of 'em are not worth goat shit. You can fertilise a field with goat shit.'

Satyrus had to laugh. It made him feel less tense, but his side hurt, his shoulders ached, and his stomach was flipping every minute. And it hurt to laugh – hurt his ribs and his cheek.

Achilles expelled a long fart, and gave a rueful grin. 'Sorry,' he said. 'I don't like this.'

Satyrus shrugged. 'Me neither. We may be about to die for a misunderstanding.' He rolled his shoulders. 'Waiting is worse than fighting,' he said.

'Any time,' Achilles admitted.

It was half an hour before the ship was landed. The crew beached it sloppily, stern first but without much care, and an oarsman leapt over the side and ran up the beach towards the military camp, clearly the herald of Satyrus's arrival.

Satyrus didn't have a high opinion of the rowers or the trierarch or their care for the ship, and then he was jumping into the surf, low gurgling waves a few fingers high. The three of them walked up the beach.

'The best sign,' Satyrus said openly to Achilles, 'is that they've left us alone with young Amyntas, who's really quite well born. I assume that if they meant us harm, they'd have met the ship with an escort.'

The sun was well up, and Achilles caught Satyrus's glance even as he started to speak. Amyntas whirled, intending either to protest or to threaten, but Satyrus took the sword out of his hand and Achilles had his sword at the Macedonian's neck so smoothly that it looked as if the three of them were practising.

'No offence intended,' Satyrus said. 'But I'm not eager to be executed by Demetrios.'

Amyntas was purple. 'He's not going to execute you!' he said.

Satyrus nodded. He exchanged looks with Achilles. Now – a little late, perhaps – there were twenty soldiers coming down the beach from the camp, led by a man in ornate armour with a leopard skin over his shoulders.

Satyrus headed up the beach. 'Demetrios!' he shouted.

The king of half the world laughed. 'Satyrus, you are the limit. But alive.'

'Your cavalryman found me – trapped me very neatly, so no shame to him. But he's the only bargaining counter I have right now.' Satyrus motioned over his shoulder, where Satyrus was confident that Achilles had the other man by the throat.

'He's my father's sister's youngest,' Demetrios admitted. 'So I suppose that I want him back.'

Satyrus took another step forward. 'As I say, he took me neatly enough.'

Demetrios nodded. 'Good for him, then. He's earned a reward – even if he did get himself captured on his own beach.'

Satyrus well remembered the bantering voice and the hard steel will behind it. 'Listen, then, lord. I will hand him over with apologies as soon as you swear to me that you mean me no harm, that you take an oath to the gods that you will not harm me or cause me to be harmed, nor that you yourself have attempted such since the siege. Swear that, and all the swords will vanish.'

Demetrios smiled – an angry smile. 'Always you seek to force me to oaths, Satyrus. An oath makes a man tributary to the gods. I seek to *be* with the gods.'

'Swear by Styx, if that pleases you,' Satyrus said.

Demetrios looked at him. 'If I kill you right here on this beach, for the seizure of one of my officers, I could thumb my nose at your sister and her allies.'

Satyrus lifted his spear. 'If you had a thumb left,' he said.

Demetrios nodded curtly. 'You are a cocky son of a bitch. Very well, I swear – by Styx, on which the gods themselves swear, on my living father and on my own dead, that I mean you no harm now, nor ever have since the end of the siege of Rhodos, nor will, unless you turn on me. And now you swear the same.'

Satyrus said, 'I swear by Kineas my father, and Arimnestos of Plataea, and all my family back to Herakles, that I intend you no harm, unless you turn on me, or we face each other on the battlefield.'

Demetrios nodded. 'And I the same – that's a clever addition, and I add it to my oath. You're a clever man. May I have my young scapegrace back?'

Satyrus motioned to Achilles, who released the Macedonian. He glared at Satyrus. 'I was perfectly courteous to you, my lord.'

Satyrus raised his eyebrows in surprise. 'You are Macedonian, are you not? I learned these habits from your kin.'

Demetrios nodded. 'I hate walking on sand,' he said. 'My best riding boots are full of it now. But you do amuse. This siege had begun to bore me to death, and there's months left in it. Will you join me for a meal?'

Satyrus sheathed his own sword. 'With pleasure,' he said.

The twenty elite hypaspists closed in around him as soon as he sheathed his sword, and for a moment he froze, but Demetrios stood at his elbow, completely relaxed.

'I had a pair of Cretan archers on you the whole time,' he said.

Satyrus looked up the beach and saw the two men unstringing their bows. 'Ah,' he said.

'I really mean you no harm,' he went on. 'Your sister has bitched my spring campaign completely on your behalf, moving my third fleet out of the Pontus.' He looked at Satyrus. 'It was Cassander, cousin. Not me. A woman – Phiale – acting for him. My spies tell me that it was planned at the wedding of your former ally, Heraklea, to that fool Lysimachos.'

Satyrus winced.

They continued to walk up the beach. 'Oh, I don't think Amastris or Lysimachos had a thing to do with it,' Demetrios said. 'Not that I wish them anything but ill, but Amastris served me well enough against Rhodes and elsewhere. A moment,' said the besieger, and he turned away to speak to a man in plain armour – an engineer, as it proved, who gave his report on the progress of a ramp of earth going against the walls of Corinth.

Satyrus turned to Achilles. 'We're not at threat.'

Achilles looked around. 'We'll see,' he said. 'But at least we're not going to be stuck full of arrows in the dawn.' He grinned at Satyrus. 'So far, I don't think much of working for you.'

Satyrus sat on a rock and cleared the sand from his sandals. A hypaspist offered him water, and he took some.

Demetrios returned. 'Let's eat. I'm not always fond of getting up this early, but the promise of food can lure me from my rest.'

They ate on the terrace of a farm that overlooked the Gulf of Corinth.

'I could envy this man,' Demetrios said as he dipped some golden honey bread in olive oil and honey.

'The farmer?' Satyrus asked.

Demetrios nodded. 'This is how a man should live.'

'But you wish to be a god?' Satyrus asked.

Demetrios nodded, his mouth full. 'I am a man still,' he admitted. 'I like the honey bread, the oil, the feel of a breast under my fingers. Hah – if the stories are to be believed, the gods like all those things themselves. But the tale of Herakles has all the clues, does it not? A man may become a god.' He looked at Satyrus, snapped his fingers, and a slave came to refill his cup. 'You think me mad,' he said.

Satyrus shook his head ruefully. 'Becoming a god has never

interested me in the least,' he admitted. 'But I should like to be a hero.' He surprised himself with his own temerity. But it was true.

'Perhaps that is why I like you,' Demetrios said. 'Many men humour me – few enough meet me on my own ground. I intend to assault the suburb at dawn tomorrow. Will you come and swing your sword beside me? It would please me,' he added, as if this was the most important thing in the world.

Satyrus shook his head. 'Not my fight, lord. And men might say that I had changed my feathers – that I was fighting against my own allies.'

Demetrios laughed. 'Cassander wants you dead. He's no ally. Your ally is Farm Boy – Ptolemy of Aegypt, and he and Cassander are no friends at all. But for an accident of history, my father and Ptolemy would be allies, and then the rest of this riff-raff would whistle for a victory and never get it.' He sipped wine. 'I will allow you to question Neron, my spymaster. Perhaps he can satisfy you.'

Satyrus shrugged, held out his cup and got more fruit juice – delicious stuff, sweet as nectar. 'I came to deliver a grain shipment, as I promised. And to see my friend Abraham. Let me offer this. If you release Abraham to me, I'll stand by your side tomorrow.'

Demetrios looked pained. 'Ah, the Rhodian hostages,' he said uneasily. 'Hmm,' he said. 'When your sister threatened my shipping, I sent my hostages away.'

Satyrus sat up. 'Where?' he demanded.

Demetrios lay back. 'Don't take that tone with me,' he said. 'They're gone to Ephesus, where I can keep them out of plots – closer to Rhodos, closer to home. I am not a harsh man. But I wanted to let you and your sister see that they were *in my power*.'

'The treaty specified Athens,' Satyrus said, suddenly worried. The whole purpose of keeping the hostages at Athens was so that they could not be used for further bargaining. Although Demetrios was powerful in Athens, the citizens there had their own opinions and the ability to keep some neutrality. Ephesus, on the other hand, was an Antigonid possession.

'Yes, well, the treaty didn't allow your sister to close the Pontus against my ships, and let bloody Lysimachos take a third of his men into Asia,' Demetrios said, suddenly angry. 'Why do I tolerate you?'

Satyrus realised that the besieger was enraged. Challenged. 'All I want,' he said, 'is for my friends to be safe and my trade uninterrupted. With Rhodes and Alexandria and Athens. I am not the one attempting to conquer others.'

Fickle as the seasons, Demetrios was suddenly playful. 'Is that what passes for rhetoric in the Euxine?' he asked. 'Perhaps if I married your sister, we might be allies?'

Satyrus almost spluttered his juice.

Demetrios slapped his thigh. 'See? I am not a dull companion. Come and storm the breach with me tomorrow, and let us see what we can arrange.'

Satyrus was on the point of blank refusal when Achilles leaned forward. Satyrus hadn't even seen the man enter the room.

'Do what he asks and then crave a boon,' Achilles suggested. 'Act as if he's bigger than you.' He was back in his place behind the couches in a wink.

'Your bodyguard?' Demetrios asked. 'A noted ruffian.'

'My only advisor, at the moment,' Satyrus said. 'Very well. I'll go up the breach tomorrow.'

Demetrios changed – again. He seemed to grow larger, and he rose to stand, cup in hand. 'That,' he said, 'is wonderful. Let us make it – memorable!'

7

An hour before dawn. The air was lighter – warmer, the promise of a deadly hot day. In armour – borrowed armour, and not particularly well-fitted – Satyrus was already hot.

'You need to pay me more,' Achilles commented. He swung his arms again, annoyed by the shape of the shoulders on the yoke of his borrowed cuirass. 'This is war – a breach assault? People die like sheep when a lion gets into the pen, in an assault.'

'Done one before?' Satyrus asked. Demetrios had been lavish in his offerings of weapons and armour – and since it was a matter of life and death, Satyrus was taking his time picking a sword.

It's odd, he thought, *that in the inn, I took the only sword to hand and grew to like it, but offered all these beautiful blades, I'm unable to choose one, much less enjoy it. Socrates would have something to say – and Philokles, too, I imagine.* He had a flash of Philokles, standing in the pre-dawn light at Gaza, silent in the face of coming battle. Satyrus had seen battles, now – on land and at sea, and a year of fighting at Rhodes that left him weary. The thrill – the simple, youthful rush of eudaimonia, a frisson of fear and lust for glory – it wasn't there. Fine weapons and beautiful armour were expressions of his status, not tools of his trade. He smiled.

He wasn't even decently nervous.

He picked up a magnificent sword, Chalkidian, with beautifully back-swept edges from a wicked, and very prosaic, armour-piercing point. The grip was ivory, the fittings gold-embellished bronze, and the scabbard would buy an inn in Attika, or a farm in Plataea. It was sharp as a barber's razor, the lobes of the leaf thin and vicious, with a heavy spine that ran down into the point.

Even through his lack of interest, the sword was good. It fitted his hand – the balance was better than his father's long machaira, and that had always seemed to him the best sword he'd ever handled.

He shrugged, pulled the sword belt over his right shoulder and drew the sword, wincing when his too-small armour pinched at his right bicep on the cross-draw. 'Where's the slave?' he asked Achilles, who went out of their tent – an enormous tent of red linen, and Satyrus had to wonder what Macedonian officer was sleeping under his cloak and bitter about it – and Satyrus heard his voice.

Two Persian slaves came in and bowed low.

'I have chosen weapons,' Satyrus said. He raised his arms. 'All of the armour is too small. I need a bigger thorax, even if it is plain leather or undecorated linen.'

The slaves helped him out of his armour. The older slave bowed again. 'A thousand apologies, lord. We will return with better armour.'

Achilles grinned and raised his arms, too. 'I like this game. I want mine larger around, with a smaller yoke, and covered in gold. With jewels.'

The Persian bowed. 'Lord, it shall be as you wish.' He looked weary. Who wouldn't, in the semi-dark before dawn?

Slaves came with torches, and set them in holders all around the portico in front of the tent, and more slaves came with a table, and they set it with gold and silver vessels – cups, ewers, plates, a huge platter. Wine appeared, and fruit, and good bread, fresh from the ovens, and olive oil, honey and milk and small onion sausages, and fresh grilled anchovies.

The Persians returned, each like Thetis bringing the armour of Achilles from Hephaeston in their eagerness to satisfy him.

Achilles laughed. 'I think that Demetrios fancies you,' he said.

Satyrus chose an unadorned bronze thorax and tried it on. The fit was close – perhaps a little tight, but the armholes were large enough and he could move his arms freely. He raised his shoulders, thrust with his legs. His ribs hurt, but he could fight.

'I'll take this,' he said.

Achilles was a larger man yet, but they fitted him on the third try.

'Had I known the kind of party I was going to, I'd have brought the right clothes,' he said.

Satyrus dipped fresh bread in olive oil and took a bite. He was finding it surprisingly easy to eat.

'I'm usually far more ... worried ... before a fight,' he confessed. 'I feel odd. Unconcerned.'

'You want to watch that,' Achilles said. 'Fear is what keeps a man alive.'

Satyrus nodded. It was lighter outside, and a large body of men was moving through the half-light just beyond the ropes of his enormous tent. He walked around the end to get a better look, and found himself face to face with a file of heavily armoured men.

'Make way for the king!' one of the men said. When Satyrus did not hurry to obey, the man raised his spear and shoved . . .

At air. Satyrus backed, swung aside on one foot, caught the spearhead, and pulled, disarming the man.

'Stop!' Demetrios ordered. 'Satyrus – I've come to share your breakfast.'

The soldier glared at Satyrus.

Satyrus handed him his spear. 'That sort of thing may work in Asia,' he said, 'but in Greece, someone might use your skin to keep crows off their crops.'

Demetrios nodded. 'I tell them all the time. I want the Greeks to love me, and my hypaspists want them to hate me.'

'We protect you, lord!' the man protested.

Slaves appeared behind the king, bearing braziers on which they cooked more fish, there was fresher bread, and fruit juice.

Satyrus ate a plate of anchovies and drank pomegranate juice, a luxury even by the standards of the King of the Bosporons. 'I envy you this,' he said.

'I might be facile, and suggest that if we were allies you could share it every day,' Demetrios said.

'Is this how you wooed Amastris?' Satyrus asked, only half joking.

Demetrios shook his head. 'A very attractive woman with a very attractive sea-port.' He took a mouthful of olive paste. 'I didn't seduce her. Not for lack of trying. It was her damned spymaster – he apparently counselled her to keep me at arm's length. Excellent advice. A very, very dangerous man.'

Satyrus smiled. 'Stratokles of Athens? Very dangerous indeed, lord. On that, we can agree.'

Demetrios snapped his fingers. 'Neron?' he said.

A tall, thin Syrian came forward. He was well-enough formed, but his limbs were long and they gave him a vaguely simian look. He had a bushy black beard and bleak eyes.

Neron bowed. 'Satyrus of Tanais,' he said. 'It is a great pleasure to see you in the flesh, after reading so many reports about you. My master here delights in stories about you. You keep me busy.'

Against his inclinations, Satyrus liked the man – his wit spoke well for his mind. 'A pleasure, sir,' Satyrus said, taking his hand.

'Does *everyone* like you, Satyrus?' Demetrios asked. 'How wearying it must be for your friends.'

Satyrus didn't have an answer for that. He shrugged.

'Ask Neron your questions,' Demetrios asked.

'What difference will that make?' Satyrus asked. 'You might have told him to tell me anything.'

Demetrios rolled his eyes and went on eating.

'Who paid to have me taken at Athens?' Satyrus asked.

Neron bowed to Demetrios. 'May I eat as well, lord?' he asked, and when Demetrios inclined his head impatiently, the spy took a cup of wine and began to pile a silver plate with fresh fish.

'You know Phiale of Alexandria?' Neron asked.

'Very well,' Satyrus answered.

Neron smiled unpleasantly. 'Many do, to their regret.' He shrugged. 'Women who sell their bodies are seldom nice or comfortable people to know – and always bad agents.'

Satyrus raised an eyebrow. 'How very Socratean of you. But I knew that Phiale was an agent in my taking – I spoke to her.'

'Ahh!' Neron said. He glanced at his master with a certain weary tolerance. 'Sometimes the most difficult source of information I have is my own lord, who does not always share everything he should.'

Satyrus nodded.

'Amastris of Heraklea was wedded some weeks ago,' Neron said. 'At her wedding, to the best of my information, Cassander arranged the murder of Stratokles of Athens. You know him? A gifted man in my line.'

'Your rival, perhaps?' Satyrus asked.

'Hmm. Not, I think, a player at my level, my lord, but only because of his ridiculous loyalty to Athens – to an Athens which hasn't existed for a hundred years. Perhaps I offend you with my frankness?' Neron sipped his wine, added more water.

'Far from it. And yet, I assume you are similarly loyal to your master?' Satyrus asked. The discourse was barbed – he wanted to show his own teeth.

'Loyal enough, in these dark times,' Neron answered. 'At any rate, the murder of Stratokles was botched.'

'I am surprised at myself, but I'm glad to hear it.' Satyrus had to laugh.

Neron answered him with a gleam of teeth. 'How remarkable, my lord, that those are my exact feelings. Stratokles has been a great help to me and a desperate enemy, and the world would seem emptier if he were to be swept from the board.' He looked around. 'So far, everything I've said is available information to any merchant. This is not. Lysimachos, Cassander, and envoys from Seleucus and Ptolemy met. They discussed things. Lysimachos met Cassander privately, as well. They discussed different things.' Neron shrugged. 'My master, as you call him, has told me to be direct with you, and I will be, as far as our interests converge – but you will pardon me if I note that you are not really our friend, and your friends are most definitely our enemies?'

'And misleading me to sow confusion among your enemies is too tempting?' Satyrus asked.

Neron looked disappointed. 'Amateurs play these pointless games. I'm sharing information.'

Demetrios nodded from across the table. Slaves brought him a chair and he sat. 'Satyrus, listen to me. I aim to be king – absolute king – of the world. I need men – men like you – to trust me. If you catch Neron in a lie today, tell me, and I will have him killed, despite all his service to me, because if men like you won't trust me, my cause is doomed. Understand? And my cause – to which I seek to win you – is the cause of justice, good government, a single empire from world edge to world edge, with courts and city states and philosophers, where a merchant or a scholar can travel from India to the Gates of Herakles without fear of pirates or robbers or tolls.'

Satyrus frowned – because Demetrios made a good argument. And because, unless Demetrios was a magnificent liar, he seemed utterly earnest – the way a man who wanted to be a god had to be. Single-minded to the point of ... insanity, or godhood.

'Ask your questions, and don't be petty minded,' Demetrios said.

Satyrus drank a whole cup of fruit juice. 'Cassander and Lysimachos,' he prompted.

Neron shook his head at Demetrios. 'Suffice it to say that they discussed matters of strategy. My master makes no secret of his intention to drive Cassander first from mainland Greece, and then from Macedon. Cassander wants Lysimachos in Asia, against Antigonus. Lysimachos would prefer to stay in Thrace and tax his Thracians.' Neron nodded. 'For a minor player, Lysimachos is wise, cautious and able. He has survived two major military defeats – the mark of a truly able commander. He refused to allow your murder when Cassander proposed it – he said that he owed you for support in former years.'

'While he married my Amastris,' Satyrus said, with more bitterness than he had known he felt.

'More an act of statecraft than lust, I suspect,' Demetrios said. 'But you understand, his possession of Heraklea – and he has possessed it, just as fully as he has no doubt possessed Amastris's welcoming body – and your sister's expulsion of my ships from the Pontus have placed me in an impossible position, as Lysimachos has moved almost half of his army across the Euxine into Asia, to the great discomfort of my father.' Demetrios rose to his feet, resplendent in armour of gold. Behind his chair, the sun was ready to rise – Dawn was coming out of her bed over the ocean. 'We have an assault to make. And afterwards – after we have swung our swords together – I hope that we can sit together as friends, and I can convince you that my side is the side of arete.' He accepted a purple cloak from a slave and slung it around his shoulders.

Neron leaned over. 'But Cassander insisted, and in the end Lysimachos accepted your death in exchange for naval support from Cassander, which he has not received, and a free hand in the Euxine, where he intends to be king after you. These, lord, are your allies.'

Satyrus raised an eyebrow. 'You have given me much to think about while I kill men who have done nothing to offend me,' he said. 'Despite your protestations and those of the king, you'll pardon me if I don't automatically accept that my allies are hot to betray me.'

Neron bowed. 'You would be both naive and inhuman if you thought otherwise,' Neron said. 'But I have told you the truth as I know it.'

Satyrus slung his sword over his shoulder and picked up the shield he'd chosen – not a real aspis, but a smaller Macedonian shield, a circle three spans and a little in diameter, with the star of Macedon in gold.

He and Demetrios walked out from the tent lines, crossing the horse pickets and walking past thousands of waiting men, slaves bringing water, men currying horses, women washing. The hypaspists closed around them when the crowds were thick, but otherwise Demetrios appeared to stroll through his army with the freedom of a philosopher walking through the Athenian agora. No man approached him – there appeared to be some sort of rule – but he would stop to address soldiers, even slaves, and their obedience was as immediate as their bows were profound.

It was all very un-Greek.

'He's very comfortable with slaves,' Achilles murmured, at his shoulder.

Satyrus thought that it was a very astute observation.

Two long bowshots from the walls, the ramp to the outworks of the suburbs began. A battery of siege engines squatted behind elaborate mounds of earth, gravel, stone, and wood. Enormous wicker baskets, filled with loose stones and sand or earth, covered the batteries. Trenches were dug both in front of the walls and behind them. Newer works were narrow and low – older works were deep, with high walls and carefully terraced interiors reinforced with heavy wooden beams.

Thousands – possibly tens of thousands – of slaves laboured like ants on the works. Men dug earth, women carried baskets of earth on their heads, children wove baskets to carry more earth or to act as forms for engineering. Everywhere that Satyrus looked – everywhere – the siege was prosecuted with a massive labour force.

Demetrios smiled. 'Have you ever seen the like?' he asked.

'Yes,' Satyrus said. 'At Rhodes. Or had you forgotten?'

Demetrios was clearly put out. 'Fine, then. But it's different when you are the prime mover. Who could prosecute a siege like this and not feel like a god? I snap my fingers, and this happens. I could order the very mountain reduced – and it would be done.'

'Hmm,' Satyrus said. He had been given a long spear, a heavy dory, and he didn't like it – liked it less and less as he carried it. Still, Demetrios had one, and he supposed it was the rule. On ship, he carried a pair of longche, heavy javelins.

The ramp stretched away in front of him, filling his vision, and his usual nerves had finally begun. His hands began to shake.

'You are not impressed by my slave army?' Demetrios asked.

Satyrus rammed the saurauter of his spear into the earth, took a handful of sand, rubbed his hands to get the sweat off, and drew his sword.

'I thank you for the sword. It is excellent,' Satyrus said.

Demetrios beamed. 'Ahh! I can please you, then. Why do you like it?'

Satyrus shrugged, caught himself grinning at the weapon. 'It is superb,' he said. 'Beautiful to look at, perfectly balanced, and not too gaudy.'

'It was made for me,' Demetrios said. 'Brought by an embassage, I think. Wear it in health. Are you ready?'

Satyrus nodded.

Demetrios motioned to the hypaspist commander. Satyrus noticed then that the commander had been in conversation with Neron – and that Neron slipped away quickly.

The hypaspist officer walked over. At a sign from Demetrios, he signalled by raising his spear, and the engines began to launch their projectiles with a *whip-crack* as their casting arms struck the retaining beams and the long slings opened. They were five-talent engines, and Satyrus watched as they cast and saw their projectiles raise puffs of powdered stone when they struck the towers at the top of the breach. He had the strangest feeling, just for a moment – the feeling that this was predestined, that he had done this before or seen it in a dream, overlaid with the feeling that he was about to assault himself – that he would find himself standing with the defenders.

'Lord?' the hypaspist captain asked him. 'Will you stand to the right of the king, and your man in the rank behind you?'

'Breeze is perfect,' Demetrios said.

Satyrus turned to look at him. 'Perfect how?' he asked.

'A little something my engineers have come up with since Rhodes. I like to fancy that if we'd had it, I've have taken the city.' He turned to a slave and took what appeared to be a scarf.

The sun was just getting a rim above the edge of the sea, and it was already hot. Satyrus was perspiring inside his armour. He had no interest in a scarf.

'Best take one,' the king said.

Satyrus smelled smoke. He stepped out of the ranks and looked around, and there they were – thousands of bundles of green brush, the fires under them just licking at the foliage. Satyrus had taken the pile for another entrenchment.

'The smoke will cover us all the way in,' Demetrios said. 'Wear a scarf.'

Satyrus took one from the slave. He noted that most of the rank and file hypaspists had them on already, making them look like a regiment of hill bandits. Most of them had magnificent Thracian-style helmets with elaborate cheek-plates fitted like faces, some with heavy beards and moustaches in black paint, enamel, or blackened silver – or even bright gold. The scarves vanished as they buckled the cheek-plates down.

Satyrus pulled down his own cheek-plates. He had a simple Attic helmet, a light thing of tinned bronze with an ordinary plume of red and white horsehair – nothing like the elaborate horsehair coifs worn by the veterans around him.

Sealed in his helmet, Satyrus's vision was limited to a few degrees off the centreline – his peripheral vision was almost completely lost. And the damp scarf was stifling his breath. The cuirass he had chosen was slightly too small, and now it seemed like a torture device, constricting his lungs even as he tried to wrench air through the damned scarf – and the smell of smoke was everywhere.

Why am I doing this? he asked himself. There was no easy answer.

The ramp stretched away, apparently to the edge of the heavens. It was almost a stade long, and rose ten times the height of a man. The first two-thirds were well surfaced in carefully laid turf, but the last third looked like loose dirt.

And then the breeze took the smoke and tossed it forward, and he couldn't see anything.

Arrows were beginning to come down from the battlements on the suburbs, and bigger, more deadly projectiles came from higher on the Acrocorinth; bolts and stones from engines.

Demetrios stepped out of the ranks. 'I am your king,' he said, 'and my eye is on you. Stand with me and be my brothers, or prove craven and go be less than men.' His eyes met Satyrus's, and he raised his spear in salute.

Satyrus returned the salute.

'Smoke is good,' coughed the hypaspist commander. 'Thick.'

'Let the engines fire again,' Demetrios said.

Satyrus stood and sweated and shook.

'Remind me why I said we should do this?' Achilles muttered.

One of the hypaspists laughed. 'This is work for men,' he said. 'You foreigners should probably sit this out.'

Achilles grunted. 'Foreigner? Where were you born, Asia man?'

'Silence in the ranks!' a phylarch called, and Satyrus smiled to think that he was going into combat as a hoplite, not a king.

'Ready, there!' the commander called.

The phylarchs answered, and Satyrus realised that as he was at the head of an eight-man file, he had best answer. 'Ready,' he coughed, through the smoke.

'Ever been in a fight before?' asked the man next to him.

'Once or twice,' Satyrus said.

'He fought us at Rhodes!' said the phylarch on his left. He laughed. 'Watch him, Philip! He'll do his part.'

Satyrus was oddly pleased at the compliment.

'Up we go, then,' said the commander.

Demetrios stepped into the middle of the front rank at the last moment, and raised his shield. The arrows were falling faster – they were walking right into the thick of them.

'Shields up!' yelled the commander. 'Right up – don't be lazy fucks!'

Satyrus wished for an aspis as he raised the smaller Macedonian bowl over his head. Arrows began to strike the surface, and something bit his shin.

The smoke was debilitating, and Satyrus was not sure, as a some-time commander, that he thought it was worth the cover. The arrows seemed to fall with wicked minds of their own, and the smoke got in his lungs and made him want to puke – he had the burning sensation in his guts that a man gets when he eats too much fat.

Up and up – his feet were still on sod, so they hadn't gone very far yet, but Satyrus could feel the burn in his thighs, and the arrows were coming faster, and suddenly a ballista bolt swept away the phylarch next to him and the man behind, a ringing, screaming chaos of death, and the whole front bent as men fell, wounded or only struck by pieces of the corpses – the headless phylarch fell back into his file—

'Halt!' screamed the commander. 'Close up!'

The smoke was thinning. The range was almost point-blank, and the enemy engines were firing *down* with more force and more accuracy, and a second direct hit cleared the rear half of another file in a wave of screams and ringing armour.

'Are you ready to be a hero?' Demetrios asked. The two of them were nose to nose. 'Did I mention that the breach is only eight men wide? We go first, whatever Philip tries to do. He wants to protect me. I want to be first on the wall.' Under his ornate cheek-plates, Satyrus could see the white rims around his eyes, the slightly mad grin.

'I'll be right beside you, lord,' Satyrus said. Then he allowed himself a smile. 'Or ahead of you, if you stumble.'

Demetrios smacked his shield face with his spear. 'I love this moment. May it last for ever in memory.'

'Forward!' Philip, the hypaspist commander, sounded panicked. His losses were already more than he'd expected, and Satyrus was, frankly, surprised that they weren't retreating. With a tenth of his men down and the breach so narrow – it looked like foolishness.

Foolishness that Demetrios was committing because he had to impress the King of the Bosporons?

Sling stones began to hit them – first a punch against his shield, and then a blow like a giant fist to the crest on his helmet. Satyrus adjusted his shield, crouched, and began to go faster. So did the new phylarch to his left.

Suddenly the ground was gone beneath his feet, and he was on loose dirt and sand, grateful for his boots. He went faster, and the sling stones were like a storm of deadly bees – zipping through the air, ringing when they hit armour, thudding when they hit flesh.

This breach is not prepared. Demetrios has made a mistake.

Self-preservation said that if he couldn't turn tail, he could run at the breach, and Satyrus did. He was suddenly conscious of how narrow the ramp really was, and how far he still had to go. He was out of the smoke, the breach was full of men, and he was … in front. If he slipped to the right or left, he would fall – probably to his death on the rocks at the base of the ramp.

And then all the worry, all the thought, all the strategy fell away, and he was running up a steep slope at men who intended to kill him, and it no longer mattered whether Cassander had tried to kill him or was really his ally, because there was only right here and right now, and a tall man in a yellow horsehair crest who seemed to fill the breach.

Satyrus paused, perhaps ten paces from the wall – shifted his weight, slowed, and threw his dory, twice the height of a man, a long thrusting spear, not a throwing spear.

Yellow Plume took it right through his shield, gave a scream, and went down.

Satyrus drew his sword, stepped on Yellow Plume, still squirming with the spear in his side, and put his shield into the next three men, who all attempted to spear him together. He caught two of the spears and the third hammered into his helmet, caught for a moment on his crest-box and skidded away, snapping his head back painfully against his chin-strap.

He got his feet under him and stepped in, passing his right foot forward to get under the spearheads and stay there. Behind the men in front was another rank, and their spearheads thundered on his shield and one ripped his thigh, a hard overhand thrust that he never saw. Another glanced off his bronze thorax.

Then he was shield to shield with the front rank, and he stabbed at their thighs and feet, ruthlessly sweeping the razor edges of his new sword across their tendons while his aspis went high. He collected their spears and pressed in like a lover against their chests.

Men began to fall.

The daimon took him, and he moved, spun, and cut as if guided by an invisible hand, or as if he was a dancer in a carefully practised routine. He stopped sensing time as a linear thing and moved through his opponents, seeing them as fractional images of the action – a descending back-cut through a man's nose guard, a wrist-roll thrust with an off-axis left foot advance that penetrated through a man's leather cuirass and his belly, a ripping blow from a heavy spearhead that chopped a piece from his shield rim – the spearman's second attack, using the spear like a long-handled axe, and his response – deflection, avoidance, inside the spear's reach, the man's terrified eyes as Satyrus cut him down ...

He saw the blow. The stop-start universe of instant to instant life and death showed him the little man's spear as it came in from his unprotected right side – he was trying to withdraw his sword from his last victim, and the fine edge was stuck in bone – the realisation in less than half a heartbeat that he could never block the blow – the enemy spear – another spear driving into it, and Satyrus was alive, his sword ripped from his last victim, and over his shoulder Demetrios was glowing with triumph as he pulled his own spear out of the little man.

'Saved your life,' he said with real satisfaction.

Satyrus didn't pause, as there were three men trying to kill him.

The beautiful sword stuck in the ribs of another victim, a few heartbeats later, and Satyrus was all but driven from his feet by a powerful blow to his shield – a man tripping and falling to his shield side, but the man was ideally positioned to topple him, and Satyrus went to one knee – spear thrusts clattered on his shield and one rang on his helmet, and his searching sword-hand found nothing in the gravel and rubble of the breach.

Achilles stabbed over his head, fast as the sting of a wasp – one, two, three – and the rapidity and force of his blows was godlike – the third blow sank the width of a man's hand through an enemy shield, and the man screamed as his shield arm was ripped open by the needle point on the spear.

Baulked of a weapon, even a broken spear shaft, Satyrus rose, grabbed the injured man's shield with his free hand, and spun the rim, breaking the man's already injured arm and dislocating his shoulder. Stepping through him, Satyrus slammed the edge of his shield into the next man in the breach, catching his shield and driving it back into the man's unprotected mouth, spraying teeth, and Satyrus took his spear as the man screamed and sank to his knees.

Now Satyrus was the point of a wedge, with Demetrios at one shoulder and Achilles at the other, and the defenders of the breach were hesitant, because the best men had been at the front and now the survivors were brittle.

The pause gave Satyrus time to realise that he'd been wounded twice, that his imperfectly-healed ribs were burning as if on fire and that the fight for the breach was almost won. One of his adversaries, bolder than the others, lunged overarm at his outstretched left leg where it projected from under his shield. He dropped the head of his spear and swept the weapon sideways as he passed his right foot forward – collected his opponent's spear on his shaft, rotated his own and thrust with his sarauter, taking his opponent off line and in the throat, killing him instantly. And he heard Demetrios grunt in admiration. He hefted his spear, pivoted, and threw it at a man who was looking elsewhere, and who paid with his life for his inattention, and then Satyrus let his aspis fall off his arm, collected a big rock – formerly part of the wall – and threw it into the enemy rank – just a little above the upper rim of a front-ranker's shield. The man raised his shield and was knocked flat as the weight of the rock took him.

Demetrios was there, and ten other men – into the gap, widening it like workmen with chisels working marble, and in the time it took Satyrus to stoop and recover his shield, the defenders were pushed back out of the breach.

'Take my sword,' Achilles said.

Satyrus turned his head, saw the offered hilt, and took it. He spat. 'Thanks,' he said. 'But I think this is done.' Nonetheless, he picked up his shield and took his time fitting it correctly on his arm.

Hypaspists pushed past them, desperate to get to their king, who was now three horse lengths ahead, and Satyrus was carried forward by the rush. Someone's spear point opened the back of his calf like a line of fire on his skin – careless bastard.

Satyrus moved to his right, and again to his right, pushed forward by the relentless pressure of the hypaspists but controlling his approach. The enemy were falling back and back, trying to rally, trying not to run.

Satyrus saw the flashes of new crests and well-made helmets over the beaten defenders – reinforcements.

'Form up, there!' he bellowed, but his accent was Greek, not Macedonian, and the eager men around him ignored him. The hypaspists pressed forward in a mob, their spears upright or pinned against them by the press.

The enemy – the beaten enemy – turned their heads, almost as one, like a flock of birds changing direction in the air. And then they opened their ranks – not well, but well enough – and let the newcomers through. The exchange of ranks took fifty heartbeats, and during that time the new enemy were vulnerable, but the hypaspists weren't in order to make a cohesive attack, and mostly they gathered around their king and walled him off from the fighting.

And then the enemy attacked. They were mercenaries – most of them political exiles with a burning hate for Demetrios and his pseudo-democratic ways, and they crashed into the disorganised hypaspists and drove them back ten paces, killing as they came, and in the time it takes an Olympian to run the stade, Satyrus was in the front rank.

His opponent had a magnificent crest on one of the new helmets – a small, fitted Attic helmet with engraving on every surface. He had a thick blond beard under the cheek-plates, and he slammed his spear into Satyrus's aspis with the confidence of the larger man.

Satyrus shuffled back to absorb the impact of the man's spear, and then stepped forward – *push* with the back, right thigh, lead left, collect balance, and he was under Blond Beard's spear, pressing shield to shield – Blond Beard trying to stab almost straight down over the locked shields. Satyrus stooped to get the pushing face of his aspis under the other man's rim, and as the man responded to that threat, sliced the edge of his sword across the other man's instep – flicked it back into the man's unprotected ankle under his greaves, and *then* powered forward against him, making him stumble back and fall into his own line ...

Now Achilles was next to him, and he put his spear point through a man's face, and the enemy line paused.

But Demetrios's hypaspists were not Alexander's hypaspists, and they were still not in fighting order. A dozen or more – twenty, perhaps – were clustered around Satyrus and Achilles, but the rest had surrounded the king and forced him down the ramp.

'We're fucked,' Achilles said.

Satyrus spat. He'd been wounded again, and the futility of the whole fight was overweighing the daimon.

He backed a step, and Achilles matched him.

He backed three more steps, and he was in the breach. The hypaspist on his left locked up, their aspides touching, and Achilles' rank partner did the same, and they almost filled the breach.

Satyrus risked a look over his shoulder.

Demetrios was screaming at someone, his voice rough with strain, but his men were forcing him out of the breach. The rest were clearly intent on retreat, except the handful already committed to standing with Satyrus and Achilles.

The enemy mercenaries were hesitating.

'Back,' Satyrus ordered. He stepped back, and the man at his back gave ground as well.

'We had them, gods curse on them!' said the man on Satyrus's left.

Now the mercenaries were preparing for a charge.

Satyrus stepped back again, and again, and now his head and shoulders were level with the outside of the breach, and he had the gritty dirt of the ramp under his sandals and between his toes. A bad position from which to fight.

But the mercenaries hesitated again.

'Back,' Satyrus said. The danger of falling off the ramp was very real.

Down below, a ballista fired, its bolt crashing into the right side of the breach and ricocheting crazily until it struck the front rank of enemy hoplites. It didn't kill anyone, but in its tumble it broke a man's ankle and knocked another unconscious.

'Give that man a bag of darics,' Achilles grunted.

Satyrus shared his view – the first ballista shot stopped the enemy at the back edge of the breach, and Satyrus and his little band were able to skid down the ramp unmolested – not even by javelins or arrows.

Satyrus reached the base of the ramp, and men hastened to hand him water, wine; they were chastened by their defeat, and aware that the last men off the ramp had taken greater risks and were the better men.

They weren't his men – it wasn't his place to berate them or demand explanations. Besides, he was bleeding in three places and the damned thorax he was wearing had cut into his waist to the extent that he could barely keep his feet. He opened the cheek-plates on his borrowed helmet, ripped it off his head, and drank air, his sides heaving.

His right leg was red to the knee.

Demetrios pushed through his cordon of guards and threw his arms around Satyrus. 'I feared you were dead. By the gods, I'd have killed the lot of these cowards if you had fallen. Say the word, and I will.'

Satyrus didn't know what to do with Demetrios's embrace – he returned the pressure for a moment, and then stepped back. Another man offered a wineskin, and Satyrus took a long drink and handed it to the man who had stood at his left shoulder.

'Satyrus of Tanais,' he said.

'Kleon Alexander's son of Amphilopolis,' the man answered, pressing his hand. 'An honour, lord. If I live, I'll tell my sons I stood with you in a breach.'

'He stood? At the breach, when they carried me down the hill?'

Demetrios said. 'You are a phylarch. Give your name to my military secretary.'

'All these men stood,' Satyrus said, his sense of justice piqued. 'And if I may – they have orders to protect you at all costs, I suspect. So they did. When you exposed yourself, they assumed the worst.'

'I saved your life!' Demetrios said. 'It was worth it.' He grinned. 'I didn't expect to take the suburbs today.'

Satyrus shrugged. The attack had been dangerous and demanding and had come within a moment of success – the golden king was rationalising defeat, a surprisingly human thing for him to do.

'As you say, lord,' he said. 'And may the gods stand by your shoulder as you stood by mine,' he added, because it was good manners – and true enough. Satyrus wasn't too exhausted to recall the unwavering spear point of the small man, calmly waiting his moment to kill him. That close. That man had been a killer – Satyrus had seen it in his eyes. Tyche had cheated him of his moment of glory, and saved Satyrus's life.

He was having trouble breathing, and the world was shrinking, somehow.

Achilles put his hand on his shoulder. 'You need to get those wounds looked at,' he said. 'You're making a puddle.'

Satyrus glanced down and saw that Achilles was literally speaking truth.

The sight of so much blood shook him, and he stumbled.

Fell.

He awoke to the thought that it would have been stupid to die fighting for Demetrios, and he was a fool for taking part, and then he was awake, his eyes gummy and his throat sandy, his mouth feeling as if he'd eaten glue – or spent a long night drinking with good companions.

'You with us?' a strange voice asked.

Satyrus had trouble focusing his eyes for a moment, and the other man's face swam and then steadied.

'Sort of,' he muttered.

'How many fingers?' the doctor asked.

'Three?' Satyrus answered.

'Close enough,' the doctor answered. 'Don't be in a hurry to raise your head. You lost blood – I had to burn your thigh, but I think you'll be fine if you don't pick up a contagion.'

Even as the man spoke, the pain in his thigh began to push through a hundred other scrapes and pains.

'No poppy,' he said.

'You've already had some,' the doctor said.

'No more,' Satyrus said.

'Fair enough. You've had too much? Fairly common soldier's complaint.' He nodded again. 'I'm Apollonaris of Tyre – I'm Demetrios's physician.'

The world was coming into focus, and Satyrus would have thought that he was in a palace, or even a temple complex, except for the odd light filling the structure. A tent then. A tent hung in tapestries and decorated with a heavy, hanging gold lamp.

'How long will I be on my back?' Satyrus asked. He had a thought of Miriam – a sharp pang of longing. *What am I doing here?* he asked himself.

'Two days, or perhaps three, unless your wounds infect.' Apollonaris grinned. 'In which case, you'll soon be dead.'

Satyrus cursed. 'This is how you talk to the golden king?'

Apollonaris laughed. He had a rich laugh. 'Yes. He likes my banter. Don't fret, lord, I won't let you infect. Apollo and I are old friends.'

'That sounds like hubris,' Satyrus said.

The doctor smiled, and while Satyrus slipped away into sleep.

Each successive sleep caused him to awake better and more restless, and there was food – mutton soup, and then ever more solid things – delicious, rich foods straight from the golden king's table, and twice Demetrios came in person.

After his third long sleep, he awoke to find Achilles at his bedside, and he grinned at the man.

'Next time tell me when I'm bleeding – a little sooner.' Satyrus took a deep breath, waited for the pain from his thigh. It was there, but definitely better. No fever.

Achilles smiled. 'The rest of the boys have come in,' he said. 'And young Jason. Still a lot of people looking for you. Jason had a go at offing Phiale and didn't pull it off – trying to avenge his master. He's here for you – claims you said you'd take him on.'

Satyrus sighed. 'So I did,' he answered, wondering how many plots he'd be saddled with if he accepted the boy as his freedman.

'Her people killed a lot of people in a brothel, and Jason brought a couple of survivors. I'm sure they can find work here,' Achilles said, with a leer. 'You planning to go into business?'

'Too complicated for me,' Satyrus said. 'You run it.'

Achilles nodded. 'I thought I might, with Memnon and the boys. That's how you serve with an army – run a string of boys and girls, protect 'em, rake in the owls. We staying here for a week or two?'

Satyrus realised the man was serious. 'I'm not going anywhere until I have Demetrios's permission. And I need to be able to walk. But if you plan to stay in my service, you have to know that I'll be out of here as soon as I recover – one way or another. Being wounded has its advantages – I've had time to think. This is a diversion. I have things I need to be doing.'

Achilles didn't seem to have listened to a word after the first sentence. 'Two weeks, you say?' he answered. 'That's fine.'

When Achilles was gone, the doctor and a pair of slaves changed the bandages and salves on his arms and legs. Satyrus was amused to see how heavily bruised he was – the breastplate itself had done as much damage as enemy weapons. When he was settled, drinking iced wine and water with fruit juice, Demetrios came in. Slaves brought him an ivory folding stool and he sat, took some juice, and dismissed the slaves.

'How are you doing?' he asked. It was a curiously human opening for the golden king – he seemed tentative, uncertain.

'I'm well enough,' Satyrus said. 'No infection. I'll be ready to leave in a week or so. Will you be allowing me to leave?'

Demetrios looked away. Then he looked back. 'I'd rather like you to stay,' he said.

There it was. 'No,' Satyrus said. Relations with many people had taught him that in situations like this, where people's emotions ran high, straight answers were better than prevarication. 'No,' he said again. 'I want to be back with my own people.'

Demetrios's face flushed. 'Have I been less than hospitable?' he asked. 'Did I not give you the best I had?'

Satyrus smiled. 'That sword is the finest I've ever held in my hand,' he said. 'Damn. I lost it, didn't I?'

Demetrios shook his head. 'No, I'll have it back for you – Prepalaus is ready to surrender the citadel on terms if I allow him to withdraw into Achaea in good order. He may even be making the right decision, but he's gutless. I wouldn't give that citadel up until my men were eating the dead.'

'The way we were at Rhodes?' Satyrus asked.

'Exactly!' Demetrios said, uninterested in Satyrus's tone, or perhaps unused to sarcasm. 'The defence of Rhodes will always be my touchstone – that's how a city should hold.'

Satyrus shrugged, and it hurt his ribs and side and all his bruises. 'Prepalaus isn't Corinthian.'

Demetrios shook his head. 'No – but can't a man love an ideal bigger than his city? He should fight as well for Cassander—'

Satyrus tried not to laugh – laughing had consequences – but he couldn't stop himself. He wheezed a little. 'Would you die for Cassander?' he asked.

Demetrios looked puzzled. 'Why on earth would I die for Cassander?'

Satyrus wheezed again, and thought, *If I live, someday I'll tell my children this story.* 'I mean, if you were merely a Macedonian spearman.'

Demetrios shook his head. 'How would that happen?' he asked. 'Honestly, sometimes you make no sense.'

Satyrus nodded. 'So you can't put yourself in another man's shoes?'

'Whatever for?' Demetrios asked. 'I am myself. To pretend otherwise would be a lie – perhaps hubris.'

Satyrus shrugged, with attendant consequences, and winced. 'Aristotle has a lot to answer for,' he murmured.

'I want to convince you to stay,' Demetrios said.

Satyrus didn't know what to say, so he said nothing. The golden king was pausing his day to woo him, and Satyrus decided that he could do worse than hear him out.

'Can we agree that the current state of perpetual warfare is a curse to all men?' Demetrios asked.

Satyrus raised an eyebrow. 'I'm surprised to hear you say so,' he said.

Demetrios frowned. 'At any rate, my dear fellow king – will you concede that? Good. So I ask you: what is the quickest, most efficient way to avoid future wars? And the answer is obvious – a single, unified government. One king, one empire – the whole world. From one edge of the girdle of ocean to the other, the whole circle. One king, one empire, one law, one set of gods. Then men will be free.'

Satyrus absorbed this for a long moment. 'Free of what?' he asked.

'Free of war,' Demetrios answered. 'And honestly – speak freely – who is more fit to rule them all than I?'

Satyrus frowned.

'I have a good staff and I am myself both hard-working and brilliant. My goal is worthy, Satyrus; peace and prosperity, a universal standard – think of it. You are a king – a universal set of coins. Of weights and measures. One language – one art – one poetry to breed excellence in men.'

Satyrus shook his head. 'This is going to make men *free*?' he asked.

'Free to build and live and raise their families,' the golden king said.

'According to your laws and the customs that you dictate.' Satyrus met his eyes. 'You would subject the Sakje to the same laws as the Greeks?'

Demetrios leaned forward. 'Not initially, but eventually, by remorseless interchange. What would seem strange to them initially would grow more familiar with trade and contact, until they accepted it of their own will.'

Satyrus pursed his lips. 'And if they did not?'

Demetrios shrugged. 'There are always malcontents,' he said.

'In other words, a war of reprisal,' Satyrus said.

'If you must,' Demetrios said.

'And when your empire collapses?' Satyrus asked.

'What?' Demetrios asked. He looked truly befuddled.

'Empires fall,' Satyrus said. 'Babylon. Aegypt. Mycenae. Troy. Athens. Sparta.'

'An empire based on the work of rational men and led by heroes and demi-gods?' Demetrios said.

'Faster than any,' Satyrus answered with derision.

'You are making me angry,' Demetrios said. 'I want you to stay. Many men follow me from self-interest or even love, but you ... are my friend. I can *talk* to you. Even if you disagree, you understand what it is to be different. You are god-touched, too. I saw you fight, Satyrus. You are greater than mortal. So it is with me. Come – let us be friends. Counsel me, and we will be remembered until the sun falls from the sky and the sea of chaos sweeps over the last men.'

Satyrus didn't feel that this was the time for astraight answer – but he thought it might be time for a straight question. 'Demetrios, may I tell you something? A human thing, about myself, that is not godlike?'

Demetrios laughed. 'I have spoken above myself and affrighted you.'

Satyrus shook his head. 'No. I dream of Herakles, and I believe in the gods. I seek to be a hero – I won't hide it. A hero. I pray that Herakles will stand by my shoulder.' He nodded. 'Why *not* aspire to be a hero?' he asked. Smiled. 'But listen. I love a woman – and she is your hostage.'

'I took no hostages who were women,' Demetrios said. 'Who is she?'

Satyrus took the plunge. 'Miriam, sister to my friend Abraham the Jew of Rhodes.'

Demetrios slapped his thigh. 'You love a Jew?' he asked. 'Well, they're a handsome race, I admit. Stiff-necked, too.'

Satyrus smiled at a memory. 'Will you release her for me – and release her brother so that she will go free? And let me go to them?'

Demetrios looked puzzled. 'Why?' he asked.

Well, Satyrus thought, *it was worth a try.* 'Because that is all I need for happiness,' he said. 'I don't believe in your universal empire. And even if I did, I wouldn't fight against my friends to help accomplish it.'

Demetrios's puzzlement was turning to anger. 'Your friends are arrogant fools who seek to limit me when I can make the world *better*.'

'Quite possibly,' Satyrus said. He shrugged. 'But they are my friends. And I find that I no longer need dominion to make me happy.'

Demetrios seemed to ignore him. 'Ptolemy? He's no hero – a fat old man with no dreams left in his head, who wants nothing but to rule Aegypt and enjoy its revenues.' He narrowed his eyes. 'Leon is a merchant – he has no honour, merely money.'

Satyrus shook his head. 'You are wrong there, lord, but let us not quarrel.'

Demetrios got a sly look on his face. 'I have it,' he said. 'Your allies tried to kill you. I told you before – Cassander ordered your assassination.'

Satyrus shrugged. 'Not the first time. Cassander has never been a friend of my family.'

'If you stay with me, together we can destroy him,' Demetrios said.

Satyrus shrugged. 'I want Abraham and Miriam, and I will go back to Pantecapaeaum and interfere no more in the affairs of the Middle Sea,' he said. 'The truth is that I have been a dreadful king, swanning about with my warships, helping this place and that, and spending my revenues on war when I could have built roads and strong places and granaries and lyceums. Time for me to stop playing king and expecting one of my friends to do the work.' He nodded, aware that he was speaking to himself, and determined in his conviction. No more time-wasting. 'I should thank you. Through you, I have seen my errors.'

Demetrios shook his head. 'No,' he said. He got to his feet. 'You will remain here with me. I would think less of you if you didn't try to recover the hostages – why not? And when I give you the one who matters to you – then you will make war on me. Your sister has already closed the Pontus against me. I would be within my rights to execute the Rhodian hostages.'

Satyrus felt anger blaze up within him. 'If you execute them, I will die fighting you and your father and your cursed universal empire.'

Demetrios nodded. 'It's good that we understand each other.'

Satyrus chose his next words carefully. 'Am I to understand that you don't intend to release the hostages on time, as according to the agreement?' he asked.

Demetrios shook his head. 'No one could possibly expect me to. If I release the hostages, Rhodes will be free to act against me – as will you. And then, I expect that your combined fleets would destroy mine, and then I might fail. So, much as it pains me, I'll just keep them until Lysimachos and Cassander have been neutralised. Two years – three at most. You want this woman so much? Speed their fall. Tell your sister to open the Pontus to me and close it to Lysimachos.' He nodded. 'In the meantime, you are my friend and will remain my guest.'

Angry denunciations crowded Satyrus's mouth, but he spat them out. He was awake enough and wise enough to know that an open break with Demetrios would serve no purpose. 'I will think on it,' he said.

Demetrios rose to his feet. 'That's the spirit,' he said. 'Swear allegiance to me, and I'll have this Hebrew maid brought here to you – and more. I felt the power that we would have together – did you not? In the breach? Oh, it makes my heart beat faster to think what we might accomplish.'

Satyrus thought: *We failed. We didn't even storm the breach.*

But he smiled. 'I'll think on it,' he said again.

Demetrios smiled again. 'I'm sure you will,' he said.

8

Three more days of dusty inaction, and Prepalaus surrendered the citadel on terms and marched the garrison away across the isthmus, headed north and west for Achaia. Satyrus didn't see Demetrios, and on the third day, as the palace tents were packed, Satyrus's bed was moved to a tent of his own – the tent he'd had the first day.

'We'll follow my lord when you are a little better,' Apollonaris noted, measuring a dose of syrup. 'Try this – it's what I give men who can't take poppy. Not as effective but not bad.'

'What is it?' Satyrus said. He put effort into his act – to seem worse than he was.

'Hmm. A concoction of roots.' Apollonaris smiled. 'Professional secret.'

'Odd taste,' Satyrus allowed.

'Your tents sound like a brothel,' the doctor said, after some grunts had been heard through the walls.

Satyrus shrugged. 'I think my mercenaries have gone into business.'

The doctor laughed. 'Well, I'll pitch my tent a little further away.'

The next morning, Satyrus got up immediately after the doctor had left him and began to exercise. Achilles came in, with Jason, and Jason oiled him and massaged him thoroughly, and he began to feel better. He tired too easily to contemplate immediate action, but he was better.

'How many men are there out there?' he asked.

'Fifty hypaspists,' Achilles said.

Jason nodded.

Satyrus kept his voice low. 'Any idea how we can slip them?' he asked.

Achilles shrugged. 'Any time. Never was a group of soldiers so happy to find a bawdy house. But they've coin left – no need to hurry. Odysseus and me, we mean to have it all.' He chuckled.

Jason leaned closer. 'Your sister has declined to open the Propontus to Demetrios unless you are handed over. I have reason to believe that Neron ordered your death – in battle, at the breach. It stands to reason, lord; if you die here, apparently serving with Demetrios ...'

Satyrus took in a sharp breath. 'I'm not as smart as I think I am,' he said.

Achilles chuckled again. 'I am, though, lord. We have these men where we want them.'

'What's your plan?' Satyrus asked.

Achilles shrugged. 'Ask me in a day or two,' he said.

Jason leaned in closer. 'I missed Phiale,' he said apologetically. 'I needed more muscle than I had, and her killer wiped out my thugs. I came away but I won't rest until I've finished her.'

'Who's paying her?' Satyrus asked. 'That's what I want to know.'

Jason shrugged. 'The word is it's Cassander,' he said. 'But the word could be donkey shit, too.'

'You two make my head hurt. Anything about the hostages?' Satyrus asked.

'He's moved them all to Ephesus,' Jason said. 'More than a month ago.'

Satyrus started. He got up from the carpet, where he had been raising his legs, and he sat on the edge of his couch, winded from a very minor exercise. 'But ... that means he sent them away before I even reached here.'

Jason nodded. 'Oh, yes. I remember the order coming to us. It was more than a week before you arrived. Perhaps two weeks.'

Satyrus cursed. 'Then he never intended to keep the treaty.' The rage threatened to overwhelm him. If he had stayed on Delos, he'd be free now, and he'd have learned this. He had come to Athens for nothing. And almost died for it. Truly, the gods knew all, and men were fools.

He thought of Cassander ordering his death, and Demetrios casually ordering the hostages to Ephesus.

There was no side that he wanted any part of, unless it was Ptolemy.

'I've been had,' he said.

Night, and Achilles' travelling brothel was hard at work. Satyrus walked out of his tent, careful in case the doctor was wandering about but eager to have a breath of air, and discovered that the storage tent had a plank across two bales of sheepskins and on this makeshift table four different knucklebones games were going on. Four large pithoi of wine were half buried in the soil behind another temporary counter, and men sat on bales of sheepskins or benches, drinking, while Memnon measured wine with a ladle.

Aella appeared from the darkness. 'Cup of wine, sir?' she asked. 'Oh,' she laughed. 'It's you.'

Satyrus nodded. 'I'll take the cup of wine,' he allowed.

She nodded. 'And there's the games, of course – are you a gambling gent? And Alex and me have got some boys and girls – local talent, really.'

'How old are you, Aella?' Satyrus asked.

She swayed, gave him a hard look, her eyes cold as ice. 'Seventeen, I think.'

'Is this the life you want?' he asked.

She met his eye easily. 'No. This is the life I have. If you pay me what you said you would, I'll never play another flute as long as I live.' She shrugged. 'Otherwise, this is my trade until my purse fills with a baby.' She stalked away.

Alex sat down with him on the bench. 'She's just angry. We know you don't have any money right now.' He shrugged. 'Besides, this is way better than Athens. Achilles put us in charge. I'm keeping more'n half of what I make.' He nodded at a young boy. 'And a quarter what they make.'

Satyrus swallowed bile. 'Send Achilles here,' he said.

The wine was not very good. Satyrus shook his head in disgust. He'd been wrong, he'd been taken, and now he was the master of a travelling brothel.

The weight of the bench shifted, and Satyrus made room for Achilles.

The man sitting next to him was *not* Achilles.

'Stratokles,' he breathed.

'Satyrus,' said his old enemy. He raised his empty hands so that Satyrus could see them in the firelight. 'I'm here for your sister.'

Satyrus started. 'What?'

Stratokles laughed. 'It's odd for all of us. But Melitta sent me, and I've brought several of your friends. It's been the deuce of a time

164

finding you, and there's men out to kill you even now. Remember the doctor? Sophokles?' Stratokles was watching the hypaspists.

'I'm unlikely to forget him,' Satyrus said.

'He's close,' Stratokles said. 'I saw him in Athens. He's after you.'

Satyrus took a deep breath.

'Apollodorus has the cream of your fleet at Aegina,' he said. 'And I have Anaxagoras and Charmides with me.'

Suddenly Stratokles straightened.

There was a sword at his throat.

'Best explain yourself,' Achilles said.

It took an hour to explain it all, and another hour to make their plans.

Another day, and the brothel closed up, counted its profits and paid off its staff. The Macedonians watched them go with mixed emotions – most of them had lost every obol they had to one vice or another.

The golden king's doctor had pronounced Satyrus fit, and Satyrus agreed to go by palanquin to rejoin Demetrios at Achaea. He paused at the moment of departure to borrow cash – half a talent – from the doctor, and he used the money to pay off his four bodyguards, who added the money to their takings from four days of fleecing the Macedonians. Then, after a last visit to the tree line to relieve himself, Satyrus was seen to climb into the palanquin, his Tyrian purple chlamys visible through the silk curtains on the travelling kline.

The four mercenaries and a handful of former brothel employees watched the strong guard march away with the King of the Bosporus as their prisoner. When they had climbed the hill behind the Acrocorinth on the road to Achaea, Achilles shook his head.

'That was too easy,' he said.

'Mmm,' Memnon said. 'Guard captain owed me more than a talent of silver.' He shrugged. 'He won't be with 'em in the morning, either.'

Stratokles looked over the four. 'Gentlemen, I consider myself among the wiliest men in the world today, and I profess myself to be a mere student before your mastery.'

Odysseus laughed. 'Aye, like enough, there's always someone to put one over on ye, no matter how swift ye may be,' he said.

Satyrus rubbed his chin. 'I still fear for Jason,' he said. 'The Theban boy was wearing his clothes. When they find out …'

'That's the beauty of it,' Achilles laughed. 'When the guard captain deserts tonight, he'll take Jason with him. And those fuck heads will chase *him*.' The mercenary laughed. 'Never you fret for Jason, lord. He was playing this game when he was in nappies.'

A day's ride over the mountains brought them to Megara, where Charmides and Anaxagoras waited. They were delighted – and so was Satyrus, who feared he might weep, he was so happy to see his friends.

'Practised your lyre?' Anaxagoras asked.

'Not as much as I should have, no doubt,' Satyrus said. He was choked with emotion.

Anaxagoras embraced him hard. 'Let me be the first to tell you: I told you so, you fool.'

Stratokles laughed aloud.

'We have a boat for Aegina,' Charmides said.

At the pier, Aella paused. 'Lord?' she asked in a small voice.

'Despoina?' Satyrus asked her.

'What happens now?' she asked.

Satyrus scratched his chin under his new beard. 'For you?'

She nodded. 'Me and Alex.'

'You can't stay here. So you come with us, and I pay you each a talent of gold, and then you settle down – in Tanais, or Olbia.'

She nodded. 'I don't believe it,' she said. 'You'll just cut our throats and dump us.'

Alex shook his head. 'No, no he won't.'

Aella was trembling. 'We're not even human to the likes of him. Here, give me something now, and I'm away. You, too, if you have any sense.' She looked at Alex.

'You cannot go back to Athens,' Satyrus said. 'Phiale will kill you.'

'So you say,' she spat. 'I am not sailing away on that ship – away from—'

Satyrus narrowed his eyes, suddenly angry. 'Listen to me, young lady. Away from Athens? Where you can sell your body until you get pregnant – and if you are lucky, keep a quarter of the proceeds? What will you have left of yourself in five years? Eh?'

'As if you care,' she said.

'I do care. You two saved my life. I pay my debts.' Satyrus regretted the words as soon as they were out.

She turned. 'Fuck you and your debts,' she said.

She crumpled to the ground when Memnon clipped her on the head. 'For her own good,' he said apologetically. 'She's got it for you bad, lord.'

'Huh?' Satyrus said, and felt foolish.

'Let's get to sea,' Charmides suggested. He smiled.

As he jumped into the longboat, Achilles grunted. 'Where to now?' he asked.

Satyrus was still chewing over his encounter with Aella. But he managed a smile.

'Ephesus,' he said.

A hundred stades away, the captain of the guards who were supposed to be escorting Satyrus back to Demetrios cut open the back of the tent where Jason was waiting, wide eyed. The two of them slipped out through the slit in the tent wall and sprinted for the waiting horses.

'Better get a good wage out of this,' the Macedonian said.

They got on their horses and walked them carefully, quietly, clear of the ring of sentries, and then back across the hills towards Corinth.

Sophokles watched his target escape the dense ring of guards with well-concealed delight, and led his group of hired men to the south, up across the old pass with its deep chariot ruts in the rock and back down above the main Achaean–Corinthian road just as the sun was rising. The men at his back were Thessalian mercenaries – good horsemen, and tough as old leather. They got to the top of the pass long before their quarry.

Satyrus and his saviour rode into the trap without any god intervening to save them, and Sophokles had the immense pleasure of seeing his own black-fletched arrow finally go into Satyrus's throat under the cowl of his chlamys. The King of the Bosporus fell from his horse and did not move, and the guard captain died a moment later with a pair of javelins in his back.

'Phiale won't like that you killed him,' Isokles said.

Sophokles couldn't stand the man, so he didn't bother to respond.

'Phiale won't like that you killed him,' the man said again in his annoying voice.

'I don't work for Phiale,' Sophokles said.

'But you said—' the man began.

'I lied,' Sophokles said. He made a gesture, and his men emerged from their ambush positions.

Isokles went to the corpses, but Sophokles stopped him with a gesture.

'No. Leave them for the ravens. No spoils. Let Demetrios wonder. And this way, Cassander can blame Demetrios – look how he was shot trying to escape? Perfect. I couldn't have planned it better myself, and I must give thanks to the gods, who have played some odd tricks on me with this man and his sister. At last it is my turn.'

'I don't like you,' Isokles said in his odd voice.

'Alas. But I shall learn to bear it. Get on your horse, eh? There's a good fellow.'

'You ain't as smart as you think,' Isokles said. 'And Phiale—'

'No one is as smart as I think I am, young man. And Phiale isn't even on the board.' Sophokles reined in his horse and looked down at the King of the Bosporus. 'How I shall enjoy telling this story,' he said, and rode away.

PART III

'And he escaped?' Demetrios asked. His tone was mild, and the hypaspist phylarch was obviously terrified.

The phylarch mumbled some sort of an answer.

'Say that again?' Demetrios said. A slave handed him pomegranate juice; Neron, his spymaster, stood close by him. He was wearing helmet and bronze thorax, that both had recent dents – Demetrios had fought, hand to hand, at the height of the pike push, and he'd been roaring in the front rank when they broke Cassander's Macedonians with their own.

'He might be dead?' the phylarch attempted, although most men would have taken his voice for a whisper.

Demetrios sprang off his stool, unclipped his cheek-plates, and tossed his helmet to a slave. 'I'm sorry, did you say dead?'

One of his strategoi was trying to get his attention. Demetrios swung his slightly mad gaze clear of the terrified hypaspist and inclined his head to Philip, son of Alexander. 'Well fought, sir.'

The strategos flushed at the praise. 'Thank you, lord. We have prisoners – thousands. Prepalaus's whole army must be collapsing.'

Demetrios's face lit with satisfaction. 'This is it!' he said, and thumped the other man on the back. 'By Herakles, Philip, if Prepalaus collapses we've won. We push our sarissas into Asia and save Pater. By the gods – I never thought this moment would happen.' He turned back to the phylarch. 'Lad, you're leaving something out. Speak. I'm in a benevolent frame of mind.'

The man stammered, mumbled. Paused.

'We found the guard captain,' he said, quite clearly. 'Dead.'

Demetrios felt his guts clench. 'And?' he asked. It seemed to him that the gods had traded his Satyrus for this victory. What a foolish way for a hero to die. *Poor Satyrus.* The man deserved better, even if he chose the wrong side – perhaps *because* he chose the wrong side. Demetrios wanted him – as a contestant.

'And Lord Satyrus?' he asked patiently. As the master of Greece, he suddenly had time to be patient.

The man began to babble, and Neron smacked him.

Later, when Neron came back bearing a cup of wine, the spymaster shook his head wearily.

'I honestly can't tell what's the truth and what's fiction,' he said. He sat on Demetrios's ivory stool without asking permission. Neron was one of the few – very few – who had such rights.

'Tell me all,' Demetrios said.

'It sounds as if Satyrus's escape was itself a trap – an ambush to kill him.' Neron shrugged. 'I have one niggling thought – one cavil, if you like. That phylarch is holding something back, something he's too scared to impart. I'm going to guess that the body he found was *not* Satyrus's.'

Demetrios sat up on his kline. 'You ... by Herakles! That would be wonderful!'

Neron shook his hands, rubbed his eyes with his palms, shook his head as if trying to shake off fatigue. 'I'm pleased for you, lord. You like him. But he's a cunning opponent and if he has got clear, it is a master stroke.'

'Nonsense,' Demetrios said. 'What can he do? We've the fleet, we've the army, Cassander's at my mercy and I can push my pikes in Asia – tomorrow, if I want.'

'If he's dead ...' Neron took a deep breath. 'If he's dead, his sister will fight you for the Propontus.'

Demetrios was dismissive. 'Let her. We'll summon the Ephesian squadrons – sixty hulls there – and move our troops straight across to Asia, and bypass the Propontus. She can watch there all summer – the war will be passing her by.'

Neron nodded. 'Your pater is hard pressed,' he said. 'We have to move fast. But you know all that.'

Demetrios drank off his juice. 'I fought well today.'

Neron raised an eyebrow. 'Time to stop that, lord. We're this close to victory – this close.' He held his fingers the width of a slim coin apart. 'You take a wound – we're done.'

Demetrios shrugged. 'I'm going to be a god,' he said. 'I don't get wounded.'

Neron sighed. 'If you say so. My last news? I have a messenger who says that Satyrus has fifteen ships at Aegina. Right now. Fishing boat saw them in port.'

Demetrios frowned.

'If Satyrus is alive, and free, he'll be aboard by now.' Neron shrugged again.

'What can he do?' Demetrios asked. 'Fight my Isthmian fleet at one to four odds?'

'Raid shipping?' Neron said, his voice impatient. 'Break up our troop movements? Save Prepalaus's army by covering his flank?'

'Not with fifteen hulls. Perhaps with fifty. If he's alive he'll do something. Good for him. Prepalaus was too easy. Unworthy.'

Neron's voice became hard, critical. 'Don't go that way, lord. If Prepalaus had been any tougher, we'd be desperate now.'

Demetrios smiled. 'Lighten up. But yes, point taken. Here, have some wine.'

Neron sighed. 'I will.' He raised his cup. 'If Satyrus lives, may he sail home.'

Demetrios shook his head. 'Avert! If he lives, may I find him at the end of my sword.'

'I got him,' Sophokles said. He was offered wine by a slave, and he took it.

Cassander let go a long sigh. He was still a handsome man, but age was beginning to tell – age, and fifteen years and more of constant campaigning, betrayal, revenge. 'The only good news of the week,' he said.

The doctor nodded. 'I heard. And whatever reports you received, it's worse than they told you.'

Cassander raised a weary eyebrow and toyed with his sandals.

'I was there – off the flank of Demetrios's cavalry when the rout began. I couldn't help it – there's only so many ways out of Achaea. Your cavalry deserted, he broke your infantry, and now most of them have gone over – Demetrios must have doubled his numbers.'

Cassander's eyes were bloodshot. He snarled. 'You're right. No one told me it was that bad.'

The doctor pretended to finish his wine. In fact, he hadn't tasted it – he'd poured the whole cup into a chamber pot while Cassander was looking at his sandals. But he appeared to appreciate it. 'Prepalaus has ceased to exist as a fighting force. Demetrios will either come after you or go to the aid of his father. Either way, he's won here. What will you do?'

He ducked as the heavy gold cup that Cassander had been using flew by his head.

The doctor smiled, picked up his heavy satchel, and withdrew.

'Everyone blames the messenger,' he said.

Phiale emerged from the antechamber tent. 'That's that evil bastard done with,' she said with savage satisfaction.

'Done with?' Cassander asked.

'I poisoned his wine,' Phiale said. 'He killed Satyrus, and I killed him. It seems ... balanced.'

'I'm not done with him!' Cassander said. 'I need ... an act of the gods. I need Demetrios to die. Or Antigonus.' He took a deep breath, and he was an old man – a pale, shaken old man. 'I need some luck.'

'Touch me for luck,' Phiale said, curling an arm around his head. 'And I'll see if I can take care of Demetrios.'

'He was in armour! Serving against Cassander! With bloody Demetrios as his butt-boy!' Ptolemy raged. 'My spymaster says that they spent days and nights together at Corinth!'

Leon sighed. His own spies said the same. Said that Satyrus of Tanais had taken a wound in Demetrios's service, and was recuperating in the palace tent.

'What am I to think?' Ptolemy raged. 'Cassander is falling apart and Satyrus is helping it happen! Zeus Soter, Leon!' The lord of Aegypt was also in armour – sitting on the edge of a hard bench in his sleeping tent. Outside, the long, Syrian twilight was giving way to true night, and the sound of insects competed with the steady, rhythmic chomping of thousands of horses eating the good grass of the Bekaa Valley.

The Nubian merchant had come cross-country from Tyre, where his own ships waited with Ptolemy's fleet, guarding its flank from the increasingly confident and aggressive squadrons of Antigonus and Demetrios, up the coast at Ephesus.

'As far as we can tell; Cassander tried to have him killed,' Leon said. He ran his fingers though his beard. 'If he knows that then he may, indeed, have elected to serve Demetrios.' He shook his head. 'But I doubt it.'

Ptolemy sounded bone weary. His cautious invasion of Palestine and lower Syria was a war of careful manoeuvre and local siege, with Antigonus's local forces responding with vigour. Just three months before, they had seemed on the verge of collapse, but now – now Antigonus seemed to have found his youth.

'How could he be so *stupid*?' Ptolemy asked.

'Satyrus?' Leon asked.

'Cassander. The useless *fucker*. He tried to kill me, remember? And now Satyrus. What for?' Ptolemy shook his head. 'If we had his fleet, we'd still be in the game.'

'Is it that bad?' Leon asked. 'I've been at sea.'

Ptolemy shrugged. 'To be honest, no. It's not that bad. It's never been as bad as when Perdiccas had Alexander's own army at the Nile forts and I had nothing but a handful of mercenaries to stop them. Nor as bad as when Golden Boy came at us at Gaza. We're in Syria. Lots of room to retreat.'

'And this looks like a good army,' Leon offered.

'All the quality money can buy,' Ptolemy said with a touch of his old humour. 'But if Cassander folds – and the bastard will fold – then they'll all come after me.'

'Lysimachos?' Leon asked.

'Won't hold long enough for Seleucus to reach him – because there's nothing to stop Demetrios from taking his soldiers to Asia. Faster than Lysimachos can move.' Ptolemy shook his head again. 'It's not cast in bronze. But I'm not going to save them. I can't beat Antigonus – and you and I both know it. If I had Eumenes ... if I had any number of the boys from the old days. But I don't, and I don't think I could trust this army to face old One-Eye.'

Leon sighed. 'I should get back. If you are right, we will have to cover your retreat.'

Ptolemy laughed. 'Yes, if we're really lucky, we'll have to fight them after all.' His sarcasm was evident. 'I'm too old for this shit.'

Leon nodded. 'Think of One-Eye. He must be eighty.'

Ptolemy nodded. 'I think of it all the time. I think if he were to die, we'd be saved.'

The last winds of the storm were still blowing hard enough that a phalangite would have a hard time holding his sarissa upright. Most of the army's tents were blown flat, and the slaves had stopped trying to get them back up.

Lysimachos was on the beach, stripped, trying with every other soldier in his army to rescue men from the sea. The corpses were so thick in the sea wrack that the waves seemed to be made of dead men.

Half his army, gone in an afternoon squall on the Euxine. Five thousand veterans, gone to the bottom. The beaches from Heraklea to Sinope were littered with corpses, and more were sinking beneath the waves or floating, bloated and stinking and black, like soft logs in the wake of the squall. His fleet wrecked.

Lysimachos continued to search the corpse-wrack, looking for men who were alive. And after hours – the hideous work seemed eternal – he found Amastris and her women beside his men. His wife – he hardly thought of her these days – was swimming about, grabbing men by the hair and pulling them to shore.

Until then, she had never been more than a tool for his desires – the desire to conquest, the desire to have a child by her, to hold her city as a port into Asia.

But watching her dare the undertow to pull a Macedonian peasant out of the clutches of Poseidon, despite the complete disaster that had just overtaken him, he smiled.

Kalias, his principal strategos, was shaking his head.

'We're done,' he said. 'First Cassander and now this.'

Lysimachos watched his wife for another minute. She was beautiful – and brave. Worthy, in fact.

'Bullshit,' he said. 'I'm not done yet.' He stripped his chiton over his head. 'See those women out in the water? Are they *better* than we?' He ran through the corpses and dived headlong, racing for a man he'd seen to move a hand.

All along the beach, weary, waterlogged soldiers rose to their feet, stripped their gear, and went into the surf.

Lysimachos made it to his man. He couldn't tell whether he was alive or dead, but he did what he'd seen Amastris do – he got a hand into the man's hair, put his buttocks under the man's back, and swam for shore.

He was further off the beach than he'd thought. He raised his head and saw that he was a surprising distance offshore, and despite his swimming, he seemed to be getting further and further away. He swam harder. He started to panic and he fought it with the long experience of the veteran warrior who knows panic like a man knows his lover's body.

At some point it occurred to Lysimachos to let go of the body. But he was sure there was spirit still in it – and in some way, some inexpressible sending of the gods, Lysimachos had decided that if he could save this one man, if the man lived, then his army would live, his cause would live, and he would save his honour. And if he could not save this one man, it seemed fair that he die here, choking water, Poseidon's victim.

It was a simple contest: Lysimachos against the sea. Lysimachos was strong, and his will was as great as his body. He was *not* a great swimmer. But he *would not* surrender to the waves, or let go the man whose hair he had.

He fought a long fight.

The land slipped further and further away – first a stade, and then another.

He kept swimming. Fighting.

He got a throat full of seawater, his nose closed, his larynx burning from the salt, and he fought panic off one more time, pushed himself up in the water. Changed grip on the body on his back – almost certainly a corpse by now.

A swirl in the water by his head.

He closed his eyes. He opened them to find a mermaid.

'You're going the wrong way,' Amastris said. She was as calm and fit as a goddess, and as beautiful. 'Here, give him to me.' She took the man's hair and had the energy to swim up under his head, stick her fingers in his mouth, and pull him up to her shoulder.

'Still alive,' she said cheerily.

Side by side, they swam for the beach.

Antigonus read the dispatches from his son with unconcealed delight, his one eye roving over the careful scribal writing like a lookout watching for ships on a threatened coast.

'He doesn't even know that Lysimachos is wrecked!' Antigonus laughed. 'By all the gods. By all the gods, gentlemen! Ptolemy is alone! Cassander's defeated, Lysimachos wrecked by a storm, Seleucus too far away, Satyrus dead!' He laughed again. 'And I was at the point of despair.'

'Ptolemy still has a mighty army,' suggested his spymaster, Kreon – a Siciliote.

'We will buy him. Offer him a generous truce, crush the rest of them, and take him next spring. Ares, I haven't felt this young in years. Get me a girl.'

Kreon laughed. 'Don't hurt yourself, lord,' he chuckled.

'Damn it, Kreon – I'm old, not dead.' Antigonus laughed aloud. 'By the gods. We've won. I never thought I'd say those words.'

Kreon flinched. 'Not done yet. They still have life in them. Lysimachos still has troops – about half his army, and all of Heraklea's resources. I understand he's marching.' He looked at his master. 'Seleucus is mighty.'

'That pup? What can he do?' Antigonus said. 'His army is a quarter of mine and he has no fleet.'

'Join hands with Lysimachos or Ptolemy?' Kreon said.

'It would take a miracle,' Antigonus said, and chuckled.

Miriam was doing exercises when she heard her brother's angry roar. She finished her dance steps – her brother had a temper and it was best not to feed it – and then pulled a chiton over her head and emerged from her room into the central garden.

They were not slaves. Far from it – they had returned to comfortable captivity, but with the threat of slavery or death hanging over them every day. They were held in a spacious private home right against the walls of the city, and there were fifty soldiers watching the forty Rhodian prisoners in the houses around them.

Abraham, when she found him, was weeping.

Miriam came and sat by him on the bench.

'Our father is dead,' Abraham said, and ripped hair out of his beard.

Miriam felt the tears well up in her eyes – painful tears. She had never made peace with the old man. And now she never would. But to say she didn't love him would have been a lie. She began to sob, but it was as if someone else was doing the crying, because her mind ran on, calm and clear, even as she heard her own rather shocking exclamation.

Abraham took both of her hands.

'And Satyrus may be dead,' he said. 'Demetrios has won a great victory in Greece, and Cassander is destroyed. Demetrios and Antigonus have ... won.' He took a long time, and she found that she cared nothing – nothing – for the defeat of her *side*.

'Satyrus is not dead,' she said through her sobs. She would know, she thought. Even though she had determined to tell him that she would not go with him to Tanais – even though Ephesus had clarified for her that she was a Jew and not a Hellene. She would be neither his mistress nor his wife.

She had decided. But she would feel it in her body if he died.

If Abraham heard her, he ignored her.

'Demetrios had him killed,' Abraham said, and his voice cracked.

Miriam raised her head. 'Satyrus is alive,' she said.

Abraham looked shocked. And in a moment – in her eyes, in her posture – he understood.

Abraham understood, and he searched for rage – rage at his sister's betrayal of her ... widowhood?

There was nothing there but his own sorrow for his father. 'You love Satyrus?' he asked.

Miriam hung her head. 'I will not wed him.'

Abraham understood in those words, and he put his arms around her. 'Oh,' he said. 'Oh, my dear.'

9

EPHESUS

Dawn. Light the colour of fresh rose petals that rouged the river where it met the sea – wave tops that showed pink, not white. Gulls wheeled away into the sky, frightened by predators or merely playful. Off the river mouth, a school of dolphins leapt and leapt again, and further offshore, a line of sea haze veiled the islands like Poseidon's coast, waiting for the heat of the sun to burn it off.

Up the coast, five big Athenian grain ships, close up against the beaches, had their sails turned from white to blinding pink by the sun.

Deep in the haze, a flash, and then another – a rhythmic flash.

Flash.

Flash.

A line of flashes, as the rising sun caught oars – many, many oars.

Ten sets of oars.

Flash-flash-flash.

Racing speed. Ramming speed. Into the dawn.

Apollodorus stood amidships, his helmet forgotten on the deck as his hair blew in the wind of his reckless race up the estuary. Ephesus lay before him, high on her ridge, and the Temple of Artemis, one of the wonders of the world, sparkled in Dawn's embrace.

Closer to hand, fifty ships' lengths ahead, lay Antigonus's Asian fleet, moored in the gentle current or beached with their sterns pulled up high above the waterline, and the great camp of their oarsmen and marines stretched up the farm fields and around isolated stands of olive and oak and seemed to reach right up to the town.

Anaxagoras stood by him, and Charmides, and Coenus, and Theron, and Eumenes of Olbia.

There was nothing to be said – nothing but the rush of the wind, the sparkle of the sea, and the enormity of their risk.

And then they were through the chops of the estuary and into the river, still racing, the crews in top training. On the shore, sentries were shouting.

'Sing the paean!' Apollodorus called, and all through the fleet, the oarsmen took up the song. The daughters of Apollo were just being hymned on the mountainside of Delphi when the first rams crushed the first helpless ships at anchor.

Out in the estuary, the second Bosporon squadron came on, with Melitta standing in the bow of her penteres, and she heard the hymn rise to the gods, and she grinned.

'Let them see who *we* are,' she said to Herakles, Alexander's son, who stood behind her, awestruck to be participating in such a mighty enterprise.

Forty warships – the entire fleet of her kingdom.

'Sing!' she commanded Herakles, and he caught the song from across the water and raised his clear young voice, and their rowers took it from him, so that forty crews – eight thousand throats – roared the paean into the dawn.

High on the hillside above Ephesus, six men heard the paean.

'Got their beaks in,' Stratokles said. He smacked his fist into his palm. 'It's a pleasure to work with such competent people,' he added happily.

Thirty stades away, a minute column of smoke began to rise, and then another and another, like threads on the horizon.

The town garrison began to pour out of the gates, men tying their armour, tossing sword belts over their heads, shoving arms through porpakes.

'Let's do it,' Satyrus said.

The six of them slipped forward, from one grove to the next, until they lost sight of the estuary and the river because they were so close to the wall.

'Follow me!' Stratokles said. He sprinted towards the wall; a sentry shouted, and an arrow flew.

Now close to the wall, which rose ten times the height of a man, course upon course of mud brick atop stone. Another arrow flew, and it stuck in the face of Satyrus's shield.

Stratokles ran diagonally across the face of the nearest tower. The sentries were sounding the alarm but of course the city alarms were already ringing, and their local bell was ignored. As Stratokles had planned.

Around a corner of the wall, where a local farmer had planted his olives right up to the tower.

Up an olive tree, into the crotch, a long step up to the course where the stone met the mud brick – a ledge. Stratokles was panting, but he pointed up the wall; a long, diagonal, like a shallow set of steps hidden by the tops of the olives and by vines.

'Smugglers,' he panted.

Satyrus cut past him and ran up the secret steps in the wall.

His bodyguards protested, but he had to do this himself, and so he did. Right up the wall, six men against one of the mightiest cities in Asia.

The sentries were alert, but either they didn't know of the secret steps or they couldn't believe anyone would attack them there – there wasn't a man at the top of the wall, and Satyrus was on the platform.

A man shouted from the nearest tower, and a fully-armed hoplite came running, full tilt, out of the door of the tower.

Achilles came up the wall behind Satyrus. 'We have to clear the towers without more alarm.' Satyrus said.

Achilles nodded, and went west.

Satyrus braced. The oncoming hoplite was a brave man. He ran like a god, and he carried a heavy spear.

His inexperience showed in everything from the way he wore his helmet to his overly ornate greaves. Satyrus tipped him off the wall with his shield and the man broke his back falling to the sheds below the wall. But he died quietly.

Satyrus ran for the open door of the tower.

The second Bosporon squadron had fire pots, and they used them, going right in on the beach and putting fire into ship after ship, but further east, on the beaches by the city, the crews were awake and moving, and they began to pour into their hulls. There were sixty ships there. Enough to overwhelm the twenty Bosporons, despite the damage they'd inflicted.

Somewhere in the chaos, Plistias of Cos was cursing the gods and rallying his men. He had five ships launched, and then ten; formed – more forming. He knew the penteres he was facing as soon as he saw it – he knew who he was going to fight.

Even at odds of three to one, he knew his men would have to keep their nerve or die here.

But they stayed steady, despite the shouting in the town, despite the ships burning on the beaches and the turtled wrecks in the estuary. He was proud of them. Then he had twenty ships formed, enough to make a fight of it, and he flashed his shield, and his squadron rowed forward to face bloody Melitta of Tanais.

Into the tower, up the steps, onto the fighting platform – two men, both half-asleep, both watching the disaster out in the anchorage and frankly unbelieving that the war was upon them. Satyrus considered offering them surrender, but he couldn't afford to lose his surprise. He put his javelin through the nearest man and drew his sword.

'Yield,' he said.

The other man shook his head, and threw his javelin. It clattered off Satyrus's shield, and then Memnon beheaded him. Satyrus never even saw the strike – just the poor lad's head sailing over the tower wall, still helmeted, to land fifty pous below in the olive trees.

Satyrus sank to one knee and panted.

Then he dropped his aspis, pulled his leather bag over his shoulder, and dumped the makings of a particularly greasy fire onto the stones of the tower top.

Memnon took a swig of vinegar and water and handed it to him, and he had a swig himself.

Got his fire laid out: tinder, carefully kept dry, wrapped in bark, with tallow.

A small clay pot, full of coals. Hot as lava.

Satyrus emptied the coals into the bark tube.

Twenty heartbeats, and smoke began to billow out.

'Get me the straw from their sleeping pallets,' Satyrus called over his shoulder.

*

Four stades away, and Nikephorus watched the tower from under the shade of his hands. At his back, eight hundred men, his best, who'd come ashore from the captured Athenian grain ships and literally crawled across the countryside since midnight.

Draco saw the smoke first. Thumped his back and pointed.

Nikephorus grunted. Just for a moment, his throat closed with some emotion, and his eyes watered. Because if this worked, his name would live for ever.

'Stand up, you bastards! Time for your morning run!' he called, and the gods laughed with him.

Melitta stood on her tiptoes to release her third shaft. She was shooting to kill Plistias of Cos. So far she'd killed his helmsman.

Ahead of her, *Oinoe* oar-raked one of the enemy ships and it fell out of line.

The noise of the fight on the river was like the noise of every battle she'd ever heard, magnified and echoed by the enclosed space and the looming hillsides above them.

An arrow scored down her side, the broad point cutting her bicep and then punching into her side, but her scale shirt turned it. She shot the archer – caught the man leaning out to follow his shot. They were half a stade apart, both ships closing so fast that she would only have time for one more shot. She drew, nocked, searching for the red crest of the enemy navarch.

He'd vanished off his command deck.

He was almost completely hidden, the length of his heavy penteres from her, with boatsail mast and all its rigging between them, and he had his helmet off – and still she saw the flash of his cuirass. She leaped up on the rail and balanced there, on her bare toes, vaguely aware that every archer on the enemy ship was now shooting at her. And then it was just her bow and her hand and her eye and the infinitely distant glimpse of bronze – no conscious thought, the lift of her fine needle-headed arrow above her target, through a waving jungle of ropes and masts and timbers ...

She loosed, and tumbled back aboard as two arrows struck her thorax. The scale held one. The other punched into her.

*

Plistias lined up his ship – bow to bow with the enemy navarch, and he had the satisfaction of knowing that whatever happened now, he'd done his best, and most of his ships would escape. Forty or fifty, anyway – enough that the enemy's whole brilliant surprise would be wasted.

He never saw the arrow that hit him – a needlepoint that plunged through his wrist and into his thigh where he gripped the steering oars, and he screamed and stumbled, his weight changed, and his whole vessel trembled as if the ship and not the helmsman were wounded.

His *Golden Demeter* fell off, and he screamed in rage and frustration as he felt the crunch – her oars were fouling against the next ship in line, and with his wrist and leg pinned he couldn't even make himself push the helm back.

The fire on the top of the tower was billowing smoke.

'Gate,' Satyrus said to Memnon and Stratokles.

They nodded – three men against a company of town militia. Then they raced along the walls, all three of them now carrying town shields. The gate was between the next two towers, and it was closed. There was fighting in the courtyard behind it – Achilles and Odysseus and Ajax, back to back to back, with twenty men around them in the yard, and four or five already down. The three mercenaries were careful, cautious – only the most over-exposed man was taken down.

Memnon didn't say anything – he simply ran down the steps by the gate, and into the back of the press, screaming a war cry.

Stratokles ignored him. 'Gate!' he roared.

Satyrus looked at him. In the courtyard, Ajax fell.

'All or nothing, Satyrus!' Stratokles said.

Satyrus knew the man was, for once, telling the truth. But it was all he could do to turn his back on the four men – four thugs he'd come to love.

But he did.

He got a shoulder under the spokes of the main drum and Stratokles got under the other. It was a six-man job.

There was no time.

Someone shouted from the other tower. An alarm bell began to ring. And another.

The bars moved by a fraction of a finger's width.

'One – two – three!' Satyrus croaked.

The bars moved – stopped – moved. The sound of a pawl in a gear. *Click.*

'Clear the gate! There's men opening the gate!' shouted a new voice in the courtyard.

A burst of eudaimonia – the sound of Achilles's roar of rage, the shouts of fear and pain ...

Click click click

An arrow that hit his greave – pain translated to strength ...

Click click

'*Get the gate closed!*' from close at hand. A panicked voice.

Click click click click clickclickclickclickclickclickclick!

Satyrus raised his head and an arrow clipped his helmet and there was blood in his nose.

He could *see* Nikephorus at a dead sprint – a stade away.

He whirled as he heard Stratokles shout. The Athenian was sword to sword with a man in full armour, and guards were pouring up both sets of steps to the gate platform.

Satyrus made it to the head of his steps one pace ahead of his adversary, and he risked everything – balance and life and battle – on putting his shoulder into the man's aspis at full tilt, trusting to the man's weight to slow him.

The man fell off the steps, and Satyrus bounced back – lost his footing – rolled over his hips and got his feet under him like a dancer, and came up facing the next man's spear-strike – wide open.

But he missed, and Satyrus had his shield up, shield foot forward – shields locked, cut low – a deep cut into the man's foot and he was down, fouling the steps. Satyrus gave half a step, and then another, and a second spearman came up – a third, bolder than the rest, vaulted to the platform from three steps down.

Stratokles was fighting brilliantly at the head of his steps – he had two men down, and his spear was licking down onto their heads.

Satyrus had two opponents, both off balance. He lunged – shield-foot first, a sliding advance that took him off line as his shield caught his opponent's spearhead and brushed it aside, and Satyrus *punched* with his shield rim, caught the other man in the helmet, took a blow, accurate but weak, in his own side, felt the blood flowing, but he stepped *across* in a pass, and used the rotation of his hips to power the full weight of his back-cut into the man's exposed right side where his partner's shield no longer covered him. He cut neck and helmet together – so that blood exploded from the wound and the helmet's base creased and the man fell back onto the steps.

The men on the steps were looking over their shoulders. And then they were running.

Satyrus heard the footsteps as clearly as if he were listening to the end of a footrace. He felt light-headed – his mouth tasted as if he'd drunk all night.

He stumbled down the steps after his beaten foes.

Achilles stood alone in the courtyard. Not, strictly speaking, alone. Memnon was across his lap, screaming in pain, his intestines all around him. Ajax was face first on top of a dozen other corpses in a little mound, and Odysseus was well off to the side, curled in a fetal ball.

The courtyard was full of dead men, a charnel house of the wreckage of brave young men who had died for their city.

Nikephorus ran through the barely open gate, and behind him, fifty phalangites put their shoulders to the doors and pushed, and the doors – giant edifices of wood, iron and bronze – hit their walls with a crash, and the city was theirs.

Plistias managed to get a new helmsman into the helm. He got a marine to cut the arrow, and he stayed conscious. He got his ship free of the enemy – two fights, a thousand flights of arrows. He was hit again, in the same thigh, and he couldn't walk, and consciousness came and went.

His men were superb, and he had himself carried among the rowers and he gave them heart, and they got clear of the Bosporon second line. By now, the whole estuary was a single mêlée, and friends rammed friends in the smoke of forty burning ships.

He no longer hoped for the escape of fifty ships. Now he hoped for victory, although his losses would be appalling. It no longer mattered. This was the whole fleet of the Bosporons, and if he beat it here – even at the loss of every ship he had …

He felt the chop first, and he peered through the smoke and haze to seaward. His ship had passed all the way down the estuary.

'Command deck,' he told the two marines carrying him, and they lifted him up.

From the slightly greater vantage point, he saw the flash of oars.

He sighed. He didn't have the heart – or the strength – to do more. In one flash, he knew what had happened – what the enemy strategy was, and how it had succeeded.

'Have the bastards taken the town?' he asked his trierarch.

'Gods!' said the man, and he was pale under his helmet. 'Why?'

Plistias glanced over his shoulder. 'Because that means that the hostages are lost,' he said. 'And that,' he pointed with his free arm, 'that there is the fleet of Rhodes.'

Herakles was standing alone when the enemy ships boarded them from both banks of oars, so that the deck was flooded with enemy marines as fast as a sinking ship fills with water.

Melitta – the Bitch Queen, as he thought of her, with no little admiration – had a heavy linen bandage wrapped around her slim torso. She'd stood naked on the deck while two of her barbarians wrapped her after one of them planted a heated axe-head on the wound. She didn't even change her facial expression.

She was next to him when the enemy came, with two of her barbarian chiefs shooting over her. Herakles was young, inexperienced and terrified – but it was obvious even to him that there was nowhere to run.

So he pushed in front of them. He had an aspis – none of them even had a shield.

The enemy marines were fighting their marines amidships, and the oarsmen were coming off the benches – morale was good, and the rowers clearly thought that they were winning. Herakles had time to take all that in with enormous, god-sent clarity, before the first wave of screaming enemy marines hit him.

The three barbarians behind him accepted the shelter of his shield and kept shooting.

Only Lucius stood by him. 'This is going to be bad, son,' he said. He locked his shield into Herakles' own, the gentle tap as they met *almost* reassuring.

His knees were trembling so hard he could scarcely stand.

An oarsman – some clod he'd never even recognised with a nod – leaped off his bench with a long Keltoi shield on his shoulder, and the touch of his hip against Herakles' hip was ... like love. Now they were a line of three.

And then the enemy hit.

Keep your shield up came Lucius's voice in his head, and so he did, through his terror. Spearheads rained on his shield like the pelting of rocks by angry boys and he all but fell, except that Melitta herself was pushing on his back with all her strength. She shot – he felt the arrow go between his legs and his immediate adversary seemed to explode in pain and shrieking – shot in the groin.

As the wounded man went down, his file partner stepped forward. There was a delay – the dying man's arms flailing, his razor-sharp spear threatening his own men – and into that infinite moment of hesitation, Herakles found that he had shot out his own blow, an overhand spear thrust at the file partner, and the spear point went in under the man's helmet and licked out like a wet, red tongue and the man fell across his file partner.

And Herakles straightened his back.

That was not so difficult, he thought. *I am the God of War's son.*

The guards had all fled.

Abraham was an old hand at sieges, and he knew the sounds – the enemy were inside the walls.

He grunted. Hardly the enemy – unless they came and killed all the hostages and raped his sister while they sacked the town.

He got the gates of their house locked. The other hostages were old men, but most of them found clubs or billets of wood.

Outside, in the alley behind the slave's entrance, he heard a voice.

'No ... this house. I paid gold for that information, Satyrus. It must be this house.' The voice was panting, like a man who had run fifty stades.

Satyrus.

'Satyrus!' Abraham shouted.

'Abraham!' he heard.

Abraham laughed until tears ran, and started to dismantle his defences.

'Satyrus of Tanais!' he shouted, and then willing hands helped him lower the bar.

Satyrus was covered in blood. Blood dripped off his sword, and down his sword arm from his elbow, and he had a wound under his right arm that seemed to be running down his right thigh from under his thorax.

Behind him were twenty soldiers, and Stratokles the informer, who Abraham usually thought of as an enemy.

Satyrus came and put an arm around his neck, blood and all.

But his eyes were elsewhere. 'Abraham!' he said.

Abraham laughed for the sheer joy of it.

He turned – all those men needed water and food, he could see – and saw his sister standing in the doorway of the garden, framed by the trellis that held the house roses. She had a sword in her hand, too – and she seemed to have been hit by an axe.

If Abraham had not already known, nothing could have kept him from reading the moment. Neither Satyrus nor Miriam had eyes for anyone else. And then, as if it was the most usual thing in the world, Satyrus handed his dripping, sticky sword to Abraham.

'Hold this, if you would,' he said.

Abraham took it.

Satyrus stepped forward and gathered Miriam into his arms. She raised her face, and the soldiers began to cheer – they were, after all, soldiers.

Stratokles produced a cloth and took Satyrus's sword. He laughed. 'So this is what we came for,' he said. He shook his head. 'Poseidon's balls.' He laughed.

Ten stades out beyond the estuary, Plistias of Cos swam in and out of consciousness in a chair by the helmsman of his *Golden Demeter*. He had three wounds, and none of them were mortal, but the combination kept him in pain – too much pain to function.

But south and west, fourteen of his heaviest ships had cut their way through the disaster – fourteen ships saved from the Bosporons and the Rhodians. On them, he could rebuild his fleet. Demetrios still held Athens, and the Athenian fleet would yet tip the balance of power.

10

Satyrus would have liked to have swept Miriam away – directly away, to a private bower with a couch, if the gods were in the mood to grant his wishes.

But command seldom functions to the satisfaction of the commander, and having seized Ephesus – the whole of the town except the citadel, and Antigonus's commander had offered to surrender the citadel for a large enough bribe – Satyrus had time to kiss Miriam, apologise for getting blood on her chiton, share some babbled inanities, and then Charmides was peeling his thorax off his torso while Miriam and Stratokles – of all people – poured warm water on the chiton where, blood-soaked, it stuck to his body. The wound under his arm was less than a fingertip deep, but the pain was intense and the bleeding periodic.

Even while he stood, almost naked, on the tiled floor of the bathing room of the villa where the Rhodians had been held, officers came to him. First Nikephorus, reporting on the willingness of the citadel to surrender, and then a report from his sister via Coenus, and hard on his heels a delegation of Rhodian officers eager to see with their own eyes that their hostages were free.

About the time that the chiton came free of his skin, Satyrus received the surrender of the citadel and a scouting report from one of Stratokles' hirelings, a Lesbian mercenary who had taken a party up the road to Magnesia the day before when Nikephorus landed his soldiers. The Lesbian's mission had been to scout towards Antigonus to prevent surprise – coastal rumour placed One Eye close enough that Satyrus and his commanders wanted to be sure.

Satyrus stared at the man – covered in dust, and with circles under his eyes as if he, not Satyrus, had been fighting – and tried to remember his name. Lykeles? Polycrates? Named after some orator – Isokles?

'Pericles,' he said.

The Lesbian bowed – bowed again to Stratokles. 'My lords,' he said.

Stratokles was sitting on a stool, carefully washing Satyrus's wound while Charmides poured wine over his washcloths and Miriam fetched honey. Stratokles looked up from his task.

'Aren't you supposed to be a hundred stades away and moving fast? I could swear you promised me that you and your men were the fastest riders in Asia.' Stratokles raised an eyebrow.

'Lords, we were sent to find Antigonus – what we found was the wreck of Lysimachos. He's on the Magnesia road; he's been defeated by Antigonus and his forces are in rout. He ... begs you to receive him.' Pericles shrugged. 'His words, lord.'

'How far behind is Antigonus?' Satyrus asked.

'His cavalry is right on Lysimachos,' Pericles said. 'I didn't linger to see the truth of it, lord. I left my second with most of my men up the pass.'

Stratokles nodded. 'You've done well,' he said. 'But now I need to know what you gave away.'

Pericles looked stricken. 'Gave away?'

'If Lysimachos is begging us for protection, you told him we were here, eh?' Stratokles asked.

The man flushed. 'I was picked up by a cavalry patrol,' he said. He shrugged. 'My own fault. All I said was that your fleet,' he inclined his head to Satyrus, 'was at Lesbos and might come to the coast of Asia.'

Stratokles nodded. 'Well said. Very well, rest yourself.' He pointed and Miriam ushered the man out.

'Lysimachos?' Satyrus asked. 'Shouldn't he be five hundred stades away?'

Stratokles shrugged. 'He's a damn good general, despite his behaviour to me. He saw what we saw – that Plistias's fleet was the key. Hit the Asian cities from the landward side and draw the teeth of the Antigonids – I'll wager that was his intention. But down here? He's hopelessly over-committed.'

Satyrus turned, caught Anaxagoras's eye. 'I need you to run – run to Melitta. And bring her back. Bring Theron, get any other senior officer you can find. Charmides ... Menedemos just passed through to see the hostages. My compliments, and would he please attend me within the hour. My *best* compliments, mind – we're allies, not overlords.'

He turned to Miriam. 'Despoina, some rough words are about to be exchanged.'

'I've heard rough words,' she said, and looked at him carefully, her eyes largely hidden under her brows.

'Good, I would value your counsel. Right – Stratokles, if you have been in Lysimachos's pay all along, now's the time to tell me.' Satyrus met the Athenian's gaze, and their eyes locked.

Neither flinched.

Stratokles didn't look away. 'He tried to kill me.'

Satyrus nodded. 'Perhaps. But just by chance, Melitta and I and all our ships and all our troops are here, on the coast of Asia, at just the right moment to save Lysimachos. You've served him for two years and you sold him Amastris. See a pattern?'

Stratokles shrugged. 'I agree. I've served him well. But not by intention – by all the gods I swear it.'

'Listen, Stratokles, in a moment my sister will arrive. Then it will be too late. If you made this happen, tell me. I won't let anything happen to you.' Satyrus noticed that he was standing with one arm raised, and this man he didn't really trust was carefully wrapping a linen bandage around his torso. He felt very vulnerable.

'Not guilty,' Stratokles said quietly.

'I'm having a hard time believing you,' Satyrus said.

Miriam laughed. 'How does it matter?' she asked.

Satyrus looked at her and smiled. 'Ahh,' he said. 'I knew you were more than a pretty face.'

Stratokles took a deep breath. 'But—'

Miriam put a hand on his arm. 'I happen to believe you, but in this case, I think your "true" allegiance is meaningless in solving the problem of Lysimachos – at least from Satyrus and Melitta's point of view.'

'You believe him?' Satyrus asked.

'If he served Lysimachos, he'd have made an excuse to ride with these scouts – and you'd have let him.' Miriam crossed her arms, suddenly aware as soldiers began to enter that she was the only woman present, dressed in a single layer of linen, with no wrapping under it.

Satyrus examined Stratokles. 'Well,' he said. 'So, give me your views.'

Stratokles nodded. 'Let me ask – what do you want?'

Satyrus shrugged. 'Miriam,' he said. 'My kingdom of the Bosporus, untrammelled by war.'

Stratokles nodded. 'Then you should load your ships and sail away.'

Satyrus nodded.

'Except ...' Stratokles smiled at his own sense of drama. 'Except that if you play no part in the last act, you can't expect to be included in the settlement – and they *all* covet your kingdom. Lysimachos, Antigonus, Cassander, Demetrios ... all of them.'

Satyrus nodded. 'I can defend my own,' he said.

Stratokles shrugged. 'Of course you can. But wouldn't it be better if you didn't have to? If you wait, war will come to you – your farmers and your vineyards. Or – you pick one to win. Now. And I think you've already made the choice by taking this city. You can save Lysimachos – save his army, save the allies. And name your price.'

Satyrus nodded. 'I've thought this, too.'

'Well, the time is now.' Stratokles nodded. 'If you decide to sail away, I'll come with you. But to be honest' – he gave a wry smile – 'if you elect to save Lysimachos, *please* consider allowing me to be the bearer of the tidings. It would give me a great deal of pleasure to be the means of saving him.'

Satyrus exchanged a look with Miriam.

'Stratokles is actually an honest man,' Miriam said. 'In a terribly bent way.'

Stratokles bowed to her. 'I begin to understand your choice, Satyrus.'

Commotion in the gateway, and Melitta arrived with Scopasis at her side. She embraced her brother, and then Miriam. 'So?' she said. 'You sent me a beautiful messenger, brother.'

Anaxagoras had stripped to run, and he stood there looking like a statue of Apollo.

'Show off,' Satyrus said.

Anaxagoras shrugged. 'I really can't help it,' he said. 'It's hot, and you told me to run.' He nodded at Satyrus. 'What's your excuse?'

Melitta laughed, passed a hand down her lover's back, then stopped herself. 'Tell me,' she said to her brother.

Satyrus took her aside. 'Lysimachos has lost a battle, perhaps just a skirmish, but his army is broken up and he's coming this way over the pass from Magnesia. He asks us for rescue.'

Melitta looked steadily into her brother's eyes. 'Your choice, brother,' she said. 'I made this war for you. You said, "Rescue Miriam".' Melitta's eyes flickered over the still figure of the brown-haired woman. 'She appears rescued. Now you want to save Lysimachos?' She shrugged.

Satyrus acknowledged her point of view with a shake of his head. 'I begin to think it's time to choose a side and see to it that they win.'

'We chose a side in Aegypt.' Melitta shrugged as if to indicate that it hadn't done them any good. 'My side rides the plains and cares nothing for this war. Eh?'

Satyrus nodded. 'Demetrios means to conquer the whole world,' he said.

Melitta smiled. 'Much good it will do him. The world will swallow him. No one but the Sakje know how much world there is.'

Satyrus fingered his beard. In the doorway, Miriam slipped away, and Menedemos of Rhodes bowed to her, eyed her breasts, and then came in. Charmides appeared with plain wool chitons, gave one to Anaxagoras and held out another for Satyrus.

'Satyrus!' Menedemos called. 'You've outdone yourself.'

Satyrus shrugged.

Melitta raised an eyebrow. 'As far as I can tell, Stratokles planned the thing and I did all the fighting,' she said. She flashed Stratokles a smile. 'I may have to think better of you, Athenian. At the very least, I'd rather you were at my side than on the enemy side.'

Stratokles flushed with obvious pleasure – so obvious that Melitta laughed.

'Are you clay in the hands of every handsome woman?' she asked him quietly, looking up at him.

He sighed. 'Now my secrets are discovered.'

Across the room, Menedemos took Satyrus's arm and Satyrus stopped trying to listen in. Instead, he explained about Lysimachos.

The Rhodian nodded. 'And you?' he asked.

Satyrus looked around. Nikephorus was just coming in with Theron. Abraham gave him a nod from the doorway.

Satyrus cleared his throat and clapped his hands, and the room quieted.

'Friends,' he said.

They all turned away from other conversations, and looked at him.

This is power, he thought to himself. *I wonder if I will ever have more than I have today.* He saw young Herakles at the back, and smiled. The boy looked … as if he'd done some growing up.

'First – thanks!' he said. 'Well done, everyone. Diokles? Apollodorus? Casualties?'

Diokles had a wax tablet in his hand.

'*Marathon* is a complete loss – hulled twice. *Ephesian Artemis* and *Pantecapaeaum* badly damaged. On the positive side, we captured sixteen useable hulls: fifteen triremes and a quadreme. Leaving the captures aside, we're short about six hundred rowers from all causes – casualties, illness, desertion.' He paused. 'Sandokes died with *Marathon*.'

Satyrus glanced at Nikephorus – more to tell him he was next than anything else – and looked back at Diokles.

'Please send my praise to every rower. That was a brilliant action, carried out at extreme risk and against odds. And tell them there's loot from the city and shares in the value of the captures – and pay out a silver drachma per man tonight.'

Diokles grinned his old, piratical grin. 'Better than your praises, I'm afraid, Lord.'

Satyrus returned it. 'I remember. Apollodorus?'

The marine shrugged. 'We lost one quarter to one third of our boys. Typical sea fight. I have five hundred marines fit to fight, and another hundred who need a week to recover – or die. If you choose to crew those ships you took, my boys'll be spread thin.'

Satyrus nodded. 'How soon could your fit men march?'

Apollodorus pursed his lips. 'Tomorrow. Not sooner.'

Satyrus looked to Nikephorus. The Greek mercenary nodded. 'Two dead, six wounded, and three thousand spears marching up from the ships now.' He allowed himself a small smile. 'Lord, you and yours did the hard fighting. My lads just held the gate.'

Satyrus flashed on Achilles with Memnon's head in his lap. 'Yes,' he said. He sighed. 'Menedemos?'

'We barely fought. If I have five dead, I'll be surprised. *Summer Rose* took a hit from one of their penteres but she'll be right as rain by tonight.' He shrugged. 'My marines weren't engaged.'

Satyrus glanced around. His fatigue was such that he thought that if he closed his eyes he'd go directly to sleep, and he had so many aches and pains they seemed like a chorus. He really didn't want to make any decisions, and he didn't want their admiration, either. He wanted to go and see Achilles, and he wanted to lie with Miriam ... and sleep.

He looked at Melitta.

She gave him a slow nod.

'Tomorrow at dawn we march east,' Satyrus said. 'It was not my initial plan but we will leave a skeleton guard in the citadel – Rhodian marines, if Menedemos will accept the command. I'll take all my men – marines and phalanx – to rescue Lysimachos. Melitta will see to the fleet. We will send a messenger to Ptolemy – best done by ship. Find Leon. If we can link Lysimachos and Ptolemy ...' Satyrus paused. The die was cast. 'Then we can end this war. And I have come to the decision that the war needs to end.'

The buzz of reaction told him he'd made a popular decision, if not the right one – except Apollodorus, who spat, and left the room; and Stratokles, who met his eye and shrugged.

'Ready for a ride?' Satyrus called to Stratokles. 'Take your scout and ... Charmides, are you fit to ride?'

The young man grinned. 'For anything.'

Stratokles nodded. 'I'd like a good bodyguard and Herakles.' He smiled. 'I'm going to make Lysimachos crawl.'

Satyrus grunted. 'Not too much,' he said. 'I want him to love me.'

Miriam reappeared, dressed as a matron. She gave him a smile, and he treasured it, but he stood, his side screaming in pain, and forced his back straight. 'I lost some men today,' he said to no one in particular. 'I want to see to them. Abraham, will you serve with me? I have ships that need captains.'

Abraham smiled. 'I will serve until One-Eye is done – until there is peace. But then?' He shrugged. Looked at Miriam. 'My father is dead, Satyrus. I am the head of my house. My life is not with you.'

Satyrus smiled. 'I might surprise you. Why not buy a nice house in Tanais? Run your empire from there?'

Abraham tilted his head to one side. 'Planning for the future?'

Satyrus nodded. 'I'd like to marry Miriam, if you'll have me.' He looked at her across the room. 'And if she'll have me, I suppose.' He laughed.

Abraham took a deep breath. 'If my father was alive ...' he said. 'You will become a Jew?' he asked.

Satyrus sighed. 'I can't do this now. I know nothing of being a Jew, Abraham. I say that without judgement. I am a servant of Herakles. I would never be a hollow worshipper of any god. But I would never interfere with your sister's worship.'

Abraham frowned. 'You are right – this is not the time or place. In our religion, she may not wed anyone ... who is not of our kind.'

Satyrus found that his fists were clenched, and he unclenched them. 'Well,' he said. 'I have business.' He took the chlamys that Anaxagoras held out, slipped a sword belt over his shoulder, and made his way to the door, his side twingeing at every step.

'Uh, oh,' Anaxagoras said.

'Herakles my ancestor, give me strength.' Satyrus muttered. 'He's my *friend*.'

Anaxagoras put a hand on Satyrus's shoulder. 'He means to do *good*,' he said. 'You are a pious man who keeps the laws of the gods – would you have him different?'

Satyrus nodded. 'I know what you say is true but that was not unease. That was intransigence.' He shrugged. Apollodorus was leaning outside, drinking wine.

'You don't like my decision,' he said.

Apollodorus shrugged. 'I'm tired of it,' he said. He took another drink.

Satyrus put an arm around the small marine. 'Let's get it over with – for everyone, then.'

Apollodorus nodded. 'I'll fight for that. About the only thing left I'll fight for – except my friends.'

Satyrus looked around. 'You'll know where the wounded are,' he said.

Apollodorus nodded, knocked back another cup of wine. 'That's right. Let's go.'

The three of them made their way through the late afternoon sun, that threatened to grill them through their light wool chitons like herrings or anchovies fresh-caught and seared on an iron skillet.

They climbed to the temple centre. The wounded were in the Asklepion. Satyrus walked among them, trying to cast off the bone-deep fatigue. He let a pair of doctors look at the injury under his arm, and he clasped hands with fifty wounded men. And at last he found Achilles, sitting with Odysseus.

The smaller man had a heavy bandage wrapped around his abdomen and his eyes were the blank eyes of a man with a great deal of opium in him.

Achilles looked up. 'King,' he said.

'Achilles,' Satyrus said. 'I'm sorry. I chose to open the gate.'

Achilles nodded – one short nod, with a variety of meanings. 'Memnon's dead,' he said. 'Ajax hasn't come to. Might be dead, might be fine – no fucking clue. And Odysseus here ... I saw his guts, and I ain't never seen a man recover from that.' He didn't meet Satyrus's eyes.

Apollodorus put a hand on the mercenary's shoulder. 'You don't know me,' he said. 'I'm Apollodorus of Olbia. I'm a priest of the Hero Kineas. Let me help.'

'There was just the four of us,' Achilles said, as if it explained everything.

Apollodorus looked at Satyrus, and his look told Satyrus to walk away.

'You and Memnon and Odysseus and Ajax – you saved us,' Satyrus said.

Apollodorus nodded, as if to say, *That's good, now go away.*

'Who's this Kineas, anyway?' Achilles asked.

'Kineas said that the nobility of the warrior lay in offering to do an ugly job so that other men would not have to,' Apollodorus began. 'He also said that in the eyes of the gods, he who does more is of more worth.' He didn't sound drunk now – his eyes were steady, and he had both of Achilles' shoulders. 'Your friends were men of worth.'

Achilles began to weep.

Satyrus walked away into the evening.

'Don't do something you'll regret,' Anaxagoras said behind him.

'I liked those men, and they're dead.' Satyrus walked to the edge of the restraining wall. Above him was the Temple of Artemis, and the city of Ephesus fell away below his sandals.

'They were professional soldiers,' Anaxagoras said. 'You told us the odds when you laid out who went where. They elected to come with you – for money.'

Satyrus shrugged. 'At least one is dead, now.'

Anaxagoras looked out at the first stars. 'I think you are more injured by Apollodorus than by their deaths,' he said.

Satyrus turned and looked at the man. 'You know, I don't always need the whole fucking truth poured on me. Yes, watching Apollodorus drink himself to courage hurts me, and yes, hearing him be a priest of *my father* frightens me. But I don't really need to talk about it.' He looked out at the night. 'They died so that I could have what *I* wanted – Miriam. What if that's for nothing?'

'Make it for something. Save Lysimachos, defeat Antigonus, end the war.' Anaxagoras shrugged.

'You make it sound simple,' Satyrus said.

'You know where we're standing?' Anaxagoras said. 'The portico of the old Temple of Artemis. Where Heraklitus taught. "War is the king and father of all – some men become kings, and others are made slaves. All of creation is an exchange – fire for earth, and earth for fire."'

Satyrus smiled. 'You are a fucking pedant, anyone ever tell you that?'

Anaxagoras met his smile. 'I'll go a step further and say that if Abraham had guaranteed you your marriage, neither Achilles nor Apollodorus would have hurt you. I tell you this as your friend – she loves you. You love her. It will happen.'

Satyrus felt dirty – bitter, angry and dirty. And he knew that Anaxagoras was right. He took his friend's hand. 'Did I mention that you're an annoying pedant?' he said. He embraced him, and then, unseen by the army and his own increasing horde of sycophants, he slipped into the temple, made sacrifice to Artemis and to Herakles, to Athena and to Aphrodite, and then went down the hill, to the army, to his friends, to the war he had started.

Satyrus slipped into the house virtually unseen, by the simple expedient of walking confidently through his own guards and in through the slave's quarters. The andron was full of officers – Charmides, holding forth on pleasure as a good unto itself, and Diokles, quietly enjoying a cup of wine, Scopasis, his eyes heavy on Melitta, and the queen of the Sakje herself, apparently unaware of how her presence in the andron might affect others, holding forth on naval tactics. At a glance, Satyrus took in that she was a little drunk, and bored – hectoring her audience rather than informing.

He kept going.

He didn't know the house, but all Hellenic houses had a logic of their own, and somewhere behind the andron and near the kitchen would be a broad set of stairs going up to the women's quarters. There was a stone tower, visible from outside – remnant of a pre-Hellenic past, perhaps.

The slaves in the kitchen were surprised at his arrival, but unlike the people in the andron, had no real idea who he was. They were, in the main, off duty. A tall, balding man rose from a cup of wine to bow.

'Lord?' he said, in Syriac-Greek. His accent wasn't heavy, sounded educated.

Satyrus raised a hand in benison and managed a smile. 'I think that the party in the andron needs more wine. Send a man, not a woman, eh?' He smiled to show he was on their side.

The balding man nodded seriously. 'There is a woman there, lord. I do not think she is lewd.'

Satyrus didn't have to push the laugh that came to his throat. 'Not lewd at all, sir,' he said. 'That's the queen of the Assagetae.' He laughed at the picture of what his sister would do to a man who thought she was a flute girl.

'May I have a cup of wine?' he asked; a young girl sprang to fetch one for him. Of course, he'd interrupted their late dinner – and the looks on every slave's face showed him what a day they'd had. The city taken; for slaves, that could be a horror beyond the worst imaginings of a free person. The fact that horror hadn't come to their house had yet to be ... proven.

Satyrus took the time to sit with the balding man, who he had picked out as the major domo. 'You are in charge of the house, I think,' he said.

'Yes, lord.' He inclined his head. 'I am Phoibos.'

'Phoibos, I am Satyrus of Tanais. I will see to it that your oikia suffers no harm.' He accepted a wooden cup of wine.

Phoibos eyed him hesitantly. 'Yes, lord,' he said, but his words suggested anything but certainty.

'Whose house is this, Phoibos?' he asked.

'We serve the great Demetrios, son of Antigonus,' Phoibos said with a certain pride.

Satyrus grinned. 'Tell him, when you next see him, that I insisted that all his possessions be preserved. If anyone offends against you or

any of your people, please inform me yourself. Demetrios and I ...'
Satyrus struggled to name their relationship. 'We are ... hetairoi.'

Phoibos gave a sharp nod. 'Of course, lord.' He sounded as if he
didn't believe a word.

Satyrus got up. 'Do you know where the Lady Miriam is?' he asked.
There was no keeping things from slaves, at any time.

Phoibos nodded. 'She is in her room. Ash, is the Lady Miriam
asleep?'

Another young woman came in. She shook her head. 'Packing,' she
said. 'In the middle of the sodding night— Oh ... your pardon, lord.'
She bobbed a hasty bow.

Satyrus smiled as agreeably as he could manage to the room at large.
'Please – eat your food. I have a few words to say to Lady Miriam.'

Carrying his wooden cup and led up the stairs by young Ash –
Ashniburnipal? Ashlar? Ashnabul? It was a common enough Syria
name-prefix – he sipped his wine and went to stand outside her door.
His hands were shaking.

'Thank you,' he said to the maid, who bowed and hurried back to
her dinner.

Satyrus didn't know whether to knock or simply enter. So he
paused, took three deep breaths, and rattled the beads that hung with
the door curtain.

'Come,' Miriam said, more imperiously than he'd heard her speak
to him.

Satyrus went in.

She was standing between two hampers; large wicker baskets –
good, solid local work, available for a few obols in the market. One
hamper was full.

She looked at him.

He looked at her.

'I came here with nothing,' she said, and shrugged. 'I don't know
where all this came from.'

Satyrus smiled. 'I don't think of you as acquisitive,' he said.

She smiled back. 'You don't know me at all,' she said, and then her
smile vanished. 'Oh,' she said.

'Miriam,' he said, and stopped. The silence between them went on
and on ... uncomfortable, almost unanswerable.

Where is my love of the siege? he asked. In his head.

'You are leaving,' he said, perhaps more harshly than he intended.

'You might at least have brought me a cup of wine, too,' she said. She took a deep breath. 'Yes – yes, I am leaving. Before we do each other a mischief.'

'I love you,' Satyrus said. There it was: the wrong thing, said the wrong way, at the wrong time.

She threw a length of linen cloth into a hamper – somewhat at random, he thought. 'And I love you,' she said. She shrugged. 'It is not ... material ... to the problem.'

Satyrus sighed. 'The problem that you are a Jew and I a gentile?'

'You are a king and I am a foreign merchant's daughter. You are a Hellene and I am not. You are a warrior – I have no time for war. Our ... feelings are nothing but the products of a year of siege.' She sighed. 'I meant to slip away and spare us both this scene.'

Satyrus sat on her bed. 'Perhaps I don't want to be spared,' he said.

She shook her head. 'I'm sorry, Satyrus. I have had time to think and ...'

She had come close enough that all he had to do was stand and gather her in his arms.

So he did.

'No!' she said.

'Really?' he said. He let her go, so that they were standing, body to body, but he with his arms relaxed at his sides. 'Really, no?'

She turned her head away, but her weight continued to rest against his hip.

He sighed. 'Not only do I love you too much to allow you to slip away, but in addition, I will not allow you to pretend that this is my doing. If you say no again, I will walk away. And when I walk away – it will be away.'

'Stop!' she said.

'No. I have come to say my piece, and I will say it. I, too, have had time to think. What I think is that in my kingdom, there are so many flavours of alien and barbarian that you can be whatever you like. Found a synagogue. Make me a Jew. So I say to you – stop making excuses. If you want me, you should have me. If you don't want me – I will endure it. I will, almost without fail, find someone else to love – that is the way with men and women, as old Nestor says in the *Iliad*. But please don't fool yourself with false piety. The gods do not expect us to sacrifice our transitory happiness for some artificial rule – I cannot believe it. What kind of god would make such a demand? I am sorry your father is dead, because alive, I might have brought him round, but dead, he is an insurmountable obstacle.'

Miriam nodded. She reached out and took the wine cup from his hand, and drank most of it. 'When I left my husband,' she said. Then she paused. 'You know I had a husband,' she said.

'Yes,' he said.

'I hated him. Not for some major sin – oh, he was older, and full of himself, but he didn't beat me. He didn't sleep with my handmaidens. He gave me money.' She laughed. 'He was handsome enough,' she said. 'But the thought of spending my life with him chilled my blood. I felt as if I was growing ... *smaller* ... every day. Less of a person. I wasn't a person to him – I was a chattel, like his best bronze lamp and his largest warehouse. He only spoke of me as a conduit to my father. He would introduce me as "Ben Israel's daughter" as if that was a title. He treated me with a dismissive condescension.' She was shaking, and Satyrus stepped forward again and took her hands.

She stepped away and withdrew her hands.

'I left him and fled to my father's house. Remarkably, my mother would have none of me. But my father: he was ... not understanding, but yet ... on my side.' She turned away. 'My father, whose law I was breaking. My mother, who had probably suffered the same at the hands of my father.'

She drank off the rest of the wine.

'I prayed for him to die. He came to the house and took me back – with the same condescension, as if I had left because I had some female brain fever.' She couldn't meet Satyrus's eyes. 'I prayed for him to die. And he died.'

Satyrus wished that there was more wine. He couldn't say anything – that much he knew. Neither to comfort nor remonstrate.

There was turmoil elsewhere in the house. He heard a voice calling his name – it sounded as if it was Apollodorus. *Satyrus.*

Satyrus stood. 'I must be briefer than I intended. Miriam, I am going to make war – to an end. The end. I intend to go to Lysimachos this morning and make him an offer of alliance – and then to back him and Ptolemy until the Antigonids are broken. I have asked your brother to serve. I would ask you to consider either going with your brother, or going to Olbia or Tanais to await the outcome.'

She raised her face. 'I will never wait again,' she said. 'I will be an actor, not the audience.' She stared at her hands. 'That much I have learned.'

In her words, Satyrus heard reason to hope. 'I am a bad man, asking you to come with me to an army camp ...'

She shrugged. 'I will consider it, Satyrus. Go. And if I run to Alexandria ... not everyone lives in a play by Menander. If I choose you ... Oh, Satyrus, I must give up my whole life to have you. Or I can run back to Alexandria, and all I lose is you. Do you understand?'

Satyrus!

'All too well, my dear,' he said. He took her in his arms. 'Cowardice is easy, is it not? I, too, think, *let her go*. The Euxine is full of beautiful young women who will lie in my bed and give me children and not force me to think about my religion – who will bring me land, cities, even. Dowry, soldiers, horses, grain, perhaps even fame. That is *easy*. But you ... you are the thing that is excellent. You are not easy. Merely ... better.'

She smiled. 'Your flattery, sir, is going to be my undoing. And such a very Greek concept.'

Satyrus!

'I think—' Satyrus had another argument to make.

'I think you should shut up,' Miriam said. She put her mouth on his and breathed his breath, twice, a kiss that sent peals of Zeus-sent lightning through his body, and then she was gone. She pushed him sharply away, and was back at her hampers.

'Take the cup,' she said. Her eyes were bright. 'Wine is *not* what I need.'

He walked into the kitchen to find Phoibos remonstrating with Charmides. Curious: the man had protected him, on no real information.

'Here I am, Charmides,' he said.

'Stratokles needs you,' the young man said.

Satyrus hurried down the main hall and past the andron. On the porch, Stratokles and his Latin lieutenant, Lucius, stood with a third man.

'Sorry to wake you, lord,' Stratokles said. He sounded so smug that Satyrus knew that he was not sorry, nor did he think that Satyrus had been asleep.

'It is nothing. What's happening?' he asked.

'I have the citadel. I need your say-so to put Apollodorus and your marines in it. Time is of the essence.' Stratokles looked at Apollodorus, who emerged from the lighted corridor to the dark of the portico, his hair shining under the temple lamp that hung in the arch.

Satyrus nodded. 'Apollodorus?' he asked.

'Ready,' he said. He had drunk too much – that was obvious.

'Charmides, go with Apollodorus. Help him.' He put a hand on the marine's shoulder.

Apollodorus shrugged. 'I'm not drunk. Just pissed off. Thought we were *done*.'

Satyrus stayed close to him. 'Last time pays for all, Apollodorus. We need to see this through – to finish.'

Apollodorus met his glance, and his eyes were hard – they sparkled in the lamplight, remarkably like Miriam's a few minutes before. 'A lot of good men will lie face down in the sand – for ever – so that this can finish.' He belched, and the smell of fish sauce floated across the portico. 'If we sail away to the Bosporus, these busy gentlemen will just have their war without us. Someone will win, and someone will lose. But we – this pretty boy here, you, me, Anaxagoras, Abraham, Diokles – we'll all be *alive*. Draco will father some sons. Your Olbians and your men of Tanais – what do they care? And if the winner decides to come after us? So what?' He looked at Satyrus, and his gaze was as heavy as a branch full of leaves falling in a forest. 'Your sister? What if she dies? Will it be worth that?'

Satyrus didn't have an answer. 'Apollodorus,' he began.

'Girl turn you down?' Apollodorus asked. 'Nice war to make it all better, eh?'

Satyrus had held his temper a long time, and under a variety of situations, and all of Philokles' instructions on the subject were starting to wear thin.

'You are—' he began.

He had pushed forward into his friend's face, and the smaller marine didn't budge by the width of a finger. 'An arse? You bet, *lord*. I'm not a mutineer. I'll go. I'll fight. I might even die. But by all the gods and

206

heroes, and especially by the memory of your father, I have the right to tell you when you are wrong.' He shrugged. 'I don't *know* you are wrong. But I think we're going a campaign too far.' He stepped back. 'Had my say. I'll go to the citadel. Don't fall in love with this bastard,' he jerked his thumb at Stratokles, 'just because you've lost the girl.'

He turned to Charmides. 'Go down to the beach and find the quarter guard. Get them up here – right here in the street, and then wake the next watch and tell them to suck it up. You take command of that watch – understand?'

Charmides snapped a salute.

Apollodorus went back inside.

Lucius laughed. 'Damn, I like him.'

Satyrus smiled. 'Me, too. And I reckon I might have had that coming.'

Lucius pushed past. 'Well, I know the details – I'll go and brief him.' He looked pointedly at Stratokles, as if to say 'see what I do for you?'

Stratokles waited until Lucius was gone. 'Is your strategos there going to be a problem?'

Satyrus gave a wry smile. 'Only if he's right.' He looked at the cloaked figure beside Stratokles. 'Am I going to get an introduction?'

The cloaked man threw the folds of his chlamys back from his head. He had curly black hair and extraordinary good looks – a sort of dark-haired Charmides.

'I am Mithridates of Bithynia,' he said.

Satyrus looked at Stratokles.

'He was in the citadel with the special prisoners,' Stratokles said.

'They were supposed to kill me,' Mithridates said. 'I bought some men and bought a few days – and the gods have provided.' He smiled, and the sharp whiteness of his teeth gleamed in the light of the multi-wicked lamp.

'Bithynia,' Satyrus said, looking at Stratokles.

'His uncle, another Mithridates, is on the throne. Put there by Antigonus when this young sprig was kicked off it for flirting with Lysimachos.' Stratokles grinned. 'He is a major playing piece to fall into our hands. If we strike fast, we can topple his uncle and put him back – and we'll own all the passes from here to Heraklea in one political change.'

'I am not a playing piece,' the young man said.

Satyrus rubbed his chin. 'Stratokles, is there any hour at which you are not plotting? At some point, aren't your hands too full of pieces – like a man winning at poleis? You have me, and Mithridates here, and Herakles, and Banugul, and Lysimachos – if you die, does the world end?'

Stratokles looked at him, and then laughed, a sudden, spontaneous laugh. He laughed a long time.

'I need a cup of wine,' he said. 'I confess you may have a point. But we can't stop now – and if we're going to meet Lysimachos in the morning, it's best to have a plan.'

Satyrus smiled at the young Persian. 'I have a plan. Much of it is the same as your plan. Let's get some sleep.'

Stratokles nodded. 'I could help you with the Jew,' he said, very quietly.

'*No*,' Satyrus said firmly.

Stratokles shrugged. 'Wine, then,' he said.

Satyrus smiled again at the Persian, and then made a beeline for Miriam. But when he got to her room, the hampers were gone, and so was she.

He stood staring at the empty room for as long as it took his heart to slow. He took a deep breath, and then another.

Done. He took a third, tried to imagine a future where Miriam wasn't part of his life and where he cared nothing for where she was or what she thought. In a year, he'd share some other woman's bed – he would, he was sure of it. In two years, he'd be in love.

He took another breath. What she had done was ... well, right. She had done the noble thing.

No, fuck that, Satyrus thought. *I don't want to understand. I want Miriam!*

His thoughts were interrupted by light footsteps on the stair, and his heart pounded again – she'd come back, she'd changed her mind—

'Brother,' Melitta said. She smiled and put a hand on his arm. 'You don't look well.'

'You're drunk,' he said.

'Quite possibly,' she said with a smile, her eyes glittering. 'But I'm not in love, so I'm clearer-headed than you.'

'I'm not in love anymore,' he said. He didn't try and hide his hurt.

'Really?' she asked. She took his hand and led him down the corridor, down the servant's stair and onto the exedra of the woman's quarters. Satyrus caught up an amphora of Chian wine in the kitchen, and the major-domo, quick on his feet, grabbed cups and a mixing bowl and followed them.

The exedra had folding stools, the kind men used in a military camp. Satyrus unfolded a pair of them and sat. The butler poured wine and water, mixed it, and retired.

'I'm tempted to take him with me to run my household,' Satyrus said. 'That man knows his business.'

'I assume that Demetrios executes anyone who isn't up to his standards,' Melitta said.

'Do you know where she is?' Satyrus asked.

Melitta shrugged. 'Yes, but I'm not telling you. Although I am on your side in this, and I will not let the advantages of . . . a relationship fade from her thoughts.'

'So she's on the ships,' Satyrus said.

'Excuse me, brother. I would like to speak to the King of the Bosporus, just for a moment. Not the love-sick Achilles.' Melitta took a cup of wine, lifted it towards the star called Aphrodite, and said, 'To love.'

Satyrus poured a libation and shook his head. 'If I could just speak to her—'

'You already spoke to her. Now speak to me. You are determined to meet with Lysimachos?' She leaned back, her shoulders against the railing of the exedra.

'Yes,' he said.

'Why?' she asked. 'Why not just load the fleet and sail away? I mean, leave Stratokles and his plots and his boy-king. They can have Ephesus. And he's got a small army – more than two thousand mercenaries he raised in Lesbos.'

'I am determined to put Antigonus down,' he said. 'And Demetrios.'

'That's good old-fashioned hubris, brother. You're the petty king of a few cities on the Euxine, several thousand stades from here.' She raised an eyebrow. 'Am I going too fast?'

Satyrus drank some wine. 'I know who I am. And what I am doing.'

Melitta shook her head. 'No. I don't think you do. You are playing as if you are a major player – as if you are Lysimachos or Demetrios.

209

But you are not. And you are spending money like water. For what? You aren't impressing Miriam. You aren't impressing me. I don't care a whit for Demetrios. You can make it personal – he kidnapped you, he tried to kill you – but Stratokles has tried to kill us a dozen times. And now he's your ally. And while I admit that he did a fine job with your rescue, he's not what anyone would call reliable.'

Satyrus tried to muster his arguments … and couldn't. Not in the face of his sister's scarred realism. Much like Apollodorus's view.

'It's what I do,' he said. 'I am a soldier king. I *like* it.'

Melitta shook her head. 'You are lying to yourself, there. You haven't liked it since Rhodes. Rhodes sucked the glory right out. You want to do it so that you can avoid going home, so that you can avoid running the kingdom, which bores you. Why did we take the Bosporus, if neither of us wants it? Eh? Is it possible that Heron really was the better king?'

Satyrus glared at her. 'No.'

'Well, I admit, we haven't started killing our own farmers yet. But the grain tax this year – so that I could send the fleet here – started some serious grumbling.'

Satyrus was smarting under the accuracy of her statements and the futility of life, as he saw it that moment. But he took a deep breath and faced it. 'Right now, however trivial you and I are to the great game, we hold a mighty city and the balance of power between Antigonus and Lysimachos. If I walk away, Antigonus will triumph.'

Melitta nodded. 'And if you stay, he will triumph just as surely. If you stay, I will not stay with you. My clans need me. There are, believe it or not, people on the plains who do not love me, and seek to make trouble for me, and I am here, rescuing you. Taking part in your ambitious schemes. For the second summer in a row. I will sail away, and take the fleet – at least, the part of the fleet that is paid for by my gold.'

'Anaxagoras will be sad,' Satyrus said.

'And yet I will go.' She shrugged.

'Have you asked him to go with you?' Satyrus asked.

'He said that he would do as you do,' she answered.

Satyrus sat, his back against the main wall of the house, and sipped wine, and watched the stars.

'If you come with me, you will have time at Tanais to talk to

Miriam – where we have a home, a palace, streams and mountains and places to make love. Come, brother. Come back to the real world. Leave the war to the men who want it.' She finished her wine and stood, a trifle unsteady.

Satyrus was angry – a rare emotion for him. 'What if I tell you that it is not your business?' he asked. 'I don't need to be *rescued*. I don't need your help with Miriam – who is done with me. Perhaps, in time, you can find me a nice Sakje lady with a thousand-horse dowry.'

Melitta shook her head. 'I have made you angry.'

Satyrus took a breath. 'No, I was angry before you started. I'm still angry. I agree, honey bee. In so many ways. But I'll see this through, and our kingdom – and all the kingdoms – will be better for it. I listened to Apollodorus tonight; he spoke as a priest of the hero Kineas. You know that? And he quoted something our father said – that the only virtue in a soldier is that he does what he does so that others do not have to. I have thought of it all evening. I will help Lysimachos finish Antigonus – so that others do not have to. Keep the war here – let it never come to the north.'

She shrugged. 'I thought you'd say that. Myself, I don't think they'll ever come to the north, either way. I think Demetrios lost his chance at Rhodes. You've done your part. I've done mine. Let's get off the stage.'

Satyrus shrugged back. 'Is that what we learned from Philokles and Mother? From Theron and Coenus? To walk away? Is that excellence, Melitta?'

Melitta crossed to the door. 'Perhaps not, but you and I could grow old and die on our beds, surrounded by people who love us, having built something to *last*. Or you can die here, fighting Antigonus. Is that *excellent*?'

As soon as she spoke, Satyrus could tell she regretted it.

'I didn't mean to say that,' she said. She shrugged once more. 'Besides, what is that but the choice of Achilles?'

'And look what it got him,' Satyrus said. 'Have you had dreams?'

She looked away. 'Premonitions, yes.'

Satyrus nodded. 'Then rule well when I am dead, sister. Make Anaxagoras king. He will be a good one. You have a son – he is my heir as well as yours. I will go and meet Lysimachos. If you say I will die, well, perhaps I will die. For, by Herakles my ancestor, I am determined to do this.'

Melitta stopped in the door. 'You *fool*. You are the one *breaking* our oath. Our sacred oath! Given at Heraklea with the gods and furies all around us! You are allying yourself with Cassander and Stratokles – who *killed our mother* – against Antigonus and Demetrios. Of course you will die! You are fighting against the furies!' She pushed through the curtain and was gone.

Satyrus stood staring out to sea for as long as it took to drink another cup of wine.

11

A slave woke Satyrus when the sun was fully above the rim of the world. He rose with the feeling of impending doom, and said prayers in the household alcove with Apollodorus and two slaves – the only others up to greet the sun.

'Garrison's in the citadel,' Apollodorus said tersely. 'I left Draco in command.'

'I told you to take command,' Satyrus said.

'You aren't allowed out without a keeper,' Apollodorus said. 'Your sister's orders.'

'Where is she?' Satyrus asked.

Apollodorus pointed. Out in the bay, one of the squadrons was just getting clear of the beach.

'Diokles is to stay to keep you clear of Antigonid ships,' Apollodorus said. 'Melitta is taking the main fleet back to the Propontus.'

'So she told me last night,' Satyrus said. 'I see Scopasis.'

'He told her she was wrong and stayed to help you. He brought another forty Sakje – ten ships' worth of archers.' Apollodorus shook his head. 'She made quite a scene. You slept through it.'

'Poor Melitta,' he said. Scopasis was a big man, and his eyes were blank. He had been an outlaw. And he looked it.

'You had other things on your mind last night,' Anaxagoras said, emerging from the courtyard. 'Melitta said she'd try to talk sense into you.'

'Hmm. If you agree with her, why didn't you go with her?' Satyrus asked.

Anaxagoras raised an eyebrow. 'Did I say that I agreed? I simply said that I would abide by your decision. Look, here I am. You know that she took Miriam?'

Satyrus had intended to try and remonstrate with Miriam one more time – and there she was, sailing away. 'I knew last night.'

'She left you all the fighting trierarchs and all her marines. She'll leave a squadron in the Propontus.' He grinned. 'Just for the record, I think she's wrong. I think we have to do this.'

Now he was being ushered out the door by his staff, who were working efficiently and who were, he could tell, all too aware of his feelings. That alone made him angry – that and the feeling of being cosseted.

The butler stood in the doorway, wearing a plain linen chiton and holding a staff. He bowed deeply.

Satyrus nodded to him. 'You like it here?' he asked.

The man raised an eyebrow – a very expressive eyebrow, which suggested that no man, no matter how comfortable, could 'like' slavery.

'If you will come and run my military household, I'll free you on the spot. Today. I'll leave your price for Demetrios.' Satyrus thought that this might be the way to propitiate the gods. Or simply to do something worthy. This morning, death seemed very near.

The man bowed. 'Lord, I am your man,' he said.

Satyrus nodded to Charmides. 'See to it. Install him as my butler and have him arrange for a tent and military equipage. A dozen slaves to do the work. I expect this to be a long campaign, friends. Get what you need here.'

Charmides nodded. 'As you say, lord.'

Satyrus nodded at the young man. Charmides reminded him of someone – especially when he was grave and dignified like this. Satyrus stared at him a moment, and took a steadying breath. He was in an odd mood this morning.

Out in the street there were a dozen horses – excellent horses. Expensive Persian horses.

Achilles was mounted on one.

Satyrus put aside his emotional confusion at the look on Achilles' face. The schooled emptiness. He went up and took his hand. 'You don't have to come,' he said.

Achilles shrugged. 'Do we have a contract, or not?' he said, his voice dead.

Satyrus flinched at the voice, but he nodded.

Stratokles was the last officer to join them. He looked old.

'Too much wine?' Satyrus asked.

Stratokles swung onto his mare's back with easy agility. 'Or not enough,' he said.

Outside the gates, they picked up an escort – twenty-four of Apollodorus's marines who could ride, each with his infantry equipment hung from his back, with a pair of javelins and a spear. Satyrus, reared to the standards of the Sakje, thought they might just be the worst troop of cavalry he'd ever seen – at least one man had no notion of how to handle a trot, and when they took their first rest, forty stades from the city, most of the men slid from their horses and walked like porne after a night at a wild symposium. Nor did most of them have any sense of horse management; Satyrus had to catch a young mare himself, and then he found himself giving one of the phylarchs – Lykaeaus, from *Olbia* – a lesson in how to set a picket line and how to hobble a horse.

Satyrus found that his preoccupation with his escort had a positive side – he crested the ridge of the Paktyes Mountains behind Ephesus and found that he hadn't thought about Miriam or Lysimachos in hours.

He found that he was quite angry at Melitta. Nor did he want to discuss his anger – rather, he wanted to treasure it, almost as if he enjoyed it. Upon examination, that seemed an unworthy approach.

And Miriam.

Lots to be angry at, really.

How could she refuse him? He didn't think her feelings for him were abated by the width of a knife's edge. So why? Because her father was dead? Because Abraham would disapprove? Because she was a Jew?

Satyrus made a note to himself to learn more about the beliefs of the Jews.

'Cavalry in the next gully – sixty or more,' said Lucius, trotting back. 'Unless they're complete ninnies, they saw us crest the ridge.'

Satyrus snapped out of his blackness. 'I'd rather not get in a fight right now,' he said, flicking his eyes over their escort.

Lucius grinned. 'That's both of us, lord.'

Satyrus glanced back at Anaxagoras, who was riding better than he usually did – but not much better. 'My sister might at least have left us *all* of her Sakje,' he called.

Anaxagoras reined in and sat back with a groan. 'I can't dismount. I might not ever get up again.'

'Here come a pair of them,' Lucius said.

Satyrus pointed at Lykaeaus, who could ride well enough, and Lucius. 'Be careful, Lucius,' he said. 'They'll be afraid and desperate.'

As Lucius trotted toward the two riders, Stratokles pulled up beside him. 'My man,' he said. He smiled, but his eyes were hard. 'Mine! Hands off.'

Satyrus grinned, happy for once to have annoyed the informer. 'Of course,' he said, in a tone calculated to mean the opposite. 'Although you seem free enough in giving orders to *my* men.'

Stratokles shrugged. 'You have so many. I have one.'

Satyrus was watching Lucius under his hand. He was backing his horse carefully, talking and pointing, but refusing to let his mount close enough to the other two for a javelin throw.

'He's a good one, though,' Satyrus said.

'You don't know the half,' Stratokles said.

Satyrus laughed. 'You know, if you don't watch yourself, I could start liking you, too,' he said.

Stratokles loosened the sword in his sheath. The wordplay ended as the situation worsened. 'I don't like this.'

Lucius whirled his horse and cantered for them, Lykaeaus at his heels.

'Form up,' Apollodorus ordered.

Apollodorus had drilled his men, and they surprised Satyrus by dismounting and forming on foot, with four men told off as horse holders. Bows appeared.

Satyrus nodded to Stratokles. 'Going to stay mounted?'

Stratokles agreed with a jut of the chin. 'If they come at us?'

Satyrus swung up to get a better view, clamping his mare's back with his knees, and made a motion with his hand. 'We go right.'

Lucius arrived in a local cloud of dust, and Lykaeaus dismounted and threw his reins to his horse holder.

'Not Lysimachos's men. Those are Antigonus's men.' He spat.

Apollodorus trotted over. 'Lord?'

Satyrus regretted a number of things, and one of them was not bringing a hundred marines. He looked at Stratokles, who shrugged. 'Yesterday, we were in contact. Today, the noose is closed.'

'I need to see ... by Herakles, I need to get through these men. Will they charge us?' he asked.

Lucius nodded. 'There's fifty or more of them. They think we're beaten.'

Satyrus turned. 'Lykaeaus – back to Ephesus. The whole army – now. Nikephorus in command, the full phalanx – everything we have. Leave a hundred marines in the citadel.'

'Antigonus has at least forty thousand men,' Stratokles said.

'And I have four thousand. I'm not planning to go down onto the plains. I'm planning to extricate Lysimachos.' He pointed at the dust cloud in the centre of the valley, off toward Magnesia. 'That must be him.'

'He may surrender,' Apollodorus said,

Stratokles looked at Satyrus, and his face showed his thoughts. 'Lucius?' he asked. The Latin turned his horse. They walked a few steps aside and had a hurried conversation.

Satyrus was watching the Antigonid officer. He was pointing out something to his prodromoi.

'How many bows, Apollodorus?' he asked.

'Six,' Apollodorus said.

'No time like the present,' Satyrus said. 'See if you can blunt him and kill some horses.' He turned back to Anaxagoras and Stratokles. 'The moment is now. I should have brought the whole army. Either we extricate Lysimachos ... or board the ships and leave. That's what it comes down to. I plan to save the bastard.'

The six archers jogged forward a few horse lengths and began to shoot.

Their first arrows had no effect. As they overshot the enemy scouts, it seemed possible that the prodromoi never saw the shafts fall. But somewhere around the fourth or fifth arrow, a barbed point went deep into the rump of a horse, which immediately threw its rider, and by luck of the will of the gods, the seventh arrow fell into the shoulder of the enemy officer. He fell like a sack of sand, and suddenly his command dissolved, men trying to rescue him, a phylarch yelling for them to rally ...

'If I had a troop of real cavalry, I could end this fight right now,' Satyrus said.

'Since you've been bold enough to commit your army,' Stratokles said, 'I feel I must do the same. As soon as we can, Lucius and I will ride for Lysimachos. To tell him to push this way.' He hesitated. 'If you trust me to do it.'

Satyrus was watching the enemy. 'I guess I have to,' he said. His scale corselet was weighing on him and the day was hot and his horse was too small for a long fight. He rather fancied the look of the enemy commander's horse, currently cropping grass by its prone master. He turned and gave Stratokles a smile and his hand. 'May the gods go with you, Stratokles. If you've planned all this ... well, you are more cunning than Athena.'

Stratokles laughed. 'I wish,' he said. 'Will you flank them?'

Satyrus caught Achilles' eye. The big man was still mounted, watching the developing fight carefully. 'We'll all go right together. If you can ride clear, just keep going.'

Satyrus noted that a phylarch had at least half of the enemy troopers in hand and moving forward. His archers were shooting cautiously. At this range, and now that they were warned, the enemy cavalrymen could watch the shafts coming in, and avoid them. Mostly. As he watched, another man fell from his saddle.

'Half done!' shouted the lead archer, indicating his quiver.

Satyrus trotted to Apollodorus. 'When they charge, we'll go hard right,' he said. 'Try and split them.'

Apollodorus nodded. 'Why don't you just ride clear?'

Satyrus frowned. 'Because I will not leave my men.'

Apollodorus shook his head. 'There's some illogic there.'

Anaxagoras spat. 'At least I have my feet under me,' he said.

'Here they come!' called a hoplite, and then all of the archers were sprinting for the line of spears. Every man in the line had a shield – the smaller Macedonian aspis. The line was only two deep, but with a deep pile of rocks – the result of an avalanche – on their left, they were solid enough.

Satyrus rode back to Achilles, Lucius and Stratokles. 'Ready? Follow me.' He rode off to the right, cantering around a copse of old oaks that briefly hid them from the Antigonid cavalry.

The enemy made a simple mistake – they were cautious when boldness would have saved them time and casualties. Their cavalry came on slowly, trotting from cover to cover. Satyrus thought that they were almost certainly mercenaries, and perhaps hadn't been paid recently. Despite overwhelming numbers, they were casualty-averse to a surprising degree.

As was so often the case in war, their caution cost them. The archers began to shoot again, the range closed, and they were loosing flat. The shafts aimed with care – and horses began to fall.

Twenty horse lengths out, and every arrow seemed to take its toll.

Satyrus had both succeeded and failed, in that his inexperienced opponent hadn't even noticed his flanking motion – four men weren't enough – but now they were coming in unopposed, and Satyrus, at least, had a bow and a lifetime of training in its use. He cantered along, riding downhill, diagonal to the enemy approach, and his small mare responded well to his knees, and he began to shoot. Five arrows caught at least two targets, and still they hadn't noticed him. He pushed in closer, changed direction so that he was riding with them, and when their flank group paused in the cover of the oaks, he reined in and shot at point-blank – emptied two saddles, and *then* they realised that he was not on their side.

Achilles cut a man from the saddle when he tried to flank Satyrus.

Satyrus rose on his horse's back and put an arrow in yet another man. There was yelling from the line ahead, and at least a dozen of the enemy cavalrymen were turning towards the two of them.

Satyrus assumed that Stratokles had already ridden clear, and he turned his horse's head and ran for the next patch of oaks, turning in his seat to flip an arrow over his shoulder like a true Sakje. His shaft was over-hasty, but it gave pause to the man behind him.

Satyrus felt his horse stumble – he reacted on rider's instinct; sliding from the stricken animal before he fully understood that the little mare had a javelin in her side. He hit the ground well enough, but his quiver caught between his legs and he was down, bow thrown from his hand, arrows everywhere.

He rolled, avoiding the lance that he had to expect in the next heartbeat, and he heard the hooves, rolled again and stumbled to his feet, but his pursuer was lying in a pool of his own blood with Stratokles' javelin in his guts, and the Athenian was riding beautifully, galloping clear after a good throw. Even as Satyrus watched, he collected the horse of a downed enemy and came back towards Satyrus.

Achilles and Lucius were holding their own, splitting half a dozen enemies and dispatching them as if they practised together every day.

Satyrus had the time to reverse the gorytos where it had tangled, get it out from between his legs, gather a fistful of arrows and drop them in the top, and find his bow – an aeon of time in a fight. He placed a shaft in a young man hanging back from the mounted fight, and Stratokles raced by the back of the fight, threw a javelin; he threw flat and hard, and Satyrus had seldom seen a man throw mounted with such accuracy.

Then he ran for the horse Stratokles had dropped off. This horse was a big gelding with odd spots – almost like a wild pony made into warhorse size. He got a hand on the reins before the gelding shied, and he almost lost his new mount right then, but he got a hand on its nose and began to murmur, and then, before the big horse had time to think about it, he had a leg over and he was up, blessing the long practice he and his sister had of riding strange horses at all hours, and he was away across the grass, headed downhill to where Achilles, Stratokles and Lucius were facing four men, sword to sword and javelin to javelin.

Lucius was down – unwounded, but his horse was running free.

Satyrus punched into the back of the knot of mounted men, and his sword licked out and caught the man whose spear was about to finish Lucius, and they broke.

Satyrus had no notion of how his bodyguard and friends were doing – the oak woods hid the main action, and he pursued his broken opponents downhill, away from the fighting.

He didn't go far – these men weren't coming back. He turned his horse the big gelding was a natural warhorse, and wanted no part of turning. Satyrus used the reins, hard the bit was soft, leather or bone, like a Sakje bit, and the gelding didn't feel a lot of need to respond. They plunged downhill.

Satyrus was carried a stade or more before he got the gelding's head turned. Achilles was right at his shoulder.

'Are you insane?' the big man asked.

Satyrus shook his head. 'This big idiot is,' he said. He started uphill, and Achilles stuck with him.

The line still stood. Satyrus could see them now, standing at the top of the pass. There was a hummock of dead cavalrymen and horses in front of them, and the rest of the enemy cavalry were spread across the pass.

Satyrus pointed them out. 'As long as they don't have bows,' he said quietly. He and Achilles rode up the centre of the deep valley, unimpeded, for two stades.

By then, Apollodorus's men were gathering their javelins and cutting the throats of the wounded, or dragging them to shelter. Apollodorus had a Syrian man over his shoulder when Satyrus rode up, and he grunted, put the man in the shade, and began to give him water.

They had six prisoners, all of them wounded.

'Lydians,' Apollodorus said, when Satyrus had dismounted. 'Mercenary officers, all militia from the towns.'

Satyrus nodded. 'Thank the gods,' he said.

'Almost had us anyway,' Apollodorus said.

Satyrus was looking for friends. Anaxagoras was giving water to a wounded marine.

'Two dead,' Apollodorus said. 'And an archer wounded. It's the next attack I'm afraid of.'

Satyrus walked around, collecting wineskins and water bottles. 'Achilles, over the ridge there's the pretty little waterfall. Fill them all, please.'

'Bodyguard,' Achilles grunted.

'I won't be dead when you return,' Satyrus said.

Achilles grunted again, but he took the bottles and rode away.

Satyrus got back on his gelding and rode up to the top of the pass, where it was narrowest. From the top, he could see movement down on the valley floor, towards Magnesia, and more on the valley's flanks – twenty stades or more.

He rode back to Apollodorus and Anaxagoras. 'Get everyone up to the top – under the big tree. Pile up rocks – we'll cut the tree when an attack comes.'

'Why not now?' Anaxagoras said.

'Shade,' Apollodorus and Satyrus said together.

Two hours, and the sun was high, stark, and hot. Satyrus and his twenty men were huddled in the shade. There was a good breeze, and all of them had drunk their fill of water.

A loose stone wall covered most of the road over the pass. There were shallow pits on the flanks, but the ground was so stony that none of them had managed to get any of their carefully sharpened stakes to sit in the holes, and when they put them in the ground in front of their wall, Satyrus could knock them down with the flat of his hand.

Satyrus looked at the rocks above them – the flanks of the ridge, which towered over his head by a stade, at least. 'We can hold a casual attempt,' he said. 'If they put archers or slingers up there, we're done.'

'I feel like a child playing soldier,' Anaxagoras said. 'We've built our fort and we have a pile of rocks to throw – didn't my father forbid this?' He chuckled.

'Your father forbid this? Mine beat us if we didn't come home with blood under our nails,' Apollodorus said.

'I can see our troops,' Anaxagoras said, and sure enough, there they were – a hundred marines, all mounted on donkeys, and another hundred archers.

The Antigonid cavalry arrived an hour later, and they didn't even try the wall, being dissuaded by the first volley of arrows. The archers rose from cover, but these cavalrymen were professionals, and they'd smelled a rat.

Satyrus watched them under his hand. 'Real troops,' he said.

Achilles nodded. 'Aegema,' he said. 'Or Companions. One of the elite regiments,' he continued. 'Look at their armour.'

Satyrus wasn't minded to allow them to block the pass, either. An hour after their arrival, he estimated there were about two hundred of them. He formed a neat line across the pass — his men in open order, archers in front, ready to form close at a trumpet blast – and moved swiftly down the top of the valley.

The Antigonid officer had never been attacked by infantry, and he hesitated … and lost men as the archers found their range. But he didn't waste any more testing Satyrus's skirmish line – that much he understood. Satyrus reoccupied his initial position without the loss of a man.

Satyrus had his men collect the enemy wounded and all their horses.

Another hour and the Apobatai, Nikephoros's elite, came over the top of the pass, jogging, and came down to form behind his line. Nikephoros was with them, and Delios, their commander.

'You made good time,' Satyrus said. He embraced the mercenary. 'Good thinking, with the donkeys.'

'Eh? That was Charmides,' Nikephoros said. 'I made him stay with the garrison, though.' He looked down the valley. 'Ah, the Aegema.

That's old Coenus, ain't it? He's got no chance with us now.'

'I'm going to push them right down past the trees,' Satyrus said. 'But I thought your boys needed a breather first.'

Nikephoros smiled. 'It's the young,' he said. 'Old men like me can run for ever – it's tomorrow I'll pay, and the next day.'

Satyrus rode up and down his line, briefing his men. They were eager – there was something *personal* about war at this level that was like a tonic, and Satyrus could lead his men in person. He could tell that they liked to have him so close – he called out names, told individuals he was watching their prowess, slapped shoulders, and he fed in return on their admiration.

Apollodorus gave him a sour smile and tipped his helmet back. 'It's fun when you're winning, isn't it?' he asked.

Then they were loping down the hill, the Apobatai all closed up in the centre, the rest of the marines spread across the hillside. This time the Aegema retired as soon as they saw movement. Like good cavalrymen, they stayed just a little more than a bowshot in front, but when they reached the valley floor, they made a dive for Satyrus's flanks, splitting neatly and rolling outwards, only to find that he'd doubled his archers at the flanks and after they lost two men, they retired.

Satyrus pressed them remorselessly after that. 'I'd give anything for twenty Sakje,' he said to Achilles. He remounted his escort – some of them on better horses – but they weren't good enough horsemen to give him the advantage he needed to press his pursuit. The Aegema couldn't close with his line, and he couldn't break them.

Early evening, and the sun ceased to be the enemy. They were ten stades down the road to Magnesia, now. The enemy cavalry had reinforcements, and they'd tried his flanks again, but the Apobatai trained against Sakje – practised charging cavalry, like Alexander's hypaspists had – and they saw the Antigonid cavalry off with a flashing counter-charge.

'If only war were like this all the time,' Satyrus said. 'It's like a good day on the palaestra.'

'Except for the dead men,' Apollodorus said.

Full evening, and the men ate olives and onions and cheese out of their bags and Satyrus watched the enemy command group, about two stades away. He could tell they were the command group – messengers rode in and out.

His own phalanx was over the top of the pass, a dark mass moving down the road behind him. New messengers were coming in across the way, as well.

Nikephorus had picked up a horse. 'He's got some satrapal cavalry, I'd guess – see the men in burnooses?' he asked.

'Persians,' Achilles said. 'Persian nobles. Look at how they ride.'

Anaxagoras was exercising – not because he needed it, he had assured them, but to stretch his riding muscles. 'We will face the Mede? How noble!'

'Only if that man is a fool,' Apollodorus allowed. 'They can't face us without some infantry. We have way too many archers, and as long as this ground is rocky and broken, our marines are their equals.'

'More messengers,' Satyrus said. A dozen men rode up – big men in armour – and suddenly, Satyrus knew he was looking at One-Eye himself.

Antigonus One-Eye was smaller than a mountain, but not much smaller. His armour seemed solid silver, and his white hair flowed under his helmet.

'Uh-oh,' Satyrus said, and smiled. The Aegema commander was getting a piece of his master's mind.

'They're going to break contact,' Apollodorus said.

'Going to attack, you mean,' Anaxagoras said.

Apollodorus nodded. 'When you speak of music, or philosophy, you are the master,' he said. 'Watch those phylarchs. Which way are they looking?'

Before the sun sank another finger's breadth, a herald rode out from the enemy command group.

Satyrus received him just as his phalanx came up, the men panting with the effort after weeks on ships.

'The King of Asia requests your leave to collect his dead,' he said. 'He has some of your men he'll happily trade for ours.'

Satyrus looked at Apollodorus for confirmation. 'We have … sixteen?' he said.

Apollodorus nodded.

Antigonus turned his horse and cantered away in the distance.

'I had hoped to meet your master,' Satyrus said. 'I am Satyrus of Tanais.'

'So we surmised,' the herald said. 'May we assume that you have taken Ephesus? In defiance of the treaty, of gods and men?'

Satyrus smiled. 'I rather think I've taken it with the help of gods and men. But yes, the city and the citadel. In return, may I assume you are breaking contact because Lysimachos is right behind you?'

The herald accepted a cup of water from Anaxagoras and nodded. 'Blast you, yes. We were so close – we had him.'

'Well, now you don't. Nor Ephesus nor a fleet.' Satyrus looked away from the herald to watch Antigonus cantering away. 'I reckon that the King of Asia will find it a whole new war now.'

Antigonus handed a cup of wine to the phylarch. The man had two wounds – in the thigh and neck – so there was no question but that the man had done his job.

'We were never close to breaking them,' the phylarch said. 'Their king was with them, all day – right in the front. They fought like heroes.'

Antigonus nodded. 'That's the way to do it,' he said. 'I thought Lysimachos tried to kill him? And my *son* was making this man his friend?' He shrugged. 'We were close. You may go – see to it your dressings are changed, young man. Narses, give him a horse – his choice. I need men who will fight with a wound in them.'

When the young man was gone, Antigonus groaned. 'Ephesus lost?'

'He may be lying,' Philip, his chief of staff, murmured.

'Really, Philip? And how exactly would he get five thousand men up that pass if he didn't have Ephesus? If Plistias was *behind* him?' He shook his head. 'One day. One arse-cunt of a day, and we'd have had fucking Lysimachos and the war would be *over*.'

Philip looked down the valley – twenty stades separated them from Satyrus of Tanais's forces. Lysimachos's routed men were still flowing by. Only his rearguard – led by the man in person – held together. 'Night attack?' he asked.

Antigonus shook his head. 'I've made two mistakes today,' he said gruffly. 'I underestimated a deadly accurate scouting report this morning, telling me that there were fresh forces moving up the pass. And then I bet everything on breaking those forces instead of caving in the flanks of Lysimachos's rearguard.' He shook his head again. 'Philip, sometimes you have to know when Tyche is *not* at your shoulder. All our cavalry is tired. Lysimachos is a wreck. Let him go.'

Philip shook his head. 'You're wrong – now or never. If we're tired, Lysimachos is ten times more tired. He can't stand a concerted attack – and he's still ten stades from these fresh troops.'

Antigonus was tired, and he felt old, and he didn't trust Philip the way he trusted his son – didn't like the man's hectoring tone. He'd been in the saddle since dawn, and he couldn't see leading a night attack from a litter.

'No,' he said.

'I'll lead it myself,' Philip said.

'Give me a cup of wine,' Antigonus said.

'He's just barely keeping it together,' Stratokles said, as soon as he rode up. He looked as if he'd been beaten with rods: tired, with bags under his eyes and his shoulders slumped. 'He asks – begs, really – that you come with some men – just to put heart into his men.'

Apollodorus put a hand on his bridle. 'No,' he said. 'That would be an insane risk.'

Satyrus looked at the last light. 'How far?'

'Ten stades,' Stratokles said.

'Let's see if the Apobatai can live up to their name,' Satyrus said.

'Foolish!' Apollodorus said.

'Shush, now,' Satyrus said. 'I can do this. And I must. I'd appreciate it if you'd trust that I have a strategy.'

Apollodorus shook his head. 'You're haring off after glory,' he said.

Satyrus reined in his temper. 'No,' he said. 'I'm gaining myself an ally. For life.' He looked around his friends and officers. 'This is *not* vainglory. This is politics. I wish to save Lysimachos *myself*. Understand?'

Apollodorus shrugged. 'I understand that I promised your sister – we all did – that we'd keep you from excess.'

Satyrus had to laugh. 'Then she should have stayed to help. Nikephorus?'

The mercenary nodded. 'If we mount all the riders we have sixty men and we can put the rest on the mules. We're wrecked if attacked, though.'

'In the dark?' Anaxagoras asked.

'Want to come?' Satyrus asked, cheerfully.

*

226

Philip carried his point by enough to be allowed to mount a night attack on Lysimachos. Antigonus would not allow him to cross the valley against Satyrus.

'That bastard is snug behind a rock wall,' Antigonus said. 'You'll lose me a hundred troopers – just from horses with broken legs. No. But a stab at Lysimachos – have a go.'

The attack started badly, when his flanking Persian cavalry vanished in the darkness. But his Greek cavalry did better, following a line of withies laid out by an enterprising officer and they burst into Lysimachos's rearguard like furies, slaying right and left. Philip rallied the Greek cavalry and the troop of the Companions he'd committed, and paused to send prodromoi to learn where the next line was – if there was a next line.

Then a band of barbarians charged his Companions – they emerged screaming from the dark, undaunted by the cavalry, with tattoos and enormous two-handed swords, and the whole fight went bad. When he fell back and sounded the rally trumpet, *all* of his cavalrymen retreated. Suddenly they'd abandoned the enemy camp – and they ran onto enemy forces moving in the dark, and his satrapal levies panicked and broke.

'Damn it, you fools, we're winning!' he screamed at their backs.

Moments later and the barbarians were dead or in flight – Thracians, he thought. But he'd lost control, always fragile in the dark, and he was a canny old hound and he knew when a night attack was a lost cause.

'There's Greek regulars out there by the olive trees,' said a scout. 'They ran off the Medes, and now they're working around our flank.'

Philip sent the scout back, sent a half-dozen Aegema with him, and waited, blowing the rally.

After a few minutes, it suddenly occurred to him that his trumpet call was giving the enemy a focus.

His prodromoi officer came back with an arrow in his side. 'They're coming,' he said. 'Hundreds of them.'

Philip didn't catch another word – the shrill *eleuelaieleuelai* of Greeks came over the broken ground, and his cavalry cantered away, stung with javelins and with their flanks threatened by Thracians.

A stade from his own camp, his rout slowed where the old man had a phalanx out on the open ground in good order, pikes braced.

They stood their ground and the enemy declined the engagement, the barbarians slipping away, the enemy peltasts, if that's what they were, forming at the edge of sight and slipping away.

Philip pulled his helmet off in disgust and rode over to the old man. 'My apologies, lord,' he said tersely.

Antigonus handed him a canteen. 'We gave them too much time. Let them go.'

Philip shook his head. 'It should have worked.'

Antigonus grunted. 'No. It shouldn't.' He slapped Philip on the back. 'I'm an old bastard and I need sleep. But next time I tell you something, just take my word for it. Eh?'

Philip took a long drink of sour wine, and spat.

Two stades away, Satyrus leaned on his remaining spear. At his side stood the Satrap of Thrace, Lysimachos.

'I owe you,' Lysimachos said. 'Gods, that was almost worth the last three days.'

Satyrus nodded, almost invisible in the dark. 'So ... can you take some straight talk? Ally?'

Lysimachos nodded, grunted. 'I like to think I'm famous for it.'

Satyrus opened his canteen, drank the vinegar, honey and water, and handed it to the Satrap of Thrace. 'No advance north of Heraklea. No dicking about at Sinope. No troops in the Sakje hinterland – and I'll know in hours, won't I? No more playing at assassination. You and me – we'll be allies. My sister will watch you like a hawk, and if I die, she'll make you a bad enemy.'

Lysimachos coughed. 'It was Cassander wanted you dead. He thought that if you and Stratokles joined forces ...' They turned, as if by common consent, and began walking back towards the pass. 'I understand the joke. You *did* join forces, and the result was my rescue.' He shrugged. 'It was never personal.'

Satyrus's voice was hard. 'It'll be fairly personal if you have me killed now. I'm just hoping you understand that. If the western Assagetae went into the Getae and Bastarnae, you'd lose all of Thrace – at least as long as the tribal fighting went on. To say nothing of what the fleet would do to your shipping.'

'What do you want me to say?' Lysimachos said. 'I'm in the wrong. And you've saved my arse anyway.'

It occurred to Satyrus – sent by the gods, or perhaps something worse – that they were alone in the dark, and that he was almost certainly fresher and a better hand-to hand fighter. That he could put Lysimachos down, and probably take his army. Perhaps take Thrace.

'When we reach Ephesus, I would like you to swear to Artemis to be my ally. I will swear, as well.' Satyrus paused.

'That's it?' Lysimachos said.

Satyrus was tempted to explain. But then he shook his head, covered by the darkness. Lysimachos was another kind of man, more like Stratokles than like Satyrus, and there was little ground between them.

'That's it,' he said.

12

'We can't hold Ephesus,' Satyrus admitted. They'd fallen back on the city, with Satyrus's fresh troops as the rearguard. Antigonus hadn't even followed them over the pass.

Lysimachos stared out to sea. 'I thought that you had a fleet,' he said.

'I never had enough of a fleet to transport your army,' Satyrus said. 'Antigonus is going to march back to Magnesia and north over the high passes to cut us off from Phrygia and Heraklea.'

Nikephorus pointed at the hastily drawn chart on the table with a meat skewer. 'South to Ptolemy,' he said.

Diokles shook his head. 'The word I have is that Ptolemy is almost back to Aegypt,' he said.

Satyrus nodded. 'That's what Melitta said, and I have a message from Leon to the same effect.' He shook his head. 'It's as if both sides are under a curse, never to get the accumulation of strength they need to break the deadlock.' He looked at Lysimachos. 'I fear that we are about to join you in retreat.'

'Ares,' Lysimachos said, and shook his head. 'If he cuts north from Magnesia, he's on the hub of the wheel, and we're on the rim. We'll have further to go.'

Nikephorus nodded. 'Luckily, his cavalry isn't worth spit in the mountains. They won't even be faster.'

Lysimachos narrowed his eyes. 'If he gets to Sardis first ...'

Anaxagoras, who had spent the conversation working a haze of red rust from his spearhead, got up, wiped his hands on a towel held by a slave, and admired his work. 'If he gets to Sardis first, we'll be glad that we hold Ephesus,' he said.

'And you are?' Lysimachos asked. His intention – rudeness – was plain.

'Anaxagoras of Corinth, musician and philosopher,' he said. 'And you?'

Apollodorus laughed, and Lysimachos's face grew hot. 'I am the King of Thrace,' he said.

'Splendid. A pleasure to meet you. Shouldn't we be marching?' Anaxagoras asked.

13

Satyrus left Apollodorus as the garrison commander of the citadel with all of his marines – the cream of his infantry, and his best commander. But Apollodorus had clear orders: to hold the city only against the lightest of opposition, and otherwise to board Diokles' ships and sail away.

'If you lose the city, try to operate out of Lesbos – Mytilene or Mythymna will be opposite our operations,' he said.

Diokles laughed. 'I can *take* Lesbos with twenty-five ships and the marines,' he said. 'I could install Abraham as governor,' he said wickedly. Abraham had looted the countryside around Mytilene years before, in another campaign. Diokles looked at Abraham, who didn't really deserve his reputation as a ruthless pirate.

Abraham smiled. 'Whatever you ask,' he said. He looked ten years younger in chiton and chlamys and armour.

'Don't take Lesbos,' Satyrus said. He clasped hands with his navarch and his best friend and Apollodorus, and mounted his horse. He was training his own cavalry escort – Charmides and twenty picked marines – chosen by Apollodorus.

'Don't go playing foot-slogger,' Apollodorus warned.

Satyrus smiled. 'I'll try and be a king,' he said.

Apollodorus flicked his eyes to where the King of Thrace stood with a mounted Thracian bodyguard. 'Not like yon,' he said.

Satyrus smiled, backed his horse a few steps, and turned away with a wave. But he felt a hand on his leg, and reined in, and there was Abraham.

'You are making me ask, and that's not the act of a friend,' Abraham said.

Satyrus shook his head. 'You must already know. Why rub salt in the wound?' He looked around to see who was in earshot, but

Apollodorus – with the look of a man who's been warned off – was taking Diokles up the steps of the citadel.

'I want you to tell me to my face. You think I'm just going to *accept* this?' he asked. He growled through the last few words – very much the terror of the seas he'd been five years before.

Satyrus finally understood that there was a misunderstanding. 'She told me *no*.' He shrugged. 'I offered to marry her.'

Abraham looked as if he'd been kicked. 'She told you *no*?' he said. 'But she's gone!' He looked around somewhat wildly. 'I assumed ... that is, I feared ... Oh, fuck it, Satyrus, I thought she'd gone to live in your tent. She's threatened it to me often enough.'

Satyrus had to laugh, although there was no comedy to the moment. 'I don't have her, brother of my heart if not by birth. She threw my religion in my face and asked me to leave her. I did. I said things that I regret – I told her I could find another, and I lied. I won't find another.' He looked around – Nikephorus was holding a messenger by the arm, restraining him physically, and the world was running on. This was too public, and neither he nor Abraham could say ... everything.

Abraham slammed his fist into his hand. 'That explains your silence, right enough,' he said. 'Where is she?'

Satyrus sighed. 'With Melitta. They were always friends back when they were children.'

Abraham shook his head. 'No note?' he asked.

Satyrus shrugged. 'Brother, I'm as far at sea as you.' He laughed bitterly. 'I guess that was for the best, eh?'

Abraham narrowed his eyes. 'You have it that bad?' he asked.

Satyrus snorted. 'Of course.'

Abraham straightened his shoulders. 'The lord does these things for a purpose,' he said. 'Perhaps there is a purpose to all this.'

Satyrus raised an eyebrow. 'Don't let Diokles and Apollodorus fight,' he said. 'Find us more mercenaries if you can. I have to keep Lysimachos from undoing himself.' He smiled. 'And teach Charmides to ride.'

Abraham looked past his friend at Satyrus's escort. 'Good luck with that,' he said.

*

His escort was tired by the second day, and hard by the fourth. Their riding improved, too, although it was almost a pleasure to watch beautiful, athletic Charmides fail at something. He was not a gifted rider, and he didn't love horses.

Lysimachos's Thracian nobles were excellent cavalrymen, as tough as Sakje – half of them were Getae, the hereditary enemies of the Western Assagetae. They were in the saddle from dawn to dusk, and aside from the handful who acted as bodyguard and couriers, the rest scoured the dusty hills to the north and east.

The army had food, and thanks to the citizens of Ephesus, who would never love them, they had baggage animals and carts, and the army's baggage marched inside a tight square of Lysimachos's most trustworthy phalangites. Satyrus kept his own troops together in one division – four thousand heavy infantry under Nikephorus, another thousand not as good under Stratokles and Herakles, and three hundred archers – armoured archers – under Scopasis, Melitta's guard captain. Many of the archers – not all, but most – were Sakje or Persian, and while they had come as archers on warships, Satyrus found them horses around Ephesus and more horses in the valleys to the north, and every horse gave him another mounted archer; a far, far more valuable warrior. So far, Satyrus had sixty of them mounted.

Horses were rare in this part of Asia. More than that, though, was that mounted archers needed more than one horse per man. At home, on the Sea of Grass, the Assagetae counted a warrior poor if he had only four horses.

The fifth day of the retreat, and the process of breaking camp had become routine. Behind a screen of mounted men and an interior screen of formed infantry, the slaves and lower-class infantrymen struck the tents and the rude shelters that the poorer men built from whatever was to hand. The Thracians built huts – and burned them when they sauntered away.

Scopasis strolled up to Satyrus while he watched a dozen slaves – all his, at a remove – striking his small pavilion that his new butler had purchased – or had made – and loading his gear on a train of donkeys. The man was very good at his job, and freedom made him even better. Phoibos was his name – Apollo had sent him.

He'd paid cash for Satyrus's baggage animals. They got the best. Most of the soldiers had simply taken the animals they needed.

'Lord of the Marching Men,' Scopasis began formally.

Satyrus grinned. The scarred Sakje was a former lover of his sister's, a former outlaw, and one of the hardest men Satyrus had known – as hard as Apollodorus, or worse – and yet, his courtesy was somehow cautious and reticent. 'Scopasis, how are you this morning?'

Scopasis bowed. 'I wish to ask a favour, lord.'

Satyrus had seen that coming. It was written in every line of the man's stance. 'Ask away.'

'I want to take my best – my own men – and leave the column.' He took a breath. 'For a few ... days.'

Satyrus also took a deep breath, held it, counted to ten, and let it go. 'Whatever for?' he asked.

'Horses,' Scopasis said with a shrug. 'Antigonus's men have them. We need them. To be honest, lord, if we do not mount my people, some of them will walk back to the ships.' He shrugged again. 'We do not like to walk.'

Satyrus winced. But he knew that Scopasis wasn't making this up.

'What's your plan?' he asked.

Scopasis laughed.

Satyrus woke to hear the patter of rain on the roof of his tent. Most of Nikephorus's pikemen would have no shelter but the Aeolian coast of Asia was not a damp climate, and he didn't expect the rain to last. He turned over on his bed of fleeces and went back to sleep.

He awoke again to waves of rain – the slashes of water hit his pavilion roof like blows from a stick.

Charmides came in, his light wool chlamys wet through. 'Zeus Hospites. Lord, Lysimachos says we must march.'

Satyrus rubbed his eyes. It was raining so hard that when a gust hit the roof of the pavilion, a fine haze of water appeared inside the tent. 'I'm surprised the pegs didn't pull,' he said.

Charmides smiled. 'There's a dozen slaves standing in the rain holding your lines,' he said.

Satyrus sighed. 'Better the slave of a bad master,' he quoted. 'Need a dry chlamys?'

Charmides shook his head. 'No point.'

'Like that, is it?' Satyrus asked.

An hour later, he was soaked to the skin, head down under a straw hat, riding like a farmer with his seat well back on his horse's rump and his feet dangling. The water wasn't cold, but it was *wet*. Shoots and falls of water decorated the steep hills on either side of the pass they were marching though, and the rocks were shining in the watery sun, and the sky was a pile of dark clouds, stacked one on another as thunderheads came in off the sea and raced inland.

That night, Phoibos shook his head. 'It is *not* dry in there, lord,' he said. He gestured at the pavilion, the lines taut as hawsers between fighting ships, the roof stretched tight. Sheets of rain flowed off it in waves of water. Inside, Phoibos had a smaller tent – almost certainly his own – set up. The inner tent protected Satyrus's bedding.

'I have some deer meat and a cup of wine, lord.' He bowed his head.

'Splendid,' Satyrus said. 'You are a miracle worker. Invite Charmides and Anaxagoras.'

They marvelled at the inner tent, drank their wine, ate skewers of meat, and complained about the weather. Satyrus sent a slave for Nikephorus and Stratokles, and he brought Herakles, all of them soaking wet and muddy to the hip, and Phoibos had them wiped clean in the outer tent.

The inner tent was packed with his friends, all praising Phoibos. The man glowed with the unaccustomed praise.

'We may be merrily dry in here,' Satyrus said, 'but the phalangites are soaked and cold.'

Nikephorus grunted. 'I was soaked and cold myself until you sent a pais.' He shook his head. 'It's unnatural. Never seen rain like this.'

Satyrus nodded. 'We have to march anyway. For all we know, three valleys over, there's no rain.'

Anaxagoras nodded as if this was the wisest thing he'd ever heard. 'Of course,' he said. 'I had never considered this.'

'How many fires are going?' Satyrus asked young Herakles. Charmides leaned forward to speak, and Satyrus shushed him.

'I don't know,' Herakles said. He was just recovering from the misery of being wet through and colder than he could remember being.

'Five? Fifty?' Satyrus asked.

'I don't know,' Herakles repeated.

'Go and find out,' Satyrus said. 'If the men have no fires, they'll be too cold to sleep and too wet to move in the morning, and we'll have desertion. By tomorrow, men will start to die. They are your men.'

Herakles shook his head. 'So what? If they die, we'll hire more.'

Satyrus's eyes seemed to sparkle in the lamplight. 'Out you go, young Herakles. That's an order.'

'It's not fair,' Herakles said. But he got to his feet. Stratokles rose to follow him. Satyrus restrained him.

'Let him learn to be a king,' he said. 'Or at least to be a phylarch.'

Herakles made a thorough job. He came back an hour later. 'Our men have fifty-four fires,' he said. 'More are being lit now. The wood is coming up the pass from the farms below us.'

Satyrus clapped him on the back.

'Well done,' he said, and gave him a cup of wine.

In the morning, the rain was less, but it was still raining, and there were head colds and sneezes throughout the camp. Lysimachos's men had had a worse night, being further from the wood, and they were slow to start. Satyrus's men stood in the rain waiting. Many of them had straw hats and straw cloaks, and Nikephorus's men marched armed and armoured, only their sarissas in the carts. Most of Lysimachos's men marched in their chitons, and they were cold.

'If they have their arms, they have something to sell if they desert,' Lysimachos said. 'Besides, with so many Thracians, I know I won't be surprised.' He had thousands of the barbarians, and they moved like waves, covering the distant ridges and the rocky valley floor. Even in the rain, they glittered with armour and gold.

Satyrus saw no reason to argue. 'When we crest that ridge,' he said pointing north and east, 'we'll see the sea. Then we need to press for Sardis.'

Lysimachos nodded. 'We need to take some time to forage,' he said.

Satyrus grunted. 'You mean, to buy food from farmers? Or just take what you want?'

'This is Antigonus's satrapy,' Lysimachos said. 'We'll take whatever we want.'

'Not that they were ever offered a choice. Why not pay? We'll get better intelligence and leave a friendly populace behind.' Satyrus tipped his hat and watched the water run off it.

Lysimachos looked at him as if he had two heads. 'No one has that kind of money,' he said. 'If we had to buy our supplies, there'd be no war.'

Satyrus just looked at him. Melitta was sounding smarter and smarter.

The eighth day, and Stratokles took Lucius and went ahead to Sardis with a picked troop as an escort. The rain hadn't ended, and Lysimachos's men were deserting. Nikephorus had lost a dozen.

'We need a siege train,' Satyrus mentioned to Jubal. The Nubian grinned. He hadn't played any role in the campaign so far – just ridden quietly with the escort. He was a natural horseman.

'I'll be happy to be at building it,' he said. 'But I'll need a few things: wood, iron, bronze. Some skilled artisans.'

'Sardis,' Satyrus said.

Jubal smiled. 'Sure.'

'Either we'll stop to lay siege, and you'll have to build us some artillery, or they'll open the gates, and you can get what you need.' Satyrus looked at Lysimachos, aware that he was ordering Jubal to take what he needed.

Jubal made a face. 'Sure,' he said. 'Lord.'

But Sardis opened its gates for a cash payment to the commander of the garrison, and Lysimachos kept his men outside. Jubal bought a pair of slave smiths and some metal and a talent in silver's worth of cut and planed wooden beams. He bought wagons and linen tarps coated in linseed oil.

Satyrus bought pots – fire pots, the type his triremes used to keep a fire going all day at sea. He bought every scrap of canvas in the city: every party pavilion, every sail from the fishing boats. A convoy came over the mountains from the seaport with more. He spent a summer's tithes from the Propontus on tentage.

It didn't stop the rain, but it earned him the thanks of the army.

The third morning at Sardis – the eleventh since they had marched from Ephesus – they marched again, just as One-Eye's scouts came over the high pass. Satyrus sent a runner back to Apollodorus ordering him to abandon Ephesus. It wouldn't matter to them – in twelve hours, Antigonus would cut the road.

Satyrus cantered over to Lysimachos, who was watching Antigonus's scouts descending the road behind them. Nikephorus came, and

Stratokles, and two of Lysimachos's Thracian chiefs and Nikeas, his escort commander and right-hand man, and Lucius.

'Two thousand stades from here to Heraklea,' Lysimachos said.

'Most of it through the mountains,' Satyrus said. 'You have a route?'

Lysimachos nodded. 'I planned to go the Royal Road from here,' he said. 'I didn't expect Antigonus to be on our heels.'

Satyrus watched the first formed troops come over the ridge. 'I don't think that the Royal Road is a good option, anyway. Until Plistias recovers, my ships on Lesbos will cover the seaward flank. I'd like to stay in touch with them. I suggest we go north through the mountains to Cyzucus on the Propontus – or to where the road goes east, at least. My ships hold the whole of the straits. From there we can move east by stages with our flanks secure.'

Lysimachos rubbed his beard. 'That means marching through Bithynia. Hostile, very hostile.'

Satyrus waved at Mithridates, rescued from Demetrios at Ephesus. 'Handy that we have a spare King of Bithynia, then, isn't it?' he said.

Lysimachos looked at him. Even Stratokles looked at him with respect.

Satyrus nodded. 'But first – if I may be so bold – we had better brush One-Eye's advance guard back, or they'll be crawling all over us.'

The fight at the fords of the Hermos River was not memorable in any way, except that Anaxagoras told them that the Ionian Greeks had fought the Lydians and Persians here. 'It is in Herodotus,' Anaxagoras said. 'Right here at the bridge – two hundred years ago, give or take a few. The Greeks held, and the Persian satrap was wounded, and the Greeks slipped away.'

'And then they won at Marathon,' Charmides said.

'Hah!' Satyrus put in. 'Not the Ionians. They were tools for the warring powers.'

'Still are,' Stratokles added. 'Too rich.'

'Too soft,' added Lucius.

Charmides narrowed his eyes. 'Now see here ...' he said.

Anaxagoras raised his hands. 'It's history!' he said. 'Not a calculated insult. Besides, didn't you tell me once your father was a Spartan?'

Satyrus turned his head. 'What?' he asked. 'How did a Spartan come to Lesbos?'

Out across the plain, the enemy scouts came forward warily, and behind them came two big squadrons of cavalry and a taxeis of pikemen, marching hard.

Charmides grew red and said nothing.

'Here they come,' Anaxagoras said, and pulled his helmet down. They were manning a barricade of stakes hidden by a line of woven matts with greenery on them – it was hard to arrange an ambush at a frequented ford with no cover for ten stades in any direction.

The scouts came to the river bank opposite but they didn't like what they saw. Ten minutes later, the enemy cavalry pushed into the river, but they didn't cross, and the taxeis halted on the far bank.

Their baggage came up, and they began to make camp.

Satyrus watched them with real respect. 'Antigonus is good,' he said.

Lysimachos, already pulling his best barbarians out of their ambush positions, nodded. 'He's the best of us who are left. Why?'

'He's laid a counter-trap, that's why. We're supposed to make a lunge at this advance guard, so far from his army, no support. But look – cavalry on both ridges.'

Lysimachos nodded. 'I've been duped by him a dozen times, and yet, I swear we could take the taxeis before the cavalry could save them.'

Satyrus shrugged. 'If that's the war we were waging. I thought we were retreating?'

Lysimachos laughed. 'We are, we are.'

Philip, with One-Eye's advance guard, made camp across the water, ready to sell his life dearly.

Satyrus broke contact and rode away behind a screen of Thracians.

And that night, Scopasis appeared in camp. Satyrus had some warning of his coming – the rumble of horse's hooves. His sentries grasped their weapons and stared into the darkness.

He had more than a thousand horses, all told. All his Sakje were mounted, and their horse herd covered the space of the whole of the rest of the camp.

'I hate rain,' Scopasis said. He grinned. 'But it is good for stealing horses.'

'How'd you get so many?' asked Charmides.

'Patience,' Scopasis said.

'Will you teach me?' Charmides asked.

'Yes,' Scopasis said.

The irony – the hand of Tyche, to some – was that Satyrus suddenly had superb cavalry scouts – the best, in fact, in two thousand stades – just as both armies entered the mountains. The plain of Sardis gave way to the rising passes of the Tennon Mountains. The Sakje were penned in with the army, crossing high, wooded passes that narrowed to the width of the tracks that followed them.

But Scopasis seemed determined to scout, so Satyrus sent him far to the north and south, marking alternative passes over the great folds of earth that separated the deep green valleys of Lydia and Mysia.

Behind them, Antigonus pushed his cavalry and light infantry to keep the pressure on.

And in the skies above them, the clouds rolled in from the sea, on and on, so that it seemed to Satyrus, riding up his third steep climb of the day, that he had been wet through for ever. Now he made a practice of riding among Nikephorus's Apobatai, calling out names and asking men for a dry chiton to get a laugh. Sometimes he would dismount, hand his horse to a slave, and march on foot with his own rations in a leather bag – not because the act had any value in itself, but only because the infantry needed to know that he was there.

Five days out of Sardis – when the rain seemed eternal, and the farmers by the road were showing signs of despair at the weather, which was flooding their fields – Satyrus was marching with the Apobatai. He found that the men sharing the trail with him were Lucius, Stratokles and Herakles.

Herakles gave him a look – half reproach, and half a request for praise. 'They told me I had to do this,' he said with a shrug.

He was carrying an oiled linen tarp, a bronze cook pot and the same big leather wallet as Satyrus – although his was covered in ornate bronze work. He was actually carrying the whole marching kit of a hoplite or a phalangite. Behind him stumbled an adolescent boy with his shield and helmet.

Satyrus laughed. 'You're carrying more than I am, lad,' he said.

Herakles smiled.

Satyrus realised that it was the first time he'd seen the boy smile.

He spoiled the effect by panting and then crowing, 'It's easy!' The combination was risible. Satyrus hid his smile, slapped the boy's back, and marched on into the rain.

Two stades up the pass, Stratokles fell in beside him. 'He worships you,' he said.

Satyrus laughed. 'He's an ephebe in a man's body.'

Stratokles shook his head. 'He asks all the time – how does Satyrus do it? What does Satyrus wear?' Stratokles smiled. 'Look at his hat – he had to find the same peasant who made your straw hat.'

Satyrus laughed, but then he nodded his head. 'Everyone needs someone to follow,' he said. 'I had Philokles. The boy could do worse than me.'

Stratokles looked at him and raised an eyebrow. 'You're an arrogant sot, you know that, lord?'

Satyrus nodded. 'If I can't be a model for ephebes as the war-king of the north, what good am I?' he asked.

'Right, then,' said the Athenian. 'I'll just keep him away from Jews, shall I?'

Satyrus counted twenty steps before he allowed himself to answer.

'Sorry,' Stratokles said. 'Meant it as a joke.'

Lucius, trudging along in the rank behind them, laughed. 'The men I've killed because of your so-called sense of humour.'

'Tell me your story, Lucius,' Satyrus said, to pass the time.

The Latin pushed forward, his long legs eating the rocky trail. Now the army was just two abreast, strung out along the passes for twenty stades and more. Satyrus and the Apobatai were the rearguard – except for scouts and archers posted to annoy Antigonus and his vanguard. When Satyrus topped a big ridge, he could see the distant, watery twinkle of iron and bronze. One-Eye.

Lucius turned and looked down the back trail. They were almost last. Satyrus had the strangest feeling, all of a sudden, that he was alone with Stratokles and Lucius and that this was just the sort of carelessness that his sister had warned him against. They weren't really alone – he knew Philos and Miltiades in the clump ahead – but he tried not to be too obvious as he eased his sword in the scabbard – felt it stick, and flicked his glance at Lucius.

The Latin was gazing down the back trail. 'I think Antigonus got up early this morning,' he said.

At the base of the ridge, in the valley they'd just left, a dozen horsemen and a thick column of infantry appeared, trotting strongly right at them.

Satyrus pulled at his sword again, and it came free of the scabbard fitfully, the blade red with rust.

Lucius looked at him. 'Where I'm from, that's a crime,' he said.

Satyrus nodded. 'If my tutor saw me with a rusty sword,' he said. Then he looked into the valley. 'Apobatai!' he called.

Heads turned.

'Philos!' Satyrus called. 'Run up the track and tell Nikephorus to start forming the rearguard – One-Eye's making a grab for us. Look on the heights above us!'

Philos dropped his shield and ran, sprinting up the steep trail with the hoarded energy of the professional soldier.

Lucius was looking at the cliffs above them. 'We're fucked,' he said.

Satyrus was shaking his head. 'I have scouts in every valley!' he said.

'They went over the ridges,' Lucius said. 'Once you climb to the top, moving along isn't that hard.'

Rocks began to roll down on them from the heights.

The first attack was really just a probe – fifty tribesmen of one sort or another, charging out of the rocks.

Satyrus stood his ground between Herakles and Lucius. Herakles was afraid – terrified – and he talked and talked, his young voice carrying over everything. He talked about his mother, and about a contest he'd won – a pitiful story – and about how he wasn't afraid.

'Here they come,' said Lucius. His first words in an hour.

By luck, good or ill, the only determined attackers – a pair of men too young to understand the word feint, or so it seemed to Satyrus – made unerringly for their part of the line while javelins fell like rain. Herakles took a javelin in his shield and stepped back half a step, reached around it to pull it free – and they were on him.

Lucius got one – a simple, brutally well-timed thrust into the man as he ran at them, full tilt. A running man is vulnerable. Most men slow when they hit the shield wall, but not these Mysians. He went down.

Satyrus tried to do the same but Herakles, in his panic, was shuffling and then – full of fear – thrust forward at the tribesman, effectively cutting Satyrus out of the fight.

The enemy spear hit him just over the heart, glanced off his bronze thorax, skipped up his neck, across his face, and past. Herakles caught the shaft – hurt and desperate – and they were face to face, and Herakles' hand went up under his arm as he was trained, caught at his sword hilt – backwards – ripped it clear of his scabbard overhand and thrust it into his attacker's face, by luck or Tyche through an eye, and the enemy – a boy Herakles' own age – went down, and his shade left his body.

The fall of javelins had stopped.

'I killed him!' Herakles said, elated. 'By the gods! I stood my ground!'

Lucius nodded. 'Yep,' he said. He flipped the two dead men over and checked them. They had nothing.

'I-I killed him! Man to man! You saw me, Satyrus!' the young man said, and he almost danced – skipped a little, and his eyes were bright.

'That was the easy part,' Lucius said. 'Now they come at our flanks. Where is Nikephorus?'

Satyrus was on the same message. 'Back!' he told the Apobatai.

'He ... smells like ... a deer.' Herakles was looking at the boy at his feet. The dead boy's lank hair was in his own blood, and flies were already landing on the mass of potential food. Slowly, and with awful certainty, the corpse voided its bowels.

'Oh ... gods!' Herakles said, and threw up on the corpse at his feet.

Lucius had his hair. He stood there until the boy was done, and Satyrus gave him some wine from his pottery canteen.

'I ... killed him,' Herakles said.

Satyrus's eyes met Herakles' eyes. 'We know,' he said, his voice as soothing as a mother's. 'Have some wine.'

'Welcome to the brotherhood of Ares,' Lucius said.

Satyrus slapped the younger man on the shoulder of his armour-yoke. 'Move faster, or you'll lie with him.'

They began to trot up the pass.

More rocks began to fall.

Just short of the top of the pass, they found Philos, dead, his throat cut.

'Uh-oh,' Lucius said.

'Herakles, stand with us,' Satyrus said. 'Right.' He had most of the Apobatai – almost two hundred men. The obvious choice was to form them in the open space at the top of the pass and hold off all comers until Stratokles or Charmides or Nikephorus sensed what was wrong.

Against that solution, the top of the pass was overhung by two big ridges within a stone's throw. The men holding the top of the pass would be bombarded with small rocks and scree – not the end of the world, but annoying. And there was a light fog – almost a haze – as far as Satyrus could see. If his messenger was dead, it could be an hour before Nikephorus inquired.

'Any great ideas?' Lucius asked.

Satyrus found he had the daimon on him, and the smell of wet cat that he hadn't smelled in years. *Perhaps I die here*, he thought. It would be like Herakles to grant his worshippers the time to get their thoughts in order so that they could die like heroes.

'Yes,' he said. He looked around for phylarchs. 'All officers,' he said. 'On me. Form your ranks, gentlemen.'

The phylarchs of the Apobatai gathered around him, and Delios tipped his helmet back, looking around through the haze. 'We can hold here, lord,' he said.

Satyrus shook his head. 'That's just what they want us to do,' he said. 'As soon as all the boys are together, we're going up the ridge – there. Don't point. All together. Men at the flanks will have to scramble and fight. But if we get up there we'll hold. Who has water left?'

No one did.

'There's a stream right there. Every file waters up. Then we go. Phylarchs, take the time to look for your way up.'

'Ares – this will suck,' Delios said. He shook his head. 'But ... you're right. Better to die like lions.'

Satyrus grinned. 'I don't intend to die,' he said. 'I intend to get to the top of that ridge and kill everything I find there.'

Delios wasn't sure if his king was joking. 'Lord?'

Satyrus nodded to all of them. 'Herakles is with us,' he said.

Behind him, he heard young Herakles say to Lucius, 'What does that mean? Is he talking about me?'

'Shush,' said the Latin.

It took for ever for the men to fill their canteens. Arrows fell on them, and javelins, and rocks with increasing frequency as the enemy filled in on the ridge above them – more men on the ridge behind

245

them. Satyrus took a heavy rock on his shield and had to skip to avoid it crushing his ankles.

Somewhere, they had friends, too. Probably the archers out with their morning scouts – there were enemy tribesmen dying up there on the ridge, and arrows going *both* ways.

'I don't get it,' Lucius said. 'Who're those bastards?'

'No idea. Don't look a gift archer in the mouth,' Satyrus said. Louder, he said, 'Dump everything but your canteen and your fighting gear. If you have a long spear, ditch it. If you can get a javelin or two – take them.'

The ranks shuffled as men stripped their food bags. Veterans took a bite of bread, or dropped a ripe fruit down the front of their chitons. Some men dumped everything – some kept everything.

Men were edging forward, eager to start, to get it over with. To get out from under the rain of death. Two men were already down – one with his skull crushed, another with a broken ankle and *then* a crushed skull.

'Wait for it,' Satyrus yelled. Above them, the Mysians were screaming war cries.

Young Herakles shuffled and spat, trying to get the taste of death out of his mouth. Lucius looked bored. Satyrus watched the hills above them, wishing that he could suddenly hear the trumpets of the main column.

It seemed an odd and somewhat pointless place to die. But the smell of wet cat was powerful in his nostrils, and his hands shook with the power of his eudaimonia. He felt the strength of ten men flowing through his hands.

'If this is your last hour,' Satyrus called in his storm-at-sea voice, 'use it to show the gods that you are a hero, not a man.'

The Apobatai, poised on the edge of desperation and defeat, heard him, and their roar of defiance was the sound of a wounded lion, crouched in the thicket, still dangerous.

'At them!' Satyrus roared, and they were away – a mad scramble, rock to rock, and the javelins flew thick and fast, and rocks – almost impossible to climb with an aspis straight-armed over your head. Satyrus got a leg up on a big rock, and something hit him in the exposed hip, and then he was up – no idea how – and instead of slipping down and climbing the next rock, he simply jumped – landed on the peak of the next giant rock, his foot already slipping, and he did it again, running from rock-peak to rock-peak while javelins hit his shield.

He wasn't the only man to run along the top of the rocks instead of picking his way.

He was just the fastest.

He went up the side of the ridge, and three bounds brought him to his first opponent – his balance was already slipping, and the man was below him, and Satyrus put a spear point unerringly into the top of the man's head as he turned to run, right through the top of his skull, and Satyrus leaped again. Now he was on a patch of grass the size of a helmsman's station, and two men stood there, one with a bow and one with an axe. The bowman shot the axe man in the back and died to Satyrus's spear, his eyes still full of the remorse of his panic-driven error. And then the Mysian tribesmen were breaking, running, and the Apobatai hunted them through the rocks to the top of the ridge, until their flight was stiffened by Agrianian javelin men from northern Macedon – professional light infantry, some of them veterans from Alexander's earliest campaigns. There were fifty of them there, and some slingers.

They were professionals, but they didn't have armour, shields, or desperation. Satyrus's men suffered from the slingers – ten men went down in as many casts – but then, out of nowhere, a dozen of his scout-archers appeared higher on the hill and let fly into the back of the Agrianians, and the ridge was taken. The Mysian tribesmen were butchered, thirty of them were taken prisoner, and the Agrianians fought a dogged rearguard action of their own, their javelins outranged by the Sakje bows of the scouts. But they knew cover and they knew how to move, and they slipped away with fewer than a dozen casualties.

Satyrus made the top of the ridge and slumped against a stone. His sword was red with blood and light rust, and when he raised the blade to point out the enemy slingers and call an order, the blood ran untrammelled down the blade and over his hand. He had one more fight – not his choice – when a wounded Mysian chose to die rather than surrender and attempted to take Satyrus with him. Satyrus had to kill him twice, a blow to the head that should have put him down and another that all but severed his head before the man fell at his feet.

And then he slumped against a rock again, the pain in his hip so intense he could barely stand, the sword stuck to his hand with dried blood.

Herakles found him first, gave him water, and then poured water over his sword hand until the dried blood ran away and he could open his hand.

'It's dry here,' Satyrus mumbled. At his feet, he could see Nikephorus coming hard with three hundred pikemen.

'Can you walk, lord?' Herakles asked him.

Satyrus laughed. 'You, too, are a king, lad. You and I don't call each other "lord".'

Herakles looked around. 'Is this ... all there is? Satyrus? Is this all there is to ... to war?' He looked at his feet – crusted with the mud of Ares – blood, excrement and dirt. 'I was *so scared.*'

Lucius came up and put his arm around the young man, and Satyrus drank wine from his canteen and rubbed his hip. The thorax had held, but now that he had time to look, he could see that the rock – he thought it had been a rock – had crushed the flange at the hip right into his skin.

'Help me get this off,' he gasped. The blood was soaking his buttocks and his groin, running down his legs.

He dropped his shield and they unlatched the thorax and folded it off him. He wished for his scale shirt, but it was thousands of stades to the north.

The wound itself was nothing; the rock had crushed the armour, and the corner of the broken bronze had cut his hip deeply and repeatedly with every stride he took – a series of fifty semicircular cuts, every one of which had drawn blood.

'That's going to make a spectacular scar,' Lucius said. 'Can you walk?'

Satyrus shook his head. 'I'll be fine. Dump the thorax – we can't fix it here.'

Young Herakles shook his head. 'And let them put your breastplate in a trophy?' he said. 'Never!' He took a rock and bashed at the place where the hip was bent in and the metal was torn asunder. In three blows he'd knocked it back into shape, the jagged edges now thrust out and away from Satyrus's hip.

'Well done, young man!' Lucius said. They got it over Satyrus's

248

head, and latched it, and Satyrus felt only the pain of the wound and some additional pressure where the weight sat on his hips. He pushed his blood-soaked chlamys up onto his hips, and managed to wink at Herakles. 'Thanks,' he said. 'Although I don't really care if they build a trophy,' he added.

'That was incredible,' Herakles said, as they started to descend the mountain. 'I feel like a god.'

Satyrus nodded. The wine had gone to his head, and all he wanted was sleep. The rain had stopped. The sun was starting to burn through the haze. Nikephorus was running to meet them, relief in his eyes.

'I had no idea!' he shouted, fifty paces away.

When Satyrus reached him, he slapped the mercenary on the back. 'Neither did I. Antigonus is one wily bastard.'

They collected the rearguard, picked up their dead and retreated over the top of the pass.

Yes, Satyrus thought. *That's all there is.*

PART IV

14

Cassander stood in the doorway of his pavilion, looking across the dusty plain towards where Demetrios was encamped, with the beach and his ships behind him. It was still dark – he could see his opponent's fires.

'Today?' he asked aloud, to the woman on the bed. 'Ares and Aphrodite. He can finish me whenever he wants, the bastard. Why wait?'

Phiale lay in Cassander's bed, contemplating her options. She had not expected Cassander to be so easily defeated. Six months before, he had been the captain general of his alliance, at the very edge of victory, and now they were on the edge of annihilation, their armies hunted across mainland Greece, their small fleet utterly defeated.

'The thankless bastards – Athens, Corinth, Plataea and Megara – none of them will stand with me.' Cassander took a cup of juice from a slave. 'Leave me,' he ordered the slave.

Phiale wondered if he would be ... difficult. Defeated men made the most trouble.

'I offered him my absolute surrender if he would leave me as King of Macedon. I offered to change sides and attack Ptolemy and Lysimachos.' Cassander stood there, the sun rising beyond him. He looked old – old and evil.

Phiale found that she was lying in the bed of an old, evil man who had lost his war. She sighed. He'd lost the Greek cities through wanton ill-treatment, but this was scarcely the moment to tell him.

She wondered if she could jump from his bed to that of Demetrios.

What if she killed Cassander? That would certainly ingratiate her with Demetrios.

The sun was just peaking over the shoulder of the world. Phiale stretched. *I am thirty five*, she thought. *Too old for this life. And soon my body will not be everything a man desires.*

'Do you know that Satyrus of Tanais is still alive?' Cassander said bitterly. 'I wonder if an astrologer could have helped me. Everything I put my hand to this year has come undone.'

Phiale sat up. As she was naked, she caught his attention.

'Ah, that gets you moving, my dear alley cat.' Cassander came over and put a hand on one of her breasts, flicked the nipple – more in cruelty than passion. 'Lie back down,' he ordered.

Phiale was not a courtesan for nothing, and she obeyed languorously. Attractively. As if his desires inflamed her. And as he mounted her, she considered him – hated him – and savoured her newfound emotion for him. Sex with hate was not new to Phiale but it was rewarding, in its way.

He didn't take long, and when he was through, she watched him go back to the doorway. The sun was up – cocks were crowing in camp. And a messenger was racing towards them across the cleared ground in front of the pavilion.

'Lord!' shouted the man. 'Lord! Demetrios is gone!'

'Hah!' Cassander said, and came and kissed her on the head. Something she hated. 'You are the touchstone of my fortune! Tyche's daughter – make love to Phiale and the world turns!'

How I hate you, she thought. And sighed.

Demetrios was the first man to leap from the deck of his ship on the Ephesian beach, but there were no enemy hoplites to kill, no heroics to be performed. Instead, there was Philip, his father's general, and two hundred men.

'Thank the gods you are here,' said Philip.

Demetrios rolled his eyes. 'I *had* Cassander. I *had* him. What happened?'

Philip rolled his eyes. 'We had Lysimachos ... and then the King of the Bosporus appeared out of the sea with fifty ships, took Ephesus, drove Plistias south, and saved fucking Lysimachos. His fleet holds the Propontus, and their armies – no match for ours – are retreating on Heraklea across the mountains. Your father wants you to sail into the Propontus, defeat his navy, and pounce on his fleet.'

Demetrios smiled. 'Oh, Satyrus,' he breathed. 'Alive?'

Philip looked angry. 'Of course he's alive!' he said.

Demetrios walked up the beach. 'You've retaken the citadel?' he asked.

'The commander simply sailed away. A deputation of citizens met us at the passes and told us that the city was open to us.' Philip shrugged. 'Satyrus stripped them of baggage animals. Your father has taken all their gold. I'm to garrison the city and return with you.'

Demetrios shook his head. 'No – no, I think I'll do just as you suggested, and hunt his fleet into the Dardanelles.' He looked at the man. 'Hostages?' he asked.

Philip shrugged again. 'The Rhodians have them back,' he said.

Demetrios cursed. 'Then we don't have naval supremacy,' he said.

All of Demetrios's ships landed their men to cook dinner and stretch their legs. Unnoticed amidst the multitude, half a dozen men in armour walked away from the camp, up the road to the town, and into the gates. In an hour, they had purchased horses – local nags, the sort of animals left behind when army after army passes through a city.

Isokles had his own men, now; men of the sort he preferred, not soft-spoken women like the Athenian doctor, but scarred men from the lower classes who didn't posture – or if they did, they postured in a way Isokles understood.

He himself was going to kill Satyrus of Tanais. And he had a plan.

Four days later, Demetrios caught Diokles at the mouth of the Dardanelles, his ships on the beach. Diokles had no idea that there was an enemy fleet so close, and he was giving his rowing crews a day of rest.

Demetrios came up from the south, and the ships sitting at the north of the beach had time to launch and flee. Diokles got his ship into the water – he was the eleventh on the beach, and the eighth was already being dragged off by Demetrios's grapnels.

Apollodorus was twelfth. He got his rebuilt *Marathon* off. Diokles could see him on the stern, calling something.

Diokles turned to his helmsman. 'Ramming speed,' he said.

He saw the hope die in the other man's eyes, but Leonidas obeyed.

Diokles' *Atlantae* turned smoothly, gathering way as the oarsmen dug deeper. The Tarentum-born helmsman smiled grimly.

'It's Demetrios,' he said quietly.

Diokles saw the golden figure by the helmsman on the next ship but one, a towering penteres whose heavy engines were already throwing big bolts into the *Atlantae.*

Diokles nodded. 'I have to buy time,' he said, apologetically.

Leonidas shrugged.

Diokles ran forward, where men were already dead from the heavy bolts coming aboard. 'Dead men over the side!' he called. He turned to his captain of marines. 'Get Jubal's fancy repeaters over the side,' he said. 'I'm not giving them to Demetrios.'

Nautarch, his top marine, smiled. 'Over the side, weighted,' he answered.

'Then fire pots – all we have,' he said.

'Bodies over the side, Jubal's engines, fire pots,' Nautarch repeated. 'We's in it bad, eh?'

'Can you swim?' Diokles asked.

'Aye,' said the marine.

'Well, pray to Poseidon and don't jump in the water yet,' Diokles said, and smacked the man on the shoulder. Then he leaped up into the bow above the ram, watching the enemy ships. Demetrios's penteres was turning, trying to decide if his attack was a feint of not. The trireme beyond was threatening to foul his oars, and if they could just run over Demetrios's stern, Diokles could put his ram in, back oars, and run clear.

He looked at the seven ships he'd lost, already bobbing together on the waves. He felt like a fool. He felt like falling on his sword, but Diokles wasn't interested in suicide.

He ran aft to the helmsman's station. His rowers weren't all on the correct benches, and only now was the rhythm settling down – a crash forward as another heavy bolt hit.

More rowers dead. That's what happened when one ship rushed twenty-five. Thirty. Quite a few, anyway.

'Hit him just aft of the bow. He can't manoeuvre – look at the size of the bitch. Want me to take the oars?'

Leonidas looked at him steadily. 'We're going to die, aren't we?' he asked.

Diokles nodded. Quietly, he said, 'Yes.'

'Then let me go to Hades my own way.' Leonidas stood straight. 'Know who colonised Tarentum, Diokles?'

'Sparta. You've told me about fifty times.' Diokles thought they had perhaps a hundred heartbeats, if the enemy engines didn't rip his bow off first.

He watched one of Jubal's repeating engines sinking away in the water behind him. One thing off his mind.

Another crash forward. Satyrus had all the archers. He had nothing with which to reply except his ram.

The enemy trireme was now clear of the penteres – they weren't going to foul each other. It had been close – the trierarchs were still screaming at each other from their command decks.

It had never been that good a chance, anyway.

The penteres was coming for him.

'Let's get the trireme,' Leonidas said. 'We can't miss – he's still turning.'

'And the penteres gets us,' Diokles said.

Leonidas nodded.

Diokles nodded.

The Tarentine leaned on the oars and they turned, the sea foaming at their bow. Diokles saw a bolt vanish into the water, a clear miss – the turn had bought them that, if nothing else.

And then they hit. The ram caught just a few feet behind the cathead and smashed the oar-box in an explosion of splinters, and men screamed. The impact was so strong, and *Atlantae* was going so fast that she pushed the stricken ship down and back, water foaming over her stern as she sank. Her stern ran aboard the next trireme's bow, and down his oars – more oarsmen screaming, dislocated shoulders, men flayed by splinters.

The penteres had them, of course. But Diokles had twenty heartbeats, and he used them. 'Throw the fire pots!' he ordered. Then he roared, 'Over the side! Swim for it!'

Men jumped immediately – they'd been waiting for it. The marines had stripped their armour, and the rowers had left their oars as soon as they struck the enemy trireme.

Leonidas stepped up on the rail. 'You coming?' he asked. The lead enemy trireme was afire, and her consort's bow had caught.

'After you,' Diokles joked, and then an enemy marine's javelin caught him in the back, just above his kidneys, punched right through him so that he had a brief glimpse of the shiny point emerging from his gut. And then he fell forward into Poseidon's embrace.

15

Achilles was dour after the fight in the pass. He hadn't stayed at Satyrus's shoulder, and he'd missed the fight, and after that he was a shadow at Satyrus's shoulder, night and day.

Anaxagoras behaved much the same way, although with plenty of self-mockery.

Satyrus just nodded. 'I roam up and down the column, seeking to put heart into men,' he said. 'I have a horse and I go where I please. You two don't have to be with me every moment.'

Achilles looked at him. 'We have a contract,' he said.

Satyrus nodded again. 'We do, at that. So far, I have no reason to complain.'

Achilles shook his head. 'I should have been there.'

Over the last ridge of the Pelekos Mountains, and down – precipitously down – to the plains by the Mekestos river – with the mountains towering on either hand. The two armies were beginning to blend – men shared fires and food, and when the three phalanxes and their auxiliaries paraded, the third day on the Mekestos, they looked like an army. It was the first time in a thousand stades that there had been room to form up.

Lysimachos nodded to the north. 'We're about halfway,' he said.

Scopasis twirled his moustache. 'So is One-Eye,' he said. 'His cavalry will be hard on us now.'

Lysimachos nodded. 'You and my Getae will have to keep them away, then,' he said.

Scopasis looked at the Getae chiefs, and spat.

The feeling was mutual.

But the sun shone for three straight days. The forage was better, the horses' coats began to shine again, and the thrush in the hooves began to smell better. Or less bad.

Scopasis led a raid on one of Antigonus's outposts and rode it down in the dark, returning with fifty horses and twenty captives, all members of the elite Aegema. Satyrus sent them with a herald, and received back the wounded Apobatai and four Cretan archers from the fight in the pass – a good trade as far as he was concerned.

But the sun made Antigonus's horsemen bolder, and there was fighting in the rearguard every day. Satyrus felt that the Getae hung back and watched the Sakje die. After the third time that Scopasis's three hundred fought unsupported, he rode up to the lead Getae chief – a man who wore so much gold he glittered like Demetrios in the sun.

'Are your tribesmen women?' he asked. He grinned. 'Not women – my sister has killed more enemies than these children.'

The old Getae just smiled, showing his scars. 'Anything you say, lord,' he grunted.

Satyrus nodded. 'I say that the Getae are all children – any man's brats. You – pais – get me water,' he said to a bearded warrior. The man flushed.

Satyrus took him by the throat – mounted – and boxed his ears swiftly, as if the man was a slave. 'Water, *boy*.'

The Getae man roared 'I am no boy, Greek fucker!'

Satyrus smiled. 'Really? You can't fight. So fetch water.'

The chief nodded. 'You could get hurt, foreign king.'

Achilles' blade appeared along the barbarian's throat. 'Lots of people could get hurt,' he said, pleasantly.

'Sakje so noble,' the Getae spat. 'Let them show us how great they are.'

'It's true,' Satyrus said. His Getae wasn't great, but he knew a few words. 'Men with penises are generally better fighters then men with no penis.' He turned his back and rode down the hill towards the column.

The next morning, Lysimachos joined Satyrus and Stratokles for a crust of bread and a cup of wine. 'My Getae hate you,' he said.

'They'll hate me worse later today,' Satyrus said. 'They don't plan to fight, and they're none too fond of you, either.'

Lysimachos nodded. 'I think they're negotiating with Antigonus,' he admitted. 'It's the rain,' he added.

'It's the Sakje,' Satyrus said. 'Stratokles has a plan.'

*

The sun was well up when Antigonus's cavalry raid – late, but determined – overran the pickets and came flooding up the valley. The Sakje were caught flat-footed. There were only a handful of them, the rest asleep or elsewhere, and the enemy Aegema poured up the banks of the river, killed a handful of light infantrymen and some slaves still bathing in the river, and continued towards the infantry rearguard. A dozen Sakje fled before them, shooting from their saddles.

The enemy wanted them badly. So badly that they pursued them over a low ridge to the left and straight into the Getae camp, where they scattered the Getae herd, killed several men's wives, and burned the Getae tents.

Then the Sakje counter-attacked, pushing the Macedonian cavalry back through the Getae camp again, back to the river, shooting as they went. They saved fifty Getae women and most of the children, and in the pursuit, they picked up most of the Getae herd.

The next morning, without orders, the Getae raided the Antigonid camp.

Stratokles was disgustingly smug. So was Scopasis.

And still they marched north, and still Antigonus pursued them.

At the forks in the Royal Road, Satyrus sent Charmides north with a message: to send the fleet east to Kios, covering the flank. Then he led the army down the east fork, towards Miletopolis and Apollonis and the Greek cities of the northern Troad.

'We're at the edge of Bithynia,' he said to Stratokles.

'I'm on it,' Stratokles said. He winked at Herakles.

Lysimachos shook his head. 'If the Bithynians put an army across our path,' he muttered, 'we're done.'

In fact, Scopasis had already located the nucleus of a local army – six hundred cavalry and some peltasts – forming on the banks of the great lake to the east, near the town Eumenes had founded at Niceas, just three hundred stades away.

'I'm on it, I said,' Stratokles insisted.

The army marched east, right into the Bithynian trap.

Mithridates the elder, uncle of the younger man who Demetrios had captured and lost, sat on a camp stool, listening to his scouts report on the army of Lysimachos, who was marching straight into his hands.

Not that that was altogether good – his own small army would have the fight of its life, even in the constricted terrain on the banks of the lake with the mountains towering above them, and he'd pay dearly.

Could Antigonus be trusted to make it worth his while?

He sat and wondered why Lysimachos hadn't at least made him an offer.

So he was unsurprised when his guards told him that there was a messenger from Lysimachos. With a woman.

That was more like it.

They were brought in; the messenger had been roughly handled, and stripped of weapons. He was bleeding from his mouth, and his eyes – he had the eyes of a killer, and just for a moment, Mithridates wasn't amused.

'You're no herald,' he said.

'If I was,' the man said, 'you'd be guilty of impiety.'

'Heralds,' Mithridates said. 'Do I look like a fucking Greek? Anyway, you have no staff. I can order you killed. I should.'

The man shrugged. 'I'd like to live,' he said through his split lip. 'I'm here to tell you that Satyrus of Tanais is behind you with four thousand Sakje, and to offer you terms.'

No commander likes to have his subordinates hear about failure – especially one whose hold on power was as poor as Mithridates III of Bithynia. 'Clear the tent,' he said, glancing at his most danger-ous rivals – the Lord of Niceas and the Lord of Apollonis, former mercenaries under Alexander, now petty tyrants in Asia. 'Hold your tongue,' he said to the man with the split lip.

He kept two guards and four slaves.

'Now tell your story,' he said. He'd had a moment to think about it, and while Satyrus might have got by him – by ship to Heraklea – Mithridates couldn't see how he'd got four thousand Sakje. It didn't hold water.

The man shrugged. 'I'm here to offer you terms.'

'You have a curious accent,' Mithridates said. 'Why the woman?' he asked. He turned to look at her, and got a dagger point in the eye.

Lucius breathed out, a long exhalation like a sigh of despair. Both of the guards were dead, and the slaves had fled, and Mithridates IV was sitting on the stool. 'That was not my best work,' he admitted.

The young man on the ivory stool raised an eyebrow and rocked his head back and forth slightly, more like a handsome philosopher than a warlord. 'Luckily, he was a fool,' he said.

'Should we be worried about the rest of the nobles?' Lucius asked.

Mithridates sighed. 'If we're not dead in fifty heartbeats, I'll be king for a while,' he said.

'Ares – that's your plan?' Lucius asked. He ran his thumb idly down his sword's edge.

The Lord of Niceas pushed his head into the tent. His eyes widened – once at the blood, and again to see the young man on the stool. The Lord of Niceas was grey-haired, Greco-Persian, tall and hawk-nosed.

'Come in, my lord, and swear fealty,' Mithridates said.

'Lord?' the man said. Then he stepped in. He seemed unsure of himself. A dozen more local warlords came in behind him – too many for Lucius to kill all of them.

'We are now allies of Lysimachos and Satyrus of Tanais,' Mithridates said. 'I will be receiving a small subsidy in gold. You will all receive a share.' The handsome young man smiled.

They all smiled back. No one likes a battle, when the alternative is a subsidy.

They began to kneel and swear.

Lucius found that he felt light-headed. *I need to get out of this business*, he thought.

Antigonus found his enemies waiting on the shores of Lake Askania, and it became clear that his shaved knucklebone, the Bithynians, had betrayed him.

He sat on his horse and watched the enemy form opposite him. Their three big phalanxes filled the shores of the lake, and they had plenty of cavalry. He outnumbered them two to one, but they had started entrenching the narrow slice of farmland between the hills and the water.

'Fucking Bithynians,' he spat.

His numbers were still great enough to push through. He was sure his Macedonian veterans could rout whatever levies they used. But things happened in battles, and suddenly he was in hostile country, and if he lost here ... well, he could forget conquering the world. He would be lucky to get buried.

Antigonus had been fighting wars since he was fifteen, and he was eighty-one. He had not arrived at this age by making rash decisions. So he halted his army on the banks of the lake and ordered his engineers forward. And he ordered his cavalry to start rounding up the population of the countryside. If their leaders chose to oppose him, the people would serve as slaves.

Besides, his son was ferrying his army over from Europe, in Lysimachos's rear. He didn't *need* to fight here.

Unless he could win. And one thing the fucking *Bithynians* wouldn't do well was sit and wait while he raped their land.

Satyrus watched as the Antigonids began to lay out a fortified camp behind the heavy screen of cavalry and light infantry – thousands of men. Behind them, two full taxeis – almost as many pikemen as all of Lysimachos's army – stood to, their pikes upright in the sun.

Anaxagoras, Stratokles and Mithridates watched with him. Slightly to the rear, Lucius and Herakles and Charmides played at dice. Herakles had begun to adopt Charmides as his role model – or his erastes. It was early days yet. Satyrus watched them with a reserve he hadn't had on earlier campaigns. His sister was right. The joy was gone from the thing. No longer did he watch with fascination as war cemented the bonds of honour and friendship between warriors. Now he watched from a distance, expecting the best of them to die.

'Why so glum?' Anaxagoras asked. 'He's doing exactly what you said he would do.'

Satyrus shrugged. 'That doesn't make it any better. He can bleed us white, once his access to food and water is secure.'

Mithridates rubbed his beard. 'You Greeks are the barbarians. He's enslaving virtually the whole population of northern Mysia to build that camp.'

Anaxagoras barked a laugh. 'Mithridates, you will be a great king but you are a poor historian. The Assyrians did the same, and the Babylonians, and the Persians, your ancestors. No people have a monopoly on barbarism. It is a human trait. All humans share it.'

Mithridates sighed. 'I believe that is a cold comfort for my people over there.' He looked at Satyrus, who was chewing an apple – a new apple, too green for eating, but the taste was delicious. 'Can we do anything?'

Satyrus nodded. 'We need wood and iron and bronze for war machines. Jubal is gathering them with the cavalry. When that is done, I will send my little band around the lake. Antigonus will do it as well. It would be best if you sent some of your noble cavalry and their retainers as far as you can – all the way into Mysia, if possible – to harry his patrols and his efforts at collecting wood. And slaves.'

Mithridates shook his head. 'If I release my nobles, they will never come back,' he said. 'Most of them are already prepared to change sides, for certain assurances.'

Satyrus nodded once, briskly. 'As I expected. Very well. Let's find Lysimachos.'

Stratokles looked interested. 'Why? I mean, from fear? Or because they already hate you?'

Mithridates laughed. 'They hate anyone greater than themselves. It is our way. And they say – with some justice – that Antigonus has done nothing to them but enslave some peasants.'

Stratokles nodded. 'Who would you say was your most dangerous nobleman? The one most likely to desert?'

Mithridates laughed again. 'I really would be hard put to choose one among all of them,' he said. 'But Darius Thrakes, as we call him, is the worst of the lot, and he leads almost a thousand riders. I can't touch him.'

Stratokles saw the look that passed between Satyrus and Lucius.

'You can do this one yourself, boss,' Lucius said.

Stratokles sighed.

Lysimachos, when they found him, was watching Jubal build war engines. He had sixty men – his own men, many former sailors and some former slave artificers – all laying out machines together, and he had another three hundred Bithynian workmen with adzes and axes.

'That is a dangerous man,' Lysimachos said. 'Would you sell him to me?'

'He's not mine to sell,' Satyrus said. 'Try asking him.'

Jubal was standing, his chiton pulled down to his hips, showing a young smith the patterns for corner plates for a torsion engine – demonstrating how to form the plates, cut them, and bend them to shape with the minimum of work.

'We need a cavalry raid,' Satyrus said.

Lysimachos nodded. 'Of course.'

'Mithridates says his men will desert if allowed out of our lines,' Satyrus said.

'Aphrodite's tits!' Lysimachos exclaimed. 'So you want my Getae?'

'And all of my Sakje. Yes.' Satyrus shrugged.

'They hate each other. Your Scopasis and my Sakarnus – they are *not* friends.' Lysimachos shook his head. 'And if we lose them ... Ares, Tanais, if we lose them, we can't cover our retreat.'

If he calls me Tanais, should I call him Thrace? Satyrus thought. Lysimachos was a curious blend of old campaigner and parvenu king. 'If we don't try, we might as well retreat right now,' he said.

Lysimachos shook his head. 'We have a few days.'

Satyrus was still mounted, and he used his height and his voice to show his discontent. 'I don't agree,' he said. 'We do not have a few days. Antigonus will have his cavalry on the south shore by tomorrow.'

Lysimachos grinned at his own staff, all waiting a few horse lengths away. 'This from your years of experience as a strategos, eh?'

Satyrus raised an eyebrow. 'Your scouting is poor at best. Antigonus owned your flanks at Magnesia and again when I found you because you won't send your best troops out into harm's way to find and eliminate the enemy scouts.'

'How nice! Lessons in hoplomachia from a Greek stripling.' Lysimachos shook his head. 'Listen, Tanais, don't turn red on me like a maiden with her first dick. I've fought Antigonus and his son for as long as most of you have been alive. Scouting – listen. I can see his camp. He can see mine. If he wants to ride around and kill barbarians, let him.'

Satyrus nodded. 'You fought for Alexander, right?' he said. 'So you really should know better.' *I should keep my mouth shut and ride away.*

Lysimachos swung up onto the back of a pretty Nisean mare, the kind of warhorse men killed for. He was unruffled. 'I remember what it is like to be young,' he said. 'I forgive you. You are a good ally, Satyrus of Tanais, and I don't need a quarrel. So I'll give you fifty Getae – no more.'

Several of his staff officers – Macedonians all – laughed. Lysimachos whirled on them. 'Keep it to yourselves, gentlemen. Remember where we'd be without these men.'

Satyrus took a deep breath, held it, counted, and listened to the inaudible sounds of a lyre scale. When he was done, his eyes were clear and his smile was genuine.

'Send me the cavalrymen at nightfall,' he said. 'And thank you.'

He and Lysimachos clasped hands.

As he rode away, Stratokles came up beside him. 'I'm going,' he said. 'And I want Mithridates to send his goat-boy – Darius what's-his-name. With fifty men.'

'I'm commanding myself,' Satyrus said.

'All the better,' Stratokles said.

Satyrus wanted a fine Nisean like Lysimachos's horse. His gelding chewed the bit constantly, and now thrust out with his head, trying to act like a stallion. Satyrus slapped his neck. 'You have plans for Darius?'

'I think he should give his life for his country,' Stratokles said. 'Can you give Herakles a command?'

Satyrus turned in his saddle and eyed the young man. 'I had intended to raise twenty cavalrymen from the mercenaries. Can Herakles be trusted to do it?'

Stratokles nodded. 'Let's find out.'

Anaxagoras laid his hand on Stratokles' reins. 'I hate to interrupt a good plot,' he said.

'But?' Satyrus smiled.

'You know that the men now know who he is, eh?' Anaxagoras asked.

'Who he claims to be,' Satyrus added.

Stratokles shrugged. 'It was bound to happen,' he said.

'Draco and some of the Apobatai are ... emotional about it.' Anaxagoras shook his head. 'If he's Alexander's son, should we be sending him on cavalry patrols?'

'Let them show their worship of him by keeping him alive,' Satyrus said. He wondered whose voice uttered those words in such a tone of hard finality.

Anaxagoras clearly wondered, too. He met Satyrus's eyes and held them. 'Have a care,' he said. 'I think a music lesson is required.'

'After the cavalry raid. Charmides, fetch me Scopasis: my compliments, and would he meet me at my pavilion.'

Satyrus's pavilion was another topic of contention. They all used it – Anaxagoras, Charmides, Nikephorus and Stratokles all sat and drank wine and used the stores of cedar oil that Phoibos had against mosquitoes, and the lavender soap and whetstones and … everything. The man thought of everything.

But somehow, with the red oiled-silk pavilion and the slaves – now more than fifteen – who attended it, he gave Satyrus the air of a potentate, of a king. Satyrus understood better than some of his men understood – that he had always lived like one of them on campaign, and consequently, the appearance of his pavilion set him apart in a way he had never been set apart before.

The pavilion offended Anaxagoras and Charmides and Draco, but not Nikephorus, who simply wanted one of his own, nor Scopasis, who never seemed to notice it, as long as a cup of wine was put in his hand as soon as he dismounted.

Satyrus understood their discontent, which was really about him. And the change he was experiencing – from captain to king. From leader of a few to leader of an army. He seldom had time to talk about philosophy with Charmides, to play his lyre with Anaxagoras, or even to discuss Miriam. He longed to discuss Miriam, but his sense of justice made him hold his tongue. Anaxagoras had his own troubles, and didn't need to talk about a woman who had, in effect, left them both.

Scopasis was waiting at the pavilion, long legs stretched before him as he leaned against a tent wall, a cup of wine in his hand.

'I greet you,' he said, formally.

Satyrus slipped down from his gelding, passed the reins to a slave, and smiled at Scopasis. 'I greet you, hipparch.'

Scopasis smiled at the Greek word. 'When did you last love a horse?' Scopasis asked.

'I was just thinking the same,' Satyrus said, and nodded. 'Too long. They die. Like flies.'

Scopasis folded his legs under him and rose to his feet. 'Let me show you something I have for you, then,' he said.

Behind the tent was a Nisean – grey like a storm at sea, with a small, high head and a pale mane and tail.

'Is Antigonus dead?' Satyrus asked. 'Where did this horse come from?' The stallion – his status was obvious – had red leather tack decorated in bronze, and a polished bronze bit in the Persian, and thus the Sakje, style, and a high-backed saddle like the Sauromatae used.

Scopasis shrugged. 'I found him wandering the plain to the south, a broken hobble on his fetlock,' he said. 'My mare wanted him.'

'He is magnificent,' Satyrus said. Indeed, he was the tallest horse Satyrus had ever seen, or close enough. Melitta had a pair of war-Niseans, and they were of a size. 'You should have him.'

Scopasis shook his head. 'Too finicky. He needs five slaves and a constant supply of grain. But in a fight ... by the gods, Satyrus, that is a fighting horse. My gift.'

Satyrus gave the Sakje a hug. Scopasis thumped his back.

'The gods must have sent that horse,' Satyrus said. 'Because I was just thinking about how poor my horses are – and about leading a cavalry raid. I want all the Sakje – all your cavalrymen. We'll have fifty Getae and another fifty Bithynians and at least fifty Greek cavalry. I plan to strike south around the lake – a long scout into the rear of his army.'

Scopasis nodded. 'High time. I will come, of course, and all my men.'

They all ate dinner together: Satyrus and Scopasis, Charmides and Herakles, Nikephorus and Anaxagoras and Jubal and Orestes, his foreman, and two of the phylarchs, chosen by Phoibos; Naxes, an Athenian thetes risen to command, and Niceaos, an exiled aristocrat from Samos who looked like a Spartan from tip to toe. It was a good dinner – roebuck and rich bread and a plate of figs so good that the men ate them to the last fruit and sat on their stools, licking their fingers and laughing like boys.

'Phoibos, you are a miracle worker,' Satyrus said.

'I endeavour to give satisfaction, lord,' the man replied. 'I must say, lord, that I find this – exhilarating. I might wish that I'd gone on campaign earlier. The challenges of maintaining the oikia in such circumstances – splendid. May I mention that our money supply is running low, lord?'

That brought Satyrus up short. 'Low? I gave you a talent of silver.'

'Yes, lord. I have a little more than a quarter of that left. You did insist that I pay for everything.' He shrugged. 'The figs were not cheap. Nor the roebuck, to be frank. The market here is very ... expensive.' The butler smiled ruefully.

Satyrus was taken aback. He was not used to thinking about money at all. But a talent of silver would pay a hundred mercenaries for the summer. 'By Hephaestus, sir – how much did you pay for the figs?'

Phoibos shrugged. 'A moment, if you please, lord?' he said, and returned with a five-fold wax tablet. He flipped it open on his knee.

'Ahh … here. Mykos did the shopping. A good pais with a head on his shoulders. Five silver owls of Athens.' He nodded and snapped the tablets shut.

'Five drachma? For figs?' Satyrus turned to his assembled guests. 'Please pardon me, gentlemen, but I need the figs back. We have soldiers to pay.'

Charmides fell off his stool he was laughing so hard.

Anaxagoras slapped his back. 'That's the first joke I've heard from you since Athens,' he said.

'Up until now, the food has been cheap,' Satyrus said back. He turned back to Phoibos. 'You are an excellent steward, and I recognise that you have the highest standards. I need them a little lower. A talent of silver has to last the entire campaign. And then some.'

Phoibos sniffed. 'Ah. Very well, lord. I will economise.'

Scopasis held out his cup. 'Do that thing tomorrow! For now, pour us more of the Chian!'

Satyrus shook his head. 'A talent of silver is the value of twenty farms north of Olbia – the whole tax of a district.'

Phoibos nodded. 'It is not cheap, to be a king,' he answered gravely.

When they gathered, it was still dark. The Getae came in early – only thirty of them instead of fifty, under a young, blond nobleman who looked more like a Keltoi than a Getae. His Greek was excellent – he was called Calicles, and while he kept his distance from Scopasis, he was not ill at ease with the other officers.

His men all came with two horses apiece, or more.

Herakles had two dozen men, most of them older veterans. Most Macedonians could ride, and the infantry was full of Thessalian peasants who had been born to riding but couldn't afford a horse or panoply. The young man looked more terrified than inflated by his first command.

'Don't fuss,' Satyrus said. 'Who's your hyperetes?'

Draco came forward out of the murk. 'I am, lord,' he said. He was grinning from ear to ear.

'I wondered where you were,' Satyrus said. *I am so far from these men*, he thought. 'You can be the hyperetes of the whole force. Get me a trumpet. Charmides, find me a trumpeter. Even if he's a slave.'

Mithridates provided the trumpeter – a young boy, no more than twelve. His trumpet seemed as long as he was, and he rode a magnificent horse – almost as tall as Satyrus's gelding, an enormous horse for a boy. 'My great-uncle's son, Artaxerxes,' he said. 'He's lucky I haven't executed him. If he doesn't come back,' Mithridates' eyes grew hard, 'I shall shed no tears.' The new King of Bithynia looked troubled in the grey light of first dawn. 'I should ride with you. If only to keep an eye on that one.'

Satyrus looked at Darius Thrakes, the lord of the northern Bithynians, a man who looked more like a Getae nobleman than Calicles who led them. But the Thracians had been in Bithynia for generations. 'We'll keep an eye on him,' Satyrus said, his eyes flicking to Stratokles.

Stratokles was tightening his girth. He was a hippeis class Athenian, and an expert cavalryman – one of the few Satyrus had. Lucius was a cavalry-class Latin – also a professional. The three of them had more professional cavalry experience than most of the rest of their Greek troopers combined.

Stratokles got his girth the way he wanted, played with the buckles on his Sakje-style bridle, and Lucius gave him a leg up into the saddle. The Athenian then turned his mare. 'I'll go make friends with him,' he said.

The Bithynians were strong – almost a hundred cavalrymen, all with two mounts. They had a baggage wagon, as well.

Satyrus rode up to Lord Darius and clasped his hand. The hand was not offered with any great willingness. 'Good morning. Fine-looking horseman, lord. Please leave your baggage wagons.'

Darius smiled. 'No,' he said.

Satyrus shrugged. He turned to Draco. 'Burn them,' he said.

Darius froze. 'We will—'

Satyrus forced himself to smile. 'You and your men will all die. Understand? War is not a game. You want those wagons so that you can ride away and leave us. That won't be happening, my lord. If it does, we will hunt you down and kill you. Every man. Understand? You think you are a wily, dangerous man. The men sitting around you have been at war for their entire lives. Understand, lord?'

He saw it all in the other man's eyes – fear, and hate, and acceptance. It made Satyrus tired.

Behind the Bithynian nobleman, Stratokles smiled mirthlessly.

By noon, they were well south of the lake, edging along the downslope behind the crest of the main ridge of the hills ringing the lake, so that they were hidden from Antigonus – unless his horsemen had beaten them to the ridge top. There were parties of Sakje and Getae all around them, and each of them had one Bithynian trooper as a scout and guide.

And Darius rode between Stratokles and Lucius, so obviously a hostage that his men understood and obeyed.

'You've done this before?' Satyrus asked Stratokles.

Stratokles grinned. 'I'm an Athenian,' he said. 'Before the Macedonians, we had an empire that covered most of Thrace and all of the Asian coast. Unwilling allies – it's an Athenian speciality. Don't worry, when we're done, the Bithynians will be as eager as Scopasis. More so.'

Lucius grimaced.

Herakles was cautious and careful of his men, and Draco had to drive him forward. Scopasis was too rash, and Satyrus had restrain him, finding a fine edge between speed and foolishness.

Anaxagoras rode at his shoulder and shared his canteen. 'You play them like I play the kithara,' he said. 'Charmides is a first rate leader.'

'But a poor rider,' Satyrus said.

'So you coach him on riding. Herakles is a good rider,' Anaxagoras said.

'But a nervous man with his first command, starting at shadows.' Satyrus dug his knees into his gelding's back and rose up, looking forward and then down the ridge to the left and south. He could see Sakje – red jacketed, most of them – away to the south on the next ridge, and well ahead, too. He longed to be on the back of his stallion, but he was saving the Nisean for the inevitable moment.

He spared a thought for his ancestor Herakles. He had dreamed of death the night before.

Anaxagoras turned to Artaxerxes. 'Tell me about yourself, youngster. Who is your father?'

The young Mede coloured. 'My father was Xerxes son of

Artaphernes. He is dead. My mother is dead. My brothers and sisters are dead. I was a hostage in Mysia when they were killed, and now I am a prisoner of my great-uncle. May I have a sword?'

Anaxagoras shook his head. 'They're worse than Macedonians,' he said. 'You can have a sword when the king and I think you are worthy of it. Do you know how to use a sword?'

'Oh, yes,' the boy said.

Anaxagoras raised his eyebrows. 'Really?' he asked.

'Your first pupil,' Satyrus said. 'All boys claim that they can wrestle and use a sword.'

'Can you play music?' Anaxagoras asked.

'I play the harp. And the flute.' The boy nodded. 'And the trumpet,' he said with disdain.

Satyrus didn't like what he was seeing to the west. He rose to his knees, shifted his weight so that he could kneel on the gelding's back. He needed to see a little farther.

'Would you rather be here with us, or in Mithridates' tent?' Anaxagoras asked.

'Here with you, lord! Mithridates has to have me killed.' The boy shrugged. 'If I grow to manhood, I will surely kill him.'

Anaxagoras clucked. 'So the trumpet has already bought you a few days of life,' he said.

There were men in a gully – Satyrus was sure of it. Almost sure of it. The sun was high in the sky, and even this close to autumn, the heat was palpable.

'Sound halt,' Satyrus said. 'One long blast.'

Artaxerxes froze.

'Now, boy,' Satyrus said.

The trumpet went to the boy's lips, and the call rang out – the first time, a spluttering sound like a flock of geese, but the second was a loud clarion that carried across the valley.

All the Sakje froze.

A few of the Getae stopped moving. The officers at least looked around.

'Enemy is front. Do you know the call?' Satyrus asked. This is what the Sakje did – using trumpets to tell distant scouts what to do. The Exiles were masters of the trumpet. Satyrus and Scopasis knew all the calls – not so the rest of the phylarchs. Herakles wouldn't know five of them, which was one of the reasons he and Charmides were close to the main column.

Anaxagoras whistled the call, and Satyrus shot him a thankful glance.

The boy put the trumpet to his lips and played. The first call was halting, but again, the second was high and loud.

Satyrus took a spear from Charmides and pointed it at the gully, three stades distant, where he had seen flashes. Far away to the front, a mounted man smaller than an insect waved a lance. Sakje riders broke right and left, enveloping the head of the gully.

They got four prisoners, and the fight was on.

The Antigonid cavalry was just coming over the ridge. The men in the gully were their prodromoi, and they had a heavy force behind them.

Satyrus brought his column forward at a trot, heedless of the sun and the thirst of his horses until he had his men well down in the shade of the valley.

'Water them by sections,' he said, and changed horses to the Nisean – The horse was a pleasure under him – calm, collected, eager. He turned to Charmides. 'Do *not* move forward until all the horses are watered. Then come up to me.' He took Artaxerxes and Anaxagoras and went sloping up the ridge towards the fighting.

Scopasis had twenty men, a dozen Getae and some of the Bithynians as well. He'd dismounted them in an olive grove – a natural growth of wild olives, high on the flank of the main ridge above the lake. The Sakje had bows, and a few of the Bithynians and Getae did as well.

The enemy had already made an attempt on his position. It was nigh impregnable; rocks spiked out of the sandy ground, and the trees provided dense cover. The ridge top fell away around them so that the last approach to the summit was steep and rocky – terrible cavalry ground. But just below the summit was a long meadow coated in late-summer flowers, and the drone of bees filled the air. At the far side of the meadow, three hundred enemy cavalry formed in two great rhomboids, and ahead of them came two dozen infantry skirmishers, moving cautiously across the meadow.

'They tried the road,' Scopasis said, pointing to the gap between two enormous rocks. The gap was filled with dead men and horses. 'Nice horse,' he said, and smiled.

'He's a pleasure,' Satyrus said.

Scopasis nodded. 'Don't get him killed,' he said. 'I like him.'

Satyrus nodded. He unslung his gorytos, rode over to a Bithynian trooper.

'Know how to shoot?' he asked.

The man grinned. He had two gold teeth, and he looked particularly rapacious. 'Aye, King!' he said.

Satyrus gave the man his bow. 'I'll want it back,' he said. 'So try not to die.'

Again, the gold glinting grin. 'Aye, King.' The man said again.

Satyrus rode back to Scopasis. 'How're the Bithynians?'

'Not bad at all. Some of them can ride.' From a Sakje, this was praise. 'How long?' he asked.

Satyrus shook his head. 'I told Charmides to water all the horses,' he said. 'And Stratokles is already west of here — he may not even know we've stopped.'

Scopasis nodded. 'He'll know,' he said. 'Here they come.'

The enemy cavalry — mostly Mysians, and some Persians, with Greek officers — came forward and met with archery. They tried to circle around the summit and found less resistance.

After fifteen minutes, they retired, leaving a dozen dead and wounded.

Scopasis puffed up his cheeks and blew out. 'Fools. Now their horses are blown and unwatered.'

Satyrus shook his head. 'Remember that up until now, they've had it all their own way,' he said. 'No reason they should expect anything else.'

The Getae and the Bithynians were beside themselves with joy — forty men against three hundred, and holding their own.

The Sakje were methodically stripping the enemy dead.

Now the enemy hipparch sent his infantry scouts out — carefully probing the ground all around the summit. They were fixated on Scopasis, and missed the main body of the allied cavalry until it was almost on them. Satyrus leaped up, gathered his reins, and wriggled onto his horse's back. His legs were already tired. It made him feel old.

'Come when you can,' he called to Scopasis. He found that his trumpeter was right with him, and he rode along the road, over the fly-infested corpses from the first attack, and into the field of bees.

Charmides was forming his files. It was odd – more like a dream than a real fight. They were on a hilltop meadow in the sun, so that all Satyrus could see was a field of flowers and distant mountaintops, as if they were fighting in the heavens for the entertainment of the gods. The drone of bees filled his ears.

Charmides was appalled at the responsibility – he'd never commanded so many men, and he'd dismounted to organise them, unsure of his seat.

They were forming well – the professional Greeks in the centre, and the Sakje and Getae on the flanks. They were still outnumbered two to one, but their horses were fresh and all the Sakje had bows. Without orders, they cantered forward and loosed a volley.

Satyrus was too late to stop them, and he shrugged.

'Surely they are helping you win this action,' Anaxagoras said.

'We didn't need to fight,' Satyrus said. 'Their horses have no water. They should have retreated. But now we've stung them, and their hipparch is inexperienced, so he'll come forward, and men will die.'

'Surely that is war,' Anaxagoras said.

'Will you be so philosophical if it is you?' Satyrus asked, somewhat pettishly.

The Corinthian pursed his lips, then fumbled for his helmet. The enemy was coming.

The first clash was hard fought. The enemy may have been tired and their horses unwatered, but they had weight of horse, numbers, and a certain determination, and the mêlée was desperate. Satyrus led the counter-charge from the centre – he put himself in front of Charmides' little troop of bodyguards, took a spear from the phylarch, snapped his cheek-plates down and pointed with the spear.

The two forces met with a crash like an avalanche in a winter valley, and the meadow packed them so tight that men were brought to a stand or knocked flat. Satyrus was at an advantage, mounted on his magnificent new Nisean, and he knocked aside a Lydian noble in scale armour on a much smaller horse. His spear glanced from the man's aventail, the man's lance missed over his shoulder, and then he was reining frantically, his hands in the Nisean's mane, trying to keep him upright as he trampled the smaller horse.

He'd lost his spear, so drew his sword – the good sword Demetrios had given him. The Lydians were well-armoured men, and the sword's point was quickly dulled against the bronze breastplates most of them wore.

Then he was in the midst of the enemy. Both sides had threaded each other, so that their files were intermixed, and his back-plate rang with blows; he was face to face with a Macedonian officer, and Satyrus got his bridle hand on the other man's elbow, put his pommel in the man's face, and took his spear from his unresisting hands as the man fell. It was a good spear, short and needle sharp, and Satyrus used it against the unarmoured rumps of the Lydian horses around him, twisting and stabbing like a viper.

And then he heard Charmides shouting to his right – he had both hands on the spear haft, and he shifted his weight and the stallion backed a few steps, as nimble as a dog, and Satyrus loved him. He shifted his weight and he backed again.

A terrific blow on his head and he was on the ground, on his feet, but a horse stepped on his foot and he was down in the dust.

The stallion stood over him.

He must have lost consciousness for some time – heartbeats or more – suddenly Charmides was right over him, and Satyrus got his feet under him and got to his feet, although his head was spinning and his foot hurt so badly he couldn't put his full weight on it. But the Macedonian's spear was *right there* and he got a hand on it, used it to hold his weight and then, as he had been taught as a boy, he put it against the stallion's back and stepped up onto the spear with his good foot, gritted his teeth against the pain in his other foot and got his leg over. He barely clung on, hung there a moment like a sack of wool, but he was up, and despite the pain reached behind and retrieved the spear.

Scopasis had come into the flank of the enemy. He could see where they were falling back, and how they had been disoriented by Scopasis's charge.

He looked around. His trumpeter had blood running down his neck – an ear, cut clean off. And his trumpet was cut in two. He had used it as a club.

'Rally!' he began to call. It hurt his head.

16

Satyrus rallied them all the way back to the summit end of the meadow, and hoped that the enemy hipparch would have the sense to just ride away. His foot hurt as if every bee in the meadow had stung him, and he had a dent in his helmet so deep that it looked as if it had been hit with an axe. The side of his head was mushy with blood.

'Send all the Sakje along the edges of the meadow into the rocks. Greeks in the centre, with the Getae and the Bithynians, formed close. A wedge.' Satyrus pointed, his voice already hoarse.

Scopasis got it, organised the flank detachments, and the Sakje slipped from their ponies and began to push forward in the rocky ground. The enemy's light infantry were there, but their javelins were no match for bows and armour, and they lost the rocky edge.

Satyrus placed himself at the point of the wedge. Some jobs came with being in command.

He had the most shocking fear. He felt lethargic, and he was *afraid*. This little skirmish was of no real moment to the campaign. And he might *die* here. Men said his father had taken a wound in one fight and that had left him too weak to last a second fight, and that's how he died.

He kept the fear from his voice and straightened his shoulders. Charmides and Anaxagoras were the next men in the wedge. Both of them were grinning like fools.

Satyrus thought of a thousand things he wanted to say. Many of them were about Miriam.

The Sakje edged along the meadow. He could see them rising to shoot – flushing the enemy psiloi from their cover – often simply running at them in short rushes, cutting down the slowest. The enemy psiloi were heavily outnumbered and finally they abandoned the fight, the remaining two dozen breaking and running for the safety of their cavalry.

Satyrus took two shuddering breaths. He reached out for his god ... for the smell of wet cat, the eudaimonia that lifted him into combat and made him one with his god.

There was nothing there, and he shuddered as if cold. His fingers were sticky on the haft of the Macedonian officer's sword. He had blood under his nails and in the fissures of his hands.

He wanted to go back and tell Miriam that he'd rather go to Alexandria with her than be King of the Bosporus.

The enemy hipparch – too inexperienced or perhaps simply too stubborn to know that he was beaten, was organising another charge. His horses were blown, but he seemed to have some fresh men. Now they filled the field flank to flank – three deep or more.

The Sakje were emptying their quivers into the Antigonids, and the Lydians, despite their armour, were suffering.

Satyrus found that his hands were trembling. It made him angry.

Was he afraid? Or was he about to charge an enemy that outnumbered him heavily because this was the moment?

He could no longer tell.

'Remember who you are,' he said aloud, and men around heard him, and took it as his pre-battle speech, and hands closed on spear hafts.

'If we just wait,' Anaxagoras said, as another flight of Sakje arrows fell on the Lydians.

'Walk!' Satyrus ordered. The wedge started forward, the men at his flanks pressing in. He looked back. As far as he could see, the formation was tight.

A little less than a stade.

The Lydians started forward. They were being galled by the Sakje, and the open ground invited them.

Anaxagoras was, of course, correct.

Satyrus swallowed the lump in his throat. 'Trot!' he ordered. His horse was perfect for the point of the wedge – he was a line breaker. He had heart, and he responded instantly between Satyrus's legs, a fast trot that threatened to leave Anaxagoras and Charmides behind. Somehow the magnificent horse put heart into the man.

Satyrus had never led a wedge before, except on a drill field. But he knew the feeling of being alone, mounted on a massive monster that rode behind him and made the earth shake. He looked back, almost lost his seat as the stallion leaped something on the ground – a corpse from the first clash.

Half a stade.

The biggest error in a cavalry charge was to gallop too early. His mother had taught him from youth, and his sister, and Coenus and Diodorus and Crax and all the Exiles ... oh, to have them at his side now.

The Lydians launched into their charge, and now the fatigue of their horses showed in the whites of their eyes and their hesitation. Right in front of Satyrus, a man spurred his charger to a gallop, went a few plunges, and was back at a trot.

Half a stade. Close enough to see the whites of the horses' eyes, the sweat on their flanks, the desperation in men's faces.

Twenty horse lengths, and Satyrus knew which man he would engage – flicked his head around to see his wedge still well closed up, even the Bithynians keeping their places in line.

His hands were no longer shaking. There was only the man on a bay horse opposite him, and the point of his spear coming at his eyes, and his own spear.

He let the horse have his head. 'Charge!' he roared. The fear was there but mostly he had conquered it.

The stallion was all heart. He bounded forward, and Satyrus raised his spear two-handed, letting him run ...

He caught his opponent's spearhead with his own, swept it up two-handed and buried his spear point in the man's body, scales flying from the point of impact like rain from a tent hit with a stick, ripped it clear of the man's corpse and got the spear haft across his body to block the sword-cut of the next man, and his mare danced under him. The rear ranker tried to overbear his horse and Charmides killed him, and the point of the wedge was through the enemy line, and the stallion was still flying along the ground at a gallop. Satyrus gave him a knee and he turned to the left, skimming the ground like a flying thing.

An arrow flashed past his head.

Satyrus put himself low on the horse's neck and pounded along the meadow in a wide curve, and he had fifty horsemen behind him – Charmides and Herakles' men all mixed, and they made the turn and came down on the rear of the Lydian line, and the Lydians broke.

Then there was desperate fighting – man to man, horse to horse, and a press as tight as Satyrus had ever experienced on foot.

He saw Herakles fall. The young man took a spear wound that pinned him to his horse, and the horse fell, and he fell with it. Satyrus's mount seemed to follow his thoughts, and he leaped over the prone prince and Satyrus unhorsed one of his attackers and the other turned away.

The dust was so thick that Satyrus couldn't see. He almost couldn't breathe but the pressure of the fight was less.

The little trumpeter was still with him – he had a spear and a sword, now. Satyrus flashed him a smile. 'Don't be a hero,' he said.

The boy's face was dead white despite his swarthy looks, but he managed a twitch of the lips.

Satyrus reined around, and there was Scopasis, already mounted, with a dozen of his archers behind him.

'That man is a dead man,' Scopasis said. He pointed at the Sakje arrow in the stallion's haunch.

'He's the best horse I've ever ridden,' Satyrus said with all the pent-up emotion of the fight.

Scopasis said. 'You are just like your sister.'

Satyrus managed a laugh. He was going to live.

As always, the aftermath was far worse than the fight. Almost a third of their force was wounded – the Lydians had been trapped by Stratokles, who was rueful.

'I should have let them go,' he said, while the trumpeter poured wine on his shoulder wound and he winced. 'ARES!' he bellowed, and then subsided. 'Oh, Tartarus. That hurts like a fucker. I should know better – I was behind them, and I should have let them go.'

Scopasis nodded. 'Trapped men fight to the death,' he said. 'Better to let them flee and then kill them.'

'How are the Bithynians?' Satyrus asked.

'Regular furies when aroused. As soon as poor Darius was killed, they were wild to avenge him.' Stratokles arched his back and stifled a scream of pain. All that came out was a grunt. 'Fuck that's deep. Lucius, tell me how bad it is.'

'Better than you deserve,' Lucius said. 'Deep. But all in fat and muscle – spear point, not a cutting edge. More wine here. And some honey.'

Satyrus didn't have a wound, but his foot felt as if it had been trodden by an elephant, not a horse, and he couldn't walk. 'Darius is dead?' he asked.

'Tragic, really,' Stratokles said. 'Ow!' he grunted.

Herakles was not dead, but his leg was broken in two places, and he had a spear thrust that penetrated the top of the thigh and emerged from the base, and while it had not severed the artery, he had lost blood and slipped into unconsciousness every time he awoke. Charmides had wounds on both arms. Anaxagoras was untouched.

So was Scopasis. He took command. With Darius Thrakes dead, the Bithynians could be mixed in with the Sakje without any deference at all.

The Getae nobleman, Calicles, had a nasty cut across his face. 'I need a better helmet,' he said ruefully. 'Never been in that close a fight before. Not really what we do. That's for Greeks.' He looked around. 'My boys feel that the Sakje might not be so bad,' he said with a half smile. 'And isn't it convenient that Darius the Thracian is dead? Can I just put in my two obols? I'm totally harmless and not minded to desert, yes?'

Satyrus didn't want to drink wine, lest he pass out, but water tasted like blood in his mouth. 'It's a nasty business,' he said. 'War, I mean.'

Calicles nodded. 'I'm a hostage,' he said. 'That's why I was sent.'

Stratokles was trying his wound, moving his left arm up and down. He looked at the Thracian. 'Save it,' he said. 'You won't come to any harm from us.' He looked purely evil, just then, with his cut nose and scarred face, but Satyrus could see that it was only age, fatigue, and self-disgust.

Satyrus glanced at Stratokles. 'Where did Darius die?'

'Our first fight – up the ridge a piece. Took a javelin in the ribs. I didn't even see him go down. Bastards desecrated his corpse. When we found him, the Bithynians went wild.' Stratokles met his eye without hesitation.

Scopasis grunted. 'Useless fuck,' he said.

What an epitaph, Satyrus thought.

*

282

They'd taken heavy casualties, but they'd never again have a chance like they had right then to capitalise on their victory. It was the Sakje way: follow victory, abandon defeat. Satyrus kept his bodyguard and all the wounded, and Scopasis took the surviving Sakje, Getae and Bithynians over the crest of the ridge at dark and into the enemy camp.

Satyrus watched it from the ridge top – not the least sorry not to be participating. He followed the line of Scopasis's raid by the sparks that flew from the fires as the Sakje killed men sleeping by them, and from the tents that burned.

In truth, the damage done was minimal. The next morning, when the raiders had returned and lay like the dead, sleeping by their horses, there wasn't a sign of the raid in the enemy camp besides a few dozen charred tents and a single corpse – a sentry killed in the dark and still unfound by his mates, but already visited by a pair of vultures.

Ten more of Satyrus's men had died in the night, some making a great deal of noise. They had almost fifty prisoners. When Scopasis's raiders were ready to move, Satyrus rode over to the Lydians.

'Cut them loose,' he said, and Draco and Charmides began cutting the thongs that held their wrists.

It would be an hour or more before they had anything like circulation in their hands.

'I'm taking your horses,' Satyrus said. 'I recommend you go home.' He left them there, at the edge of the meadow where their fellow men had died.

His foot still hurt. His back hurt. He hadn't been in the saddle this long since he was nineteen.

But Antigonus had lost the southern ridge, and that meant that he could not outflank their position on the lake. Satyrus left Scopasis and the best of the Bithynians and Sakje, and took the rest of the men back to camp, their dead thrown over the captured horses.

Lysimachos was unimpressed. 'You wanted to go play horse,' he said, looking at the line of dead men. 'My Getae will not love you after this.'

Satyrus twitched. 'Is it nothing to you that we burned part of the enemy camp? That we, not Antigonus, hold the southern valleys?'

Lysimachos nodded. 'It is not nothing. But while you were gone, the old bastard moved his siege engines forward a stade and he's pounding my first-line forts. Only my best pikemen will even go up there.'

Satyrus nodded. 'Plenty of war for everyone, then,' he said heavily. To the east, storm clouds were gathering. He limped off to find Jubal.

Jubal was building a third line of forts – earthen mounds reinforced by timber, with embrasure-mounted engines. They weren't very well made, but they were there.

Jubal clasped hands. 'Lord,' he said. He nodded. 'Lysimachos, he's going to lose the first line, eh? Let him. I can build them faster than he loses them.'

'Ares,' Satyrus said. 'What a way to fight a war.' But he had seen this kind of war at Rhodes, and it held no surprises for him – unlike the meadow full of bees.

That night, Lysimachos's best pikemen set fire to the timbers of the first line and retired in good order. An hour later, the engines of the second line dropped mythemnoi-sized baskets of gravel on the former first line and the Apobatai charged forward into the survivors of some of Antigonus's peltasts, shaken from the bombardment and broken by the charcoal-blackened mercenaries.

The Apobatai retired again with the dawn, leaving a smoking ruin. The first line had cost Antigonus more than three hundred men, and all it had cost Lysimachos was a few bushels of rocks.

The rains came back the next night, and Antigonus assaulted the second line under cover of rain so fierce a man couldn't raise his face to it without pain. The fields between the armies turned to mud, ankle deep or worse. Jubal's entrenchments had drainage, and the fields in front of them didn't; the Antigonids gave themselves away squelching through the mud, and the Lysimachids were ready for them. But after a desperate fight shot with lightning, the old Macedonian veterans pushed the younger men out of the second line forts.

But Jubal already had a fourth line prepared, racing against the rains, and the engines of the third line poured his carefully hoarded stones onto the Antigonids, who discovered that the second line forts were designed to offer no cover from the third line. Antigonus tried again two nights after the rains returned, and they were stopped cold – and bled – in the lightning-soaked ditches. They were still there in daylight, and Satyrus fought in the mud with Charmides and Anaxagoras on

284

either side of him. He threw javelins, yelled encouragement, and for heart-breaking minutes faced desperate men coming up mud-soaked ladders from the ditch. At the end, they offered surrender to the enemy men trapped at the top of the forts, and they accepted gratefully, dropping their shields and sinking to their knees in the mud.

It was probably those prisoners, when they were returned two days later, who told their mates that there was a son of Alexander, alive, in the enemy camp. The wound in his thigh was inflamed, but the Lord of the Silver Bow had not sent red contagion to kill the young man, and the doctors were confident he would recover.

Satyrus rode with a dozen men as escort under Nikephorus, and Lysimachos with twice as many. Antigonus was waiting in the mud at the edge of the lake, and the rain fell like the contempt of the gods.

Satyrus had heard of the old man all his life, but never met him. Now he saw Antigonus, and his respect – bordering on awe – went up threefold. Antigonus was as straight as a sarissa, wearing armour that would make a younger man tired. His white-haired arms were corded in muscle, and the bronze of his cuirass probably covered more of the same.

Satyrus saluted him – the pankrationist's salute.

Antigonus One-Eye nodded. 'You'll be the King of the Bosporus,' he said.

'That's right,' Satyrus said.

Antigonus ignored Lysimachos as if he wasn't even there.

'I reckon you won this round, boy,' the old man said. 'I'd like a day to recover my dead – if I can find them in the mud – and two days free to retreat. In exchange, I won't come back this year.'

Lysimachos spat. 'The year's over, old man. These are winter rains.'

Antigonus's gaze never left Satyrus. 'I hear the wind sighing,' he said. 'Three days' truce.' He shrugged. 'Or I put it to the boys that we're in trouble, and I put my whole army into your lines and see what I can do.'

Lysimachos grinned. 'Even if you won, you'd be done. Seleucus or Ptolemy would eat you alive.'

Antigonus's face was stone. 'Tell the foolish wind that it would make no difference to him. He'd be *dead*.' Antigonus was an old man, but his voice held ... power.

Lysimachos narrowed his eyes. 'Bring it,' he said.

Satyrus shook his head. Lysimachos's Thracians had been deserting for days, headed home across the Propontus. And the pikemen weren't much better. Even Stratokles' men – even Nikephorus's men – had desertions. The weather was appalling. The mud was an awful place to die.

Satyrus rode over to Lysimachos. 'I know you hate him,' he said quietly, 'but if we *win* a pitched battle, the best we'll get is retreat. He's offering to retreat. Let him go with honour.'

Lysimachos took a deep breath. He seemed on the edge of a speech. But the hint of a smile crossed his lips, and he nodded.

'Yes,' he said.

In two days, Antigonus was gone into Mysia.

But the rains continued, and with winter, the pestilence came.

PART V

'You have to hand it to him,' Sophokles said to the empty air. 'He has more lives than a cat, and he has changed the war.'

'Isokles will kill him for me. You have failed,' Phiale said. She was on a swing, well over his head – one of the divertissements of Lycurgus's new Temple of Aphrodite. Sophokles was practising his knife pass, over and over, and apparently talking to the wall – or to the statue of Aphrodite as a war-goddess.

'Isokles may be a dab hand at terrifying prostitutes, but he's not exactly a man-killer,' Sophokles said.

'He's quite mad. Perhaps god-possessed. Who knows?' Phiale's voice was dreamy.

'Well, if so, perhaps he has a chance, because Satyrus and Melitta are, between them, quite the most god-helped pair I've encountered. I look forward to killing them' – Sophokles flicked his dagger from right to left hand before making his lunge – 'because it appeals to my highly developed sense of hubris.'

Phiale leaped from her swing and landed like the dancer she was. 'Satyrus has a lover,' she said.

'That's not really surprising,' Sophokles put in.

'Shush, you are ingracious. His lover is, if you can imagine, some barbarian girl of Alexandria. I want you to take her for me.' She smiled over her shoulder at him and did a back flip, which stripped her, as her chiton fell away at the top of her leap.

Sophokles collected her garment, dabbed at his face with it, and handed it to her. 'You have a superb body, despoina. I will not kill some barbarian slave in Alexandria for you. It is beneath me.'

Phiale kicked off her sandals. 'I could say that a barbarian in Alexandria might be your speed. If I was in a cruel mood.'

Sophokles stopped moving, tossed his dagger into the base of the statue of Aphrodite, and watched her. She was naked, standing on the balls of her feet, her very pose an inflammation.

'Am I being seduced?' he asked.

'No. Seduction is subtle.' Phiale stepped inside his guard and ran a thumb up his thigh, brushed his penis with her fingers, and slipped away from him with the same sort of motions he used in combat. 'This is more direct,' she said.

She turned, her eyes never leaving him, and lay down on the side altar.

She had two killers to suit her needs, and she could bind them both with simple tools – her body, hard silver. But in the Temple of Aphrodite she was a priestess, and with a partner she could work the most powerful and dangerous magics.

Sophokles rutted away – in this, he was no assassin, but merely a typical man – and she chanted her spell to his rhythm. And she built the force of it in her head until it was a black dove, and she sent it winging away across the sea.

Isokles had a house in Heraklea and a pair of slaves, and his six men terrorised the neighbourhood. It was a good life. Isokles had messengers from Phiale, and from Cassander, and he revelled in his role as a dangerous man, courted by important people. He had wealth and position. He had been received by Amastris herself. He paid bribes to a dozen of her court functionaries, and he bribed her slaves, and if Stratokles had still been in her employ, he would by now have caught the intruder and punished him. But Amastris had made a different choice, and her captain of the guard was one of the men Isokles paid so well.

Isokles drank wine, forced sex on his slaves, and waited for spring, like a hideous spider waiting in a nearly invisible web.

Diodorus lay on a couch in the heat of Babylon. Sappho, his wife, lay on a separate couch. It was that hot.

'Will Seleucus go?' Sappho asked.

It was the question on the lips of every informed man and woman in the city. Lysimachos had requested that Seleucus come north and west with his army. It was an open secret that Lysimachos had almost been destroyed in the autumn, that Cassander was a wreck, that Ptolemy had retired to Aegypt in disgust.

It was said that Antigonus had two hundred elephants and eighty thousand men.

Diodorus was sixty years old. It lay lightly on him – his chest was still as well muscled as his breastplate, and his arms were like the arms of a statue of Ares. But his hair was entirely white. He sat up, and a slave fanned him harder, mistaking his motion for a demand for a cool breeze.

Diodorus looked at the woman he loved and shook his head. 'Want to go back to winters?' he asked. 'I can't go back to Alexandria. And I think I'm getting too old for this. Time to retire.'

'Tanais?' she asked.

'We own about a third of it, you and I,' he said.

'So?' she asked.

'So Seleucus has summoned me for the second hour after the sun is at its peak to speak to him about Satyrus of Tanais,' Diodorus said. 'He has no love for Lysimachos.'

'I could go home,' Sappho said.

'Home?' Diodorus asked.

'Olbia, where my life changed. Or Tanais.' She smiled, and rose from her couch. 'Babylon is too hot,' she said. 'And the bugs are oppressive, and the locals are too subservient. The only people to talk to here are the Jews and the Medes.' She laughed. 'Listen to me. I was a *slave* for six years, and now I talk like a Macedonian.'

Diodorus bent and kissed her. 'May I make a confession?' he said.

'You made love to my new washerwoman? In that case, you can wash your own fighting clothes.' She hit him with her fan.

'The one with the squint, or the one with the strange skin disease? No. I wish to confess that I want to take the Exiles north and fight. If Seleucus goes, this will be the end. One way or another. The last cast of the dice.' He shrugged. 'It's my curse.'

'Damn that Kineas. He had to tell you that he left you all his battles.' Sappho had heard the story a hundred times.

'If he was alive, he would be there.' Diodorus waved a slave towards him.

'If he was alive ...' Sappho said, and smiled. 'I hear Satyrus made a brilliant campaign.'

'He changed the war,' Diodorus said with satisfaction.

'He is like his father,' Sappho said.

Diodorus shrugged. 'Yes and no. Kineas was a mercenary with the heart of a king. Satyrus is a king with the heart of a mercenary.'

Sappho shook her head. 'No. I know him better than you. He is a man of worth. Like my brothers. Like you, my dear.'

Diodorus raised an eyebrow. 'That is my yearly compliment – I had better treasure it. I hope he is a man of worth, my dear, because he has become the linchpin of this year's campaign. I'd best be going.'

'Give Seleucus and his paramour my deepest obeisance,' Sappho said.

'With or without the sarcasm?' Diodorus asked, but the question was apparently rhetorical, as he didn't wait for an answer.

Sappho called for her body servant, and asked for a stylus and a tablet.

Leon sat back on his kline and read Sappho's letter for the third time. By his side, Nihmu lay with her head on the armrest, her eyes out to sea.

'You will go again,' she said.

'You could come with me,' he said.

'To Tanais?' she asked. 'To the Sea of Grass?' Her breath caught.

Leon shook his head. 'We'll rally the fleets at Rhodes,' he said. 'I expect that the fight, when it happens, will be in Asia – probably far from the sea. Plistias is at Miletus. Demetrios holds the mouth of the Propontus.' Leon shrugged heavily. 'All my ships, all Ptolemy's and what Rhodes has left – all together, two hundred hulls. Demetrios and Plistias built all winter – no idea what they'll have. But I'll be surprised if they have *fewer* than two hundred hulls.' Leon shook his head. 'Everyone has their eyes on the armies and the elephants. A fleet of two hundred hulls has as many men as an army of fifty thousand.'

Nihmu sighed. 'Yes, dear.'

Leon passed a hand down her back. 'This is the end. Or at least, all of us will try to make it the end.' He looked at the letter. 'Diodorus and Crax and Sappho are coming up from Babylon with Seleucus.'

Nihmu looked out over the sea. 'All of Kineas's people, one last time.'

Leon looked at her, and she was crying.

'Did he know what was to come?' she asked. 'I never saw this.'

Leon smiled. 'Why cry? We will see all of our friends.'

Nihmu managed a small smile. 'Yes,' she said. 'And then we will die.'

Leon smiled. His wife had been a prophetess, and she was wont to say such things. Sometimes they had meaning, and sometimes they didn't, and sometimes the meaning was subtle. So he smiled, kissed her, and got to his feet. 'The children of men are born to die,' he said.

Nihmu nodded. 'I should practise my archery,' she allowed.

Antigonus sat on a leopard skin thrown over a stool, and watched two oarsmen wrestling for a prize.

Demetrios sat beside him, and the boy's presence made him ... whole. Happy. Even if the young fool wanted to be a god. That was a young man's fantasy. Antigonus One-Eye had eighty-two years' worth of pain, wounds, and age. He no longer wanted to live for ever, but he was damned if he was going down easily.

'I have the best army I've had since the king died,' Antigonus said.

'You mean Alexander,' Demetrios said. 'You and I are kings, now.'

'I mean the king. He was king. We ... are fighting in the ruins of his temple.' Antigonus watched the sun setting over the sea. 'Bring me your whole army – everything. Leave fucking Cassander holding his limp dick and come over to Asia. Let's do it – one throw for everything. I'm tired, and I've been *this* close ten times, and I want to *win*.'

A slow smile spread over Demetrios's face. 'You and me ... together? One army? Nothing will defeat us.'

Antigonus nodded. 'Nothing ever has,' he said. 'Mind you, buy every fucking hoplite in Greece before you come. Buy *everyone*. Bloat yourself. Buy them even if it is just to deny them to fucking Cassander. Buy all the Thessalians you can find.'

'You have cash?' Demetrios asked.

'You own Athens, son. Don't expect cash from me.' Antigonus grunted. 'I met your Satyrus,' he noted.

'You liked him!' Demetrios said.

'He's worth fifty of Lysimachos. Not a bad little strategos – fell for an old chestnut in the mountains, then put one over on me.' Antigonus chuckled. 'Wish you could buy him. Since you can't, I've paid to have him poisoned.'

'Poisoned! Pater, he's a hero!' Demetrios shook his head. 'That's womanish.'

'My child, I'm eighty-two years old. I can be as womanish as I want.' The old man smiled, though. 'You know why we'll win?'

'Because I'm going to be a god?' Demetrios asked.

'No. Not by a long chalk.' Antigonus drank some wine. That part of life remained good. He still liked good wine. And strong bread with a crust. And the sight of a field he'd won.

'Because we have Athens and Tyre and all the money?' Demetrios said.

'I won't pretend that won't help,' Antigonus said, and chuckled. 'But no. It's because Cassander is a useless fuck, and Ptolemy wants it to end, and Lysimachos can't find his arse with both hands in the dark, and Seleucus is an arrogant pup ... and they all hate each other. You and me, son, we trust each other, and when the bronze meets the iron, that's what will count.'

Demetrios put his arms around his father and kissed him. 'I'll be there when you call,' he said.

Antigonus drank off his wine and tossed the cup into the sea. 'Then sod 'em all,' he said. 'We'll be kings of the world.'

The caravan came to Heraklea with fifty camels and a hundred horses, laden with spices and silk and fine cottons, wool shawls from the lands east of Hyrkania, swords forged by legendary giants, and twenty loads of lapis lazuli quarried in the high, high passes of Sogdia and Bactria.

The caravan was commanded by a woman, and her tribesmen called her 'The Widow.' She was rumoured to be beautiful, and her voice was gentle, but the tough, dark Sogdian mercenaries told the boys in the souk how she had killed a bandit in the high passes with her steel, and how she had killed another – one of their own, who thought she might warm his bed – with a thumb into his brain through his eye.

Covered in dust, robed to the throat and wearing a Persian burnoose, she was slim, but that was all that could be said of her. And rich – she was certainly about to be rich. The lapis alone was the largest cargo of the fine stone to arrive in thirty years.

She spoke Greek with rapid, accurate fluency. The traders of the souk loved and hated her at once, and her vicious guards, who caught a thief by the camels, gutted him, and staked him by their lines as a warning to others.

She was still covered in dust when she finished bargaining with a jewel merchant for a handful of uncut rubies – the only sale she was interested in making – and it brought her a bag of gold darics and the eyes of every thief in Heraklea. Only her eyes showed, which the jeweller thought was an unfair advantage in making a deal, but they were beautiful eyes, large and liquid and a remarkable, lapis-dark blue, and besides, for all her bargaining, he'd just made a year's wage. He felt beneficent when she asked her question.

Leon the Nubian? Of course he still had a factor here. Directions were provided.

The widow shouted orders, and men did things, and the souk made room for fifty camels and their attendants. She had an astounding number of Sogdian mercenaries, and some Hyrkanians. Their horses alone were enough to excite envy.

She walked, accompanied by two Hyrkanians, through the alleys behind the agora to the warehouse she'd been told to visit. Really, an old Greek home sandwiched between two warehouses.

Leon's factor was a young man with a black beard and dancing eyes – hard to see that he had been a slave since birth, or perhaps all that joy was the result in ending free. He bowed; informants had already brought him word of her arrival, but he was stunned to have the agora's new star descend on his doorstep.

Before her heart had beat a hundred times, she was reclining on a couch with a cup of wine in her hand. A slave helped her roll the burnoose off her shoulders and head, and under the folds of her dusty Persian coat, she wore a man's chitoniskos. Her Persian boots were replaced by gold sandals from her bag.

Leon's man, Hector, raised his cup. 'To Hermes, god of travellers, who brings you to my door. And to whom should I pledge this cup, lady of the beautiful eyes?'

She had a playful smile, for a matron of mature years. 'Your master and I have been more rivals than friends,' she said. 'Nonetheless, I believe we are allies now, and I have brought a cargo to help finance an army.'

Hector shook his head. 'You have the better of me, my lady. If my master had a rival such as you, I would surely know.'

'Bah,' she said, and the lapis eyes flickered. 'I am an old woman and the world has forgotten me. My name is forgotten. But when I was young, men called me Banugul.'

Hector knew her then: the woman that his master called the 'Viper of Hyrkania'.

But as she was proposing to *give* him the contents of the richest caravan in thirty years, he was hard put to see how she might be plotting against him.

By the end of the day, she and her men had largely taken over his house. It worried him but she allowed – insisted, in fact – that he write letters to Tanais and to Alexandria. He sent a third copy to Rhodes. And then he was busy, as he found himself in control of the lapis market. It was a delightful way for a merchant to live.

Miriam sat on a couch, her legs stretched out before her, and opened the scroll. She did a great deal of her brother's business – it kept her from thinking. And thinking made her feel ill.

But the letter from Heraklea was for Leon, not for Abraham. She hesitated, but the name *Satyrus of Tanais* leapt off the page at her, and she couldn't help herself. At some point in the long missive, she pivoted her legs from couch to floor, rose and walked out of the garden – lovingly restored – across the tile floor of the former andron, now part of the larger reception hall, and up the short steps to her brother's warehouse.

Abraham, dressed in the long robes of a Jew, stood with Daedelus of Halicarnassus. They were old comrades, of course, but her brother's eyes positively glittered.

Miriam was suddenly conscious that she was not dressed to receive. But she was in the warehouse, where women were not welcome, and she couldn't bring herself to leave and change.

Abraham grinned at her like a fool. 'Leon's on his way!' he said. 'Ptolemy has sent part of his fleet – I'm to have a command!' He caught himself, tried to restore the imperturbable demeanour of a man of worth. Failed, and grinned again. Then tried to put his grin away, all too aware how Miriam was going to feel when he rowed off to fight alongside Leon ... and Satyrus.

'This letter is for Leon,' she said. She shrugged, an eloquent shrug that suggested that she, as a mere woman, made these mistakes, and she'd read it, and really, no one should chide her for it – all in a shrug. 'Banugul of Hyrkania is at Heraklea with a convoy of goods to be made into money for her son to buy mercenaries.' She held out the letter. 'Almost a thousand talents, the letter says.'

Daedelus shook his head. 'A thousand talents? By Hephaestus's forge – that's enough to buy Antigonus.'

Abraham scratched his beard. 'She's ... an enemy. But of course, her son is with Stratokles, and Stratokles ...' He looked at his sister.

Miriam sighed. 'Stratokles is a side all by himself.'

Daedelus made a face. 'I've heard of her, too. Alexander's mistress. But what does this change?'

Abraham shook his head. 'Nothing. But we couldn't get a message back through anyway. As soon as the winter storms are off the heavens, Demetrios will close the Propontus. As it is, the captain who brought the letter must be a madman.'

'Insane,' said a voice from the warehouse door.

Miriam's heart stopped.

'I thought that the winter winds were a safer bet than two hundred triremes,' Satyrus said. He had on his ancient, pale blue chiton and his sea boots, and he looked more like a fisherman than the King of the Bosporus.

Abraham threw his arms around his friend.

Satyrus had the good grace to look at his friend while he embraced him. Then his glance went back to Miriam.

'I came to try you one more time,' he said. He seemed unembarrassed to have Daedelus and Abraham present.

The hardened sea-mercenary grew red. His eyes met with Abraham's.

'I ... think I hear my mother calling me,' he muttered.

'Cup of wine before you go?' Abraham asked.

'Jews are the most hospitable of men,' Daedelus said.

He reached out for her hand, and she gave it to him. They sat – uncomfortably – on a chest of Athenian blackware and wood shavings. For a time that would have bored an onlooker, they said nothing.

'You must be Poseidon's own son,' she said quietly.

'Surely your Jehovah doesn't tolerate Poseidon,' Satyrus said. 'As he's a jealous god.'

She grew red.

'There are Jews in Tanais, now. I tried to get their priest to teach me Hebrew. He had to admit he wasn't very good at it himself.' Satyrus shrugged. 'We spent the winter talking Greek, instead. He's building a temple – a small one. I'm paying.'

She looked away.

'I can't be a Jew,' Satyrus said. 'Please look at me, this is no jest. I understand that it is the religion of your people. I can respect it, but I heard nothing from that good man in Tanais that would cause me to leave the worship of Herakles ... or Apollo, or Athena, or Pythagoras or Socrates or even Aristotle. But to me, it is a list of rules – rules made to govern people in a place far from my people. Perhaps every religion is such. But Herakles cares nothing for my taste in meat, only that I be excellent. That I pour everything I have into that excellence, and never allow myself to settle for second-rate. And it occurred to me, this winter, that you were the most excellent person I had ever met – that I would not settle for some Greek girl or some Sakje princess with a thousand horses, any more than I would allow other men to settle the world while I watched.'

'You might have died, sailing here.' She was angry.

He nodded. 'I thought that I would die last autumn. Melitta thought so. There was an augury.' He rubbed his chin. There was salt in his hair, making him look older than he was. 'I am not a stripling. So I won't tell you that I will die without you. But I would certainly *live* with you.'

She nodded. 'Shouldn't you be at Heraklea with Cassander and Lysimachos? Preparing for the last act of the war?'

He looked into her eyes. 'No. That's for Stratokles. He should be there by now. My sister and I have sent out the word, gathered our taxes, talked to our farmers and our tribesmen. Stratokles can negotiate for us.'

'You trust him?' she said, her eyes wide.

Satyrus smiled. 'There is some magic to him,' he said. 'I have come two thousand stades across storm-racked seas to see the woman I love, and we are discussing Stratokles.'

They gazed at each other.

'If you will live with me – wife, mistress, friend, whatever role you choose – we can look into each other's eyes for ever,' he said.

She licked her lips, then looked away. 'No,' she said. 'In time, it will lose its savour. We will argue about raising our children, about the rights of Jews in the town, about the way you levy tolls. About Stratokles. About war.'

Satyrus got to his feet. 'Yes, I agree. I think it sounds like a lovely way to pass the time. I'd rather argue acrimoniously with you than grow restless with the dull smiles of a princess and feel guilty while I fuck her slaves.' He turned back to her. 'Was that too blunt?' He took both her hands. 'We survived a year in the siege of Rhodes, and I saw you tested in the crucible of Ares – and you wanted nothing.'

She took a deep breath. He saw it in her face.

'Must I beg?' he asked.

She shook her head. 'Listen, Satyrus. Stop your chatter and listen. After Ephesus, I asked myself this: if I am not a Jew, what am I? Who am I?' She shook her head. 'And inside my head, I hear the same voice I have heard since my husband died. Since I told my father that I wouldn't go back to him.' She clenched his hands *hard*, as if she was drowning and he could save her. 'I think that you imagine that I am strong, and I am weak. I fear to fail you, and I fear to find that you have subsumed me – that I will become a body and a complacent smile. I am not your match.'

He was smiling. His smile annoyed her.

'You think that you know *everything*,' she said pettishly.

'I know you. What you say is true, but you are *you*. You think I lack these fears? Last year, I nearly lost my life and my kingdom through ignoring the counsel of my counsellors. I am ignoring my sister to plunge my kingdom into debt to fight a war that may not be my business. I am more like Demetrios than I would admit to anyone but you, and to be honest, my love, I am giving my all to defeat Demetrios and Antigonus, and I'm all but sure that they are the better men. I am tired of war and I'm no longer sure of what my motivations are for fighting. My road here is littered with corpses of people I loved – Diokles died in the autumn, Helios died here, Philokles, Nestor – like paving stones in the road, and when I am drifting off to sleep, I wince and roll and roll again, trying to be someone else, someone who does not kill people every summer. And despite all that, I enjoy my wine, and I love the sea, and I would trade the rest of my life to lie tonight in your bed.'

She flushed. 'That was too blunt,' she said with a smile.

'No it wasn't.' He put his arms around her.

She kissed him. He had hesitated, because forcing his kisses on her was far from his intention. She didn't raise her face and wait – she locked her hands behind his head and kissed him.

299

'You ... changed your mind?' he said.

'No. Listen, love. I will talk to Abraham, and if I have his agreement, I will try you – us – a day at a time.' She shrugged. Kissed him, and stepped away. 'And you will not be in my bed tonight. Curse it. But once you are there, I suspect that I will never have you out of it.'

Satyrus grabbed her, ran a hand down her side to her hip, and she squealed, and he laughed.

The sound of their laughter carried into the garden.

'The King of the Bosporus is seducing my sister,' Abraham said, and raised his cup for more wine.

'I'll drink to that,' Daedelus said.

Stratokles arrived in Heraklea like a priest going to a festival. It was, in every way, the high point of his life, the culmination of his work, and the discovery that Banugul of Hyrkania was living in the house of Leon's factor added to its savour. And the money she had, of course.

Her arrival pointed up something he had believed all his life, jumping from web to web across the plots of lesser men. That if you planned well, worked hard, and did your very best, the gods would grant you luck. He had never planned on Banugul. But the cash she brought made his job easy.

Cassander came to Heraklea, a broken reed, but still strong. He had raised a new army in Europe, and a small fleet. Lysimachos was there, with Amastris; now undisputed lord of Mysia and the Troad, with thirty thousand professional soldiers, twenty elephants, and a fleet of heavy ships.

Aiax Seleucus, the King of Babylon's nephew, was there, representing fifty thousand men and a hundred elephants, already said to be marching across Asia up the Royal Road to Sardis.

No one spoke for Ptolemy, but Stratokles had his letter in his scroll bag, telling of two hundred ships gathering in the harbour of Rhodes to open the Dardanelles when the summer winds began to blow.

Mithridates of Bithynia was there, lord of ten thousand cavalrymen, master of the gates of Asia, and now their firm ally.

It made Stratokles laugh, as he lay by Banugul in a house he had once stormed to kill Satyrus and Melitta of Tanais – where he was now an honoured guest. He stroked her side and thought of how, a year before, these same 'allies' had elected to murder him. And now, as the captain general of Satyrus and Melitta, his money and his acumen and their soldiers were the porpax of the alliance – the handle by which all the other rivals grasped the shield.

'I have never seen you so happy,' Banugul murmured.

'Nor I, you,' he said into her ear.

'My son is a better man,' she said. 'And more important – he is *alive*.'

'He is a fine man, and one who has, I think, found that he does not want to be Alexander's son. He wants to be his own man – perhaps King of Hyrkania.' Stratokles smiled.

'Meaning you no longer need him,' she said.

Stratokles rolled over, kissed her, reached across her and took the wine cup from the table by the bed, sharing it with her. 'I cannot help who I am,' he said. 'I have plots, and plots, and plots. Some succeed, and some fail. And my greatest flaw is that I hedge my own bets, and some of my plots are rivals to other of my plots.' He lay back and grinned into the lamplit darkness. 'I had planned to use your son to drive Cassander mad. As it is, Cassander has placed himself in my hands, and your son doesn't want to be a tool. So I have become wise enough not to struggle.'

'I have put money into a rumour,' Banugul said. 'That he is the son of Eumenes of Kardia.'

Stratokles laughed. 'Well played, lady. No Macedonian would cross the street to serve a bastard son of Eumenes.' He reached for her shoulders. 'But he is Alexander's son.'

'Perhaps,' she allowed. 'Are you really friends with Kineas's son? Will this alliance last?'

He chuckled, and gave her no answer, and they passed the time with other things.

But in the morning, with Lucius at his back, Stratokles walked up to the Temple of Hera.

He was dressed in his very best – a chiton with flames of Tyrian red licking up the shining white wool from the hems, themselves so thick with embroidery that the gold pins that held it together were difficult to push through the cloth. Over his shoulder hung a chlamys of pure red-purple, embroidered in gold, and on his brow sat a diadem of gold and red-purple amethysts, worth the value of a heavy penteres all by itself, without reckoning the other accoutrements he wore – gold sandals with gold buckles, gold mountings on the dagger under his armpit, gold rings on his fingers. It had cost him extra time and effort to reassemble the costume, but the effect was worth it. For his chiton and his diadem proclaimed to all of them: *You tried to kill me, and here I am, and I hold the reins of this chariot.*

It was no longer about Athens. Stratokles had loved Athens all of his life but Demetrios was sucking the marrow from Athens's bones. And when he fell – if Cassander could be destroyed with him – Athens would be free. Or as free as a city could be in the world of monsters that Alexander had created.

So he walked up the steps. Nodded to Lysimachos, bowed to Amastris, smiled at Phiale, and laughed at Cassander, whose eyes flashed with venom.

Once, this man called me a viper.

They mouthed pious nothings.

'And where is your new master?' Phiale asked.

'Satyrus of Tanais?' he asked, as if unsure who she meant. 'Elsewhere, engaged in more important business.'

The shock that this statement engendered was worth all the torments of the last year.

'His sister?' Lysimachos asked.

'On the Sea of Grass,' Stratokles said. 'They send their regrets.'

'Ares!' Lysimachos said. 'They have deserted the alliance?'

Stratokles smiled. He had all the time in the world. 'I have their instructions,' he said.

'This is intolerable!' Cassander said.

Stratokles smiled, swirled his wine, and contemplated an excellent image of the goddess – imperious, matronly, and yet beautiful. Not his favourite goddess – and yet, and yet.

'Allies,' Stratokles said. They all looked at him. He bowed to the priestess of Hera. 'My instructions are that we all swear an oath in the names of our principles, to support the alliance until Antigonus is defeated – and for one year after. I have taken the liberty of drawing up copies in advance.'

'I do not take orders from a petty king, nor from his petty minister,' Cassander said. His face was puffy, and his fingers under their rings were bloated, like those of a corpse left in the water.

Stratokles didn't need the doctor to tell him – Cassander had oedema. He wasn't fat, he was bloated with water.

Oh, the gods do what a man cannot, Stratokles thought.

'These are not orders,' Stratokles said. 'We are here as allies – as peers.'

'I am the King of Macedon, and you are a paid informant.' Cassander had once been the handsomest of mortals. Now he was hideous, and he seemed unaware of the change in his physique; speeches that had once seemed imperious now seemed pathetic.

Stratokles turned to the other kings. 'I had no intention of offending. It was our intention to plan a campaign – we had assumed that all were in favour of it.'

The younger Seleucid nodded. 'Stratokles of Athens, it is my brother's intention to march west with his elephants and his cavalry. But if Cassander will not come ...'

'I am the King of Macedon,' Cassander said again. 'I am the head of this alliance.'

Lysimachos took the man by the elbow. Stratokles saw the King of Macedon wince in pain at the touch.

Lysimachos spoke quickly, his voice low, and when Phiale attempted to step in close to her lord, Lysimachos straight-armed her away – almost a blow. She turned on her heel and walked away down the steps of the temple.

If only I had thought to have assassins waiting for her. Stratokles watched her, and then looked back at Cassander, who was nodding. He looked at Lucius, and Lucius gave the smallest nod towards Phiale, and Stratokles blinked once. That was all. Lucius was gone in the swirl of his chlamys, away down the steps, apparently in the opposite direction from Phiale.

The King of Macedon brushed his cloak, bowed to the priestess of Hera, and walked carefully to Stratokles.

'I'm sorry,' he said. 'I'm in pain in the mornings, and I get pettish. We all know' – the words seemed to come out of him like gallstones from a surgeon's patient – 'how much you've done for the alliance.'

Damn, that was good, Stratokles thought. *I could die now.*

Cassander lowered his voice. 'I will not forget this,' he said.

Stratokles met his eyes. 'You mean, you will not forget that despite your best attempts to have me killed, I continue to serve your interests? I forget nothing, sir. I would have to offend you for *years* before I would hold myself avenged. But,' he said mildly, 'I am not master in this house. The object of this alliance is the destruction of Antigonus. Are we agreed?'

It took four days. But it turned out, in the end, that they had this in common – they hated Antigonus more than they hated each other.

Phiale broke every cup in her borrowed house. She went to the slave quarters and started on their pottery.

'Satyrus isn't even here!' she roared.

Isokles shrugged. 'He'll have to come. Then I kill him.'

'He isn't coming!' Phiale said. 'Aphrodite, he must be guided by the gods. Or you have a spy in this house.'

Isokles crossed his arms. 'Despoina, shut up. Listen. This is the heart of the alliance. This port receives their soldiers – this is their supply base. Ares' rock-hard dick, he will come here in time, and I'll have him. I have people in every warehouse, every pier, on the beaches, gate guards ... this town is mine.' He grinned. 'He will sail in here, or march in here, and I'll have him.'

Phiale threw another pot – a heavy water jug. The smash was satisfying.

'What if he never comes here?' she asked.

The Latin returned with a cut on his arm. 'It's like kicking a beehive,' he said. 'The killer she hired in Athens? I saw him. He's got twenty soldiers and some local thugs.'

Stratokles made the same face that an armourer makes when looking at another craftsman's shoddy work. 'Amastris is getting sloppy,' he said.

That evening he had a long talk with Banugul, one professional to another.

'I need you to befriend Amastris,' he said. 'As one queen to another. She could be a useful ally, and she's been infiltrated. Cassander – or Phiale – or maybe even Demetrios's Neron. I'm not sure who they're all working for but this town is full of bribes and traitors. And we *need* this town.'

Banugul smiled. 'I admire your version of love talk.' She nodded. 'Heraklea would make me a good ally. Will you introduce us?'

Stratokles grinned. 'Best she not know that we share ... anything.'

'I still think you were her lover.' Banugul flicked a finger into his side and made him jump.

'She's too young for me, and besides, not every woman can see through my ugliness to the worthy philosopher inside.' He laughed.

She tickled him. 'You are a fool.'

'Would you marry me, if we live through the year?' Stratokles asked.

Sophokles knew that Satyrus of Tanais was on Rhodes as soon as he landed. It wasn't exactly a secret, but the news was new enough not to have made it across the straits to Miletus.

He had gone to Alexandria on her orders and found no quarry at all. Her information was wrong. Sophokles, released from the spell of her presence, had a profound and abiding temptation to ride away into Asia and be shot of the whole thing. He had no interest whatsoever in killing the Jewish girl. No challenge – and as like as not, Phiale was wrong about the whole thing. She was – he allowed himself to think it – cursed. Perhaps mad.

Sophokles also suspected that she was working for Neron, Demetrios's spymaster. A double or even triple agent. And that made her tasks too dangerous even to contemplate, because he wouldn't know the consequences.

But Satyrus of Tanais – that was a worthy target. Beloved of the gods, or so men said. And as Phiale, Cassander, and Antigonus all offered substantial rewards for his death, he was the most valuable contract Sophokles had ever had. That *anyone* had ever had.

Balanced against that, Sophokles had only failed a dozen times in his life, and most of them had involved Satyrus to one extent or another.

The memory of the twelve-year-old boy's searing contempt was burned into his head.

Sophokles took rooms in a house that rented to merchants, and began to make his plans. He had four men, and he used them carefully – the agora, the warehouses. It took him three days to establish for a fact that Satyrus was living with Abraham the Jew. Was surrounded by well-armed friends. Was deeply in love with the Jew's sister – no secret here on Rhodes.

*

'Miriam?' Satyrus came into the garden with three big men – big even by the standards of a tall woman with a tall warrior brother.

She rose, and they touched hands. They had reached a stage where they couldn't help but touch each other in public – the tension was a delight and a temptation and a deep frustration. Satyrus suspected that the slaves were laughing at them. He knew Anaxagoras was laughing.

'These are friends of yours?' Miriam asked. They were a frightful trio – like Titans come to life. Easily the grimmest men Miriam had ever been confronted with.

'These three are Achilles, Odysseus and Ajax,' Satyrus said, and grinned.

Miriam smiled. 'I can believe it,' she said.

'They have served me well. And deserve better than being dragged through a war.' Satyrus shook his head – just being with her clouded his wits.

Achilles laughed. 'You two're a picture, you know that, eh?' He stuck out a great hand to Miriam. 'Satyrus wants us to be your guards.'

She looked at them. 'I will be the envy of every matron in Rhodes.'

Odysseus leered at her. 'Yep,' he said.

Ajax stroked his beard, looking at the house. 'I could learn to like it here.'

Achilles looked at Satyrus. 'No strings? This is it – look after this woman?' He nodded. 'I'd think you'd done right by us, and more.'

'Until the horde of barbarians attacks,' Ajax said.

Miriam put her hands on her hips. 'You know what I see? Three agora toughs who are going to make all my slaves pregnant and drink all my wine. Why do I need guards?'

Anaxagoras came in with her brother. He saluted her on the cheek, clasped hands with Achilles. 'Ask that again, despoina?'

'Why do I need guards?' Miriam asked.

'Satyrus is here because we convinced him that there were so many different people trying to kill him that he should evade the net, do something unexpected, and vanish.' Anaxagoras put a hand on Satyrus's shoulder. 'Satyrus thinks that everyone in the world knows ... well, that you and he are close.'

Miriam flushed.

Abraham raised an eyebrow. 'Everyone on Rhodes, anyway.'

Anaxagoras nodded. 'My point exactly. So Satyrus has brought these three fine men, ' he aimed a little bow at Achilles, who grinned, 'to protect you.'

Miriam raised an eyebrow. 'And you? Are leaving?' The slightest tremor touched her voice.

Satyrus shook his head. 'I'm a fool, Miriam. I should have started with this. Yes – I won't wait for Leon, much as I want to see him. I'm going by sea to Aigai, then overland to Seleucus. I have the plan of the summer campaign. And I'll deliver it in person. It seems unlikely to me that anyone will manage to assassinate me on the Euphrates – indeed, no one will even know who I am.' He took a breath. 'But you will be a target. And if you are not then these three n'er-do-wells will have a place to have a well-earned rest.'

'Well,' Miriam said. 'I see. No need for me to complain, then.'

Satyrus, it turned out, was a hero of epic proportions to the Rhodians.

Sophokles hadn't lived so long in his business by being a fool. No murder on Rhodes – an island – would be survivable. The Rhodians would torture the man who killed their hero. He could see ways to make the kill and escape but the risk was enormous.

Worse, the Jew girl suddenly had three very dangerous-looking bodyguards – huge, showy men who had the eyes of the real thing. Sophokles saw those eyes in the mirror. He knew the type.

His men were scared of the new bodyguards.

Best, he thought, to bide his time.

Sophokles liked Rhodes, and he was in no hurry. He felt as if he was at the hub of the world. He lay on his hard linen mattress and listened to the world turn. All news came to Rhodes; that Seleucus had marched from Babylon, that Antigonus was marching to meet him. That the allies had signed a compact at Heraklea, and that Stratokles had directed it. Sophokles raised a cup of wine to his former ... comrade? Co-contractor? The man had turned the tables on Cassander – widely held the wiliest of the Diadochoi.

Demetrios had an army and a fleet in the Dardanelles, and was marching east to oppose Lysimachos. His fleet was waiting at Abydos to face the combined fleets of Rhodes, Aegypt, and Cassander.

And Satyrus of Tanais was lying on a couch on Rhodes, apparently taking no part.

Sophokles took a week to develop his informants. Abraham's house was virtually impossible to penetrate, he found; instead of slaves, the man had Jews, and they were immune to bribes. Or rather, as Sophokles found to his cost, they took the bribes and reported them.

The next thing he knew, one of his local thugs was bleeding to death in the street, and one of the big bodyguards was pounding on the door of his rooming house, and the other two were watching the back of the building.

Sophokles had not stayed alive by being a fool. He was off across the roofs in a moment. In an hour, he was back on a ship for Miletus, a step ahead of the men who had started watching *him*.

He was sitting in a wine shop on the old harbour in Miletus, watching fish rise to his breadcrumbs and considering, once again, the possibility of giving up the whole thing and riding away, when he saw a triakonter come into the harbour like a racing boat – oars flowing like the legs on a water bug, flashing in the watery spring sun. And then the boat turned end for end, slowed in the chops of its own turn, and backed stern first onto the beach, almost at Sophokles' feet. The men took a meal, and hired a pilot for the Cilician coast. And Satyrus of Tanais leaped into the shallow surf. Several of his friends leaped after him, calling for wine.

Satyrus of Tanais was ashore in enemy-held Asia, with a handful of friends and no escort.

Sophokles was so tempted by the immediacy of it that he strung his bow and put an arrow to it before he reconsidered. He couldn't guarantee a kill at this range.

He followed them as they purchased food – always expensive on Rhodes – and two slave rowers, who they freed on the spot. Sophokles watched them all night, but they were in among the wealthy men of the town and Sophokles had abandoned his men and had no henchmen.

And in the morning, the lithe triakonter sped away south, towards the distant shores of Cilicia and Aigai, their destination. That much, Sophokles had gleaned.

Sophokles gathered new men, waited a day, chartered a boat, and followed. He was excited enough that he had trouble sleeping. The gods were handing him his prey.

Ten days later, they landed at Aigai, and Sophokles was a day behind them. He landed up the coast, rode in disguised as a Jew – the irony

308

was not lost on him – in time to hear them buying horses – good horses, at an exorbitant rate in the agora. They weren't quiet men, and the two most handsome bickered constantly, and bragged to the horse-wrangler that they were going to ride 'clear across Asia'.

All the time in the world, then. Sophokles brought in his men, purchased a pair of thugs who passed as caravan guards to bulk up his force, and tried to decide whether it was better to sell Satyrus to the highest bidder, or just kill him.

17

'This is the safer option,' Satyrus said.

He was lying in the light of a small campfire, with Anaxagoras's travelling lyre in his hands. He'd played his best piece, and no one was very impressed.

'Safer than what? Suicide?' Anaxagoras asked.

'We can't sail back through the Dardanelles,' Satyrus said.

'Agreed,' Apollodorus said. 'Lunatic to try the first time.'

Jubal nodded, took a bite of apple, and winked.

'It will be two months before Lysimachos gets the army down to Sardis,' Satyrus said.

'So, naturally, we should ride to meet Seleucus,' Charmides added. They all laughed.

Charmides' light young voice rose over the laughter. 'It's like one of Plato's arguments; where only one side is properly argued.'

'We know the terrain and he doesn't,' Satyrus said, insistently. 'If Antigonus goes for him he'll be isolated in the mountains east of Magnesia.'

'Admit it – Miriam dared you,' Anaxagoras said.

They all laughed until Satyrus picked up a handful of sand and threw it across the fire at Anaxagoras.

Apollodorus finished the wineskin, rose, and wandered off. 'I have to find a rock that needs a libation,' he said.

Charmides ambled down their small valley, and Satyrus could see him, gathering sticks by the dying light of the sun. Jubal went to help him. They had no slaves, no servants, and no hypaspists. They'd decided it on Rhodes.

'Why, really?' Anaxagoras asked.

'The risk isn't bad. And the truth is, there were two poisonings this winter at Tanais. Another try at Olbia – one of Eumeles's own slaves. Stratokles told me to stay away from Heraklea.'

'He would know,' Anaxagoras said. Alone of Satyrus's inner circle, Anaxagoras liked the Athenian.

Satyrus's newly purchased chestnut mare snorted, and Satyrus rolled to his feet, dumping his wine from his horn cup as he stood.

'Herakles,' he said quietly.

He could see his mare, and she was tossing her head and pulling at her picket. She was new to him; he'd left all his good horses with his sister, to travel with the horse herd. But this was some kind of signal. Unfortunately, with a horse he didn't know, it could mean anything from a pain in her gut to a desire for food to a fear of dogs or wolves.

'Hush, girl,' he said, walking towards her. He got a hand on her bridle and she froze, head up, lips off her teeth, breathing hard.

Bow. He heard the voice as clearly as if the god stood with him at the edge of the firelight. His bow hung in his gorytos from a tree where his mare was picketed. He stepped to it – never question the god – and buckled the waist-belt as he crouched.

Anaxagoras was standing in the firelight.

'Down,' Satyrus said.

Anaxagoras dropped.

Satyrus had an arrow on his bow, the horn nock smoothly fitted on the string.

Something moved in the almost-dark.

As he raised his bow, Satyrus remembered that Apollodorus was out there.

Sloppy.

He went back to watching.

He heard Jubal and Charmides laughing.

Satyrus wasn't sure whether he should call a warning or remain hidden. But as the waiting lengthened, his resolve weakened.

'Alarm!' he roared.

The results were spectacular.

Just the other side of the horses, a man rose to his feet with a bow. He was at full draw but by luck or fate, the tree that had held Satyrus's gorytos was partially between them, and he paused, trying to make his shot count.

Anaxagoras rose from the rocks to Satyrus's left. He was armed only with a rock, but his throw was sure.

The archer twisted to avoid the rock, which hit his shoulder as he loosed – his arrow went wide. Satyrus shot him in the side – the range was so short he could hardly miss – and the man's attempt to dodge Anaxagoras revealed him from crotch to shoulders.

The next arrow came from well to Satyrus's left – from beyond Anaxagoras, who was back behind his rocks – and it hit Satyrus's bow case, penetrated the bronze and two layers of leather, cut an arrow in half, and punched into Satyrus's thigh.

He got another arrow on his bow but he couldn't even see the new archer. 'Alarm!' he bellowed.

He reached up for his javelin case, pulled out two hunting javelins, and threw them carefully – without exposing himself – towards the rocks where Anaxagoras was hiding.

He saw one of them picked up. Then he saw that there was another man right in among the horses. The last red glow of the sun threw confusing light, but something gleamed.

Satyrus felt hot and cold by turns, but the eudaimonia was on him, and he drew his next barbed point until the fletching touched his cheek, leaned out until he fell on his back, and shot through the legs of the horses. A horse thrashed, wrenching its picket pin from the ground … and a man screamed, shot through the leg just above his ankle.

Satyrus had to contort himself to get at another arrow. It took a long time, and what little light there was was fading. The downed man kept screaming.

Satyrus knew he had to sit up to have any more shots. And he knew that when he sat up, he'd be revealed to anyone above him on the hillside. He scraped along on his back, the gravel cutting into him, trying to get his shoulders behind the tree. Darkness was falling like a curtain – he could no longer see the next ridge, six stades away. Somewhere, he could hear sheep bells.

Now his back was on pine needles. He must be close to the tree.

Movement – way up the hillside – scrabbling and roaring, like a pack of wild dogs – and then the sound of falling rocks.

And closer to hand, a movement just beyond his tree.

The man he'd shot screamed again.

The arrow between his fingers felt wrong. Too heavy. But he didn't dare move his eyes.

He sat up – the assassin in the bush turned and shot – he shot – there was a scream and his mare let out a long snarl and Anaxagoras's spear flew across the horses and then there was silence.

As he fumbled for another arrow, Satyrus realised that the first scream had been his arrow. He'd shot a whistle-arrow.

Artemis must be laughing.

He heard moving, rolled against his tree cursing the growing pain in his left leg, and Anaxagoras appeared out of the dark, a second javelin in his fist.

'I missed. Who are they?' asked the musician.

'Bandits? Who knows?' Satyrus rubbed his thigh and cursed. There was a lot of blood. 'I'm hit.'

The bushes moved twice in the next hour. The feeling gradually left Satyrus's left leg; he was lying on it, and the pins and needles feeling told him to move, but he didn't dare.

'If they get the horses, we're cooked,' Satyrus whispered.

Anaxagoras bent down. 'I'm going to get the arrow out.'

'No, you aren't.' Satyrus was cold, and in pain, but his wits were sharp. 'That takes both of us out.'

Long silence. The man with the arrow in his legs wasn't screaming any more.

Satyrus took to watching his mare. She was cropping grass.

'I think they're gone,' he said.

'Jubal?' called Anaxagoras.

'Right here,' he replied. He was down by the fire, where the weapons were.

'Charmides?' he called.

'Here!' came the younger voice. Also by the fire.

'Apollodorus?'

Silence.

'Apollodorus?' Anaxagoras called.

'Right here,' said the marine. He emerged from the horses. Even in the dark he looked bad: blood flowing down his face, all the knuckles split on both hands.

Charmides went on watch, and Anaxagoras opened his leather bag and salved Apollodorus's wounds – two long cuts on his arms – while Jubal washed the blood off him and oiled him.

Then Anaxagoras built up the fire while Jubal and Charmides went out into the dark beyond the horses to give them a zone of safety. They swept all the way around the camp and came up with three corpses: a man battered to death with a rock, a man with his throat slit and an arrow through both legs, and a man with an arrow through his side.

Apollodorus agreed with the count. 'Bastard came at me while I was ... busy,' he said. 'I heard the alarm shout – he cut me.' He shook his head. 'He was fucking strong.' Shrugged, a figure of blood in the firelight. 'I was stronger.'

Anaxagoras gave him more wine. 'You, sir, will hurt like the devil in the morning. Don't add a hangover. I have poppy ...'

Apollodorus shook his head. 'Had too much. Just like Satyrus.'

Anaxagoras threw two pine bows on the fire. Now it was too hot where Satyrus lay, and the clearing was as bright as day.

Anaxagoras made a clucking sound.

'Poison,' he said. 'I fear.'

He had an odd little tool – a wicked-looking thing like a folding spoon. 'This is going to hurt a great deal,' he said. 'This is an arrow spoon. I have to put it into the wound to extract the arrow, because it is barbed. And then I have to try and get the poison out. You understand?'

Satyrus looked at his friend. 'Yes,' he said.

'Good,' Anaxagoras said. 'I've never actually done this before,' he added, and those were the last words Satyrus heard.

Pain came, and he was gone.

18

Unconsciousness lasted only a few hours, and Satyrus regretted it because the next few days were amongst the most painful he'd ever experienced. He was in a fever, and he came and went from full consciousness, and he was hot and miserable, and despite all that, Apollodorus had taken command and was moving them – fast – across the valleys of western Asia, going due east on the Zeugma road.

A lifetime of riding left Satyrus capable of staying in the saddle even when fevered. But the experience was horrible – he had delusions, his wound was inflamed and jarred by every fourth step of the horse, and when they trotted, his leg felt as if it was being broken with every bump.

And the constant ministrations of his friends wore on him, day after day. He felt a burden. He *was* a burden.

But on the fourth day the fever broke, and he lay in his own sweat and was irritated by insects, and the fact that he could be irritated by insects was itself a source of joy.

Anaxagoras crouched by him with an oil lamp. He moved very quietly.

Satyrus sighed. 'I'm awake,' he said.

'Ah!' Anaxagoras said. 'Fever?'

'Not so much,' Satyrus said. 'Ares, I feel like horse dung.'

'Philos, you *look* like horse dung, as well.' Anaxagoras brought him a clay cup. 'Eat all of this if you can get it down.'

'Was I poisoned?' Satyrus asked.

Anaxagoras shook his head. 'I don't know. I'm not a doctor, but you can't attend a Temple of Apollo without getting some basic training in healing. Unfortunately, while I've watched doctors smell wounds and prescribe herbs for poisons I have no idea how to do either.' He sat down. 'The arrow smelled like shit ... pardon me. Apollodorus says it might have been smeared in pig dung – that's apparently a potent poison.'

'Did I hear my name?' Apollodorus asked.

'Satyrus is better,' Anaxagoras said.

Apollodorus grunted. 'Then everyone should be allowed to sleep,' he said.

The next day, Satyrus rode more easily, although trots were still brutal and the wound in his thigh gushed blood and pus when Anaxagoras pushed at it. 'Not done yet,' he said, shaking his head. He poured wine and honey into the wound.

That night, Apollodorus bought a heavy boar's bristle brush from a farmer in the hills north of Zeugma who offered them shelter in his fine stone house. 'Satyrus, we're all worried by the pus in your wound.'

The fever was returning, and Satyrus nodded heavily.

'I know a trick. A soldier's trick.' He was speaking slowly and clearly.

'And?' Satyrus asked.

Apollodorus held up the brush. 'It's going to hurt like Hades,' he said.

Satyrus nodded. 'Try,' he said. He had little idea what they were doing.

Anaxagoras unwrapped the bandage, and the wound was red like Tyrian linen, with tendrils of infection running up almost to his groin and down his leg towards his knee.

'We should take it off,' Anaxagoras said. 'But I don't know how.'

Jubal rubbed his short beard. 'He'll die,' he said. 'Men need to be strong to lose a leg.'

Satyrus was scared by his leg. It didn't look like part of him. It looked as if it had taken on an evil life of its own.

'Let me try,' said Apollodorus. 'This is going to hurt like ... well, give the king something to bite down on. Pour this bowl full of wine.' He washed the brush in the wine, and then – remorselessly – he began to scrub the wound. He flayed the pus sores open, and scrubbed them, and the brush went right into the mouth of the wound and Satyrus vomited from the pain. Anaxagoras held his head.

Then he blacked out.

Then he resurfaced, to more pain. The bowl was black with crud from the wound – the smell of the pus was everywhere in the little farmhouse. Satyrus could see the farmer's face – the 'O' of his shocked mouth.

'Don't scream,' the god said. 'Don't scream. Heroes do not scream.'

Satyrus tried to smile at Herakles, whose body filled the bank of the stream. 'Lord,' he said. He wondered why he only saw his god when he was in pain.

'The ability to withstand pain,' Herakles said, 'is a path.'

Satyrus could hear a lyre playing, the notes cascading like water down a waterfall.

'Oh,' said Herakles. 'The musician. Well, he's fair enough as a healer. Do well, boy. Be excellent.'

Satyrus saw that Anaxagoras was playing for him, as he had when Satyrus had marsh fever on Rhodes. But the music seemed to have colour and texture – the notes flowed across the room, dancing like butterflies on the late-spring air and often coming to light on his fresh-bandaged wound.

Anaxagoras's face was anguished. Just like the man to blame himself.

Satyrus wished that he could see Miriam with the clarity he saw Anaxagoras. He wondered if he was dying. He didn't feel like he was dying, and that alone worried him. He was sleepy, and his leg didn't hurt. In fact, he couldn't feel it.

They'd cut it off, after all.

He tried to sit up, to look. Amazing how difficult it could be to see your own leg. Surely, if they had cut it off, there'd be a sign.

Or it would hurt.

He rolled his hips back and forth, and there it was: a piercing pain from the wound. Satisfied, he rolled back, just as Apollodorus came and pinned his shoulders. 'Rest,' he said.

Satyrus was afraid that if he gave in to the sleep, he would die. He tried to see Miriam – he wished that they had made love. Yearned for her, and wished to tell her so, and no words would come out of his mouth.

Odd, to die like this in a cottage in Syria. Of all places.

And then he was gone.

*

Coenus cut his beard, chose his horses, packed his saddlebags, and took his two best spears off the wall where he'd been happy to leave them since his last hunt. His servant, Boras, fussed over food and his own mount, and then they rode to the shrine of Artemis on the hills above the Tanais River and offered sacrifice.

'I'm pretty sure I won't make it back,' Coenus told his servant. In the morning, the arthritis was bad enough that he had to work on his hands to get them to open and close, and sleeping on the ground no longer held any attraction at all. He was sixty-four years old.

He stepped up to the altar with a young fawn he'd caught wandering in the woods after he killed the mother with a spear, and he slashed the animal's throat on the altar. He was the priest, here.

And as the blood flowed away, Coenus prayed for his friends.

Most of them were shades in the underworld. Niceas and Philokles, Kineas ... friends of his youth and middle age. Lovers – where was Nihmu, now, he wondered? On the earth, or under it? Leon? Remember beautiful young Ajax? Remember Nicomedes? Good men, who died in valour.

'If this is my last time,' Coenus prayed, 'Lady, let me be as good a man as they.'

Then he rode down the Tanais towards the city. There were changes on both banks – more farmers, Greek and Sindi and Maeoti, and more Sarmatians on the high ground – Sarmatians who had come to stay, whether they won or lost their battles with the Sakje. When they won, they pushed in, and when they lost, the survivors simply joined the Sakje clans in the old way of the steppe.

At the fork, where the road crossed the last ford over the river, there were a hundred horsemen waiting – Sakje of the old school, in red coats, with horsehair ropes at their saddles, most with a pair of gorytoi, each with its own bow and arrows, and a string of horses.

Ataelus sat on his best horse, a tall Persian in storm grey. Beside him sat his sons. Ataelus was older than Coenus, and they were the lords of this land, and they embraced gravely.

'Not for going,' Ataelus said.

Coenus was taken aback. 'But ...'

Ataelus pointed at his sons. 'They go. For being old, friend. Too fucking old to fight in fucking desert.' Ataelus pointed out over the Tanais high ground, towards the distant Caucus mountains, towards

Asia. 'Stay and drink wine for me, Coenus, Greek brother. Let young men fight for Satyrus. Old men for the fireside.'

Coenus grinned. 'No. No, my friend. This is the last fight, and I'll go. I wouldn't miss it.'

Ataelus grunted. 'No fucking last fight, Greek brother. Never "last fight".' The Sakje lord pounded his fist against his chest. 'I for fighting sixty times – never beaten. Lost wife for Satyrus and Melitta – lost sons. Lost horses.' He looked out over the steppe. 'Lost my heart for Kineas. Twice I've been dead. Eh? Now stay home, guard flocks.' He sat straight. 'Go, Greek brother. Ataelus will die in bed.'

Thyrsis saluted his father. He turned to Coenus. 'Temerix is home in his forge. They decided together ... to stay home.'

Coenus saw Maeton, Temerix's lieutenant in the wars with the Sarmatians. He rode over. 'Temerix is staying at home?' he asked.

Maeton shrugged. He had more than a hundred men on ponies, men with heavy bows and axes. 'Temerix says, I was Kineas's man, and I am old. Let the young men ride to war.'

Coenus looked at Maeton and Thyrsis. 'Who will I talk to?' he said. But he rode to Ataelus's side, and they embraced for a long time. Ataelus said something in his ear – something about Kineas.

Coenus could only picture the drunken barbarian riding back into their camp.

Kineas turned and looked over his shoulder. A lone horseman was trotting to the paddock. Coenus laughed.

'Ataelus!' bellowed Kineas.

The Scyth raised a dusty hand in greeting and swung his legs over the side of the horse so that he slipped in one lithe movement to the ground. He touched the flank of the horse with a little riding whip and she turned and walked through the gate into the paddock.

'Horse good,' he said. He reached out a hand for the flagon.

Coenus handed it to him without a moment's hesitation. The Scyth took a deep drink, rubbed his mouth with his hand. Then Coenus caught the Scyth in a bear hug. 'I think I like you, Barbarian!' he said.

He hugged the Sakje harder, and then he raised his hand.

'Ready to march?' he asked.

Eumenes, archon of Olbia, gathered his hippeis in the hippodrome that Kineas had ordered built when Leucon was archon. They made a fine show, but only fifty of them were good enough to go to war. He'd already chosen them.

And he would lead them himself, because Melitta had asked in person.

They'd hollowed out a pair of triremes captured from Macedon in Kineas's day. They took eighty chargers, the fine Olbian breed that Ataelus and Niceas had started thirty years before, heavy geldings resulting from cross-breeding the Sakje plains horses with the biggest Persian mares.

When Eumenes stood on the beach, watching his hippeis load, he felt as if Kineas was all around him – from the hero statue in the agora to the very horses his men rode, Kineas had been the architect.

He was a fair man, and he owed Kineas one more ride. Even if it would take him past Troy.

He kissed his wife, and gave his will to his son, who he was not taking. He gave the ivory stool to Lykaeus. He had held the archonship for Kineas, and now, as an old man, he could keep the seat warm for Eumenes.

Melitta reined in her horse. She was, almost literally, covered in gold – from the tip of her helmet to the base of her long, caribou-hide coat, she shimmered with gold plates, gold signs, gold sigils, gold scales. Her gorytos cover was beaten gold, showing the gods dining on Olympus, and her shield had Artemis – a mounted Artemis – worked in gold.

Her reins were gold. Her high-backed war saddle was worked in gold. Every handspan of her tack had a gold plate. Her horse towered over other horses – a Royal horse, his coat the colour of steel.

She touched her heels to his sides, and put pressure on his bit, and he reared – as he would in battle – and his hooves lashed the air, and the Assagetae screamed their approval.

Behind her, the best of her knights – Scopasis, Sindispharnax, and the rest – formed a neat wedge.

The Assagetae filled the plain south and east of Tanais – their tents went on for stades, and if there were more Sarmatian-style yurts than ever, it was a fair representation of the changes coming to the Sea of Grass. The lord of the Western Sarmatians now rode freely over the ridges of the Tanais without hindrance. His people came to council on the Euxine.

The queen of the Assagetae rode at the head of her golden knights, along six stades of tribal warriors – Stalking Wolves, Standing Horses, Grass Cats, Cruel Hands. At the southern end of the line, Nikephorus stood with a token force of pikemen and Eumenes and Coenus waited with two hundred Greek cavalry and Maeton with his scouts and Thyrsis with his. Nikephorus's taxeis had already sailed to Heraklea – the Apobatai hadn't even left the city after the fall campaign.

Coenus saluted her, and she raised her war-axe to her helmet.

'Ataelus stayed at home,' he said.

'I know,' she said. 'I'm the queen. People tell me things.' She pushed her Attic helmet back on her head, and Coenus thought that she had never looked so much like Athena.

'I tried to change his mind,' Coenus said.

'Why?' Melitta asked. 'He's the wise one. My brother's the fool. This is not our war.'

'That's why we're all going?' Coenus asked.

'I know,' Melitta said, raising her axe to salute Maeton. 'Philokles would tell me that if I go, I'm as responsible as Satyrus. And I am. But my heart tells me that we should sit home and prepare to trounce the winner.'

'Hence you take a tithe of your strength,' Coenus said.

'A tithe would be too much. I take a *token* of our strength, and that is too much to lose.' She shrugged. In armour, it scarcely showed. 'All told, I'll take a thousand warriors, and I'll leave half of them at Heraklea. And Parshevaelt – he's staying. I need someone here I can trust.' She smiled. 'On the other hand, I've invited *all* the Sarmatian chiefs to accompany me.' She laughed. 'All our friends want to come. But as queen, they're just the ones I want to stay home. All our foes desire that we fail. So naturally, they're the ones I want where I can see them.'

Coenus looked at her knights. 'These men alone could turn a battle.'

Melitta nodded, and her face was the face of Smells like Death. 'That's why I keep them around. Let's ride.'

Coenus fell in with Scopasis, and behind them, the chosen men and women of the Assagetae, the Keepers of the Western Door, the Royal Scythians, and their remounts and slaves and wagons joined the column, and the rest of the Assagetae cheered them until their dust cloud rolled out of sight. And then they went back to the grass.

19

When he awoke, Satyrus's first thought was *I am not dead.*
It was an altogether pleasant thought. And before an hour had passed, Anaxagoras had unrolled the bandage on his leg and shown him the flesh – the lines of red were gone, no longer lines of death reaching for his groin and heart.

He was weak, but he was a veteran of many wounds and he knew the drill – he began to eat anything he could lay hands on.

They let him rest for three days.

His friends were out all the time – riding. Mostly, Satyrus saw the farmer, Belial. He sensed that there were daughters hiding up in the rafters, and that the whole house was afraid of them. But he ate, and watched.

The third day of rest, he was alert enough to figure out that his friends were patrolling. Jubal came back with a twisted leg – a bad fall from his horse.

'Men trying to kill you, eh?' he said, and grinned.

Satyrus shook his head. Even here – three thousand stades from Tanais. 'Who are they?' he asked.

'Don't know. Big bunch – a dozen or more. We hit their camp, only caught three of them.' He shrugged. 'Rest were off east. Setting an ambush?'

Satyrus hadn't seen Charmides in days. 'And Charmides?'

'Apollodorus sent him east for Seleucus. He's supposed to be at Zeugma. Apollodorus is afraid he's already passed us.' Jubal rubbed his beard.

The horses were stirring outside.

'Uh-oh,' Jubal said. He got a bow from his case and went to the window. As soon as he looked out, he popped back. 'Party of men.'

Satyrus was flat on his back, too weak to pull a woman's bow.

Above him, a small girl, no more than seven or eight, waved a hand. 'We hide,' he said.

Sophokles was still hobbling from the arrow he'd taken in the fight five days earlier – the luck of the gods that the arrow had been a whistler, or he'd be dead instead of bruised. He dismounted with a curse, having covered all the ground from the mountains to the Euphrates and missed his quarry.

He wanted a good night's sleep and a chance to regroup. Seleucus was less than a day away to the east and Sophokles didn't fancy the odds of tracking his quarry amidst the biggest army in Asia.

He dismounted with a curse, and was immediately on his guard. The farmer's body language gave him away. He was hiding something.

Of course, that could be food or horses or a beautiful daughter. All of which Sophokles would be happy to take. 'We mean no harm,' he said, raising his hand.

The farmer nodded. 'How can I help you?' he asked. He had two slaves with him – big men, but not trained to arms.

'Feed us, give us all your horses, and stay out of our way,' Sophokles said. 'And we'll be gone tomorrow.'

The farmer's eyes were everywhere. 'You could go in the barn, I suppose,' he said.

'Are you a fool?' Sophokles was in pain, and tired of peasants. 'I don't ask you to suppose anything. I'll have the house.' He tossed his reins to one of his men. 'Clear the house. Don't touch his family. Slaves are fair game.'

There were stools on the lower exedra, and Sophokles lowered himself on one. 'A cup of wine might improve my mood,' he said to the farmer.

The man's wife brought it herself. She'd mixed herbs in it. Sophokles had a moment to picture himself poisoned by a farmer's-wife in Phrygia, and the thought made him smile. He drank it off.

'Not bad,' he said. 'Honey?' he asked.

She nodded, her eyes huge.

Telon, his lieutenant – an intelligent man, for an oaf – jogged up from around the stone house. 'There's horses in the barn,' he said. 'War horses.'

Sophokles reached out to grab the farmer's wife, but she was faster

323

than he expected – her fist held an iron poker, and it clipped his shoulder and his head, and he was down.

Telon killed her – cut her nearly in half with a big kopis.

Sophokles felt distinctly queasy – something in his gut, and the blow to his head. He threw up and felt better. Telon was pushing at the barred door of the barn and shouting for help, and his men were trying to get in one of the windows.

Sophokles got to his blanket-roll, and it took all his will to untie the leather thongs that held it shut.

The bitch poisoned me.

His brain was processing very slowly. He got the knots open – the blanket unrolled of its own accord. He got a hand into the leather wallet at the heart of the bundle – found the flask. Got it to his lips.

No time to measure. Only his vomit reaction had kept him alive *this* long. He took a sip, swallowed it . . .

Vomited, and vomited again. His men were calling out.

By all the gods, that had been close. One of his eyes was gummed shut from blood.

They'd killed the farmer and one of his slaves.

He took a breath and then another.

Looked up. Heard the hoof beats – saw the dust cloud.

Shook his head in weary disbelief.

'Mount up!' he croaked, and stumbled towards his horse, abandoning his blanket roll.

Telon, at least, had the wits to listen. He abandoned the barred door and leaped for his horse. Seeing the two of them mounted, the rest ran for their horses. The last man was shot dead trying to get a leg over, but the rest of them were away.

Satyrus found the act of climbing down from the hiding hole in the rafters to be as much adventure as he could handle, but worth it, because the big ginger-haired man holding the ladder proved to be Crax. Behind him was Charmides, and half a dozen troopers Satyrus had known since childhood.

'Did you get them?' Satyrus asked.

'Got one,' Crax said. 'They killed the staff.'

Out on the exedra, the daughters had begun to wail. Charmides went that way, and Satyrus dragged himself along, supported by Crax.

'You haven't aged a day,' Satyrus said.

Crax laughed. 'Tell that to my hips on a cold morning,' he said.

The two daughters were eight and twelve, and their parents and most of their slaves were dead. The casual side-product of war.

'They died for me,' Satyrus said wearily.

Jubal nodded. 'They'll be related to someone round here.' He went over to the girls and put his arms around them, and they threw themselves on his neck.

Satyrus found himself standing on someone's blanket roll. It was vaguely familiar, and he assumed it was Jubal's. Despite the pain of his wound, or because of it, he subsided to the planks of the porch and began to roll it up.

Crax was seeing to his men.

There was an alabaster vase – fine workmanship – on the blanket roll, and Satyrus picked it up, opened the stopper, took a whiff. Memory flooded him.

'Sophokles,' he said. Ten years had passed but he knew that smell, and that jar. He rifled the rest of the wallet – glass ampoules, worth a fortune, with powders. A folding tablet and a beautiful gold stylus. A scroll of recipes.

Two poems by Sappho.

A note, written on a scrap of papyrus, with an address in Alexandria. Ben Zion's address.

Satyrus let the breath go from between his teeth, and hoped that Achilles and his friends were enough.

It was hours before Apollodorus and Anaxagoras returned, riding wearily on jaded horses. They were picked up stades away by Crax's men, so they already knew of the events of the day by the time they rode up to the farm.

By then, a dozen local men and two women had taken charge of the farm and the girls. Satyrus had time to wonder what would become of them – whether they'd end well-dowered or as slaves on their own land.

He slept there one more time, and Crax's men helped bury the dead, and then they all rode out for Zeugma.

*

The first sight of Seleucus's army told the whole story. The elephants could be seen from stades away, plodding up the Euphrates. They were huge, and the rumour was that Seleucus had traded all of the Indian satrapies to an Indian king for five hundred elephants. If he had, he'd brought less than half. Satyrus counted more than a hundred before pain and boredom took over, but there weren't more than two hundred.

Still, it was the biggest concentration of elephants Satyrus had seen since Eumeles. And it would give the alliance the same odds as the Antigonids, at least.

Satyrus rode down into the walled city of Zeugma in time to meet the King of Babylon himself as he offered libations to the river god at the bridge. Seleucus was leaving the Euphrates and turning west, towards the sea and Phrygia, and he was bidding farewell, as the King of Babylon, to one of the country's deities. Satyrus watched him and felt dirty.

When he was done, Seleucus came forward, surrounded by courtiers. He was a middle aged man losing the hair on his head, and he had the square-jawed Macedonian look, but he had never been a heavy drinker, and age had brought him dignity as well as thinning hair. Satyrus had last seen him riding in Ptolemy's staff at Gaza covered in dust. Satyrus bowed.

Seleucus returned his bow. 'I am stunned to see you here, Satyrus,' he said. 'But delighted, of course. Diodorus says you have the rally point and a chart of the campaign.'

Satyrus took his proffered hand and clasped it. 'I see that you have not stinted,' he said. 'Thank the gods!'

Seleucus gave him a wry smile. 'I brought my best ... and my worst. The cream of my troops, and the bastards I can't trust at home. Ptolemy?'

'Sent his fleet to Rhodes.' Satyrus shrugged.

'Cassander?' Seleucus asked.

'Emptied Europe for Lysimachos, who now has Prepalaus to contend with. I doubt there's a man fit to wear armour left in Europe.' Satyrus was getting tired.

'A stool for the King of the Bosporus,' Seleucus Nicator called. 'Diodorus said you'd been wounded. You look well enough.'

'I am – a few days and I'll be fit. May I accompany you west?' Satyrus subsided onto the stool with relief.

'My pleasure. And your Exiles will be delighted to have you – the famous Satyrus of Tanais? Worth a thousand men.'

Satyrus smiled up at Seleucus. 'You didn't used to be such a flatterer.'

'I wasn't King of Babylon, then,' Seleucus said, seriously.

Six days, and the advance guard was across the Taurus Mountains and making camp at Cybistra, in Lycaonia. The elephants were still in the high passes of the mountains, and the rearguard hadn't left Zeugma.

Diodorus sat by a fire with Crax and Andronicus on either side of him. Sappho passed the wine. She rode astride with the men, and refused to be with the baggage. She'd made more campaigns than many of the veterans. Satyrus felt like embracing her every time he saw her.

She and Diodorus moved him the most – perhaps because they were the eldest. Diodorus was *old*. Satyrus had never expected it; the man had remained adamantine, proof against time, throughout Satyrus's childhood, and now he was a stick figure, all sinews and scorched skin with deep furrows in his face and his cheekbones so sharp they could cut. And Sappho's beauty was blasted – she was an old woman, and no one would mistake her for a great beauty.

So it had taken him two days to discover that looks deceived, and that the people who had raised him were essentially unchanged. No one had told them how old they were. Diodorus was not in his dotage – when his voice lashed a trooper, the man wilted. Sappho had much the same effect on Diodorus – and Crax, and Andronicus, and soon enough Satyrus himself, who discovered that she felt he was cosseting his wound when he might have been exercising.

'What a Spartan you would have made,' he grunted, when she forced him to bend his left leg to her satisfaction.

'I am a woman of Thebes – a far, far better place than Sparta, with better men. Ask them at Leukra.' She nodded, another argument won, and directed her slave to help him bend the leg again.

So ... two days, and he had returned to being their child. It was not so bad.

Especially when he was treated as an adult child.

'What do you think One-Eye will do?' Diodorus asked. He sat back on his cloak, and Sappho joined him, burrowing into his arms like a much younger woman.

Satyrus shifted, winced, and looked at Apollodorus. 'He'll try to defeat us in detail. About now he'll be getting his first reports that Seleucus is really on his way. So he can come east to us, or go north to Lysimachos.' He paused. 'It's not that simple, though,' he added.

Diodorus grunted. 'It never is,' he said.

'There will or won't be a fleet action in the Dardanelles. That could change everything. Or Demetrios might march inland and join his father – and *that* would change everything.' He paused. 'Or ... Hades, I don't know. Demetrios might go off to crush Cassander and leave his pater ...'

'Never happen,' Diodorus said. 'That's their edge on us. That they have each other. Demetrios won't abandon his pater. Will he win in the Dardanelles?'

Satyrus took a cup of wine from Charmides. 'Doesn't matter,' he said, as if repeating a lesson for Diodorus. How often had he gone from Philokles, having just had Plato beaten into him, to repeat the lesson for Diodorus, as he sat in his armour?

'Ahh,' Diodorus said. 'Why?' His tone said he liked the answer.

'If we win, then our troops move freely on the coast of Asia. But Alexander and Lysimachos have both shown that even if our ships *lose*, the army can move across the Troad into Phrygia without hindrance. We have Bithynia. That one change is everything. Lysimachos doesn't need a fleet to move an army down on Antigonus, and his supplies will be safe.' Satyrus sat back, feeling fifteen.

Diodorus nodded. 'Well, you've commanded more armies than I have, son. But it seems to me that the navies will still have two effects. First, morale: if we win, it *will* have an effect on the troops. And second, if our ships win, then Antigonus *can't* go far from his logistics, for fear that Lysimachos will land behind him. You know that we're in contact with Ptolemy's fleet?'

Satyrus hadn't heard.

'There's twenty triremes shadowing us on the coast.' Diodorus nodded. 'Pray to Poseidon, son. A victory at sea would save us a world of trouble. But otherwise, your analysis is correct. He's got to go for one or the other of us, as soon as he can. I reckon he'll go for Lysimachos – he's beaten him like a drum, and he's never beaten us.'

Satyrus rolled his hips. 'I just hope we don't fight for ten days,' he said. 'I can barely ride.'

Sappho laughed. 'But you will,' she said.

'It'll take ten days to get the rearguard up to here,' Diodorus said. 'Our army is spread across six hundred stades of crappy roads. But ten days ... that's about it. Ten days will see us near enough that we'll be fighting.'

Five days, and two days of rain. Satyrus could ride well again, and he exercised hard, sparring with Anaxagoras, and Crax, whose Keltoi sword was three palms longer than any Greek sword and who used it in an alien way, snipping with long sweeps and cutting straight into attacks.

Five days brought them to the shores of the Karalis Lake, more than a hundred stades from the sea and covered in gulls. The rain filled the water courses and, uncomfortable as it was, it allowed the vanguard to move faster – suddenly, water for horses was abundant.

Seleucus knew the business of war, too. Every night, when they halted, there was an agora of merchants from the nearest towns – even if those towns were fifty stades distant – with wagons full of produce, sheep, goats, fodder for horses. All they required was cash, and Diodorus's war-chest seemed to be bottomless.

'No point in being a rich mercenary if you can't keep your horses fed,' he said.

On the evening of the fifth day, Crax came in from a long scout north and west – he'd taken six men and gone as far and fast as a string of ponies would take them. Seleucus and a dozen of his officers came up the column from Iconium to hear the report.

Crax was drinking cider. He was covered in dust, he appeared to be a wraith; and the men who had ridden with him simply fell from their saddles and lay like the dead.

Crax was uncowed by having Seleucus present, although he bobbed his head to the King of Babylon – rather, Satyrus felt, like one Maeoti farmer greeting another on the road.

'Well?' Seleucus said.

'Antigonus is supposed to be at Sardis, trying to link up with his son, who's coming south from the Troad with eighteen thousand men. I didn't see any of them, lords, but there's a detachment of Antigonus's cavalry up the road a piece, north of the mines at the road junction. Locals call it Kotia. I took a man there – he hasn't been paid since the festival of Ares in the autumn – and he talked. Said that they expect us at Gordia, and they have troops ready to march that way and hold us in the passes.'

Seleucus nodded. 'It is *so* helpful that One-Eye thinks I'm a fool. Still, if they expect us at Gordia ...'

'Send some of your satrapal levies marching that way,' Diodorus said.

'Sardis ...' Seleucus began. 'That's six hundred stades. Where's Lysimachos?'

Crax shook his head. 'I don't know, lord, and my prisoner doesn't know either.'

Diodorus swore, and so did Seleucus.

Satyrus finished the wine in his cup. 'Give me a dozen men with six remounts a man, and I'll find him,' he said. 'I know these hills – I campaigned around Sardis last year.'

Diodorus nodded. 'I'd rather send—'

Satyrus shook his head. 'No – no assassin is going to follow me across Phrygia.'

'I was considering what would happen if one of One-Eye's cavalry patrols got you,' Seleucus said. 'But I need information more than I need you, Satyrus. If you'll do it ... go with Athena and Hermes.'

Satyrus took his friends, as well as Andronicus the Gaul and a dozen troopers – all with strings of horses. And Crax. The Bastarnae man was unstoppable, and he was awake at first light with his own horses.

They were off before dawn, and they rode until dusk, slept with their reins on their arms, and were off in the dark again, sweeping around the north end of the lakes, then across country to Akmonia, through tribal territories where people lived high on the hillsides in villages that seemed to hang from the sky. They weren't troubled.

They picked up the Sardis road at Thyrai and went due east, into the rising sun. They left the road when their vedettes saw soldiers and rode along the ridges above the Kogamas River.

'Welcome to Lydia,' Satyrus said. He felt wonderful – his thigh hurt, but in the usual ways of an injury. Three days in the saddle, and he was like a god. And free of the plodding columns.

The Valley of the Kogamas was full of men. When they made camp, the light of their fires stretched away east as far as they could see.

'That's Antigonus,' Crax said. 'I didn't get this far, but here he is. He's east of Sardis – where's his son? Where's Lysimachos?'

Andronicus grunted.

Anaxagoras dropped to the ground and unrolled his blankets.

Satyrus laughed. 'You know, Anaxagoras, I've done my sister a great service the last two weeks.'

Anaxagoras was already in his blankets. 'Yes?' he asked.

'You can ride,' Satyrus said. 'Like a Sakje. Now she'll marry you.'

'I'm not sure that equine riding is the skill she'll marry me for,' Anaxagoras said. He smiled, turned over, and was asleep.

Another day of careful riding – walking, often, and it was the slowest day they'd made yet – and they were clear of Antigonus. His cavalry was on the roads, but the high ground on the north flank of the valley was empty of everyone but refugees.

They had news – all of it conflicting. Demetrios had won a great victory at Kallipolis – had lost his fleet – had abandoned his fleet and marched inland – defeated Lysimachos – been defeated – everyone was dead.

'See why scouting is such a pain in the arse?' Crax asked.

Satyrus shook his head. 'Crax, you know that I've been conducting campaigns as a strategos for eight years, eh?'

Crax slapped him on the back. 'And see, you still have so much to learn.'

'Crax, my mother taught you to scout.' Satyrus was tired of the patronising lectures.

Crax laughed. 'Ataelus taught me to scout, young king. And if you know so much, why do you sit and argue with an old tribesman while the sun to anyone in the valley below silhouettes you? Eh?' He laughed. 'Your mother would know better.'

Satyrus shook his head and resigned himself to being a perpetual adolescent to these men.

Tyateira, and Satyrus, riding as a vedette with Apollodorus, met a messenger and took him. He had a scroll from Demetrios to Antigonus.

Satyrus read it, handed it to the messenger, and said, 'On your way.'

The young man, a Lydian, terrified with Apollodorus's knife at his throat, relaxed. 'Thank you, lord.'

Satyrus bowed. 'How far to Lord Demetrios?'

The messenger remounted, took his satchel and his scroll tube, and saluted. 'Forty stades, lord. Stratonika. And marching this way as fast as his pikemen will go.'

'And Lysimachos is pressing him?' Satyrus asked.

'Hard. But we're holding.' The messenger saluted, gathered his reins, and rode off, and Apollodorus shook his head.

'I'm going to guess that bastard is off to tell One-Eye something you actually want the bastard to know.' He shrugged. 'Otherwise, we just had the best piece of intelligence we could have had, dropped on us by the gods, and you're letting him ride away.'

'He's marching to meet his pater, and he's sent the fleet back to Athens rather than face ours. And he's telling his pater that our troops are at Gordia.' Satyrus took a deep breath. Suddenly his hands were shaking. 'Athena – we may yet pull this off. Let's find the others.'

That night, all of them gathered around a fire no bigger than a man's head. When Satyrus went off to piss, he couldn't see even a flicker of light. They crouched, cloaks spread to catch the heat and hide the flame, and Crax fed it patiently from scraps of wood.

Satyrus explained the situation to every man.

'The whole war may turn on one of us getting back to Seleucus,' he said. 'I need every man to know. Antigonus and Demetrios are about to join forces – perhaps tomorrow – on the plains north of Sardis. Then they can either go north against Lysimachos or east against Seleucus. They think Seleucus is way up north by Gordia.' Satyrus tried to choose his words carefully, trying to imagine a cavalry trooper reporting this to the King of Babylon. 'If Seleucus marches like lightning, he can pass west of Antigonus and join Lysimachos.'

Drawing in the stony dirt and using bread pills to mark the positions, he built a little map complete with ridges marked by rocks.

'Understand – if we get this wrong, Seleucus will face Antigonus in the plains, alone.' Satyrus looked around. They looked like they understood.

'So ... we all ride for it in the morning?' Crax asked.

'You ride for it. I'm taking Anaxagoras, Jubal, Charmides and Apollodorus and riding west for Lysimachos. We're so close we can't afford it if he rests for a day or hesitates ... or heads for the coast to link up with the fleet.' Satyrus shook his head. 'A day – a few hours – and we could lose.'

Crax nodded. 'Well,' he said. 'I guess you're all grown up.'

In the morning, they all shook hands – every man with every other – and the two parties split.

Before the gulls had descended to eat the beans they left on the ground, they were five stades apart.

20

It cost them two days to get around Demetrios and his army; two days of climbing higher and higher on the ridges north of Sardis; two days of hiding among the rocks and the scrubby wild olives. Two days of short rations for man and horse.

On the third day it rained. The water poured down as if the gods were upending buckets on them, but they seized the moment to move – visibility was less than two horse lengths. The rocks were slippery, and Satyrus and Apollodorus, who took turns in the lead, both had falls, and Apollodorus had to put one of his horses down.

Late afternoon, and even Apollodorus was unsure as to their direction. They had angled away from the ridge, looking to make up time, and now, as they rode through the deluge, heads down, Satyrus was worried that they had in fact ridden off in the wrong direction. Descents can be more difficult than ascents.

The sun was setting, somewhere beyond the endless clouds, and a wind was picking up, lashing the water against them. Their cloaks were long since soaked through. The light was tricky, and Satyrus was afraid that they were riding due south – right into Antigonus – and worried again that they were losing time.

The ground was levelling off.

Satyrus pushed his tired horse to a trot and drew level with Apollodorus.

'I want to go downhill to the road,' he shouted. 'I want to be sure where we are – I want to make some time.'

Rain poured through Apollodorus's straw farmer's hat and down his face, soaking his beard, and making him look old. Old and worried.

'Do it,' the man shouted back.

Satyrus felt his way down the ridge, pushing his horse when she hesitated. He didn't love the mare but she was the best of his string and he had to hope that she could find her footing in the tricky light and pouring water.

They went down and down and down ... and Satyrus began to worry again. He couldn't imagine that they had climbed this far – couldn't imagine that he'd have to ride back *up* all this rock to find his friends.

It occurred to him that, hurry or no, the wisest course was to go back up the ridge, find his friends, and make some sort of miserable camp until the rain cleared. One glance in sunlit daylight would show them where they were.

Down and down. Now Satyrus was sure he was lost – he could see a watercourse at the base of the valley, and the darkness was coming down like the water – too damned late to climb the ridge.

And then he saw the road.

There couldn't be a road at the base of every valley. It had to be the Sardis road – the Royal Road.

He sat on his horse's back for a moment, and then slipped down to give the animal a rest and let her drink from the gushing rainwater in the conduit by the road. He had a handful of grain and he put it in his straw hat and she ate it, ravenously, and his hat went with the grain. He had a lump of honey-sugar, almost as big as his fist, in his bag – a sticky, sodden mass, but he ate half and gave the other half to the horse, and she flicked her ears forward as if acknowledging that this, at least, was worth her time.

For the first time, he loved her.

'Good girl,' he said, and patted her neck.

Now he had to climb the ridge again.

He was so busy with the horse that he missed the men.

They came along, heads down in the pouring rain – more than a hundred cavalrymen, sodden men in sodden cloaks on sodden horses.

Satyrus was in the middle of the road. He managed to leap onto his horse's back – he had that much time – and then they were all around him.

'Get off the road, you stupid fuck!' shouted a phylarch.

He hid his head and walked the mare clear of the mass of men, so that she was fetlock deep in the conduit of rainwater. He sat there and watched as Demetrios's Aegema, his elite cavalry, marched past in the very last light. Five hundred cavalrymen, and in the midst of them,

Demetrios himself and two men Satyrus knew at sight – Neron, his spy, and Apollonaris, his physician.

Satyrus pulled his sodden cloak over his head and sat as still as he could.

Neron looked at him.

Demetrios looked at him. He was laughing – in a torrent of rain, he laughed like Dionysus. He was confident and happy.

That alone shook Satyrus as much as anything. And Demetrios and Neron were talking, but Satyrus couldn't hear them over the rain.

Neron turned his head, looked back at Satyrus, and shouted.

Satyrus held his breath.

A pair of soldiers rode forward to Neron.

Satyrus backed his horse, step by step, along the conduit that ran by the road – now the water was deeper, and icy cold. Poor beast.

Satyrus prayed to Herakles, and his prayers were answered in the form of a small path – probably the route that the road's maintainers used to get at the conduit walls.

More shouts behind him.

'Up,' he said to the horse, and put his heels into her sides, and gamely, she rose and made the jump – trusting him – and then she was on the barrow trail, and he didn't hurry. There was now a thin screen of acacia between him and the road itself, on the other side of the ditch. He rode a few steps, dismounted, and put his cloak over her head.

'There was a man – right there by the road,' Neron insisted.

Demetrios nodded. 'No doubt as miserable as we are, my friend. May he find warmth and shelter.' He slapped his spymaster on the back. 'Probably one of your own prodromoi.'

'That's what I thought,' Neron said. 'I'd kill for a report – any report – on where Seleucus is.'

'Let's not look too far ahead,' Demetrios said. 'Or put another way – fuck Seleucus. We've slipped Lysimachos, and now we join up with Pater and the world is ours.'

Neron rode on, but he looked behind him every hundred heartbeats until the rain stopped.

*

336

The two cold, wet men were careful. They searched the edge of the conduit and the trees. Then they searched *in* the conduit, but by luck they were up the hill twenty horse lengths, stabbing their spears down into the water.

Demetrios – and Neron – were well served. They weren't giving up.

Satyrus waited for the rain to get fiercer, and when it did, he walked his horse north along the conduit. He didn't hurry and he didn't look back.

In half an hour, the rain eased off, and by the end of an hour, he'd made ten stades and was on the road, and the rain had stopped.

He considered going back, and decided that the risk would be insane. He had one horse, no camping gear, and no weapons but the knife under his arm.

The sky cleared as he walked on the road, and the moon came up, and it was cold. He mounted up and rode, mostly to keep himself warm, jumping off every couple of stades and running alongside.

His mare was flagging. He searched his sodden leather bag and found a sausage. She ate it. A morsel of wet, stale bread. She ate it.

A linen napkin rolled around his fire-making kit. In the bronze tin, he remembered, he'd put pressed dried grapes from the farm where he'd hidden. The mass of grapes was dry, and the size of his fist. He broke off a piece and gave the rest to his horse.

It was full night. His good campaign chlamys was wet through, but it was still warm, or better than nothing, and the horse was warm. It was the horse that worried him. He needed her alive. In fact, he'd come to like her.

They walked. He didn't remount. He needed her for an emergency, and short of that, he'd just keep going.

Morning. A beautiful morning, with the sun rising above the ridge to the east like the figures of the poet – long, gentle rays of red-pink reaching across one ridge to lick at the next. Rosy fingers lasciviously teasing earth.

Satyrus was mostly asleep, plodding along. Trying to think of a name for his mare. It seemed like an important thing to name her before she lay down and died. And she was exhausted. And he had no more tricks to play, no more sugar, no more warmth.

But somewhere on the hillsides above him, there was a man with a fire. He could smell it. It gave him hope. He pushed forward, one step

337

in front of the other, up a steep climb. He remembered this stretch of road, and knew just where he was – entering the Mysian Gates.

Near the top he saw the smoke, and then saw the fire, and then saw the men – he laughed.

They'd been watching him all the way up the pass, cooking breakfast.

He kept walking. They were Sakje – he was pretty sure he knew the tall, dark-haired man by the fire as Thyrsis, the Achilles of the Assagetae.

'Thyrsis!' he yelled.

Every head came up. Two men he hadn't seen emerged from cover and let their arrows off their strings.

Thyrsis put his cup on the ground and ran down the road to him, wrapped him in an embrace.

'What are you doing here, oh king?' Thyrsis said.

'Scouting,' Satyrus said. 'Would you be so kind as to feed this excellent horse?'

A young Sakje woman took his mare, and he sat on a rock by the road.

The next thing he knew, he was waking to a bright day with his wounded thigh burning and stiff but he felt so much better that he chuckled.

'Soup,' Thyrsis said.

The Sakje maiden gave him a cup, and Satyrus drank it all off, and three more like it, and ate some stale bread.

'How far to the army?' he asked.

Thyrsis laughed. 'Six hundred stades,' he said. 'We're just a feint.'

Satyrus rubbed his thigh and chewed his bread. 'I need three horses and a partner. I need you to push south; find Anaxagoras, Apollodorus and Jubal. They're up that ridge somewhere. We thought Demetrios had Lysimachos right behind him.'

Thyrsis laughed and slapped his thigh. 'We are the *best*. There's two hundred of us, and Eumenes and his Olbians. We've had him running for sixty stades.'

'Lysimachos?' Satyrus asked.

'With the queen – up by Helikore, the Bithynian capital.' He smiled at Satyrus's discomfiture. 'Your sister and the King of Thrace get along very well. They are waiting at the Royal Road junction for news.'

Satyrus groaned. 'I have the news,' he said. 'I just have to get there.'

Satyrus took the time to visit his mare, who was sound asleep, lying flat, the sleep of an exhausted animal. Then he mounted a Sakje pony, and with Thyrsis himself at his side, galloped for Helikore, two hundred stades to the north.

Sunset, and Thracian cavalry pickets – Getae, who had no love for Thyrsis, but a certain wary respect. Satyrus rode into the largest army camp he'd ever seen. He lost count of the tents, the huts, the wagons ... there were easily twenty thousand men, and he suspected that the mass of them was still smaller than Antigonus's fires in the valley below Sardis.

Calicles, the Thracian nobleman, recognised Satyrus right away, and took him to Lysimachos while he dined.

Melitta saw Satyrus and nodded to him as if his arrival was the most natural thing in the world. He kissed her on both cheeks.

Lysimachos embraced him. 'You have news?' he asked.

'I've seen Demetrios retreating, and his father – and I come from Seleucus.' He raised his hand to forestall a babble of questions. Bowed to Prepalaus – Cassander's general. 'Strategos, we met near Corinth,' he said.

The older Macedonian nodded without warmth. 'I seem to remember that I was at the point of your spear,' he said.

Satyrus bowed again. 'Your master had recently ordered me killed,' he said, 'and yet I regret serving with Demetrios, even out of spite.'

The old Macedonian pursed his lips. But rather than say what was on his mind, he shrugged. 'Tell us where Antigonus is,' he asked.

'Antigonus is at Sardis. That was four days ago – I doubt he's moved. He's there to effect a junction with Demetrios, who must have joined him by now.'

Lysimachos looked serious.

'When I left Seleucus, he was in Cappadocia. Antigonus believes he is at the Gordian Gates, and he is not.' Satyrus seized a parchment provided by his sister and started rendering a chart, just as he'd learned among Ptolemy's pages in Alexandria. 'Here's Gordia. Here's Dorylaeum. Here we are in Bithynia. Here's Seleucus – over here, at Koloneia in Cappadocia. See it?'

Prepalaus saw it first.

'We need to go east to Dorylaeum.' The Macedonian scratched his head. 'But Antigonus can be there before us.'

'Antigonus and his son will, almost certainly, thrust up the coast at where he thinks you are – in the passes north of Sardis. Going for Ephesus … or Sardis. Yes?' Satyrus had it all in his head – the grand strategy. He could see it as if he were Zeus's eagle lording it in the heavens, watching men crawl like ants along the valleys of Asia.

Lysimachos nodded at Melitta. 'That's what we wanted to do all along – sweep east and pick up Seleucus on his line of march.' He nodded at Cassander's general. 'Some were more cautious.' Hungrily, Lysimachos leaned forward. 'How many men does Seleucus have?'

'Twelve thousand Persian cavalry, that again in satrapal levies, and two hundred elephants. And his household troops.' Satyrus shrugged. 'Some infantry, but not as good as ours.'

Prepalaus stood up. 'I'm not the cautious old fool that Lysimachos would have me – I just never thought Seleucus would actually come.' He gave them a wry look. 'Don't look so superior, King of Thrace. If you and I have anything in common, it is that we've both been beaten badly by young Demetrios.'

Lysimachos winced.

Melitta shook her head. 'We can bicker while we march.'

With a thousand cavalry and two thousand infantry, the Bosporon contribution was so small as to be almost negligible, but Prepalaus and Lysimachos needed a foil, or a balance, and they listened to Melitta.

'Are we agreed?' Melitta asked.

Lysimachos nodded.

Prepalaus rubbed his grey chin and nodded. 'This is where we cast the die,' he said. 'If Antigonus is ahead of us in the mountain passes, we have to retreat. And that will leave Seleucus alone.'

A slave handed Satyrus wine, and he collapsed onto his sister's couch. She kissed him, and he almost fell asleep on the spot.

'Let's do it,' Prepalaus said.

When Satyrus awoke the next morning, he found himself in a camp all but empty of soldiers. Tents and huts had become mere piles of straw; horse lines were nothing but small mounds of dung. Slaves toiled to fill in latrines.

The sun was in the middle of the sky. He'd slept half a day away.

He was in his own camp bed in his own pavilion, and Phoibos had a breakfast of sweet bread and pomegranate for him, washed down with grape juice and sparkling water from a spring.

Satyrus felt old. His muscles were stiff. But food helped, and a slave came in after breakfast and massaged him with a thoroughness verging on violence, and then he slept again.

Phoibos served him dinner – lamb on skewers and Chian wine. Scopasis joined him, left behind by Melitta to run his escort and collect the Sakje scouts and Greek cavalry of the feint. Thyrsis was already gone away back down the road towards Sardis.

It was odd to sit in the fading sunlight and look out over a dwindling camp. There were men left behind – sick or lame, tending spare mounts, or simply in charge of the last baggage, some regretful deserters and some hopeful recruits, late for the fair.

Satyrus went to sleep for the third time in a day, considering what the remnants of an army looked like, and awoke to the stiffest legs he'd ever had. But he couldn't hide in his tent like Achilles for ever, so he allowed Phoibos to dress him in a Tyrian red chiton and matching chlamys with gold embroidery. His best sword was either on his pack horse with Charmides and Jubal, or lost, so he took another, lighter and longer.

Mounting was no pleasure – riding was worse. Satyrus trotted a riding horse around the camp for half an hour, easing his muscles to their task, and then he mounted his warhorse; a horse he'd scarcely ridden since acquiring him on this very spot, more or less.

Phoibos and his slaves had the tent down and all the gear packed on a dozen donkeys and a wagon. Their little baggage train was already moving but Phoibos had two stools, a table, and a cup of wine waiting in the open where the pavilion had been – and one last donkey waiting to receive them.

Satyrus sat on the stools and the masseur rubbed some of the pain out of his calves and thighs, especially where he had taken the wound. The flesh had closed.

Satyrus drank the wine. 'You are the very best of servants, Phoibos.'

'I endeavour to give satisfaction,' Phoibos said. 'If I might be so bold, lord, I gather that we are at war with my former master, Demetrios?' he asked.

Satyrus nodded. He drank the wine off. 'Yes.'

341

Phoibos nodded. 'I think it would be best if I avoided falling into his hands. He wouldn't be forgiving.'

Satyrus smiled. 'I'll do my best to keep that from happening.'

'May all the gods bless you, my lord.' Phoibos held Satyrus's horse while he mounted.

Satyrus had the whole day's ride to contemplate how in two days he'd gone from starving fugitive to King of the Bosporus.

Philokles would laugh, he thought.

Satyrus had no problem catching the army. They made a little more than one hundred stades that day, but their vanguard managed to go almost twice that, coming up to Trikomia on the Hermos River, almost close enough to Dorylaeum to touch the walls.

An hour after Satyrus came into camp, Melitta was sharing his dinner in his pavilion, and Thyrsis, Eumenes of Olbia and Scopasis came in for a cup of wine – the Olbians and the Sakje had retired out of the Sardis Road and Mysia.

'Demetrios is north of Sardis with thirty thousand men,' Eumenes said. 'His probes up the passes were pretty cautious yesterday. We took a couple of prisoners but they didn't know anything. We let them go.'

Satyrus passed on a second cup of wine. 'I'm still tired,' he said. 'Did you find my friends?'

Eumenes smiled. 'They found us. Your marine – he's some sort of hero from epic poetry – he wanted to mount a fresh horse and come with me. But the boy ... Charmides? Went to sleep on his horse, and had a fall. I left them with my prodromoi.'

Satyrus shook his head. 'When I was lost in the rain, I couldn't imagine it would end this well.'

Before the first rays of the sun shone down the valley of the Hermos, Satyrus was up, and he'd built a small altar on a rock above the cavalry camp. He sacrificed a lamb to Hermes for protecting his friends, and another to Apollo for the healing of his wound. Then he rode down into the camp, spoke with Nikephoros and Lykaeaus who was temporarily leading all the marines. Then he mounted his bay riding horse, had a slave lead his charger, and headed east with his twenty horse marines – as the other Bosporons now called them – under Draco, who laughed at him and reminded him that they'd crossed this country together when Satyrus was a boy.

Lysimachos was with the vanguard – he had a thousand Thracian cavalry, and they were enthusiastic burners, so that the limits of their exploration could be read on every horizon. It was a brutal form of war but Satyrus, sitting with Lysimachos, had to admit that it did keep the commander informed of his men's progress.

'This is all enemy country,' Lysimachos said.

Satyrus doubted that the peasantry of the hills were really allies – or friends – to any man. And the first village they rode through showed the Thracians' savagery – dead men, dead women, and dead animals. All the roofs burned.

Melitta came up in the late afternoon with Scopasis and all her people. Her knights were stripped of their armour – it was off with their wagons, somewhere in the baggage behind them – and their adolescent men and women were armed only with a bow and a knife.

Melitta saluted Lysimachos with her whip. 'Give your Getae a day off,' she said. She said it so pleasantly that only Satyrus caught the violence with which she said *Getae*. 'We'll pass through them at sunset.'

Lysimachos shrugged. 'I don't think they need to be called in. We're making good progress.'

Melitta slapped her leather-clad leg impatiently. 'My people can make twice the time, and we don't stop to rape the animals.' Her true feelings were coming through, and the scars on her face burned red. 'And if we're as close to Antigonus as Prepalaus thinks, we need to keep the smoke off the horizon, eh?'

Satyrus had seldom loved his sister as much as that moment – Lysimachos accepted her suggestions with a smile. It was a condescending smile – that of a man in his prime to a mere woman – a woman play-acting a cavalry commander.

Melitta shrugged off the implied insult, accepted the part of his agreement she needed, and cantered away with her knights at her horse's heels.

Lysimachos shook his head. 'She actually fights, I hear,' he said.

Satyrus looked at him and smiled, albeit for a completely different reason. 'She actually wins,' he said. 'You know what the Assagetae call her?'

'Long legs? Lovely eyes?' Lysimachos chuckled.

'Smells Like Death.' Satyrus smiled at the King of Thrace. 'Our

343

mother was called Cruel Hands. And not for nothing. Ask your Getae.' Then he bowed, waved to his horse marines, and cantered off in his sister's wake. He had to ride quickly – Draco was threatening to spit on the King of Thrace.

They rode through Dorylaeum, and no one tried to hold it or the passes beyond against them. The Sakje crossed the Hermos ford at a gallop, caught an Antigonid patrol off guard and captured the lot – five troopers and a phylarch. The men had nothing worthwhile to report, but their shock at the appearance of the Sakje told its own story, and their phylarch was not so ignorant.

He claimed that there was a division of Antigonus's army behind them – half a day's march south, at Kotiaeio.

Satyrus heard the name and dismounted. He took his working scroll out of his saddlebag and made a mark.

'Crax talked about Kotiaeio,' Satyrus said. 'Ares, that was ten days ago. Ask the phylarch where Seleucus is.'

The man shook his head in silence.

Satyrus pointed his finger at Scopasis and waved at the prisoners.

Draco dismounted and moved the little 'x' of Kotiaeio further west. 'I've been there,' he said.

A pair of Sakje took them under guard, headed north to Lysimachos.

Satyrus pointed at his new estimate of where Kotiaeio was located.

'Let's say Antigonus has discovered that we're not north of Sardis … day before yesterday. So he marches north and east through the Mokedene. He had a garrison in the east – at the Gordian Gates – and now he's racing to them? Or to find us? It really doesn't matter. He's beaten us to the crossroads at Kotiaeio, and we won't fight through there. And we want to join up with Seleucus – who's down here – and we want to meet Antigonus on the plains – the high plains. Where we can use our cavalry.'

Melitta sat on her horse watching him. 'I'd like to contribute to your monologue but this is all empty space to me.'

Satyrus shook his head. 'It shouldn't be, sister. We walked down this valley pretending to be slaves. We went south and east from here, right along the Sangarius River. Remember?'

Melitta smiled. 'You were an odd boy. I was scared out of my wits. All my energy went to carrying that damn basket.'

'And a very fetching slave you made,' Draco put in.

'You had no eyes for me, Macedonian. My slave girl, now ...' They both chuckled.

'Aye, she was a tender morsel. Very much to a soldier's taste.' Draco licked his lips lewdly.

Satyrus made a face. 'You were scared? You acted as if this was a game we were playing.'

She shrugged. 'You think perhaps I should have run around screaming?' She shrugged. 'In other words, you've decided where the army should go.'

Satyrus scratched his beard. 'We should consult with Lysimachos and Prepalaus.'

Their eyes met. The smile they shared might have lasted a generation.

'Thyrsis,' Melitta called. 'Guides back at the ford, and guides every five stades. A pair, with remounts, and as soon as the vanguard comes up, they report and ride to us.'

Thyrsis looked bored. 'This is children's work. I want to fight.'

Melitta stared him down.

He shrugged. 'Yes, Mother,' he said, and some of the Sakje laughed – some at him, some at them both.

'I need Anaxagoras back,' Melitta said. 'The boys are growing restless. They need to see that I have a stallion of my own.'

Satyrus sighed and took his horse marines forward. They were fine cavalrymen now. In fact, they could, most of them, manage a bow on horseback. But two days with the Sakje and they were tired and sore. And they didn't have enough remounts to keep up the pace.

Satyrus gave them the horses from the captured Antigonid patrol, and several Sakje leaders added to the string of remounts. Two men who couldn't make the pace were left as guides. The rest of them pressed forward, heading east and south, Draco leading. His years of service – with Eumenes of Kardia, with Alexander, with Heraklea – left him with a good knowledge of the area, and he brought them unerringly to the ford of the Sangarius, well west of Gordia ... and unguarded.

They camped across the ford, and every man slept with his weapons to hand, his horse ready bridled – they had pickets over a stade from camp. They woke in the darkness before dawn and rode south and west now. Melitta sent Scopasis and half her tribesmen back along the river, prowling due west, looking for contact with the enemy.

Satyrus rode up every ridge. The ground was flat – increasingly agricultural. They were on the high plains of central Anatolia, and when they camped again, Scopasis rolled out of his blankets as if stung by a scorpion, and came to Melitta, wonder on his face. In his hand was a pair of arrowheads – carefully cast bronze points, tiny trilobate heads such as only the Sakje used.

'Our people have been this way before,' Scopasis said.

'Oh, yes,' Melitta said. She sang them one of her mother's songs, of the Great Ride against the King of Phrygia.

Draco sat with his back against Satyrus's, polishing the blade of his dirk. 'She's quite something, that sister of yours,' he said.

They were off with the sun again. Satyrus sent one of his horse marines back along the chain of guides – a chain that now stretched almost six hundred stades. They'd started to get guides back but Satyrus wanted a progress report.

Mid-afternoon, and Satyrus climbed a low ridge – shallow and long, ten stades across. There were wild grapes all along the crest, hard riding, and he had to dismount; he heard his troopers curse him.

But at the western edge of the ridge there was a mound, and below it was a bluff, and the ground fell away to the south and east. To his right, he could see Melitta and her scouts as puffs of dust on the path across the lower ridge.

And way off to the east, twenty stades away or more, was a line of dust that rose to the heavens like burnt offerings from a hundred altars.

At his side, Draco gave a whoop.

Sophocles had long since given up on catching Satyrus. He had no intention of trying to follow the King of the Bosporus into the Seleucid army. It was the sort of thing that men did in Persian songs, but Sophokles intended to live to old age.

So he rode north, around the King of Babylon. He had to stop for two days when his guts rid themselves of the last of the farmer's-wife's poison. His thugs deserted him, and stole all but one of his horses.

But they didn't kill him, and he thanked the gods for that, and rode north again. It rained so hard he couldn't see.

All in a day's work.

It took him four days to find Antigonus's army, and another whole day to get an idiot cavalry officer to lead him to the old man himself. He gathered from the men who held him – gently but firmly – that Demetrios had joined his father just the day before.

By the time he faced the father and son, his news was nine days old. But it was valuable nonetheless.

Demetrios had heard of him. And Neron. Neron came. And then the serious questioning began.

Sophokles had made his decision before riding in. He was changing sides. He no longer knew – or cared – which side Phiale was on. He needed the protection of a side, and all the signs and portents he could see shouted that Antigonus – with the bigger army and the giant herd of elephants and the brilliant son and the bottomless well of Asian riches – would win.

And Sophokles had had enough of obeying people with bad intelligence.

So, patiently, he told everything he knew.

And he knew a great deal.

Neron asked him questions all day – a full day, with two tattooed barbarians standing by. Sophokles didn't like torture any more than the next man – and he kept pointing out that he'd have more value as an agent than as a tortured corpse.

Finally – after a day – Neron came over and gave him a bowl of soup. 'One more time – you were after Satyrus of Tanais?'

Sophokles, who had answered this ten times, shrugged. 'Yes.'

Neron looked angry, but Sophokles had figured out long since that he, Sophokles, was not the target.

'And you lost him?' Neron asked.

'Twice. Lost him at the edge of the Euphrates – Zeugman – twenty days ago. Then I shadowed Seleucus for a few days, until ... well, I had a wound. Then I lost him again. He went north.'

Neron put his face in his hands. 'Satyrus of Tanais sailed around our fleet to join Seleucus. And then he left Seleucus riding north. That's what you are telling me. Satyrus is the linchpin between their armies. And he went north.'

347

Sophokles found the soup more interesting than the theory. He made the sound men make when they don't care to speak.

Neron left him for a while, and then returned.

'We want you to go back to Seleucus,' he said. 'And spy.'

Sophokles shrugged. 'Better Seleucus than Lysimachos. None of his easterners will know me, and my Persian is pretty good.' He finished the soup. 'And kill Satyrus?'

Demetrios the golden, in his second-best breastplate and with his helmet under his arm, came in. 'Absolutely not. If I hear that he was assassinated, I'll see you cut in quarters and burned. Am I making myself clear? I am the man who will kill Satyrus – in single combat. I have dreamed it. He is the worthy opponent of my story, and I will not have him killed.'

Neron raised an eyebrow.

Demetrios sighed. 'Neron, I know you have our best interests at heart. But we have more than two hundred elephants, fifty thousand hoplites, and the finest cavalry in the world. And Pater, and me. Don't you see? *We want this battle.* This is where we get them all together and we smash them like a pot. With just a little luck, we kill Seleucus and his idiot son and Lysimachos and Satyrus. The lot. Cut the heads off the hydra, and we're done.'

Neron shrugged. 'I understand the plan. I feel it is … optimistic.'

Demetrios beamed his golden smile. 'Neron, sometimes I wonder which one of us works for the other. Are you the tool of my imperial ambition? Or am I the tool of yours? This is a command. Please obey.'

Neron turned to Sophokles. 'There, you heard it from your prince. Observe, spy, and report. Do not kill Satyrus, or anyone else.'

Sophokles nodded. 'Of course. In the meantime, might I have more soup?'

21

Satyrus rode up to Seleucus in the middle of his column, with dust rolling over them like storm clouds, and the plains of High Asia stretching on either hand, rolling land as far as the mountains.

Antiochus saw him first, and left the column with a whoop, and then Satyrus was abreast of Diodorus, and they clasped hands.

'Where, by all the Titans, did you come from?' Diodorus asked.

'The west.' Satyrus felt his heart swell to see them all – to know he'd done it. He'd ridden all the way around Antigonus in twenty days, and unless Lysimachos was asleep, the juncture of the armies was only a day or two away. 'Lysimachos should be on the Sangarius by now.'

Antiochus had a parchment map. Satyrus got his out of his shoulder bag – it had wine stains, food stains, water stains, but he knew it as if it was his own body.

'Antigonus is in Arginousa. His rearguard was at Kotiaeio two days ago.' Antiochus slapped Satyrus on the back again, looked over his shoulder. 'There's a woman!' he said.

'My sister,' Satyrus said. 'The queen of the Assagetae. The Sakje scouts on your right flank are ours, and there will be more coming in.'

'You all know each other,' Seleucus said. His normally serious expression was replaced with humour, as Melitta embraced Diodorus and then Crax.

'Party in the prodromoi camp tonight,' Crax shouted, ignoring the presence of the King of Babylon. Most of the prodromoi of the Exiles were Sakje tribesmen.

Seleucus put his head down over the notes on the paper. 'I need to press north up the Doryleaion road,' he said after a moment. 'That shortens Lysimachos's route to me and puts pressure on Antigonus so that he can't press down the river valleys and fight Lysimachos alone.' He smacked his fist into his palm. 'It's ours to win, now.'

Suddenly, the tribe of rich, aristocratic Macedonian officers around

Seleucus came into their own. Seleucus decided his arrangements in seconds, and sent his son and Diodorus north with his guard cavalry, the Exiles, and the cream of his Persian cavalry.

'As fast as you can go – up the throat. I care not whether you win or lose but I want you to engage his men *today*.' His voice snapped like a whip, and a dozen young Macedonian noblemen rode away with particular orders – to the satraps, to the most trusted Persian nobles, to the Exiles and the Aegema and the Companions. The rest of the army – even the elephants – turned almost as one man and left the road. In ten minutes, there was nothing to show but eddies of dust, and then the cavalry came – most of them moving at a fast trot, six files wide, filling the road, their harness making the music of Ares as they went. The Exiles were already twenty stades north. The Aegema had to ride up from the rearguard, the elite regiment changing horses on the march. The Persians were the best mounted and most colourful – four thousand picked riders.

Melitta broke free from Sappho to whisper to her brother. 'We should go back east,' she said. 'Lysimachos needs to know.'

'The king and queen of the Bosporus shouldn't have to be messengers,' Seleucus said. 'And the Exiles are, technically, your troops.'

'Thankfully, I am not paying their wages,' Satyrus said. 'And Melitta and I know where to go from here. Your scouts might waste a day.'

Seleucus waved to Crax. 'Tell me the towns north of here – and their distances.'

'Prumnessos – six stades. You can see the roofs. Then Akroinos – just a border castle. And then Ipsos. About ninety stades.' He shrugged. 'But the road curves.'

Seleucus put the point of his dagger on Satyrus's stained map. 'Akroinos,' he said. 'Ipsos if Antigonus hesitates this afternoon.'

'Akroinos or Ipsos,' Satyrus said. He clasped the King of Babylon's hand.

'Day after tomorrow dawn,' Seleucus said.

It was odd to leave the army. But Satyrus was beginning to enjoy the war in the spaces between. A war that depended on stamina and navigation. It was like fighting at sea.

'This is what the Sakje do,' Melitta explained. 'We ride the Sea of

Grass, and we come and go. We know where we are – and no enemy knows as much.'

They were back over the long low ridge from which Satyrus had seen Seleucus in the morning. They had fewer than two hundred tribesmen, and fifteen of Draco's men. Draco had had to bow out.

'Too damned old,' he said. 'It burns me, but I'll just slow you down.'

Satyrus left him with Sappho.

Nightfall – the hardest day yet. Two hundred stades. Satyrus had used all four of the horses he had behind him. They were edging north of their easterly back trail, looking for the men Melitta had sent upriver with Scopasis.

Scopasis's scouts found them at last light, at the confluence of the Parthenios and the Sangarius. The water roared away, and the Sakje were on the other side of the river. Satyrus prepared himself to ride east to the ford but the Sakje threw ropes to each other, put a line of horsemen across the river to break up the heavy flow, and Satyrus rode across, cooled if not refreshed.

Now they were on the north bank of the Sangarius, with six hundred horsemen.

Scopasis led them to a fire and gave them koumis. Satyrus thought that it tasted so foul that he usually avoided it, but tonight everything was delicious, and he drank deep.

'Antigonus has horsemen all across the plains to the west,' Scopasis said, waving his eating knife in the last light of the red sun. 'They scout like children playing a game – they only ride the easy paths.'

'Today or tomorrow there will be a fight due west of here,' Satyrus said. 'Where is Lysimachos?'

Scopasis sighed. 'Somewhere behind me. They are so slow, we wish to fight without them.' Scopasis pointed north. 'They should be at the ford tonight.'

Satyrus wanted to go to sleep but he was haunted by the idea that after all their work, Antigonus could end up engaging Seleucus alone, because the man had boldly lunged forward to save Lysimachos.

'If you two took all the Sakje straight west along the river – before first light – moving like Sakje ...' He drew it in the dirt, by firelight.

Scopasis saw it first. 'With luck, we appear on their flank when they face Diodorus. With no luck, we alarm their sentries and cause them to act like ants in a nest when the bear comes.' He nodded.

Melitta stretched. 'Why wait until dawn?' she said.

They were gone into the moonlight before Satyrus was done with his barley soup.

Satyrus wandered over to his troopers. 'Relax,' he said. 'I'm not riding until dawn.'

That got him a cheer.

Two hours after dawn, and he was embracing Apollodorus, and Charmides.

'You ride too fast for me,' Charmides said.

'I'm getting you ready for a nice Sauromatae bride,' Satyrus joked. 'Pack up, gentlemen. The battle is now.'

That stirred them.

'Where?' Apollodorus and Anaxagoras asked together.

'A hundred stades from here.' Satyrus shrugged.

Apollodorus ran off. Nikephoros came up, heard the news, and ran off to the Apobatai.

Satyrus didn't dismount. He rode to Prepalaus, who was inspecting his Macedonians, gathered his staff, and Lysimachos. He spent ten minutes explaining. The scraps of his map were redrawn on virgin parchment.

Satyrus writhed in an agony of their indecision for as long as it took a smith to pour a bronze ingot. They were quite a contrast to Seleucus.

He debated saying something – he, the youngest, and by far the least of them – but the one who knew the terrain.

But he sensed that Prepalaus wanted an excuse to delay battle, and that the man's dislike of him could be the excuse.

Satyrus rode down the column and fetched Stratokles, who was with the mercenaries.

The man embraced him like a long-lost brother. Satyrus was surprised at the Athenian's enthusiasm.

'I need you to shepherd the alliance,' he said. 'Every minute counts.'

Stratokles had been standing with his men, and with Herakles – now the taxiarch of two thousand Ionian hoplites. Herakles saluted smartly. Satyrus waved, and Stratokles mounted, and they rode back up the column.

Stratokles took Lysimachos aside and spoke to him – low tones, urgency.

Then he came back out of the tent to Satyrus and mounted. 'The thing is done,' he said. 'I'm going to lead my men.'

Satyrus went back into the tent – already too hot. Lysimachos was putting on his armour.

'You may stay here,' he told the Macedonian strategos. 'The Bosporons and my Thracians are marching. And we will march all night.'

The first cavalry skirmish was so obviously a feint that Demetrios ignored it and led his cavalry east, looking for Lysimachos. But before the day was two hours old, his pater sent a recall, claiming that there were thousands – that was the word the messenger said – thousands of cavalry coming up the lake road from Synadda.

Demetrios's men were in high training, and they responded perfectly, so that his rough skirmish line going west changed front to the south in half an hour, and they began to sweep back south and west. The centre of the line contacted enemy cavalry north of the road, and Demetrios ran out of daylight trying to cut them off. But at nightfall, he rode the line of his campfires. He had secured his father from surprise. And his best men picked up a pair of prisoners that confirmed his suspicion. He was facing Seleucus. From the south.

'Good for Neron,' he said.

In the mists before true dawn, he brought up the best of his own Companions. He briefed his officers in the courtyard of the temple at Cybele, and many of them prayed there. The omens were all auspicious.

His enemy's omens must have been auspicious, too. Demetrios came down the hills into the denser mist of the valley floor, his cavalry line formed parallel to the road, visible across the plain, and the enemy charged him – formed wedges of professional cavalry on superb horses.

Both sides charged twice. They were well matched. Demetrios killed a Macedonian officer in the second charge – someone important – and then there were armoured troopers in blue cloaks on his southern flank, and he extricated his Companions as carefully as he'd engaged them, picked up his Greek mercenaries and came down the hills a third time, to find the road empty.

Throwing out scouts in all directions, he followed them.

He caught them again just as the last mist burned off – a brilliant day with a few high clouds. And there were the blue cloaks – almost a thousand of them. He was close enough to see that their leader was an old man.

Demetrios knew them. They'd captured him as a boy. He nodded.

'Horns of the Bull,' he ordered his Greek cavalry on either flank.

And then the folds of earth north of the road sprouted Persians, like Jason sowing dragon's teeth.

Demetrios had to allow himself to be pushed all the way back to his hills. Only there, when he linked up with his father's cavalry, could he rally.

But with four thousand more cavalry, he could rule them. He turned about one more time, despite the fatigue of his best men, and pushed down the hills one more time.

The blue cloaks and their Persians had to give the ground now. There was no fighting at all. Both sides were too professional to waste men on a declined engagement. The blue cloaks retreated south down the road, and the Persians covered their flanks.

And then something struck Demetrios in the left flank like a thunderbolt.

Scopasis reined in, wrenching his lance from the corpse of the man he'd gaffed like a fisherman would gaff a salmon in the Tanais River. It took both hands and the strength of his horse to drag the head clear. And the point was bent – the spear ruined.

Melitta put her head down and galloped clear of her own line, headed uphill. Her trumpeter stuck with her. They climbed away from the fight until she could see.

The sun was setting and the road shone like a silver ribbon in the pale green fields on either side. The dust clouds of the cavalry moving below her looked like dandelion tufts.

She was in some enemy's flank. Her people had ridden all day for this moment, and she wasn't going to stop them, even though below her a pair of adolescent girls were beheading a man, and another was being scalped, alive.

She took a deep breath.

'Blow "look at me".'

The trumpeter put her gold trumpet to her mouth and blew, long and hard, and every tribesman's head turned.

Melitta raised her spear and pointed south, into the rear of the enemy formation. They outnumbered her twenty to one, but the sun was setting at her back, there was dust in the air, and fleeing men count every foe thrice. Or so the Sakje said.

Demetrios heard the trumpet and his heart sank.

More Persians, or worse, their Saka allies. All the way around his flank – they must have slipped along the ridge.

Demetrios ordered his companions back. The rest, mercenaries and allies, were realists. They'd begun retreating as soon as they heard the trumpet.

They lost men, but they fought through – the enemy were either timid, or far, far fewer than fear had made them. But Demetrios couldn't risk a defeat – Seleucus was rich in cavalry. So he retired all the way back to his hills, and his horsemen camped where they had started.

But the enemy did not. It was only when dark fell and fires were visible that Demetrios saw that the blue cloaks had broken contact. The road south was empty.

Some of his men cheered. But Demetrios felt alone, and he sent three messengers to his father.

'You thought perhaps I'd march away and leave you?' Antigonus said the next morning. 'We have Seleucus. Lysimachos may still be up near Heraklea – scouts out as far as Gordia and no reports at all.'

Demetrios drew on a wooden table with his dagger. 'What if Lysimachos were east of us – on the Sangarius?'

Antigonus nodded. 'It's possible, but if we strike today, it won't matter a damn.'

'Pater—'

'I make the strategy, boy. Knockout blow. We don't piss on them – we kick them in the crotch. Right down the road, fast as we can – you cover my left.' He looked at the scratches in the table. 'With a little luck, we catch them in mid-afternoon and that's the war.'

*

The moon was high when Satyrus found Melitta. Her men were mourning their losses – two gone to the shades.

'You are too far north,' she said. 'We need to fall back to the ridges.'

'I'm already south of here – there's a village, Malos, twenty stades south. Nikephoros is resting the infantry there. I came for you.' Satyrus sat like a statue in the moonlight.

Melitta took his hand. 'You have finally become a Sakje, brother,' she said. 'How many stades have you ridden this week?'

'All the stades the winds crosses,' Satyrus said, wearily. 'And now we need to cross twenty more.'

Even in the moonlight, they could see that the plains at the base of the ridges were alive with moving men and fires. Lysimachos had been even more daring than Satyrus had hoped; he'd launched his army in a race across the plains, and trusted that he'd have time to sort them out if a battle occurred. The best units – Prepalaus's Macedonians, Lysimachos's veteran mercenaries, the Thracians – had moved almost as fast as cavalry.

Satyrus found Lysimachos, Stratokles and Prepalaus under the vine trellis of a tavern in Malos. The streets were packed with soldiers, and men were simply lying down on their shields and sleeping.

'If Antigonus catches us tonight, we're done,' Lysimachos said. 'But we marched a hundred stades today, and crossed a river. We couldn't have done more.'

'Seleucus fought a delaying action today,' Satyrus said. 'We need to march at dawn. I'd like you to agree to give me all the cavalry at first light – even the Thracians. I can be up with Seleucus by midday.'

Prepalaus shook his head. 'You can have my cavalry and welcome, but it is our infantry that Seleucus needs.'

Satyrus nodded. 'But our cavalry will show that we are near. And perhaps ... perhaps Antigonus will make a mistake.'

Demetrios had to admit that the blue cloaks were excellent cavalry. He ushered them around the valley floor but he couldn't corner them, and their Persian allies stayed loyal, despite gifts of money sent blatantly across the valley to them. Neron came back from one such foray shaking his head.

'I spoke to a noble named Darius. They are all named Darius. He said that such behaviour would be despicable, and did he look like a Greek?' Neron shrugged.

Demetrios sent more and more men up the ridges, trying to flank the Persians or cow them into retreat, and by late morning he had moved them back. But his horses were still tired from the day before and needed water and better food – grain.

The sun was high above them, grilling man and horse together, when the blue cloaks turned by squadrons to the right and formed four deep rhomboids, the points facing him, and their outriders, armed with bows, began to gall his Greek cavalry.

Demetrios looked back up the road to the north. He'd screened his father rather well, he thought – the pikemen were coming on in long columns of files, ready to form at a moment's notice but free to walk their fastest, and their pikes travelled in carts to save their energy in the broiling sun.

Demetrios shook his head at Neron. 'He can't actually mean to make a stand,' he said, pointing at the old man on the horse, a stade away.

'That is Antiochus with him,' Neron said. 'I have it from a prisoner.'

'My would-be rival,' Demetrios said. He rubbed his chin. 'Apple.'

His groom-slave handed him an apple.

Demetrios took a bite and gave the rest to his horse. 'Have we got a charge in us, Philip?' he asked his phylarch.

'Not unless the horses can smell water, King.' Philip shook his head and dismounted.

Demetrios agreed, but this was taking too long. That's all the old bastard over there wanted – to waste his time.

'That can't be good,' Philip said from behind him. Before he was done speaking, Neron swore and galloped away, headed for the ridge, where a little knot of Greek cavalry were rallying, silhouetted against the ridge line.

More men came streaming over the ridge.

'Lycos, go with Neron. Get me a report and bring it to my father.' Demetrios turned his horse and trotted his horse all the way to where his father sat, sweltering in his armour. He and all his officers were peering up the ridges.

'Kick them in the crotch, I said.' Antigonus shook his head. 'You're pissing on them.'

'Pater, my horses are blown and need water, my remounts are all with you, and the fucking Persians have outflanked my stupid Greeks again,' Demetrios said.

Antigonus cursed. 'Why didn't you tell me you needed to water your horses?' This from a man who grumbled 'don't trouble me with details'. 'Aphrodite's quivering cunny, boy, if we need water, we'll water. I'll push the pikes at them. Bring the cavalry back through us. I'll put elephants on my flanks. They have no infantry – they're not going to stand, are they?' He motioned for his officers.

Neron rode into the command group like a lightning bolt. 'It's Lysimachos,' he said. 'The cavalry behind our flank are *Thracians.*'

Antigonus paled under his tan. Demetrios thought he saw something go out of his father then – perhaps the daimon that men spoke about.

'Lysimachos,' Antigonus said. He was looking down the road towards the blue cloaks, who had just faced about and begun to retreat. And they were cheering as they went. 'Ares fucking Aphrodite and all the gods watching. Missed him by that much.'

Demetrios sighed. 'We can still push forward.'

Antigonus shook his head. 'No. No ... we'll roll the dice we have. Camp here, rest everyone. Fight tomorrow. Edge us west until our flank's on the Kaistros river. And fortify the front. Let's not make it easy for them.'

Six stades away, Satyrus sat with Diodorus and Antiochus, Crax and Melitta, Andronicus and Scopasis, Calicles, Anaxagoras and Charmides. On the ridge just east of the extreme flank of Demetrios's cavalry line, the rightmost file of the Persian satrapal cavalry was linked up with the leftmost file of Satyrus's bodyguard and the Thracians. Their line was continuous, and Melitta's knights had already turned the flank further north. The Greek cavalry were retreating as fast as they could out of the shower of arrows, and Melitta's men were stopping to retrieve every shaft they shot. The impetus had already gone out of the fight.

Coenus rode up out of the dust with his Tanais hippeis, and Eumenes of Olbia with his. Satyrus embraced them both.

'Will your men be my Companions?' Satyrus asked Coenus. 'Will you command them?'

Coenus shook his head. 'No. I dislike command. Let Eumenes have it – he has the spark. But I'll ride at your side.'

Satyrus turned to Eumenes. 'It seems rude to offer second best,' he said.

Eumenes smiled at Coenus. 'It would be odd if you offered it to me before you offered it to my teacher.'

Charmides was delighted at the news. 'Too much responsibility for me,' he said.

Eumenes put his arm around the young man. 'You remind me of a young man I once knew.'

Coenus remained mounted. 'That's the problem with age and nostalgia, Eumenes. After a while, they all remind you of someone.'

Almost at his feet, Apollodorus came toiling up the ridge, two hundred hoplite-armed marines at his back, running like the athletes they were, and behind them, the Apobatai, running just as hard, with Nikephoros.

Apollodorus stopped at the top of the hill, tilted his helmet back on his head, and bellowed, 'Finish as you started!'

The laggards put on a burst of speed, and the column closed up. Apollodorus stopped at Coenus's feet and saluted.

Coenus laughed. 'You want to impress the crap out of the King of Babylon,' he said, leaning from his mount. 'He's the well-dressed fellow – right there.'

Apollodorus smiled and led his marines over the ridge.

Coenus watched as he ran up to Seleucus. Saw Seleucus salute.

Satyrus came up next to him. 'I have that feeling,' he said.

Coenus nodded. 'As do I. Do me a favour?'

Satyrus turned to the older man. 'Anything.'

'The night before battle, your father did a thing: he gathered his friends and made sacrifice to the gods. And we sang – sometimes the *Iliad*. And then we drank together. Do it tonight. Most of us are here.'

There were tears in the old man's eyes.

'Most of us still alive, I mean. And the shades of the rest ... they'll be here, too.'

Satyrus looked over the fields below him on the ridge. Almost at his feet, a stone-walled farm with a big yard was like a small fortress at the edge of the plain, and the dusty Asian fields rolled away, littered in shining scarlet poppies as far as the eye could see to the haze raised by the opposing army. In the distance, the small hamlet of Ipsos rested on dry stream bed. Irrigation made the farther fields a lurid green, while the higher fields of poorer farmers were a greyer, sparser colour. All would be tramped flat on the morrow, rich and poor together.

Satyrus thought on that a moment.

'There will be more shades yet, this time tomorrow,' he said.

22

It was a perfect summer evening, and the camps stretched away from the ridges on the east flank to the river on the west, and no man present had ever seen such a confrontation – not at Gaza, and not when Alexander still walked the earth.

Satyrus informed Phoibos, and he made the symposium happen as if he arranged wine for two hundred guests every day – perhaps he did.

There were Sakje. It was not possible to invite just a few Sakje – they had no notion of invitation. A party was for drinking. The first man on a pony arrived at Satyrus's pavilion an hour before sunset, while Phoibos and his slaves were still stacking the wood for four concentric bonfires. Other slaves brought sheep, goats, a pair of cows and a bull.

Phoibos, now an accepted part of Satyrus's military household, found Draco – a trusted retainer, in his eyes, if a heavy drinker and a dangerous fornicator – already at the slaves. Phoibos caught the killer's eye. 'Sir, I need an errand that only a gentleman can run for me.'

Draco tore himself away from the contemplation of a willing accomplice in lechery. 'Whatever you need, laddy.' The word 'gentleman' had gone to his head. Phoibos knew his way around soldiers.

'I need a priest ... a decent priest, a Greek with a civil tongue. Otherwise Lord Satyrus will do the sacrifices himself, which is not seemly.'

Draco clucked. 'The things you worry about, Phoibos. But ... you do this stuff, and I don't. Antiochus has a priest of Zeus. An Athenian. I met him yesterday.'

'Would you be so kind? ' Phoibos asked, already holding out the Macedonian's dusted and re-pressed cloak.

Draco nodded and set off across the camp. He took a horse, and because he had to go to the horse lines, he put on a sword. And when he thought of who he would be addressing, he stopped and changed his chiton as well.

*

Well before dark, Phoibos presented Satyrus with another quandary. Having invited his friends – his father's friends – and the Sakje, now some of the other officers wished to invite themselves. The sight of a line of wine jars the width of a phalanx, and a set of bonfires like the funeral pyre of Petrocolus, and a herd of sacrificial meat big enough to feed the army . . .

'Lord Antiochus wishes to attend,' Phoibos said. 'The King of Babylon. The King of Thrace. The strategos of Macedon.'

Satyrus looked grim. 'Not the party I intended.'

Melitta shook her head. 'Of course it is. If Mater and Pater were here, wouldn't they do just this? What can better hearten the army than to see the chiefs together in piety and amity?'

Satyrus smiled. 'Very well. We host the world.'

'Very good,' Phoibos replied. 'I have already taken the liberty of telling them so.'

It wasn't yet full dark, and the Sakje were clamouring for the fires to be lit. There were quite a few eastern Saka with the satrapal levies, and now there were two hundred of them alone flooding the area set off for the symposium. Most of them had enough sense to bring wine, and pallets to lie on.

A tall, handsome man with a big nose and beautiful dark skin like fine wood bowed low to Satyrus. 'You don't know me,' he said. He had the voice of a Greek actor playing a Persian.

'Darius,' Satyrus said.

They embraced, and Darius embraced Melitta. 'Where's Leon?' he asked.

'Out on the sea, covering our flank,' Satyrus said.

'Ahh. He will be sad to have missed this.' Darius looked out at the Saka and the Sakje. 'I apologise – many of them are mine, Persae and Saka. So I have brought some wine and some extra hands to serve.' In fact, every man behind him had an amphora of wine – a veritable fortune.

'I am not a poor man,' he said with a smile. 'Seleucus has given me high rank.'

'You will be in the morning if we drink all that,' Melitta said.

'And this handsome man?' Darius asked.

362

'My friend, Anaxagoras,' Satyrus said.

Melitta laughed. 'My husband, whenever he troubles to ask me.'

Satyrus had the pleasure of watching Anaxagoras blush in consternation.

Old friends crowded around to offer their congratulations, but Melitta gave her shout of war and they stilled. 'He has to ask me,' she said. 'I'm Greek enough in my heart that I cannot ask him.'

Anaxagoras grinned, bowed ... and vanished.

Satyrus wondered if he was angry. Anaxagoras was not easy to hurt – perhaps he had not liked this public denouement.

Hard to know.

Old friends pressed close once more, and Satyrus forgot in a whirl of reminiscence.

Sophokles needed to get clear of the compound and ride for it. He knew everything – everything useful that he could get.

He'd spent the day wooing Seleucus's physician, a man who had never been to Athens and needed all the help he could get. Sophokles gave him good advice, shared two of his best drugs, free of charge, and discussed bandages and poisons. In exchange, he asked nothing except to sit one tent wall from the command tent and listen.

He didn't like how confident the Seleucids were. But he had the fault lines of their alliance firmly in his head, and now he could tell Neron which of the satraps could be bribed; he'd heard it from Antiochus himself.

He bowed to all, and hurried out of the palace complex of tents – hurried too fast, so that the sentries in the outer cordon stopped him. It was the sort of mistake he hated to make. He vowed never to make it again.

Draco dismounted at the officer's picket line, near the King of Babylon's tents. His horse hated the smell of elephants, and he drove her picket pin in to the ring. Then he walked up to the sentries, dusting his hands to get the sand off.

There was a handsome enough man just passing out of the palace of tents, walking too fast. The soldiers didn't like it – Draco applauded their professionalism – they stopped and asked his business.

Draco thought that perhaps he knew that voice. He froze.

When the man finally passed the cordon, Draco followed him into the streets behind the palace of tents, where the companion cavalry and infantry were camped.

Indecision was not in Draco. He watched the man walk, and he was sure.

He followed him down the main street of infantrymen, and then along a side street, past the petty-wine shops, the men who sold olive oil and new pans to soldiers.

He followed the man right to the door of his tent, and there, without breaking stride, he plunged his sword into his back.

Then he rolled the man over. His eyes were glazing.

'Know who I am?' Draco said. 'I hope so. Here – eat this, you fuck.' He buried his sword in the man's mouth, so the point came out the back of his neck. Draco put a little more pressure on the point and snapped the vertebrae, sawed messily a little and beheaded him. He sighed when he remembered that he was wearing his best cloak. But he wrapped the head in the cloak.

Pushed the corpse to bleed out in the door of the tent.

Picked up the head and went looking for a priest of Zeus.

Anaxagoras returned to the party like a thunderbolt. He was mounted, and he had – of all people – Scopasis and Thyrsis at his side, and they rode through the party like an enemy charge, scattering the guests, but not a one was injured. It was a pretty feat of riding, and it was made better by the agility with which Anaxagoras snatched the Queen of the Assagetae from the conversation she was sharing with Sappho and the Lady Thais, Antiochus's concubine, as well as Lucius and Stratokles. One moment she was talking to them, and the next she was across his horse, riding away.

His arms were strong, and his grip on her was like a band of bronze.

'Marry me?' he asked.

The sound of her laughter trickled past the sound of his horse's hooves, back through the party.

It made a fine way to launch the festivities, especially when they came back, dismounted and more orderly, and announced their betrothal. Phoibos glared at Draco, who entered looking rumpled, drunken, and soiled, but had indeed brought the priest, who hastened to do his master's bidding.

But Satyrus insisted, as host, in sacrificing the bull.

Even the Sakje were silent.

No man – no worshipper, no priest, no pious aristocrat – sacrifices a bull lightly. Not just the money – but the cut. A bull does not die as easily as a lamb or a dove. A priest might slash the bull's throat with a sharp knife, but a soldier was expected to do it the old way.

Satyrus believed in the old way. He stepped up to the altar and handed the rope to Anaxagoras, who pulled it tight, stretching the animal's neck across the altar. The old way.

Satyrus looked off into the heavens, into the last light in the sky, and it seemed to him that he saw an eagle there, or perhaps a raven, on the auspicious right side of the sky – spiralling away – and just for a moment, he wished that he was there in the sky, high above the needs of men and women.

He sent his thoughts up to Olympus, to Herakles, and drew – rotated his hips, and brought the blade down.

It was not his fighting sword, it was the heaviest sword he could borrow. And Tyche was with him: his blade went between the vertebrae of the neck as if the God himself had his hand on the hilt.

The bull slumped – the last morsel of flesh tore with the weight of the body – and the head rolled free, falling at Anaxagoras's feet.

The roar of the soldiers was like an avalanche of sound.

Seleucus – dignified, gracious Seleucus – slapped his back as if they were wine-bibbers. 'Spectacular!' he shouted over the crowd.

Satyrus wiped his blade clean and bowed to the priest, who gave him the look of a man with a hard act to follow.

But the priest did a competent job, making his way through lambs and goats, and the pool of blood under the altar grew deeper and deeper – libations were poured, and smoke rolled into the heavens from the long bones wrapped in fat and laid on the fires on the altar. A pair of acolytes cut the meat and passed it to Phoibos – a dignified Phoibos in a shining red chiton – who cut it into slices with an expertise and speed that made his flaying look like magic.

Satyrus, his act of piety complete, felt like a hero, and he poured a special libation and then stood with his friends, passing a cup of watered wine, watching the priests – a sacrifice to Athena, a sacrifice to Hera, a sacrifice to Aphrodite …

Seleucus came up by Satyrus. 'Thank you, King of Tanais. This was well thought out – a proper way for men to show their respect for the gods on the eve of battle. A proper show that we are Hellenes, here in the land of the barbarians.'

Satyrus was looking at a crowd of Darius's tribal Saka gathered around Melitta, and smiled. But he appreciated that Seleucus was trying to be genial, to overcome his habitual reserve – and besides, the two had shared Ptolemy's court.

'Great king, your praise is sweet in my ears,' Satyrus said.

'I don't call myself "Great King",' Seleucus said.

But you will, Satyrus thought.

'Is there news from the fleets?' he asked.

Seleucus nodded. 'Our fleets are already dispersing. Demetrios's fleet is in Athens and Corinth. There were two actions – Plistias declined both times. I understand that your friend Abraham, the Jew – how well I remember him from Alexandria, always the handsomest of the young men – distinguished himself in the Dardanelles. But each time he was offered battle, Plistias rowed backwards and tried to draw our fleet into disarray.' Seleucus shrugged.

Antiochus, his son, grinned. 'Lord Leon insisted that the fleet row and row. He would never allow them to raise their sails, not even on the reach from Alexandria to Cyprus. And Leon made sure the rowers were paid every month at the full noon. Strong, well-paid rowers – that's all anyone needs to know about naval tactics.'

Satyrus nodded. 'Leon was one of my father's men, and they are all gathered here. I was hoping he'd make his way over the mountains.'

Antiochus shook his head. 'Lord Leon and Abraham the Jew and your Aekes – what a polyglot crew your people are! He's a Spartan helot, isn't he?'

'I think that he is now a Bosporon navarch,' Satyrus said.

Antiochus didn't take offence. 'Oh, of course. At any rate, they took some city on the Propontus less than a week ago – Plistias's last garrison. So now the grain fleets can sail, and our allies have both sides of the Propontus. They must be twelve hundred stades from here.'

Lysimachos came up and offered Satyrus wine in a gold cup – unwatered wine. Satyrus had a sip. 'Thanks for doing this, Satyrus. The troops like a display of piety. Makes the prospect of battle easier to swallow. Eh?' He smiled and drank.

The priest was sacrificing the last ram – a black one, for the god many called 'Pluton', god of good fortune. But every Hellene present knew that the priest was invoking Hades, god of the underworld.

He poured a heavy phiale of wine onto the altar, and with the stinging copper scent of blood, the rich aroma of cooking fat, and the spiced and steaming wine over the spitting, burned bones, the air was full of the smells of the gods.

'Pluton, lord of good fortune – husband of Persephone, who brings the spring in all its abundance, Demeter's lovely daughter; brother of Zeus, all powerful under the earth, lend us your daughter Tyche and withhold your hand from us. And let the shades of our friends drink deep of these libations of wine and blood, and remember when they were men, and walked the earth beneath the kiss of the sun.'

The sun was just setting – a red fireball on the distant horizon of the ridges to the west.

Coenus was there. He was born of one of the oldest families in Greece, who claimed descent from Zeus, or so the poets told, and he was unmoved by Macedonian kings.

Seleucus extended his arm. Coenus had been an intimate of Ptolemy's at Alexandria, and the two men knew each other well. They clasped hands, and Coenus embraced Diodorus, who had made his career with the King of Babylon.

'If he raises the shades of all of our friends,' Coenus said, and there were tears in his eyes.

Seleucus nodded. 'All the men that Alexander took to Granicus, Issus, Arabela, the Jaxartes River and the Hydaspes, Persepolis, Babylon, India. There must be five armies there.'

Lysimachos habitually wore an air of irony, as if there was nothing he took seriously, neither life nor death, danger, scorn, even defeat. But as the sun sank below the horizon, he shook his head. 'Why did the priest say that? Those shades – they would outnumber every man here, in both armies.'

Coenus nodded. 'Perhaps the night before a battle is the time to remember the fallen – as we may well join them tomorrow. When you are cold and rotten in the ground, brothers, would you not want to

367

think that other men will pour wine over your memory from time to time, and think of all your deeds, and praise you?'

They were a great circle of men and women around the altars, then – the sun was going down, and he cast a last blaze of bronze colour over everything.

Unbidden, a man – a Macedonian – spoke up. 'I remember Granicus,' he said. 'I remember trying to climb the river bank, and Memnon and all his fucking hoplites at the top, killing us. My brother fell there.'

Dozens, perhaps hundreds, of voices came out of the dark. 'Aye!' they shouted, and they said aloud the names of the men they'd known who fell there.

Diodorus held up his wine cup. 'I remember Chaeronea, brothers. I stood with Athens against Macedon, and I saw my father's corpse, and two of my boyhood friends died there.'

And again, the chorus – smaller, this time. Again the shouts of names.

Coenus took the cup. 'I remember Issus. I was with the allied cavalry. Kleisthenes fell there, where we broke the Persian nobles.'

Now the chorus from the dark was louder, hundreds of voices raised, and the list of shouted names went on for as long as a man might drink a cup of wine, on an evening under the stars.

'I remember Arabela,' Seleucus said. 'I was with the Companions, when we won Asia. So many of my friends fell there ...'

And again, louder yet. Hundreds of voices, hundreds of names.

'Ectabana!' shouted one of the pikemen.

'The fight in the passes by Persepolis!' shouted another.

'Hydaspes!' shouted one of Seleucus's staff officers. 'The elephant fight!' And the chorus had become a throaty shout.

The names of battles continued from the dark around the fire as the sun finally settled below the horizon – the siege of Tyre and the battles of the Lamian War, named in order by Stratokles, the first contests of the Diadochoi ... skirmishes of which Satyrus had never heard.

His sister came and put a callused hand in his. The names came from the darkness – never strictly chronological, but as men drew the courage to shout a name – famous battles and skirmishes, an eternal litany of war and the victims of war. And sometimes the voices in the dark were women's voices.

Eumenes of Olbia raised the cup. 'The Ford of the River God,' he said.

The Sakje roared their approval.

Lysimachos shook his head. 'Zopyron died there, and four thousand Macedonians, farm boys and veterans, and Thracians – not the wisest choice to mention.'

'Jaxartes River!' Melitta called into the darkness, and again the Sakje roared, and all the Saka, and many of the Bactrians and Persians.

'Kineas fell there, defeating Alexander!' Melitta shouted again.

Lysimachos growled but Seleucus nodded as the Saka and Persians were emboldened to add their dead. But Herakles, Alexander's son, looked at the fire. And Lucius put his arms around the boy and led him apart, lest he be recognised and acclaimed, or worse.

It was fully dark now, and the bonfires roared, full force, their fire an exchange for the sun.

And the veterans of a hundred battles continued to shout the names of their fights, and their absent friends – Raphia, Tanais River, Cyprus, Gaza, – land fights and sea fights, skirmishes and battles, and now the chorus was the roar of a thousand lions that filled the darkness.

The priest of Zeus came and bowed to Seleucus. 'My lord ... I had no idea ... my apologies. I did not mean this to happen.'

Seleucus poured wine on the ground from the cup that Phoibos pressed into his hand. 'I can feel them pressing in – and I am no superstitious man, priest.'

Apollodorus, emboldened by wine, shouted at the commanders, 'You helped make the shades! Now endure them!' and hundreds of voices roared approbation.

It might have led to a fight—the contest of victories and the bitterness of the lost friends. There stood Persians with the men who had killed their fathers, and there were Macedonians with the Saka who had fought them on every field.

But Phoibos kept the wine flowing, a legion of slaves carrying amphorae as far as the firelight carried, with wine bowls that were, by day, wooden campaign bowls, or mess pots, or simply fire-hardened clay that had a sticky feel and stained black with the wine – and the Sakje shared with the Persians, with the Macedonians and the Greeks, the Ionians and the Syrians – the wine passed, and with it, some of the fear.

And then Anaxagoras began to play.

He may, indeed, have been playing for an hour – the sound of a lyre is not loud enough to compete with the roars of five hundred men. But as silence fell, respectful and tired, his lyre song rose above the whispers in the dark.

And when he was sure that he had them, he played the paean of Apollo.

Of all the songs of the Hellenes, the paean of Apollo was one that the Sakje and the Bactrians knew as well. Lysimachos began to sing, and Prepalaus, and Diodorus and Antiochus and Seleucus, and Coenus and Apollodorus, Melitta and Scopasis and Charmides and Thyrsis and Draco and Phoibos – even the slaves sang, so that the song rose to the night with the wine and the blood.

A little away from the fires, Stratokles wept. Lucius put an arm around him. 'At least this time, we're on this side of the line,' he said.

Stratokles laughed through his tears.

Four stades away, Demetrios stood looking at the glow coming from the south-east – the left end of his enemy's camp. Roar after roar came from the glow, and now he could hear the unmistakable sound of the paean.

A man came out of the dark – an officer, short, stocky, with blond hair that shone in the firelight. 'Lord,' he asked, 'what is the watch-word for the night?'

Demetrios didn't recognise the officer but he wasn't worried about a night attack. 'Zeus and Victory,' he said.

The officer stopped, listening to the sound of the paean. 'Ahh,' he said. He seemed disappointed.

He turned and began to walk towards the distant fires, and Demetrios wondered who he was. But when he turned to call out after the man, there was no one there.

He shrugged and went into his father's pavilion. Antigonus was subdued – he ate a good dinner, but he was neither ribald nor dismissive of their enemies – not his usual pre-battle performance at all, Demetrios thought.

'I have had such dreams, the last few nights,' Antigonus said.

'Something you ate, I suspect,' Demetrios said. He shook his head.

'Pater, one more battle. We've got them where we want them – all of them, except Ptolemy.'

Antigonus raised his head, and his half smile and cunning eyes were those Demetrios had known all his life. 'Aye, lad. We have all of them in a basket. But I begin to wonder: can a pack of hyenas make themselves into lions? Have you heard the sounds from their camp?' He shook his head. 'And where in the great girdle of Mother Earth has Seleucus found so many elephants?'

Demetrios had never been the one to reassure his father – it felt odd. 'Pater, relax. Are you not the one who always tells me that elephants are a gimmick? That they have little effect on a battle?'

'Two hundred elephants can have a mighty effect,' Antigonus said. 'I intend to put all of ours into the front line – spread at intervals to add weight to our skirmishers and overawe their elephants.'

Demetrios shrugged. 'There you are, then. I'll take the right flank cavalry—'

'You'll have most of the good cavalry. I have planned a little surprise for the morning.' Antigonus drank some wine.

Demetrios nodded. 'Which is?' he asked.

'What, afraid you'll miss the sound of the trumpet, boy?' Antigonus asked. 'Just because I'm old doesn't mean I'm past mark of mouth. You'll get my orders with all the other officers – in the morning.' He sipped his wine. They were singing again, four stades away. Antigonus shook his head.

'I don't like the sound of that,' he said.

Charmides sang the *Iliad* – almost the whole first book, the Rage of Achilles, like a reminder of how pride and anger could divide an army of allies. His voice was beautiful, his postures noble, and Anaxagoras's notes fell from his lyre like flames of a fire, igniting the imaginations, soothing the fears, and Charmides sang the poet's words until his voice was gone.

Satyrus sang a poem of Sappho, and when he sang, he sang to Miriam, a thousand stades away.

Melitta sang a bawdy song of Theogonus, about a man who loved boys too much – funnier than ever, from a woman – and the Greeks pounded their thighs and laughed, and then she sang a Sakje song about a maiden who avenges the death of her lover by killing his murderers, one by one, and the Saka howled their shrill war cries.

Sappho came to the fire, poured a libation, and stood still in the dark for a long time, and then came and stood with Diodorus, Crax, Antigonus and all of the 'old men' who had served with Kineas and Diodorus.

Satyrus found that he was weeping. He watched Sappho embrace Diodorus, and he watched Apollodorus sacrifice a lamb – chanting a prayer to Kineas, with half a hundred men.

'Will we win tomorrow?' Satyrus asked Coenus.

Coenus shrugged. 'I am not a commander,' he said. 'But these men are in high heart.'

Stratokles, who had been talking to Antiochus – plotting, Satyrus suspected, and plotting without conscious thought – stopped talking. He came and offered his horn cup full of wine to Coenus. 'I feel that we will win,' he said.

Seleucus extricated himself from Prepalaus, who had drunk too much. 'We will not lose,' he said. 'We have a good army and a safe retreat, and this evening has done much to bind our army together.'

Satyrus made a wry face. 'I'm not satisfied to avoid defeat,' he said. 'Wine has made me over-bold, perhaps, but I am not in this war to avoid defeat. I'm in this war to see it over. I am twenty-eight—'

'Not for nearly a month,' said his twin.

'I am nearly twenty-eight, and I have been at war since I was twelve. The men around these fires know no other life. They deserve an end.' Satyrus crossed his arms, having said more than he intended.

Anaxagoras smiled. He took the cup and drank deeply. 'Playing that long is like an athletic competition,' he said. 'Listen, Satyrus, I agree that this war should end. But consider, if you will – there are fifty *thousand* men around these fires, and the enemy has the same again. And the last thirty years – by the gods, Satyrus, the last *fifty* years – have given men the habit of war. Hellenes have lost the habit of peace. They settle everything by war. One battle will not fix that. The losers will creep away to rebuild, the winners will squabble among themselves.'

Stratokles nodded. 'How will these men make their livings, Satyrus? War is an honourable profession – should they be bandits? The gentlemen – where will they go? Back to the cities that exiled them, back to ruined farms and dead families? The smaller men – to what shall they return? The cowards who stayed at home – the young men who stayed with the loom and the potter's wheel and the blacksmith's shop – they have all the jobs. They rise in the trades. What, exactly, is a man who has been the file leader of a file of hoplites for twenty years to do, back in Corinth? Go back to his dye vat? Serve as an apprentice under a man ten years younger?'

Satyrus took the wine cup – freshly filled by Phoibos himself – and drank. Pure water with a little vinegar; Phoibos was telling them all it was time for bed. He nodded.

Melitta agreed. 'I wouldn't be here at all but my brother insisted we tip the scales so that the allies could end this stupid dream of a universal empire and everyone can return to their own grass.'

Anaxagoras smiled at her, but he shook his head. 'It has become fashionable to blame King Alexander for everything,' he said. 'But I am a student of history, and I say that Ashniburnipal and Darius and Xerxes – and Agamemnon and Priam – Sargon – the dream of universal conquest is everywhere. Alexander didn't start it.'

Seleucus nodded. 'I know those names from Babylon,' he said. 'Sargon – you are an educated man. But Alexander did more than any man before him.'

Anaxagoras nodded. 'Perhaps. But smashing Antigonus will not smash the restless urge to conquer. Nor will you, Lord King, give up your spear-won lands – nor Ptolemy, nor Lysimachos, nor Cassander.'

Seleucus nodded. 'It is true.'

'War is the king and father of all,' Anaxagoras said. He shrugged. 'I do not know how to make men make peace. To be honest, I'm not even sure it would be a good idea.'

Satyrus handed the vinegar water on. 'I'm sure that it is a good idea for me,' he said.

Water was sent out to the revellers. And Satyrus walked from group to group as they dispersed, with his sister and his friends, clasping hands and wishing men good fortune. He found Draco regaling a crowd of Macedonians with some tale.

'Bed,' Satyrus said. Draco was so drunk that his face was flushed bright red – so flushed that it was visible by the flicker of firelight.

'Killed that fucking doctor!' Draco said, throwing his arms around Satyrus.

Satyrus's thoughts were far away – he had no idea what the drunk veteran was saying. 'Who?' he asked.

Draco had a cloak rolled under his arm, and he laughed. 'Wait a mo,' he said, and howled with laughter. He unrolled the cloak with a practised flick, and the Macedonians cursed when they saw what was wrapped in the folds – but they laughed.

Melitta didn't flinch. She picked the head up by the hair. 'Sophokles,' she said with satisfaction.

Satyrus spat to avoid retching. 'Where'd you find him?'

Draco guffawed. 'Wandering about the camp like the *fucking* spy he was.'

Satyrus shook his head. 'I hate to think how many other spies Antigonus has with us,' he said. 'Stratokles, have you seen this?'

The Athenian looked at the head for a long time. Then he took it from Melitta. 'I knew him,' he said, with unusual candour. 'Sometimes we were comrades. May I take this for burial?'

Draco nodded. 'Sure. Listen, I could take you to his body. I left it in his tent.' He laughed.

Anaxagoras watched the two of them go off into the darkness together. 'What does peace hold for them?' he asked.

Satyrus shook his head. 'I take your meaning,' he said, 'but there must be something. Draco is more like the ruin of a man than a man.'

'I do not speak this way because I love war,' Anaxagoras said, 'although I confess that it does have sharp joys, like love. But merely because of what I observe. Draco lives *here*, the way a farmer lives on his farm. And he killed that assassin. Without him ...'

Satyrus nodded. And sighed, and clasped his sister's hand. They walked to the fire, and poured libations – one for their father, and another for their mother, and a last for Philokles. He could feel them, right there in the darkness.

An hour later, Draco and Stratokles came to the fires. They had burned well down, but the piles of embers were as high as a man's thighs, and Draco went off into the dark and returned with Phoibos and a file of slaves, and they piled one fire high with fresh logs – old cedar, from a fence up the valley. And then the Macedonian picked up the corpse of the Athenian doctor and hoisted it onto the fire, burning his leg in the process. And Stratokles put the head with the corpse, and poured wine and oil on the fire. Stratokles went to put oil on the Macedonian's burns, but the man stumbled away into the dark.

Lucius found Stratokles sitting alone, wrapped in his chlamys, watching the fire burn down.

'He was no friend of yours,' Lucius said.

Stratokles nodded.

'By the gods – he wasn't working for you?' Lucius demanded. 'We are ... I thought you'd chosen a side.' He spoke with sudden suspicion.

'I have,' Stratokles said. He sounded tired. 'I've chosen a side, and tomorrow, I will stand in the front rank of my own phalanx and do my best to see Antigonus defeated. But Sophokles and I...' He looked away. 'We started together. We ended differently. But I wonder, sitting here, if tomorrow my body will go in a pit – a life of scheming, and a few moments of brutality.' He shook his head and reached out for Lucius's canteen, which was handed to him, full of heavy, sweet wine. 'We started together. I don't think it's too late for us to end together.' He drank.

Lucius took the canteen back and took a drink. 'Stratokles, you've been a good boss. And I've made money ... piles of money. But win or lose, tomorrow is the end. I've had enough for a couple of years ... to go back and buy my exile off.' He shrugged, sat back. 'So let's stop being so fucking maudlin and enjoy tomorrow.'

'One more time?' Stratokles said. 'You'll keep me alive?'

'Have I ever let you down?' Lucius asked. 'You're alive, aren't you, you thankless Greek?'

They laughed.

23

Seleucus assumed that he was the commander, and neither Lysimachos nor Prepalaus gainsaid him, so when he summoned the strategoi at dawn, they came, still full of the good fellowship of the night before.

Seleucus was back to his reserved, cautious and dignified self. He nodded as Satyrus came up, and handed around cups of water. 'If you expect a complex battle plan,' he said, 'you are in the wrong tent.'

While they chuckled, he led them out onto the open space in front of his pavilion, and then up the hill to its highest point, where they could see the broad, flat extent of the plain from the low ridges to the east, all the way to the river on the west – a patchwork of small fields wearing the colours of summer in the first light of day.

Lysimachos nodded agreement without a word being said.

Prepalaus frowned. 'We are facing the subtlest and most able mind of the age,' he said.

'We have more cavalry and more elephants, and with this many men from this many lands, the best we can hope for is that we all go forward together and we don't fight among ourselves,' Seleucus said. 'I wish to put all the infantry in the centre – Prepalaus and all of the mercenary foot – Prepalaus on the right, by the single olive tree. That is where your rightmost file will form – clear of the village, and facing the open ground.'

Prepalaus nodded, a man reserving judgement.

'My sense is that our phalanx is smaller. We will only fill the plain to the walled farm ... no, there, to the left.' He was pointing with a baton, and Satyrus shook his head.

'That's ten *stades*,' he said.

Seleucus nodded.

Antiochus smiled. 'Twelve stades and some odd paces, Satyrus. I paced it off myself. Enough for a phalanx formed sixteen deep and three thousand four hundred files wide at the normal order.'

Satyrus thought of his largest battle – at Gaza—and the only one where he had commanded an army, at the Tanais River. At Tanais, both sides would have vanished into fifty thousand men, and that was just one phalanx.

'He will overreach us on one flank or both,' Seleucus said. 'Out-guessing Antigonus is a waste of time. So let us assume both. We will divide our cavalry evenly on both flanks. Lysimachos, I wish you to take the right-flank cavalry. I wish all of the Saka and Sakje there. My own cavalry will form on the left, under my son. Diodorus will hold the extreme left of the line, with his leftmost files on the river.'

Seleucus turned to Satyrus. 'I regret that I have, in effect, broken your contingent among all the commands – your cavalry is with Lysimachos, your infantry with Prepalaus, and the Exiles are with my son.'

Satyrus nodded. He was irked – he was not an inexperienced com-mander, and he'd just been deprived of a command.

Every eye was on him.

He thought, *None of them are satisfied. Lysimachos wants more cav-alry. Prepalaus wants command of the whole centre. And if I voice my complaints, I do not help the alliance. And why am I here?*

And next to these men, I am *the least experienced.*

He nodded. 'I will hold myself in reserve, then,' he said. 'Where will you be?'

'I will keep a thousand cavalry and fifty elephants in reserve,' Seleucus said.

'Fifty elephants!' Prepalaus exclaimed. 'But we could have them in the front line.'

Seleucus nodded. 'Perhaps. But they are mine, and I believe that a battle of this size can only be won with a massive stroke – a knockout blow. This will not be a dustless victory, gentlemen. My plan – if it can be called a plan – is to abide. To take the best punch that Antigonus and Demetrios can throw, and to have one more punch to throw back. I will echelon the phalanx – Prepalaus and his Macedonians on the far right, and every taxeis eight files back, like a set of steps.'

They nodded. That was the formation that they had all known since Philip's time.

'The right-hand cavalry forward, the left-hand cavalry back behind the leftmost phalanx – your Nikephoros's men, I think. They can hold the left end of the line.'

'We let them approach us?' Lysimachos asked.

Seleucus shook his head. 'No, that's bad for morale. No, when we are formed, we will go forward. But the left flank cavalry – I want you to hold back. Wait my signal.'

Satyrus leaned in. 'Where do you plan to throw your knockout punch?' he asked.

Seleucus shook his head. 'I have no idea,' he said. 'If the battle goes as I plan – and I don't expect it – I will throw them at the junction between their right-flank cavalry and their left-end phalanx.' He raised an eyebrow. 'But that is pure hubris. I will throw them where I must.'

A slave – or perhaps a freeman, but certainly Seleucus's secretary – walked around the group, handing out wax tablets bound in wood.

'This is the order in which I wish you to form,' he said, 'with the name of every contingent. All of the psiloi and all of the peltastoi into the centre. I doubt that their order matters very much – they won't last long.'

'Don't let the useless fuckers disorder my phalanx,' Prepalaus said.

Lysimachos was not quite so contemptuous of his Thracians. 'Form with gaps,' he said. 'Files double back so that the peltasts can come through. It's foolishness to ask them to go out and discomfort the enemy phalanx and not take some precaution for their exit from the centre.'

Prepalaus shrugged, obviously uncaring.

Satyrus leaned forward again. 'I wish to support the King of Thrace in this,' he said. 'If there are gaps then even cavalry can be committed to the skirmish battle in the centre. And when the peltastoi retire, they can be collected and added to the reserve.'

Prepalaus snorted, but Antiochus agreed, and Seleucus was swayed. 'It is true,' he allowed, 'that it seems wasteful to leave the peltastoi to die, but there's no room for them on the flanks. Very well. If every taxeis has four files pulled in the centre of its line, that's a two-horse gap every stade.'

Prepalaus shook his head. 'Those gaps will collapse shut every time we lose, and those men are lost out of the line,' he said.

Seleucus crossed gazes with the older Macedonian. Finally Prepalaus shrugged. 'On your head be it,' he said. 'But listen, King of Babylon, you are going head to head with Antigonus One-Eye at even odds. I would rather we were trying *something* – a feigned retreat, a night march, a fight in the rain. Anything. None of us have ever beaten him. Eh? And your plan is to accept whatever he does and *then* attack.'

Satyrus nodded. 'That's how you win a sword fight,' he said. 'Or pankration.'

'Oh,' Prepalaus smiled grimly. 'And you are an expert?'

Satyrus nodded. 'Yes,' he said.

Antiochus laughed. 'You sure you're not a Macedonian?' he asked.

They poured libations, first to Zeus Soter, and then to Athena, and then to Alexander.

'Gentlemen,' Seleucus said, 'I wish that Tyche may stand by one shoulder of every man while Athena guards the other with Nike at her side, and the Eagle of Zeus over all.'

Even Prepalaus smiled.

'Go with the gods. Let's get formed. If we form well, that's more than half the battle.'

Lysimachos saluted and went to his staff, standing apart, and started issuing orders. Prepalaus had his son with him – he sent the younger man running to the Macedonian camp.

Antiochus clapped Satyrus on the back. 'Don't let the old bastard get to you,' he said.

Satyrus shook his head. 'I thought that it would be Lysimachos refusing to play the tune. I worried that someone would play traitor. I didn't expect Cassander's general to be an old fool.'

Seleucus shook his head. 'He's no fool, King of the North. And I expect he'll be steady enough when the bronze is in the air. And all his griping tells me that he's planning to fight. If he stood silently, accepting my orders ...' He said no more, but he didn't have to.

They all dreaded treason, even now.

Antigonus had slept poorly, and he swore in answer to his son's greeting.

'The so-called allies are forming,' he said.

Antigonus stood still, a slave helping him drink pomegranate juice while two more slaves armed him. He had a heavy horseman's thorax of solid bronze.

'I don't want this thing,' he said. 'I'm going on foot with the phalanx. If those bastards don't see me there, they won't stand their ground.'

Demetrios motioned to the slaves. 'Wear scale, then, or leather.'

'Are you a complete fool?' Antigonus asked one of the slaves pettishly, and struck the boy so that he fell. He didn't whimper.

'I feel like shit,' Antigonus said. 'Something in my guts. Have any dreams?'

Demetrios shook his head. 'Not really.'

'I did – I dreamed about a lot of good lads from Pella who've died following me around.' The old man shrugged, his shoulders free of the heavy armour. 'Something light – that's the way,' he said to the same slave he'd just hit.

They had a thorax of white leather and heavy linen, carefully quilted. 'That's what I want,' said the old man. 'And greaves.'

'You aren't going in the front rank?' Demetrios asked.

'I'm the fucking king,' Antigonus said. 'What kind of king hides from a fight he started himself? Eh? I taught you better than that. When kings hide from their own fights then the world will have gone to Hades.'

Demetrios hugged his father, quite spontaneously. 'Let's win this thing, and rule the world,' he said.

Antigonus grinned. 'You are a good boy,' he said gruffly, his voice thick. 'By the gods ...' He slapped Demetrios's back.

Together, they walked to the door of the pavilion. The arming slaves were just getting a pair of sarissas so that the king could have his choice of weapons. The saurauter of the nearest was on the carpet as the slave took it down from the loops on the side of the tent, and it was on the old man's blind side. The saurauter caught his ankle, and he fell flat in the door of his tent, the wind knocked out of him, his left wrist pressed right back against his body. He shrieked with pain, and every head turned for a stade to see their king lying on his face.

Demetrios hurried to his side, and got him quickly to his feet, and men cheered, but many of them turned aside to mutter to their mates.

'Superstitious ninnies,' Antigonus growled. 'My wrist hurts like—' He glared at a man who was staring at him. 'What's the matter with you? Never seen a man as ugly as me?'

The man stammered and retreated into his friends, and Demetrios laughed.

'No one can say you aren't yourself, this morning,' he said.

Antigonus walked towards the open-sided pavilion where he issued his orders. 'I'm *not* myself,' he said. 'If Seleucus offered me a three-years truce, I'd take it. I never thought they'd pull together an army that big.'

Demetrios shook his head. 'It is no bigger than ours. And you are the greatest general of the age.'

Antigonus made a face. 'My arse,' he said. 'The greatest general of the age likes to have a healthy advantage in men and elephants.' He shook his head. 'But I have a few tricks, it's true.'

All the Macedonian officers rose to their feet as Antigonus entered. They saluted. Antigonus nodded curtly.

'Let's keep this simple,' he said. 'Form as you are camped – just as you are camped. Form the phalanx twenty deep – we'll still be the same length of line as their line, and that much more solid.'

'We could overlap their ends ...' said Philip cautiously.

'When you are the fucking lord of Asia, you can order your phalanx any way you like, Philip,' Antigonus said.

'Someone's touchy this morning,' Philip said, and the old man smiled.

'I am,' he agreed. 'So don't make me cross. Lakshaphur, take all the elephants and string them across the centre as we discussed last night. Five horse lengths between every beast should do it. The beasts will crush their barbarians and their psiloi in the centre and then – I hope – scare the crap out of their phalanx. Some of their men can't be worth a fart ... after all, we have all the old veterans.'

Philip raised an eyebrow.

'Demetrios, you will have the right-flank cavalry. Philip, you will have the left.' Both men nodded. 'At my signal, the elephants go forward. Drum beats and bugles, eh?'

Lakshaphur, one of the last of the Indians who had taken service with Alexander twenty-five years before, gave a curt nod.

'And then,' Antigonus said with finality, 'Philip will take all but the levies from the left and ride behind the phalanx to the right. All the cavalry – one big attack into their left. Shatter their cavalry and pour into the weakest part of their phalanx before they can recover.'

'It leaves our left naked,' Philip said.

Antigonus smiled. 'Are you the only one with the balls to argue with me?' he asked.

'Balls?' Philip shrugged. 'Wives do it all the time,' he said, and everyone laughed.

Antigonus nodded. 'I know the danger. So I'm putting the foot companions and the remaining Argyraspids there. And besides,' he said. 'We know we're going right. They won't expect it – who attacks the enemy's shielded flank? And they *won't* know. I'll wager a talent of silver to a single turtle that Seleucus has his useless son or Lysimachos there, with orders to hang back.' He laughed. 'If they hang back an hour, we have them. Demetrios will blow through their cavalry, turn their flank, and the thing is done.'

'I will,' Demetrios said. He was proud – delighted – to be given the position of honour and maximum responsibility. He was playing Alexander while his father played Philip. The difference was, his father loved him. 'I will cut through them like a hot pin cuts wax.'

Antigonus beamed with pride. 'See that you do, boy,' he said. 'It's all on you.'

Demetrios was busy for two hours, arranging the right-flank cavalry to his own satisfaction, riding back and forth along the line, watching as the rightmost files of his father's elite phalanx formed, adjusting and adjusting again. He decided in the end for brute force over surprise. He arranged his best squadrons in wedges all along his front, with the best armoured men at the points of the wedges; eight deep triangles of his finest heavy cavalry, and the rest – the Lydian levies, reliable men but not well drilled, and the Mysians and the Phrygians – in compact rectangles, six deep, angled off to the right to cover his flank, and a long screen of barbarians – the Thracians of Asia minor – as a screen. The Lydians and Phrygians left wide gaps between squadrons – where Philip would insert his lancers.

The enemy was forming, too. Immediately opposite, he saw the blue cloaks form. They were good troops, and they formed so quickly that their grey-beard commander ordered them to dismount, and they stood with their reins in their hands.

Demetrios wished to order the same, but he wasn't sure it was a practical idea. Any delay in mounting would disorder the whole front.

He watched under his hand as the day grew hotter and the sun climbed. He was facing Antiochus, he was sure – the enemy commander had a grey Nisean, not a Macedonian horse at all. And he was young. Demetrios was glad – glad because he had no doubts of his ability to take Antiochus. But he looked for Satyrus, especially among the blue cloaks – they were his men, but he and his silver helmet were nowhere to be seen.

Demetrios was unconcerned. He would find Satyrus, and overcome him – man to man. At the culmination of the day. That was the way of these things, and this was his day.

He rode to his father's side when he was sure of his arrangements.

'Don't you have some cavalry to command?' his father said, by way of greeting.

'All ready,' Demetrios said. He and his father embraced. 'I have Antiochus,' he added.

'Aye, and Philip has Lysimachos.' Antigonus was leaning on his spear. 'I'm eighty years old, and I'm too fucking old to carry a spear all day, so let's get this over with.' But he grinned. 'I think – I think we've got them,' he said carefully, avoiding a claim of outright hubris.

Both armies formed at roughly the same speed, although senior officers on both sides could get a useful idea of the quality of their immediate opponents by the speed and manner of their forming. Antigonus sent a messenger to Philip to ask if he was ready, and both father and son watched a particularly inept phalanx form near the walled farm on the end of the enemy line.

'I can't wait to tear into them!' Demetrios said. Individual men straggled into ill-formed lines, some actually dragging their pikes behind them. They looked already beaten.

'As soon as Philip is ready,' Antigonus said. His elephants and the enemy elephants were only two stades apart now, and they and the clouds of skirmishers – also a line ten stades long – were raising dust. In an hour, the two sides would be invisible to each other, unless they started forward.

But of course, they all knew that.

'Go with the gods,' Antigonus said to his son. He paused. 'I think this will be the largest battle the world has ever seen.'

'How wonderful,' Demetrios said, delighted.

They embraced again, and Demetrios rode away.

*

By the farm, Apollodorus and Nikephorus and a dozen taxiarchs harangued their men as they wandered aimlessly through the fields and ambled into a deeply flawed line.

'Look like militia!' Nikephorus said for the fiftieth time, catching yet another file whose idea of slouching was to march more slowly.

Apollodorus thought that the men dragging their spears behind them were over-acting, but the charade seemed to put the whole phalanx in tearing high spirits, whatever effect it had on the enemy. There are few things a soldier likes better than the feeling that he is putting some cleverness over on the enemy – and the effort distracted the men from the chaos to come.

In fact, Apollodorus had planted a line of ash stakes to mark the real front, and another to mark the deeply bowed front that amateurs would make. He'd spent the morning on them, and he was quite pleased with the effect. His marines looked particularly vulnerable at the edge of the farmyard – a loose string of men, too far apart for support, and with the rear files already edging back over the crest of the low ridge behind them.

There was no missing that the enemy cavalry was coming, and coming hard. They had eight great wedges pointed at Diodorus and Antiochus, and Apollodorus had his doubts about the quality of the Seleucid satrapal levies. Since they were the leftmost part of the army – the last to advance, and only when the whole echeloned line had formed – he sent servants back to camp to have the marine women and slaves bring up javelins and bows. And he sent another runner forward into the dust cloud to order his marine archers out of the psiloi line.

Nikephorus narrowed his eyes. 'We don't have the authority,' he said. But he watched the enemy cavalry squadrons and nodded. 'But … I agree.'

Satyrus rode up from the reserve, almost a stade behind the phalanx, where his charger and his riding horse were equally offended by the big squadron of elephants. Indeed, the Olbians, serving as his body-guard, had trouble all morning, and Eumenes had coaxed one of the Indian mahouts into bringing a single elephant out of the formation so that he could lead his horses around the beast – one at a time, blindfolded, and then with full sight, the riders standing at their heads and murmuring to them. It was a Sakje trick – the Scythians had long experience of elephants – and the horses had calmed considerably by the time Eumenes was done and thanking the mahout.

He saw Stratokles first, and rode over to the Athenian. Herakles was pale under his helmet, but he was smiling, and laughing at something Lucius had just said in his ear. Stratokles had his helmet under his arm.

'I hate waiting,' he said. 'And I hate not being in control.' He frowned.

Satyrus shrugged. 'At least you have a thousand men to command,' he said. 'I'm a well-dressed trooper under Eumenes, a man who was leading cavalry when my father was alive.'

'Trade you,' Stratokles said.

To the left of Stratokles, Nikephorus and Apollodorus shared a canteen.

'Ares!' Satyrus said. 'When are you going to form line?' As the paymaster, he was outraged to see his troops straggling over a stade of ground. Some of Apollodorus's marines were snoring away on the porch of the enclosed farmyard.

Both men smiled. 'Got ya,' Apollodorus said. He explained, and Satyrus rode away happier – except for his sight of the wedges of Demetrios's cavalry gathered like storm clouds on the horizon on a harvest day.

He rode all the way to the left, to where Diodorus sat under a tree with a slave holding his horse.

'We are in for a storm,' Diodorus said. He pointed across the plain at the wedges. 'When you go back to Seleucus, tell him that Antiochus and I can't hold all that for very long.'

'Apollodorus has filled the farmyard with archers,' Satyrus said, pointing to the farm that was the linchpin between the infantry and the left-flank cavalry.

Diodorus nodded. 'That,' he said, 'may save a lot of us. Listen, Satyrus,' he said, wiping the sweat off his brow, 'Sappho has the baggage train. She's already moving.'

'What?' Satyrus said.

Diodorus nodded. 'I don't trust Antiochus's satrapal troops – I trust Darius, but the rest are sheep. And some of the mercenaries ... anyway, it is a precaution that I've taken for years. Send all your followers and Phoibos and your people to her – she's to wait back at Akroinus.'

'That's a *parasang*!' Satyrus exclaimed. 'Thirty stades!' He looked around. Crax had Diodorus's reserve – a hundred troopers in heavy armour, with scale armour on their big Nisean horses like Persian nobles or Sarmatians. Indeed, Satyrus could see both in the ranks. He was standing with his horse, and he winked.

Andronicus was lying in the shade of the tree. Satyrus hadn't seen him. But he raised his head. 'If this army breaks up, we want our girls out of reach of the bastards,' the Gaul said.

'Tell Nikephorus to be ready to form an orb,' Diodorus said. Satyrus embraced him, and Crax, and Andronicus, and a dozen other men, and then saluted the hipparch.

'Your father would be proud of you,' Diodorus said. 'You're a king.' Satyrus smiled at the compliment. 'I feel useless,' he said.

Then he rode down the line to Nikephoros, and told him to be ready to form an orb.

Melitta didn't question the placement of her Sakje – they were on the left of the right-flank cavalry, and so they were pressed close between the Macedonian phalanx and the Getae nobles to their right. Her people would have been better off in the open plains to the far right, but Lysimachos hadn't trusted them – or her – and had sent his Companions there, instead.

The enemy had sent crack troops into their own left – Melitta watched files of pikemen come up and countermarch to reform their line, a complex manoeuvre carried out with contemptuous efficiency. She munched an apple quietly, gave the core to her horse, and nodded to herself.

Her knights were in full armour – a wedge of gold at her back. They were standing dismounted, and behind them stood another block of horses with a handful of warriors holding their heads. No Sakje noble went into battle without a remount ready to hand. Her skirmishers were to their rear. They could accomplish nothing in a head-on fight. So she kept them where they would live. And as her men – and women – had the best armour of all the cavalry on the right, it was possible that their placement was the best, after all. But she longed for open ground and room to manoeuvre.

And she felt, rather than saw, something wrong with the enemy dispositions. There was too much movement – that was the best she could describe it. She wished she had her brother to talk to – he had a much more intellectual approach to war than she did. Or Coenus.

Scopasis stood behind her, talking to his horse, with Thyrsis on his right. She considered speaking to them about what she saw, but they were too busy preparing themselves to fight – to kill. To rival each other.

Stupid boys. She loved them both.

And like the answer to a prayer, Anaxagoras rode out of the dust. He didn't embrace her – he knew when she was *Queen of the Assagetae*. Instead, he saluted.

'Satyrus says I may ride with you,' he said.

She smiled so widely she felt as if her lips hurt. 'Perhaps,' she said. 'But if you love me, you'll run an errand first.'

Anaxagoras nodded. 'Anything,' he said, with a remarkable lack of male bluster.

'Find Lysimachos and ask him why the enemy is moving so much, and then tell him I think we should attack. Then, when he ignores you, go and tell Satyrus. Then come back to me.'

He was off at a gallop.

She saw him reach Lysimachos, with his command group in the centre of the cavalry. And then, on her left, the enemy elephants trumpeted, and rolled forward.

Anaxagoras was a patient man, but Lysimachos showed no sign of allowing him to approach. He gave no sign, his whole being focused on watching the centre. The Macedonian officers around him looked at Anaxagoras with veiled disdain – he was a Greek on a Sakje horse, and he was already dust covered.

He waited what he thought was a courteous amount of time, given the circumstances, and then he rode past the line of aides, right up to the King of Thrace. A hand reached out to take his bridle but Anaxagoras was prepared for that, and he made it to his target.

'Melitta of Tanais wishes you to look at the cavalry opposite us. She says that they are moving, and she wishes to attack.' He spoke too fast, he thought, but the man turned and heard him out.

Then he surprised Anaxagoras, who had him pegged as an arrogant windbag of a Macedonian, and looked for a long time at the cavalry formed opposite them.

'Eros's tiny prick,' Lysimachos swore. 'They're either retreating, or changing flanks. Ride to Seleucus and tell him I want to attack, and if he approves, to sound his trumpets.'

Anaxagoras changed horses and rode for the centre, six stades away. The elephants in the centre were less than a stade apart. Lysimachos sent three of his Macedonians with the same message – the dust clouds were starting to obscure everything, and he wanted to be sure the message got through. As if by agreement, the four men spread out over the plain, going for where they imagined the command group might be.

Anaxagoras was wrong, and by some distance – too close to the front line, which was starting forward by the time he realised his error, and he could hear the sound of elephants shrieking. A gust of breeze, and a gap in the dust ... and he saw one of the other messengers and what had to be Seleucus, and he turned his horse that way.

Seleucus wasn't on the hillock where Anaxagoras assumed he'd be – he was well to the left, where he could see Demetrios's cavalry. Anaxagoras galloped up and dismounted to spare his horse.

Seleucus looked at him. 'Ah, the lyricist,' he said. 'You are the very scion of Apollo.'

'Today, I'm here for Hermes,' Anaxagoras said. 'Lord King, Lysimachos sends—'

Seleucus was looking past him, to his right. 'I have heard,' he said curtly.

'Melitta also wanted you to know. She wished to attack.' A bit of a stretch, really – Anaxagoras was surprised at his own presumption.

'She is a veteran cavalry commander?' Seleucus asked. It did not appear to be a rhetorical question.

Satyrus nodded. 'Of fifty fights on the plains, and several battles of Hellenes.'

Seleucus was watching Demetrios's cavalry.

'In a whole day of battle, a commander usually makes only two or three decisions,' he said. He watched Demetrios for a while, and the sounds of elephant versus elephant drifted across the ground to them – the shrieks, the trumpeting, the screams of men caught between the beasts. The best of the psiloi on both sides would be pressing forward into the dust. The worst would already be running.

Satyrus nodded. 'I know,' he said.

'Is Antigonus reading me, and luring my rash Lysimachos into a trap? Or has he decided to retire his inferior cavalry flank? Or are they unreliable? Or is Lysimachos mistaken, and they are simply late in forming line?' He sighed. 'Ares, it is hot. Already. Imagine what it's like in the phalanx. I don't even have my helmet on.' He took a drink of water – Anaxagoras hoped it was water – spat, and looked back at Demetrios.

'Satyrus, tell the reserve that these trumpets are *not* for them. Do it!' he said.

Satyrus, the highest-ranking messenger on the field, rode away. His riding horse was still terrified of the elephants, and he had the hardest time communicating with the Indian prince who led them. It took him several minutes to inform all of the reserve himself. By the time he did, his riding horse was done. But he made it back to Seleucus in time to hear the trumpets sound, all together, with a peal like the music of the gods.

Lysimachos couldn't imagine what was taking the King of Babylon so long – especially as it became increasingly obvious that cavalry units were peeling away from the mass opposite him. The enemy cavalry left behind spread out into dispersed bands and started forward, ready to skirmish with javelins and bows.

He was trembling with a mixture of anxiety and excitement when the distant trumpets sounded, and three more of his young men immediately mounted their horses and rode for their assigned locations, to order his cavalry forward into the dust.

He waited until he could see the messenger reach Melitta – the best-looking of his cavalry commanders by a long shot, and he hoped she knew her business – and then he took his helmet, pulled it on, and lashed the cheek-plates together. A slave handed him a heavy lance, and he took it. Raised it above his head, and rode to the front of his companions.

'Forward!' he shouted.

Philip rode up next to Demetrios as the rest of his Greek cavalry trotted past, headed for the far right.

'I think Lysimachos is on to me,' he said. 'I see dust, and there were trumpets.'

'Don't be an old woman,' Demetrios said. 'This is our time.' He took a pair of heavy spears from a slave and rode the front of his own personal wedge of Companions. 'Now for victory!' he said, and led them forward.

Satyrus had a near-perfect view of the first charge by Demetrios. The new breeze had cleared the dust from the western end of the field, and he could see Diodorus mount his troopers as Demetrios started forward.

Some of the satrapal levies broke immediately. In heartbeats, thousands of cavalrymen were racing to the rear.

And Demetrios hadn't reached his enemies yet.

The Seleucid counter-charge was too little and too late – even the crack companions were unsettled by the defection of half of the satrapal cavalry, and the reliable Persians raced west, seeking to flank and harass, instead of charging straight forward to a certain doom.

As Satyrus watched, only Diodorus's Exiles and Antiochus's Companions stood in the way of the charge. There were not quite enough of them to face all of the wedges.

In the last seconds before impact, Andronicus sounded his silver trumpet and the blue cloaks responded like dancers in the Pyricche, ranks flowing right and left – their horses were perfectly fresh, their discipline firm. They formed three deep, wide anti-wedges as fast as a school of fish changes direction in the sea – their points aimed at the gaps *between* the Antigonid wedges.

Antiochus and his wedge of Companions crashed headlong into the fourth Antigonid wedge, and the crash, the frightened neighs of rider-less horses, and the screams of men rolled across the plain – the war cry of Ares. To their left, Darius and his household cavalry tried to meet the fifth wedge of Demetrios's men – Darius died there, trying to cut his way to Demetrios himself, the first of the men Kineas had trained to die that day, with his relatives around him – and the fifth wedge was blunted and blown facing them.

But the rest of the wedges – and the Lydians and the cavalry from the eastern flank – were virtually unopposed, and they swept forward mercilessly, cutting into the stragglers of the Persians and the satrapal troops. The Persians had to fall back, and fall back again, and the victorious Antigonids rolled on, killing the laggards and pressing the fleeing troops as hard as their tired horses would permit.

And just like that – in one blow – the day was won and lost.

But Diodorus – the cunning old fox – was not lost. His counter-wedges blew through the gaps between the enemy wedges, threading them so that the deep formations collapsed each other and ended the charge as deep columns – facing nothing. The Antigonids pressed straight on, seeking for the fleeing Persians, or turned into the centre of the fight, where their young king was.

Diodorus reformed his columns, turned, and came trotting back to the farm. Satyrus was relieved to see him still with his men, and then the breeze died, and the dust came again.

The skirmishers were coming back through the gaps that some of the taxeis of pikemen had left. They looked like ants scurrying out of a series of holes – like water leaking through a dyke.

No one seemed to care about them, so Satyrus changed horses, left his helmet and his charger with the Olbians, and rode forward with Charmides and his horse marines.

If the peltastoi were surprised to be greeted by new orders, they weren't disobedient. Just tired and elephant-shocked.

'Over to the left. Form on the hillock. See it?' Satyrus said, over and over. By his tenth or twelfth group of tired men, the first group was already on the hillock – some of them sitting, some lying down, but their position was obvious. Men started heading there before he even reached them, and he swung wide, up the low ridge into what had been their camp the night before, to get a view west to where Melitta and the Sakje glittered in the sun.

The enemy cavalry – those that remained – were heavily outnumbered, but they were resilient and had no intention of fighting a head-on cavalry charge and losing. Rather, they dispersed along the front like professionals then tried to skirmish, closing to throw javelins into Lysimachos's Companion cavalry and the Greek mercenaries.

But when they did the same to Melitta's knights on the left end of the right-wing fight, they discovered that every Sakje had a bow.

In two volleys, the Lydian cavalry opposite them was shredded –

decimated, or worse, and the survivors broke – destroyed without being able to reply.

Melitta swept forward, widening her wedge to cover more ground. The enemy phalanxes were echeloned away from her – a long, angled line of dust and glittering pikes. The far end, twelve stades away, was level with her new position after her charge – the nearest end was still two stades distant, disciplined and professional and already forming a neat and virtually impregnable orb.

She looked to her left, where the Antigonid elephants and the slightly fewer Seleucid elephants were tangled together with all the psiloi. The Seleucid line was getting the worst of it. But the Antigonid light infantry and their elephants were more than a stade in front of their own pikes – more like two.

All this in a glance, dust or no dust.

'Thyrsis!' she shouted.

Her Achilles came up from his place.

'Back to the boys and girls – all the skirmishers. Left – right there – into their skirmishers and plough a furrow, as deep as you can. Don't fight the elephants – fight the men.'

Thyrsis saluted. His eyes sparkled. 'I will!' he shouted, and rode away to where her adolescents waited in the rear. There were more than five hundred of her light cavalry – fresh, eager, and too young to know that they couldn't face elephants.

Then she wheeled her knights the other way, to the right, and pushed forward, using her knights and their bows to clear the Lydians away, like a farmer's-wife shooing flies with a broom.

Satyrus saw the Sakje outriders pouring into the gap on the Antigonid western flank, and rode his second horse of the day to exhaustion to tell the King of Babylon.

He nodded. His whole attention was on Demetrios and his cavalry. Antiochus was wrecked – the young man himself was missing, and no messages were emerging from that flank. Demetrios's golden helmet and his trumpeter's golden trumpet were already two stades behind the Seleucid line, threatening to roll up the allies like a carpet. And Demetrios didn't hesitate to savour his victory. His men were rallying like professionals ... at least, the professionals were. The Lydians and

Mysians and Phrygians were already three or four stades away, on blown horses, pursuing the broken satrapal levies.

But his elite cavalry, and Philip's, had turned to face east.

Seleucus watched for another minute. He turned, looking over the whole battlefield.

'Lysimachos is victorious?' he asked.

Satyrus nodded. 'Sweeping the enemy cavalry away.'

Seleucus grunted. 'I hope he remembers to fall on the rear of their phalanx,' he said. 'Battles are not won by cavalry.'

He watched the battle for as long as a man might dicker for a sausage in the agora. Then he nodded sharply.

He smiled at Satyrus. 'Well, here we go. I will send all the elephant reserve into Demetrios. If you will take the right with your Companions, I will take the left with mine.'

Satyrus bowed in the saddle. 'I'm honoured.'

Seleucus shrugged. 'It's where they are posted. Go, now.'

The reserve changed front to the left with surprising fluidity. The elephants were fast – well watered, well led, and rested, they wheeled ponderously, but Satyrus was surprised by their speed. He brought his cavalry over the hillock where the rallied peltastoi waited.

'Hold here,' he told them. He identified a Greek officer – at least, the man spoke good Greek, although he was dressed like a Thracian. Satyrus reined in and changed to his beautiful warhorse while he explained.

'Organise them as best you can. What's your name?' he asked.

The man grinned. 'Alexander,' he said. He had a lot of teeth missing, and he seemed to be the size of an elephant, and Satyrus wasn't sure if the giant was mocking him or not.

'Fine. You're the strategos of the peltastoi. Form a line right here – four deep or whatever suits you. See the farmyard?' he said.

Alexander grinned. 'I grew up on a farm, boss,' he said. 'I know what a farm looks like.'

'When I say, you will go down there and help the men in the farmyard fight the enemy infantry,' Satyrus said.

'Sure, boss,' the Thracian said. He grinned again, and Satyrus had no idea whether the man understood, or what he intended.

Satyrus vaulted into his high-backed Sakje saddle on his magnificent Persian charger.

393

Gap-tooth Alexander saluted smartly.

Satyrus took his long-handled Sakje axe from where it hung at his saddle bow and saluted. 'Just be here and ready when I come back,' he said, and trotted forward to where Eumenes had his Olbians formed in a rhomboid, half a stade on and half a stade distant from the elephants – the closest the cavalry could go, even after a morning to get used to the big beasts.

'Ready?' Satyrus asked Eumenes.

As a reply, Eumenes pointed to the front, where Demetrios was already coming forward, elephants or no elephants. He had completely turned the Seleucid flank, and his second charge was already into Diodorus and the Exiles, who were making a counter-charge at the edge of the farm fields, protecting the flank of the infantry.

Satyrus could see that if he waited for the elephants, Diodorus would be swept away. Seleucus was probably willing to sacrifice a mercenary, for a prize this big.

Satyrus was not.

It was hot.

This had become the defining point of Stratokles' existence; the heat, the weight of his panoply, the sweat that rolled down his back and between his pectoral muscles, down his groin, down his thighs. His bronze thorax sat well on his hips, but he had lost weight and gained muscle in the last year, and the armour, so carefully fitted in a shop below the Hephaestion in Athens, now needed padding where the shoulders latched and down along his belly – padding that was made of lamb's wool, hot and itchy and now sodden with sweat.

He had a Phrygian cap under his helmet, and it fitted well enough but it was wool, and it, too, was full of the water of his body. His helmet weighed twice what it had when he donned it, an hour before when the peltasts ran by; he cursed the brave display of horsehair on top, adding a pound to the weight.

He had greaves on his legs, shining bronze with silver buckles, and on each leg was a standing figure of Athena worked in silver, holding Nike aloft. Lined in leather, padded in wool felt.

On his shoulder was a bronze-faced aspis, half a man's height in diameter, with a bronze porpax and bronze fittings over willow wood. It weighed more with every hour.

Over his shoulder was a sword of Chalcedonian steel, gifted him by Satyrus, and in his hand – wet with perspiration – was the shaft of a pike, three times a man's height in length. Not a proper Macedonian sarissa. Stratokles' mercenaries preferred a shorter pike – lighter, easier to wield close in.

He knew that he looked magnificent. But he hadn't shifted by so much as a foot, and he was soaked in sweat, pounded by the sun that seemed to rise ever higher just to slay *him*, uncooled by the fitful breeze.

And Stratokles was not a new boy. He was an old veteran. This would mark his third time in the front rank, and he knew that the men in the middle of the formation were hotter and had no chance of the breeze.

'That can't be good,' Lucius said.

Stratokles turned his head – the effort of it – and saw a riderless elephant wandering back and forth to their right. The beast stopped to trumpet, and headed off into the dust to the north.

Herakles drank from his canteen. Then he looked around. 'I suppose that if I have to piss, I have to do it right here,' he said.

'And then every man in your file walks through it,' Lucius added. Men laughed. All the mercenaries liked Lucius.

'It'll help cool their feet,' Herakles said, and began to take care of it. The man behind him guffawed – quite naturally. Other men in the file caught the joke and they laughed, too.

'Your piss is cool?' a wag shouted.

'I drink nothing but iced wine,' Herakles returned.

'Fuck walking through it, I'll drink it,' shouted a man who'd lost his youth in the Lamian War.

Stratokles found that he was grinning. These were men, like the men with whom he'd grown to manhood. Many of them were Athenians or Ionians – a smattering of Spartans and Spartan rejects, some Corinthians. Greeks. Men who knew what a gymnasium was for; men who could read *and* fight.

A boy – naked but for a red cloak – came running down the line. 'Lord Stratokles!' he shouted.

Stratokles held up his shield – Athena in gold on red. The boy ran to him.

'We are going forward, lord. The whole line. You are to *echelon*,' the boy put especial care into the word, 'echelon on the taxeis to your right.'

Stratokles released his cheekpieces and tilted his helmet back. He twirled his pike in his hands – a muscle memory from youth, a display of talent he still had – and placed the long spear horizontal to the ground at his head height – as if bracing the front line. With his back to the enemy, he called out, 'Ready to march!'

Men looked right and left, measured the distance, sometimes tapped their shields together. A few of the front rankers had the old aspis – Stratokles did, and Herakles, Lucius, and a pair of Athenian exiles who called themselves Plato and Gorgias. The rest had the smaller, lighter Macedonian aspis.

Which, of course, had been invented by an Athenian.

'Forward!' Stratokles called, backstepping in front of his taxeis. He'd never been a taxiarch before – never would have been, in Athens – but he knew the drills and the dances as well as most of the useless political appointees that had led the boys at Chaeronea and all through the Lamian War.

In fact, he was terrified. But like most men of a certain age, he'd been terrified so many times that terror was an old adversary, one he could best in single combat with more ease than he bested lack of sleep, heat, or insect bites.

Step by step, forward. His aulos player picked up his steps and played them – a good lad, that one. He looked at the phalanx to their right – still moving, a little ahead, with a gap widening at the critical juncture where the two came together. But to try and fix that now would disorder his men.

Later might be too late.

Politics was easier, and at the moment, assassination looked *far* more efficient.

The shaft to his back was the first warning he had that there was an enemy in the dust, and then, suddenly, there were Phrygian highland-ers – as surprised to have hoplites come at them as Stratokles was to be struck – again – by a javelin in the back. Luckily, his bronze was the best money could buy and all he had to show for the man's best throws were two deep divots in the surface of his back-plate.

It took Stratokles a long, long heartbeat to understand that he was in combat.

Not Lucius. He rammed his spear over the Athenian's shoulder, catching the crescent-shaped shield of the peltast and knocking the man flat.

Herakles put his pike point into the man – reversing and shortening his pike in two practised motions, ramming the spear point home, stepping forward over the corpse.

Stratokles saw it all – running slowly, like a dream – and had time to think, *He's no boy. He's twenty-seven and this should have been his life. And now I want him to live and get away, not die here trying to be Alexander.*

But he's more like Alexander every day.

The Phrygians melted before them, as fast as they had appeared. There was a shower of javelins – blows like punches on the face of his shield – and his golden Athena was no longer unmarred.

The taxeis had quickened its step – any veteran knew that the way to get rid of peltasts was to plough over them. Not only had they closed the gap with the right taxeis, now they were overtaking it – the front ranks were almost even.

It occurred to Stratokles then that not only were there elephants out there in the dust, but that his taxeis and Nikephorus's were going to be matched against the very finest soldiers in the world ... that is, whatever old One-Eye chose to put on the *right* of his line.

Stratokles risked a look to his left ... and there was nothing there at all.

'Athena,' he said aloud. *Too late to wonder where in Hades Nikephorus was.*

His men were trotting – well closed up, but moving a top speed. He was proud of them – worried – terrified – but he suspected that hitting at this speed would be an advantage, unless they went into elephants, and even then – he had a thought, under the sweat and grime – elephants might flinch from the wall of spear points if it moved this fast.

'You've lost your mind,' Lucius panted.

'Good to know,' Stratokles grunted.

Now his front rank was losing cohesion.

The taxeis next to him had started to trot, as well.

'Spears! Down!' Stratokles called, and all along the front, the pikes came down to chest level, throat level, and now they were running, and instead of the paean, the Athenians had started the war cry: *eleu eleu eleu eleu* in the back of the throat, rising to a scream.

The hint of a breeze, like a cat making one lick at a sticky spot on her fur – one lick of breeze, and there they were, the front taxeis of the enemy, the rightmost of the line. No, the rightmost but one. There was another, well separated in the dust. And they had the star of Macedon on their shields, and the Ionian war cry rose to a shriek.

No man in Stratokles' band had any love for Macedon.

Too late to stop and dress his line. Too late for order, too late for second thoughts, though his head was crowded with them.

The enemy made mistakes, too. Like pausing in their advance to rest with their sarauters planted in the deep earth of farm fields. The Ionian mercenaries appeared out of the wall of dust with a shriek. Just to Stratokles' front, a lone elephant bolted at the shriek – turned, riderless, and ran straight into the Macedonians behind him. The animal's flanks were gored red – blood flew off her when she turned.

Just to the left were two *dead* elephants – mere mounds of meat. But the pair of them were like terrain, covering his flank, if only for a few heartbeats.

Many of the Antigonids got their spears out of the ground and down. A spearhead struck Stratokles squarely in the shield; he stumbled, twisted, and would have lost his footing except that three or four more spear points hit his aspis and held him up. He raised his aspis until the spears scraped by over his head, and plunged in under their shafts, into the rage of Ares. He was screaming *eleu eleu eleu eleu* at the top of his lungs, and the world – Aristotle's entire universe – was only as wide as the eye-slits in his Attic helmet.

His spear point skipped off a rimless aspis, rose with the working of his hips, and rammed into a man's undefended throat.

And he roared.

Diodorus was already wounded. Something had gone into the gap at the base of his breastplate and scored his thigh – it hurt, and worse, the blood was pouring down his leg and over his white horse.

He had most of his men together. He'd lost Crax and the heavy squadron in the first fight, and Ares alone knew where they were – if they weren't all dead. But his three line squadrons were well formed, watering their horses in the farmyard by rotation, and his prodromoi were prowling the edge of the dust cloud beyond the farm while he sat and bled and watched Demetrios win the battle.

The bastard.

Diodorus turned to Andronicus – technically his hyperetes, the cavalry version of a hypaspist, but the old Gaul was hardly a subordinate in any meaningful way.

'He moved all his left-flank cavalry to the right, to face us,' Diodorus said with professional admiration.

'He didn't need them,' Andronicus the Gaul answered. 'The Persians were men. The rest of them were like children.' He spat, drank from his canteen. 'Retire?' he asked, after watching Demetrios reforming, his best squadrons virtually untouched.

Diodorus looked over his shoulder, where Satyrus's friend Apollodorus garrisoned the farmhouse and walled farmyard and barns, and just beyond, where Nikephorus – a mercenary, but a long-time retainer of both Satyrus and Melitta – had advanced cautiously, keeping one flank of his double taxeis anchored on the farmhouse. The man was clearly trying to cover a gap – he'd already wheeled a quarter to the right, and then he'd extended his right, halving the depth of his phalanx – a desperate move, really.

Diodorus took his helmet off and tossed it to his field slave, Justus. He accepted water, poured some on his head. Emboldened, he raised the edge of his corselet, terrified that he would see a curl of intestine. His hands shook.

He had a scar like a woman's birthing scar, where the spear point had crossed, riding on the inside of the bronze instead of punching through his body.

'Gracious Athena,' he said, immediately feeling better. Far from a mortal wound – a contemptible wound. Hurt like fire. No matter. 'If we bugger off, the whole flank goes,' he said. He was a far more confident man than he had been moments before.

Andronicus shrugged. 'Battle's lost,' he said with professional acuity.

Diodorus tucked a knee carefully under his backside and stood on his horse's back. The animal was patient – they'd done this a hundred times.

To the west, Demetrios was preparing his second strike: the hammer blow to finish Seleucus.

To the east, Prepalaus had given the order for the phalanx to advance. He probably had no idea of the disaster on his western flank. Or he knew about it, and by advancing, made Demetrios's job more difficult, and hid the disaster from his own men.

To the south, suddenly, out of the dust came a thick column of elephants, fifty animals, at least, every one with a heavy war harness and a crew of four or five – pikes and bows, javelins. They were forming line from column even as he watched. Squadrons of cavalry were forming at either end of the massive beasts.

Diodorus pointed his spear at the nearest.

'Look,' he said. 'It's us.' He laughed, and Andronicus laughed too. The Olbians – younger and prettier – wore the same blue cloaks over beautiful armour, a fortune in horseflesh.

'Back when we were young and beautiful,' Andronicus said.

Diodorus couldn't tell whether that was Gallic sarcasm or genuine regret.

Diodorus nodded, flexed his hand on his spear shaft, and looked out under his hand, trying to read the signs. Out in the dust, past Nikephorus, he heard the war cry of Athens – *eleu eleu eleu eleu*. He smiled.

'This is our fight, my friend.' Diodorus had made his decision.

Andronicus burnished his trumpet on a scrap of cloth. 'Or rather, these are our friends, so we fight,' he said.

Diodorus took one last look. Demetrios's squadrons were starting forward – eight wedges, with solid blocks of lesser cavalry on either flank.

'It will happen here,' Diodorus said. 'If the farm is lost, the day is over.'

Andronicus laughed. 'The day is already over. You are like a pankrationist who refuses to accept the choke hold until he falls, unconscious or dead.'

Diodorus sat carefully back down in his seat and took his helmet from Justus. 'Perhaps. Sound attention.'

Now Demetrios's cavalry were rolling forward at a fast trot. Diodorus cantered to meet his squadron leaders.

'That flank cavalry – Lydians. Horses already blown. Let them come to the edge of the farm fields – let the archers in the farmyard gall them. Then charge. We've practised it a thousand times – straight to a gallop from the stand. Got it?'

Then they were gone, back to their commands, and he was alone.

Once he sent them in, there would be no way out.

He thought of Kineas.

Satyrus led the Olbians forward, watching Demetrios, whose line of elite cavalry stretched away to the north and south, overlapping both ends of Seleucus's reserve line. He had big blocks of Lydian or Phrygian cavalry at either end of his line of wedges – already cocked slightly in, like the horns of a great equine beast, planning to envelop the reserve.

Satyrus smiled an acknowledgement that Demetrios was responding brilliantly to Seleucus's reserve ploy.

Diodorus was going to send the Exiles into the Lydians at the north end of Demetrios's new line.

Satyrus aimed his rhomboid at the tip of the northernmost Antigonid wedge.

He wished he had more men, but he didn't.

He lowered his lance, grabbed it with both hands, and rested his lower back against the pads of the Sakje saddle. 'Trot!' he called.

His Olbians – half Sakje, half Greek, horsemen from birth – went forward. They were not untried – most of them had served as body-guard at Tanais River, nine years before. The men in the centre of the rhomboid would be readying bows, lances upright in lance buckets and straps, bows out of their gorytoi. Even a few arrows lobbed high in the moments before contact could wreck an enemy formation – plunging fire into the rumps of enemy horses. Kineas, his father, and Eumenes, and Urvara and Srayanka his mother had perfected it, out on the Sea of Grass before he was born.

The leather lace that held his cheek-plates together was loose and cut into his neck under his chin at every rise of the trot, but this charger had the finest, lightest trot he'd ever known.

'All closed up!' Eumenes called. Satyrus managed a glance over his shoulder – the rhomboid was like a single living thing.

A stade.

He could see the man who would be his first opponent – the point of the Antigonid wedge. An aristocrat, a man born for war.

Through the narrow opening of his helmet, what Satyrus saw was a man who did not ride well, on a horse far smaller than his.

Individual shafts began to *hiss* past him as the best archers let fly. Hard to miss, even at this range and from a moving horse, against a target that filled the horizon.

The Antigonids had no bows.

More arrows, now – half a stade, and there was nothing to life but the rhythm of the trot, the ripping cloth sound of the arrows in flight, the man he would fight.

Fifty horse lengths.

Twenty horse lengths.

'Now!' he shouted to Artaxerxes, his trumpeter.

The calls rang out, and the tip of the wedge gave their horses their heads, and in one stride his charger was at a gallop – whistle arrows screamed over them in a volley, making untrained horses shy. There were tumbling horses all along the Antigonid front, their wedge tearing *itself* apart as rear rankers tried to ride over the dead, or worse, wounded and thrashing mounts – Satyrus's lance crashed *through* his chosen opponent, the point of the enemy wedge – crushed his breastplate and then burst through like an awl punching heavy leather, carrying the man right off his horse . . .

Satyrus dropped the lance – the head would never come back out of the wound – and drew his sword as his horse rose on her haunches and punched with her feet – two rapid blows and an enemy stallion dropped, dead, rider trapped under the hooves, and Satyrus was up on his horse's neck, chopping with his sword – heavy blows, falling on men's helmets and armoured backs, but they were *shattered* and his men had knocked them flat. Their horses were tired, smaller, had come further across the plain, and the arrows from the sky were a surprise, the whistling arrows spooked their horses, and they were dead men.

Panic, his charger, carried him effortlessly, despite his armour, seeming to skim the ground. It was like elation, like the daimon of combat magnified by the daimon of speed.

But I'd rather be on the deck of a ship, he thought, inconsequentially. He wondered where Abraham was – where Miriam was. He had a firm picture in his mind of the meadow below Tanais, where he'd ridden as a boy – where he'd killed a Sauromatae girl.

He was clear of the tail of the Antigonid wedge. Instead of going straight through, he could see that his rhomboid had collapsed the wedge and then gone at an angle. He looked back – the tired enemy horses were unable to flee, caught against the bigger mounts, going down into the dust.

Even as the victor, it was horrifying.

To his left, Demetrios's men were throwing spears at the elephants, clearing their crews. It was hardly one-sided – only the bravest of the Antigonids dared face the beasts, and many horses baulked or fled – but the elephant crews had a hard time inflicting casualties on the riders, too.

Satyrus couldn't see Seleucus at the other end of the line.

Closer, on his right, Diodorus charged the Lydians, and the fight flowed right to the walled enclosure around the house – men pressed in close, horses breast to breast, the fire of the Exiles against the depth of the Lydians. The Marine archers in the farmyard poured their shafts into the Lydians' unprotected horses from the flank.

And then something gave. The Lydians shifted – even through the dust, Satyrus saw the movement. He'd been about to order Artaxerxes to rally his knights to the right, to support the Exiles, but the Lydians bulged, and men began to look over their shoulders – terrified men.

Crax had ridden into the rear of the Lydians, out of the olive grove below the farm where he'd lain concealed, a Sakje trick. They were a hundred men against two thousand, but their flashing scale armour and their appearance in the enemy's rear turned the fight, and suddenly the Lydians were urging their tired horses back – back.

Like Diodorus, less than a stade away, Satyrus had come to the conclusion that the farm was now the key to the battle. Diodorus and Apollodorus held the farm.

Satyrus waved his sword and pointed south, towards the flank of the next wedge. 'Sound rally – rally left.'

Nikephorus had extended his right as far as he could without surrendering any hope of his men holding when struck. Despite his efforts, there was a gap a taxeis wide between his rightmost file and Stratokles' left – and the Athenian had charged off down the field with his flank in the air – vanished into the dust.

Elephants came out of the dust – mostly riderless, some with crews.

The gap had this advantage – elephants and peltasts funnelled harm-lessly down it, an alley between the spear points.

Two elephants came together, just a few spear lengths west of his position – both with crews intact– and the two animals reared up, trumpeted, and their sounds were more terrifying than their savagery. Quick as lightning, both beasts seemed to be sweating blood – tusks ripped, and shattered – the pikemen in the opposing howdahs thrust at each other and at the opposing animal, and the archer in the Seleucid howdah shot furiously from a long, cane bow, his heavy arrows taking the Antigonid crew, one at a time, until the Antigonid beast stopped fighting – despite the blood, despite the continuing efforts of his ad-versary – to place a gentle foot on the dead meat of her master, fallen from his perch between his ears. Then he turned away with a sound like a mother mourning a dead child, and fled.

Nikephorus's men roared their approval.

And then Antigonus came out of the dust.

They came slowly, carefully – spears down, marching at the slowest pace. Nikephorus saw Antigonus immediately, near the very right file – a proper man.

His own taxeis was only half depth on the right so he had to go forward or risk being broken. Nikephorus stepped out of his line. 'Spears down!' he roared.

And as the points glittered, he lowered his. 'Nike!' he roared.

Three thousand voices answered him. 'Nike!'

'Forward!' he bellowed.

And then the elephant, wounded and furious, stumbled into a run between the two closing phalanxes. Men flinched away on both sides and in a few heartbeats, both sides were like tangled skeins of wool yarn, files every which way, all order lost as the pain-maddened elephant crashed back and forth, taking long, deep wounds from brave men's spears, but snapping them, trunk flashing, bronze-capped tusks dripping blood and ordure and he slayed men and no more men could touch him. It was every soldier's nightmare – a mad elephant trapped in a phalanx. Men died like wheat or oats scythed down at harvest time.

Nikephorus stood fast, put his spear into the elephant's side – mad beasts have no allies – and drew his sword.

'Close up!' he cried. 'Get in your files!'

His men began to give ground.

'Apobatai!' he shrieked 'Hold the line!'

His very best men died there, putting their shoulders behind their shields, trying to push at Antigonus's best men while they defended themselves from thousands of pounds of pain-crazed war-elephant. They dug in their heels and pushed, they cut high and low with their swords when their spears broke, they punched and bit when they lost their swords.

Nikephorus aimed himself for Antigonus, and killed – forward, a step at a time, an eye for the elephant, still wreaking havoc to his right – but in the chaos of the mêlée, where there were no ranks, no files, just the vortex of death that was the elephant and the sight of Antigonus's gold helmet and red plumes, he pushed himself to the limit, cut, step, shield up, step—

He was six men from Antigonus when the world went black.

'Go for their rear!' Melitta shouted to Lysimachos. 'We'll do this!' She pointed her axe at the solid wall of Antigonid pikemen, formed in a tight square, like a hedgehog, with steel and bronze points bristling from every wall and every corner.

Lysimachos either understood or came to his own decision, and his spear rose above the rout of the enemy cavalry, and pointed north then west. His Companions rode with him. So did Calicles and the Thracians.

They thundered past the two thousand pikemen holding the left of the Antigonid infantry line – men who had faced cavalry at Arabela and Issus, for whom lance and javelin and flashing hooves held little fear.

Melitta rode clear of her people, called her chiefs to her, raised her bow in her fist and punched it at the pikemen.

Before she reined in, the arrows had started to fly.

Unable to reply, the pikemen closed up, lapped their shields, and endured.

But the Sakje had no threat to contend with, and they pressed closer, shooting at feet, at shins, at faces – individual young men and woman began to compete at acts of daring. A girl barely in her teens, ash-blonde braids bound to her head, rode along the front face of the phalanx, a hand's breadth from the reach of the sarissas, shooting

405

down into the ranks. Assagetae cheers followed her. And behind her, a boy, bolder or crazed with battle, rode into the gap an arrow made – a gap that lasted for a few heartbeats – pushed his pony into the gap, and the horse's hooves and his short sword wreaked havoc until he was killed, ten sarissas in his chest and horse. At one corner of the scrum, another girl lassoed a phylarch and dragged him from the ranks into the dust – he cut the cord, killed her in two sweeps of his sword, but was shot full of arrows like a pincushion. Before his body could fall, Thyrsis leaped from his horse on the man's back, cut his throat, and ripped his helmet off his head and scalped him in full view of his men, raised the flapping hair and screamed, and all the Sakje screamed.

Desperate, the Argyraspids charged, scattering the Sakje, who ran like flies from the swatter, but the phalangites didn't catch a single rider. And the Sakje turned and shot as they rode free, and old men died – men who had survived fifty battles.

Melitta halted with her fishtail standard by a well.

'Change horses,' she ordered.

Stratokles had been fighting for so long he couldn't think. His sword arm rose and fell by itself; he ducked, his shield jarred on his shoulder, his mouth was dry as parchment, and still they pressed on.

He no longer knew which direction was front and which was rear.

He'd lost Lucius, lost Herakles, and only the sharp barks of *eleu* told him that the men behind him were his own.

He wanted to slump to the ground.

His hand was red with other men's blood, and his own, and his fingers were stuck to the hilt, and he thought his jaw might be broken.

His sword arm rose and fell.

Someone was screaming like a stuck pig.

Satyrus had his knights in hand. He had a moment to snatch a drink of water – to pat his horse's neck.

'Well done,' he said to his trumpeter. The Persian boy was as brave as a lion.

Artaxerxes grinned.

Pointed past Satyrus, who turned to see another Antigonid squadron forming against him. Another wedge. They formed so fast, Satyrus

406

suspected they must be Companions before he saw the gold helmet and the purple plume and the white horse.

Demetrios himself.

Satyrus pointed to Eumeles.

Eumeles nodded. 'What we came for,' he said.

Satyrus slammed his sword back into the sheath under his arm. Some superstition – some piety – told him not to fight Demetrios with his guest gift. He took the long-handled Sakje axe from his saddle bow. Hefted it.

'Demetrios is mine,' he said. He took a deep breath against the weight of his breastplate and his fears, and his nostrils took in the smell of a wet cat.

Demetrios was annoyed that his best cavalry couldn't seem to penetrate the line of elephants, but they merely blunted his attack without breaking it. Almost none of his men were killed – their horses simply refused to go forward.

It was the greatest frustration he had ever known – that victory was visible – the backs of the enemy phalanxes were just past the elephants. He could *see* them. The farm was open to him – as soon as he defeated either the elephants ...

... or the cavalry covering their flank. He could *see* his father's phalanx – the foot companions – pressing forward to the east of the farmyard.

This was the moment.

He raised his spear. 'Blow rally,' he ordered. Pointed to the right, into the flank of the blue cloaks by the farm. By the time he shredded them, the elephants would be bypassed. Forgotten.

Enemy cavalry began to emerge from the collapsing mêlée just to the south.

He laughed, for he was the King of the Earth, and threw his sword glittering into the sun, and caught it by the hilt, and his Companions cheered him.

There was Satyrus of Tanais, a stade away, at the head of his knights, and nothing – *nothing* – could have given Demetrios the Golden more pleasure in that moment than to ride to victory over his chosen adversary.

His men, as aware of victory as he was himself, raised the paean.

*

The sky above the dust was blue and in the distance, far out over the plain to the west, mountains rose in purple and lavender, the most distant golden in the noonday sun. Up there, in the realm of the ether, all was peace. An eagle, best of omens, turned a lazy circle to his right. Or perhaps it was a raven.

Satyrus spat water and raised his axe.

'Forward,' he said. He twisted in his saddle, his last plans made. To Eumenes, he said, 'When I go for Demetrios, stay tight. Don't follow me.'

Eumenes looked surprised. Behind him, voices started the Song of Athena, that the hippeis of Olbia had sung since Kineas led them.

Come, Athena, now if ever!
Let us now thy Glory see!
Now, O Maid and Queen, we pray thee,
Give thy servants victory!

Satyrus was fifty horse lengths from Demetrios when he put his heels sharply into Panic's sides, and she shot forward like a bolt from a bow. Demetrios was covered in armour.

His horse was not.

Satyrus's actions were hurried, but he had all the time in the world, because this is what Srayanka made them practise from the time they could ride. And because he held the battle in the palm of his hand. His left hand. His bow hand.

He didn't need to kill Demetrios. But he had to stop him. Absolutely had to stop him. At any cost.

His axe was on his wrist, the haft back along his right arm just off axis from the shaft he had ready there, and his bow came into his hand as if he was practising with the girls and boys on the Sea of Grass, and an arrow fitted itself on the bowstring, the horn nock seating home and the string back and back – his draw thumb against the corner of his mouth …

Demetrios's look of shock as his horse went down, Satyrus's shaft buried to the fletching in its neck. His bow in its gorytos because Mother would yell, his axe up and the flick of his wrist that sent the

408

second man in the wedge to Hades, and Panic lived up to her name and rode through the lesser horses like they were blades of grass.

Satyrus knocked another man from his charger, and had time to think *I unhorsed Demetrios* before a blow caught him unprepared. He saw it come ... knew he would never parry it in time ... raised the haft of his axe ...

Stratokles wrestled his opponent, punched the man with his shield rim, with his fist – that hurt – and when he crumpled, tried to take his spear, but he could no longer get his right hand to close. The spear fell away from him, and Stratokles watched it dumbly.

As far as he could see in the dust, men were killing other men.

He raised his shield on nothing but instinct, got his numb right hand onto the porpax to add strength. Took a wound in his thigh and kept his feet.

'Down!' shouted Lucius, and Stratokles let himself fall.

He turtled under his shield, so he didn't see Plato and Gorgias cut into the men he'd been facing – killing two. Didn't see Lucius behead a man with a single back-cut of his kopis.

Then Lucius offered him a hand. 'I had no idea you were such a hero,' he said.

Stratokles couldn't tell whether it was said with irony, so he just smiled. He lacked the energy to say ... anything.

Even drinking from his canteen was almost too much.

There was shouting to the left.

And cheers to the right.

'We aren't fighting anyone,' Stratokles ventured.

Lucius stopped, listened. 'Ares, he's right.'

'Where's Herakles?' Stratokles asked.

'Down. Dead or wounded – I don't know.' Lucius shrugged. 'I followed you.'

He had something of his taxeis – it was hard to tell, but most of the men around him had been front or second rankers. The cheers from his right could be anyone's, but if they were Antigonid cheers, then the whole line was shattered, fuck it all. If they were Seleucid cheers, on the other hand ...

After all, they had beaten their opponents – hadn't they?

The sheer ignorance of his position made him want to laugh.

409

Stratokles the Informer – the master spy – lost on a battlefield where he didn't know friend from foe.

'What's funny?' Lucius asked.

'Me,' Stratokles said. 'We're wheeling left! Rally, you bastards! Athena! Athena!'

Apollodorus led his third charge out from the farmyard into the flank of the enemy phalanx. He had become aware that the only thing that was holding Nikephorus's men together was his own hornet-sting attacks.

Every man in the farmyard was fighting for his life – Andronicus had thrown his own elite taxeis and every man he could rally at the walls.

Apollodorus knew he was holding the linchpin of the alliance. He knew that the Exiles were dying in the fields to the south and west to keep him alive, and he did his best to support them with arrows and javelins. But they were dying.

'Nikephorus is dead!' came a panicked shout from the right.

Apollodorus wished there was someone to tell him what to do. But he was not a man to waste time.

He ran along the wall itself, jumped down into the flank file of the wreck of Nikephorus's pikemen and grabbed a sarissa from a frightened man.

'Nikephorus will live for ever! And so will we! Forward!' he shouted, and the echo of the stone wall, or the voice of Athena at his shoulder, seemed to amplify his voice to the voice of a god.

Perhaps they never went forward. But for as long as a running man's heart beat fifty times, they held.

And then they heard the shouts: 'Athena, Athena.'

Soldiers have ways beyond the rational of understanding the carnage and the chaos and the fear, of navigating where no man could sail with his mind intact, of holding firm when the merely rational demands flight. Like sailors, soldiers are superstitious because they know in their hearts that the world of the mêlée is beyond the comprehension of the rational.

Nikephorus's men – horrified by the elephant and demoralised by the death of their commander – had held. And as soon as they heard 'Athena' they *knew* that they had not lost.

They had won.

It was not a rational decision, because where they stood they were pinched between Antigonus's finest infantry and the first signs of Demetrios's cavalry, a few scattered riders trickling past the Exiles or past Satyrus's Olbians, enough to have sent them reeling in panic just two minutes before.

Now, they raised their shoulders, set their hips, put their faces to the enemy, and pushed.

The second time forward, and Melitta led her knights halfway round the enemy formation, shooting as they rode – flowed her knights from a long, shooting file to a three-deep line facing the westernmost corner of the enemy square – and the arrows began to fall in sheets.

On the opposite face, the youngest tribesmen went too close and were gaffed like fish, but they shot and shot, from so close that a heavy war arrow might punch through an aspis and into an old man's arm, or skip off his rim to break his nose. And old men's shields begin to slump – who can keep a shield nose high for an hour?

The Macedonians charged again.

This time, Melitta's knights didn't flee far ... and then they turned their horses. Melitta hauled her mare around on her haunches, perilously close to toppling, and was away. The Macedonians had spread in their charge and she was in among them, killing with her axe, and then they had closed their ranks again, leaving a carpet of dead and a smaller square.

They were superb.

Melitta intended to kill them all.

But it was Thyrsis and the young warriors who did the deed.

A boy – an eager boy – shot a phylarch above the knee, gave a whoop, and put his pony into the gap. An over-eager file closer thrust his spear into the boy's horse; the horse twisted and fell, dumping the boy into the face of the square, falling on six men and twenty pike heads ...

Quick as a trout takes the lure in a mountain stream, a pair of girls struck into the opening, shooting as they rode – one died, cut in half by a kopis, but the other girl's horse crashed into the effectively disarmed men of the sixth and seventh ranks and died there, her rider cutting at men's sandalled feet with her knife. Another boy raced through the widened gap, threw his weight forward, and died, punched from the horse's back by a pike driven with the precision of a twenty-year veteran ...

Thyrsis rode into the gap, killed a phylarch with his axe, and as his horse sank onto its haunches the Sakje Achilles urged him with his voice and the horse rose, powered by back legs the size of fence posts, and leaped – and Thyrsis was loose in the centre of the Argyraspid square.

And then, faster than even Melitta could understand, her people closed in, the dust cloud raged, and then ...

There were only Sakje.

Satyrus came to with Eumenes under one arm and his Persian trumpeter under the other, and he was lying on the hillock above the farmyard, and the sound of battle – the lungs of Ares – made it all but impossible to hear what Eumenes was saying.

His head rang, and there was pain ... everywhere.

'Your helmet – you owe the bronzesmith!' Eumenes said. He held a wet cloth against Satyrus's head. 'I don't *think* your skull is broken.'

Memory returned slowly. 'I dropped Demetrios!' he said.

Eumenes nodded. 'We tried to hold his body. His men fought like lions.' The archon of Olbia smiled. 'So did we. We got your corpse and they got his. It seemed a good trade when we found you alive.'

Satyrus sat up and wished he hadn't. It was as if he had a girdle of spikes on his head. 'Herakles!' he said aloud.

Eumenes put a hand on his shoulder. 'Win or lose, we're done. My horses wouldn't go forward again, and our remounts are six stades away, behind the elephants.'

'Get me to my feet,' Satyrus said.

A huge, hairy hand appeared in his peripheral vision, grabbed his arm and pulled.

'I waited,' Alexander said. 'You look like shit. Now what do we do?'

Satyrus forced a smile. 'Herakles,' he prayed.

The farmyard was a charnel house. And the Exiles were giving way to yet more Lydians – or perhaps Phrygians or Mysians. Not giving way so much as dying.

But on the other side of the farmyard Antigonus's phalanx was in trouble.

Satyrus made himself turn his head. 'Charmides, dismount the escort.' He took a drink of wine – unwatered wine – from Eumenes. 'You are my favourite,' he said to the archon.

'Are you insane?' Eumenes asked with admiration. Behind him, Coenus shook his head.

'Alexander, form your peltasts as tight as you can. We go *through* the farmyard into the enemy phalanx.' He met the giant's eyes, and the man nodded.

'We can do that,' he said reasonably.

Charmides formed the surviving marines across the front of the crowd of peltasts. The Olbian hippeis left their horses and fell in. All in all, they had quite a few men, tipped with a thin front rank of men in full armour – head to toe armour, in fact.

Satyrus drew his sword, took a deep breath, and swallowed bile. He had to fight the reflex to retch. There was no time.

He took another swallow from his trumpeter – water – and Herakles cleared his head, so he could see it all: he saw Crax die under the tree behind the farmhouse, the last man in a knot of brave men, and a ring of enemies at his feet. He saw Diodorus, still mounted, still fighting, and Carlus, the German, with an axe, covering his back. He saw Apollodorus in the front of Nikephorus's phalangites. And he saw Antigonus – a tired old man, pointing to the near collapse of the Exiles and shouting.

'Now or never, lad,' Coenus said.

'Follow me,' Satyrus shouted, and ran down the hillock into the farmyard.

They crashed through the enemy hoplites trying to storm the farmyard from the flank – scattered or killed them – then the horse marines and the Olbians plunged into the open flank of the Antigonid foot companions, heavily armoured men with axes and swords.

The peltasts had other ideas. Not for them the desperate mêlée. As soon as the farmyard was clear – Apollodorus's surviving marines cheering like heroes, hunting the last Antigonids out of the barns – the peltasts ran to the walls and threw everything they had – every carefully hoarded javelin, every spear, and then rocks from the walls – down into the right front corner of the Antigonid phalanx.

Satyrus found himself virtually alone, breast to breast with fresher men, fighting for his life. He had no idea, but two horse lengths away

Antigonus One-Eye, terror of Asia, the greatest strategist of his era, was dead, with a pair of javelins in his breast and his helmet crushed by a rock thrown by a Thracian peltast. And with his death, the phalanx seemed to die. Again, the knowledge of his loss seemed to be transmitted instantly to every hoplite of his army.

The Foot Companions broke.

By the olive tree behind the farm, Diodorus sat on his exhausted charger, the big gelding's legs straddling the corpse of Andronicus the Gaul, killed by ten men. Half a dozen wary Lydians faced Diodorus. He'd already killed two. He had a spear in his hand, and since this was the end, he had no need to surrender – to live to see a day of defeat.

Victory, or death without knowledge of defeat. Wasn't that what men asked of the gods?

Goodbye, Sappho, who made my life a joy.

Kineas, I'm coming, and taking at least one more of these bastards with me.

He backed his horse a step, and shortened his reins, and saw a wave of peltasts come over the farmyard wall behind the Lydians. They were so wild, he thought they must be panicked, routed men.

The Lydians turned their heads, almost as one man.

One took a rock in the side, and fell. Diodorus's spear licked out and took another.

Diodorus could see men he knew – the archon of Olbia, the boy Eumenes – not a boy any more, but one of the old ones. He had an axe, and he was waving it, and suddenly the Lydians were gone.

Diodorus's horse died gracefully – he gave Diodorus time to slide from his back, and subsided to the ground, faithful to the very last. Diodorus was left standing in the shade of the olive tree, a spear in his hand.

When Eumenes came to embrace him, he had fifty troopers gathered around him, and they managed to form something like a line on the spot Andronicus the Gaul had died because, like Diodorus, they weren't dead. And that meant that they had to keep to their standards.

Eumenes hugged him. 'We ... won!' he said, as if he didn't quite believe it.

Diodorus let out a long, deep sigh. 'I guess I'm alive, then,' he said. He thought of Niceas and Graccus, of Philokles, of Crax and Andronicus and Kineas and all of them.

One of his youngest troopers – a new boy out from Athens, named Niceas, too – was drinking. 'Can I offer you some, sir?' he asked Diodorus.

Well-mannered boy. 'What's in that canteen, lad?'

The boy smiled. 'Wine, sir.'

Diodorus took the canteen and poured half of its contents into the blood-soaked ground. 'Nike!' he said.

24

Miriam arrived at Tanais after the fall of the last of Plistias's garrisons opened the Propontus to allied ship traffic, and she rode the first ship north into the Euxine. Her brother's ship.

She landed at Tanais, and Theron took her to the citadel, where she felt like a stranger. He took her to the agora, where she felt like a stranger, and to the synagogue, where Alexandrian Jews she'd known from infancy made her feel ... like a stranger.

If I stay here, she thought, *this will be my life. Always an outsider.*

She stood in the agora, on the third uncomfortable day.

'Recognise him?' Abraham asked her, pointing at the gilded bronze statue on its marble pedestal.

She shrugged. 'I can read,' she said. 'I met Philokles, but I don't remember him being plated in gold.'

Abraham laughed. 'And this is Satyrus's father, Kineas. And this woman must by the famous Srayanka.'

Miriam nodded, her heart thudding in her chest and her breath short. What she felt was like rage. 'No statues for our parents, of course,' she said.

'Miriam!' Abraham said.

'You know, brother, you wear armour when it suits you, command a fighting ship, when it suits you. Play feed the flute girl ... I've heard. Stop affecting to be shocked by your sister. There are things in the world I don't love right now.'

'You want to go?' Abraham asked.

'No, brother, *you* want to go. You want to go and stand in the phalanx and save him. You burn, even now.' She crossed her arms over her breasts.

Behind her, Achilles and Ajax looked at each other and took a few steps away.

Abraham held his temper. 'It is too late,' he said. 'If Leon is right,

416

they fought a few days after we carried the city.' He shrugged. 'I knew when I took command that I might miss the fight. It is Leon I feel for.'

'Why must you be so relentlessly *good*?' Miriam asked.

She whirled to see her three hardened killers dissolve in mirth.

Theron dined with them – insisted that Achilles and Ajax and Odysseus recline, and they were served by the chief steward.

Theron's physique was unaffected by the years ... apparently. He looked magnificent by lamplight, and he led them in some poetry, poured wine for all of them, and did his best to make Miriam happy.

The next morning, he appeared at the door to her room. At his back was a lovely woman – perhaps thirty.

'I am Kallista,' she said, entering Miriam's room. 'Theron seems to think you need cheering up.'

Miriam shook her head. 'I don't know.'

Kallista smiled. She was beautiful and had the gracious good manners of great ladies. Great Hellene ladies. 'You are the woman Satyrus wants. If you want him, that's all you need worry about.'

Miriam looked at this lady, and hated her, at least in part for her perfectly plucked eyebrows, conical breasts and neat hair. 'I am a Jew,' she said with tragic finality.

Kallista nodded for a moment. 'You never met me in Alexandria?' she said.

Miriam shook her head.

'Nice Jewish girls,' Kallista said, 'don't meet prostitute-slaves. I was a porne, and then I was a courtesan – slave, then free. And now I am Theron's wife. In Alexandria, it would be a shame to him. In Tanais,' she said with calm happiness, 'we are whomever we want to be. That is all I can tell you. You bring what you have here, and make what you want.'

'You make it sound easy,' Miriam said. She was embarrassed – mortified – that this woman must have overcome ten times the obstacles that she had overcome.

'My husband says that every fight is the only fight – that's what he says about pankration.' She shrugged. 'It is true for all people. Your challenge: can you be a queen? Because Satyrus wants a partner, not a bed-mate. I've known him for a long time.'

'And been his bed-mate?' Miriam asked with an acerbity she regretted.

Kallista rose to her feet, the picture of elegance. 'Perhaps, and perhaps not – I would never tell, and you, my dear, should not care either way, as that would belong to a different world, would it not? I have never been his bed-mate in Tanais. I sleep with just one man here, and only when I desire him. It is like paradise for me. Now – I can go, or I can entertain you with music and poetry.'

Miriam found herself on her feet, feeling very ungracious. 'Stay and drink wine.'

Kallista smiled, and sank into a chair. 'Tell me about being a Jew,' she said.

Banugul sold her cargo, put money with bankers, and cooled her heels. Once she drank too much and cried for Herakles and for Stratokles. For what she would lose if they were gone.

One of Leon's ships swept into harbour, borne on the wings of its oars. Borne on the wings of Nike.

Leon was on board in person, and Nihmu, his Sakje wife, and they came to visit her. They told her that Seleucus and the allies were absolutely victorious, and that Herakles would lose his left arm at the elbow, but was strong.

'He will never fight again,' Leon said. He clearly didn't know how this news would be received.

Banugul rose on her toes and kissed him. 'Hah! I love his lost arm!' she said. 'He is coming home?'

'When he can travel, he will come here,' Nihmu said. 'And Stratokles is alive. No more wounded than other men, and much in demand. Sends you this letter.'

Banugul read the letter, and then she cried so hard that the kohl ran out of her eyes, and only the man who truly loved her would have found her beautiful.

Nihmu and Leon, who had expected a very different reaction, rose to go.

'Stratokles swore it would make you *happy*!' Nihmu said. 'Bastard.'

Banugul rolled the letter away. 'It does,' she said. 'I have been alone for too long with only my guards. Which reminds me ... a piece of unfinished business.'

She explained.

Leon saw Amastris alone as his next visit, gave her the official letter from her husband Lysimachos, and she, too, wept. Then Leon craved the loan of her captain of guards, who followed Leon out the door and was immediately taken into custody by two files of Leon's marines.

Who further blocked six alleys and two streets in the foreigners' quarter with the ruthless efficiency of victorious men with too much to lose to want to take any chances. And they'd cleared a great many neighbourhoods in the last few summers. They knew the business.

Banugul's Hyrkanians and her Sogdians had done the scouting, and they stormed the building, killing everyone, slave and free. Isokles and his people were so surprised that his retainers were mostly unarmed. The Hyrkanians were not disturbed by such things.

Isokles was dragged out into the street, cursing in his curious voice.

'I have friends here – every man in the guard, every courtier is mine. You are a dead man,' he said to Leon.

'Name them,' Leon said.

After he had, one of the marines opened his neck.

And Phiale – taken screaming – watched with growing horror, and finally threw herself violently at Leon's feet. 'He would have killed me!' she shrieked. 'Oh, Leon, you were always my friend!' She grabbed his knees. 'Mercy, lord!'

Leon hesitated. She was beautiful. He could remember her dancing at a party . . .

She was not so beautiful when Nihmu put an arrow in her throat.

'There is my mercy,' Nihmu said. 'I didn't ruin her face.' She looked at her husband, and smiled.

'Men,' she said, and bent to retrieve her arrow.

EPILOGUE

Satyrus landed from his own flagship to find that Theron and Leon had arranged the sort of reception that Alexandrians regularly provided Ptolemy – in miniature, and at a greatly reduced cost, as both of them assured their king with grins wide enough to split their faces.

The Olbian cavalry performed one last duty for their king, escorting him to his palace, and hoplites lined the streets, and farmers – Thracians, Maeotae, and Sindi and Sakje – all the men and women who hadn't felt the ice-cold touch of war – pressed against their backs and yelled themselves hoarse.

In the agora, the Exiles dismounted – the survivors – between the statues of Kineas and Srayanka.

Diodorus mustered them one last time, and paid them.

And the priests of Apollo and Herakles, Athena and Zeus made sacrifice, and all the people gathered to sing the paean.

Satyrus embraced them all; man after man, his father's friends and his own friends. His patience was unbreakable ... because he already knew that she was here. She was waiting.

He went from man to man. And finally, when gods and men were done, he climbed the steps to her.

He wasn't thinking it, but he had never looked better in his life – in his blue military cloak, armour and a fresh white chiton.

The steps seemed quite remarkably long, and he was not without doubts, although Abraham had embraced him at the foot of the steps as if they would never be parted.

But when he saw her with Banugul and Sappho, and Kallista, he knew his case was made, and the jury was all his own.

Their eyes met.

She gave him the grin – the impish grin – he remembered from her father's house. She stuck out the tip of her tongue.

Something flowed out of him, then – some lingering effect of

wounds, or the last spirit of the blow to his head, or just some lingering poison of evil, and he was filled with eudaimonia. He walked up
to her and – greatly daring – bent to kiss her in public.

Her eyes suggested he would pay later for this familiarity, but she
stood her ground.

'Marry me?' he asked.

'What, no foreplay?' she asked. 'I hear you make pretty speeches.'

'Marry me?' he asked again.

'This is your notion of wooing?' she asked.

'It is when all the people I love are together – and I'm in a hurry.'
He grinned.

And she grinned.

And somewhere beyond the rim of the world, armies marched –
Pyrrhus of Epirus prepared to invade Sicily, and Cassander laid siege
to Corcyra, and busy, busy plotters and hardened killers up and down
the Inner Sea faced each other across tables and battlefields.

But north of the Euxine, the grain grew in endless plains, unburned
by war. The farmers tilled the ground, and the groves gave olives, if
only small ones, and the horses grew fat on the plains, and cattle grew
fat in the fields, and the Sakje and the Sarmatians, the Maeotae and
the Sindi, the Greeks in the cities, from the lowest to the highest,
put their shields on the walls and their swords and axes above their
hearths and made babies. And grain, and silver and gold. And older
men told boys what it had been like when Niceas held the dooryard in
Hyrkania, when Philokles fell saving Alexandria, when Kineas defeated
Alexander, when their king warred the One-Eye and saved Asia.

But they were also careful to tell their sons and daughters that in
war there was blood and torment, fire and loss, many losers and few
victors.

It might have lasted for ever, this paradise.

In fact, they had less than thirty years.

But they used them well.

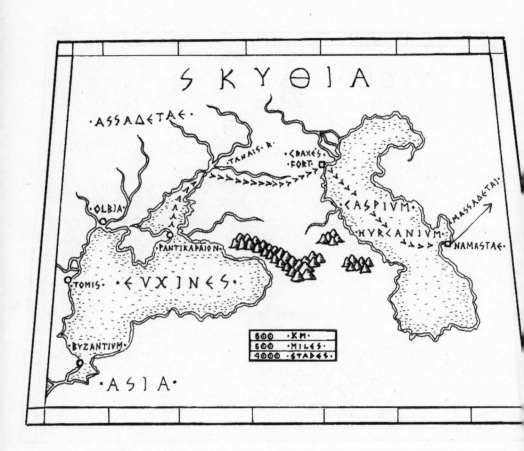

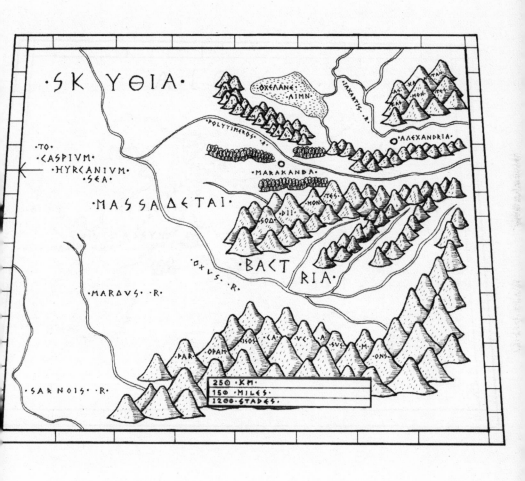

·SK Y ΘIA·

·ΟΧΕΛΑΝΕ·
·ΛΙΜΝ·

·ΙΑΧΑΡΤΙS· ·R·

·AS· ·KA· ·ΤΑΒ·
·MON· ·ΤΕS·

·ΡΟΛΥΤΙΜΕΡΟS· ·R·

·O· ·ΑΛΕΧΑΝDRIA·

·ΤΟ·
·ΚΑSΡΙVΜ·
·ΗΥRΚΑΝΙVΜ·
·SΕΑ·

·ΜΑRΑΚΑΝDΑ·

·ΜΑSSΑ ΔΕΤΑΙ·

·ΤΕS·
·MON·
·ΔΙΙ·
·SΟΔ·

·ΟΧVS· ·R·

·BΑCT RIA·

·ΜΑRΔVS· ·R·

·ΟΡΑΜ·
·ΙΟS·
·CΑ· ·VC· ·A·
·SVS· ·M·
·PAR·
·ΟΝS·

·SΑRΝΟΙS· ·R·

| 250 ·KM· |
| 150 ·MILES· |
| 1200·STADES· |

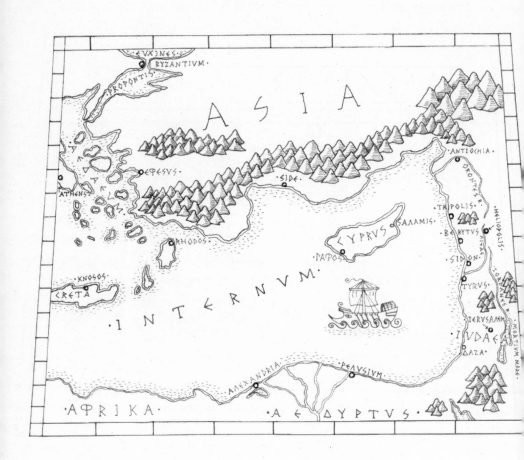

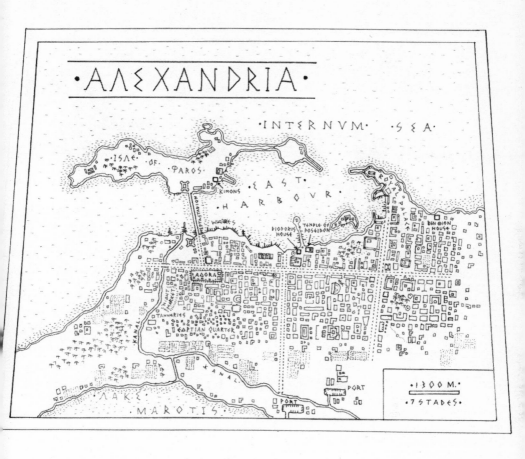

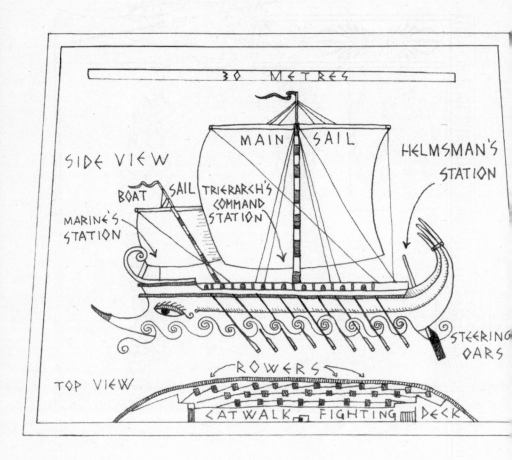

30 METRES

SIDE VIEW

MAIN SAIL

HELMSMAN'S STATION

BOAT
SAIL
TRIERARCH'S COMMAND STATION

MARINE'S STATION

STEERING OARS

ROWERS

TOP VIEW

CATWALK FIGHTING DECK

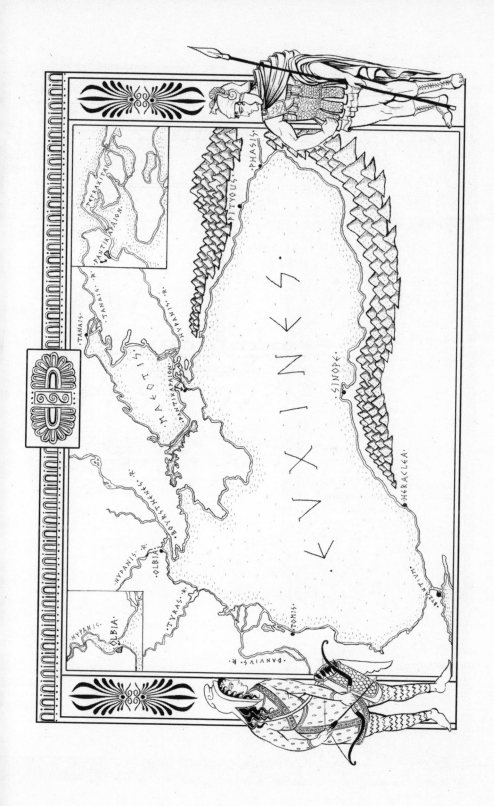

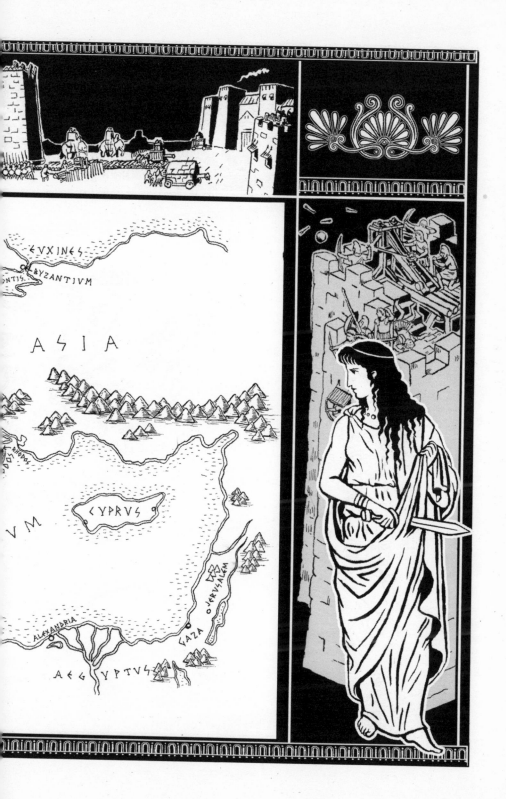